KATE HILL

KNIGHTS OF THE RUBY ORDER

ELLORA'S CAVE
ROMANTICA®
WWW.ELLORASCAVE.COM

An Ellora's Cave Publication

www.ellorascave.com

Knights of the Ruby Order: Lock

ISBN 9781419964329
ALL RIGHTS RESERVED.
Knights of the Ruby Order: Lock Copyright © 2004 Kate Hill
Cover art by Syneca.

Electronic book publication February 2004
Trade paperback publication 2011

KNIGHTS OF THE RUBY ORDER: LOCK

ଞ

Dedication

❧

For Mum

Prologue

ဆ

The Archipelago of SothSea shone like green jewels upon rippled blue satin. The most beautiful islands in the world existed in that tropical sea, but their name alone raised fear and apprehension in the strongest men and women. The Archipelago was home to the Pirates of SothSea, the largest group of thieves and murderers in the tropics. Their reputation extended to lands far north, into waters of ice and kingdoms scattered across the tundra. If the Pirates of SothSea organized, they would rival the conquering kingdom of Zaltana, but the seafaring warriors were too independent and greedy to unite under one ruler, though some were looked to as unspoken leaders during times of crisis. A few were grudgingly respected for their prowess and cunning, but only one was feared by even the worst of the lot.

Lock the White, tall, long-limbed, with a body formed of big bones and hard muscle, stood on the water's edge of a secluded cove behind his home on SeaSpider Island, south most in the Archipelago. Cutoff trousers covered his legs just past the knee. As waves broke on shore, they buried his bare feet and splashed his calves, pasting sparse, dark hair to the curve of muscle and bone. Lock's face remained stoic as he stared at the sun-speckled water, his eyes, the same clear, pale blue as the sea, a stark contrast with his dark brown skin. His face was a sculpture of sharp angles and planes, his cheekbones like those of some great cat, his forehead broad. Tendrils of long, kinky hair grabbed the muscles of his perspiring chest. He wore a beard, wiry in spite of constant trimming. Though Lock had only recently past his thirty-first year, white streaks had seeped into his bark-colored hair and beard a decade earlier and had continued to spread each year since, inspiring his name among the Pirates of SothSea.

The scourge landed hard across Lock's broad back. The blow upon already torn and bleeding flesh should have staggered him, but his posture remained straight, only his pale eyes blinking slowly with each strike revealed that his mind was not floating in some merciful trance.

The whip fell again. Blood sprayed into the sea, dripped down his back, and stained the waist of his trousers, belted around his narrow waist with a rope of braided leather.

"That's enough," said Karl, the dark-skinned, green-eyed first mate of Lock's ship. The man dropped his arm to his side, the bloodied whip dragging across the packed, wet sand.

Lock turned, his blue eyes glistening like broken glass. "You'll stop *when I say*. Raise that scourge, or it will be the last thing you ever feel on your own body!"

Karl knew better than to hesitate. Lock's threat wasn't empty, and if his order was disobeyed, he wouldn't hesitate to have his first mate whipped to death.

Turning back to the sea, Lock counted ten more blows before he jerked the whip from Karl's callused hand. He tossed the leather device back at the seaman and motioned with his head for Karl to disappear.

The darker man melted into the jungle, his thickly muscled body soon indiscernible through the trees and vines as he took the quickest route to the village.

Lock stared into the water for a moment, willing his heartbeat to slow. He knew what came next, understood the pain, as he'd felt it so many times before. He strode directly into the sea, gasping as his lacerated back immersed in salt water. He felt momentarily dizzy from the pain, but recouped quickly and waded in deeper. The water would cleanse his wounds and help prevent infection.

He knew his sailors and servants thought his self-punishment was madness, but to Lock it was a way of life. Pain tolerance was required to survive in a vicious world.

He'd begun with small tests, burning with hot wax and candle flames, scarring with needles. During his travels to the Kennas, he learned a system of empty-handed fighting arts and practiced barefoot on the rocky shore at the opposite side of the island until his soles were tough enough to walk across beds of hot coals. For the past five years he'd trained himself to tolerate flogging, pushing himself to endure past the moment when he needed to scream, but kept his silence. He'd had a nightmare years before -- a nightmare so real that he'd awakened gasping, drenched in sweat, his entire body trembling. He'd been amidst a crowd of foreigners, shackled to a platform in a village square while bounty hunters' whips slashed him nearly senseless. Others were punished with him, but women paid their fines and bought them as slaves, taking away their freedom, but also their pain. No one made a motion to pay for Lock, and the bounty hunters waited to hear him shriek...

They'll never have the pleasure, Lock thought, stepping out of the ocean. He climbed over sand dunes and rocks to his home overlooking the dock where his ship, The Shana Whore, spitefully named after his mother, awaited its next trip to pillage.

Speaking of his mother, he and his servants had a delivery to make to her brothel. His last excursion had been a pleasant success without even sailing out of the Archipelago. He'd taken an Empress's ship laden with silks, spices, and precious metal that could be melted down, made into weapons, or sold. After he'd taken what he wanted, he'd ordered the ship's sails ripped and the crew left drifting. He'd run the Captain through with his own sword, just to warn others who dared venture into the Pirates of SothSea's domain. He might have spared the man had he not flung useless threats. He'd acted like a single magistrate attempting to arrest a thousand thieves in their own den. Royalty and those who served them were so smug, so self-assured, though most of them thieved as much as any pirate. How often had he been paid handsomely by queens, mistresses, kings, and emperors

9

to steal and plunder one another's kingdoms? They smiled and made treaties to each other's faces while secretly raiding the land of sworn allies.

Not that Lock didn't appreciate a good betrayal, but he couldn't be bothered with lies, not when he had the power to live as he chose, to take what he wanted, and defend himself with sword and hand. It was simpler to be loyal only to himself, and no one had ever given him reason to believe otherwise. He'd learned long ago, before he was old enough to take up a weapon in defense, that if he didn't take first, he'd be taken from — and more likely than not left for dead.

* * * * *

Two floors fashioned from clay, wood, and colored tiles made the bordello. The roof was shaped at a wide slant, like the caps worn by the village fisherman. Narrow wooden porches surrounded both floors. Women of all ages, shapes, and coloring lingered outside dressed in sheer pantaloons and multi-colored scarves barely covering their breasts. Some wore nothing at all, just long hair draped over their shoulders, their breasts bouncing in the sunlight as they waved at patrons. Several young men wearing scanty loincloths strutted among the women, parading their wares to those who preferred masculine flesh. Lock knew from experience how many of the pirates paid for the use of boys as often as women. His childhood had been spent catering to their desires while his mother, then a simple working whore, had collected a fee from the madam each time Lock had been rented. Lock had left the bordello when he was twelve years old, after slitting the throat of a patron who had used him many times before. Afterward, he'd signed on a ship as a cabin boy and learned the ways of the sea and pirating.

As he approached the bordello, the mingling smells of perfumed oils, pipe smoke, and sweat struck him with the force of a whip, except flogging didn't sour his stomach as much as the odor of the whorehouse.

He strode past several women who called to him, wiggled their hips, and shook their bosoms, more as a joke than a solicitation. It wasn't that Lock didn't use whores when the mood took him, but he was not a man to be lured by anyone or anything, except the desires of his own dark heart. Everyone in the Archipelago knew about Lock, and most cleared the path when he passed. His temper was as foul and spontaneous as a tropical storm, and no one wanted to be caught in the vicinity of either.

The front door of the bordello led to a main hall where more women waited, some sharing chairs with patrons, others sipping the wine and smoking the pipes arranged on a wooden table at the back of the room.

Lock's mother—who was also the madam—sat on a chair by the winding staircase leading to the bedchambers. Though a woman of late middle-age, she retained a youthful body, full, firm breasts, and blue eyes lovely enough to sink a man to the bottom of the sea. Like Lock, she was tall and long-limbed with dark brown hair she regularly treated with herbal dyes to wash out the patches of gray. Her hair wasn't as sensually streaked as her son's, and several times she'd revealed her jealousy over his curly, two-toned locks.

She stood upon seeing him, her voluptuous body draped in a sheer black gown adorned with a silver girdle.

"My crew is carrying in the silks," Lock told her. "You can pay me as soon as you've inspected them."

"Hello to you, too," she said in a husky voice, approaching him and stopping so close that their bodies almost touched. She tilted her face up to his, her eyes tracing the shape of his lips while her fingertip trailed down one of his sharp cheekbones.

"Do you want to inspect the goods or not?" he demanded.

"I thought I was."

Lock took a step back, his features arranged in his usual impassive expression. He wondered if his disgust was apparent in his eyes.

"You weren't gone very long this time," she continued. He didn't reply. She took a step closer and slid her arms around him, her palms slipping up his back, her fingers gripping solid muscle.

He drew a sharp breath, her touch sending a streak of pain down his lacerated back. She took his gasp for one of desire and smiled.

Lock grasped her shoulders and shoved her back into the chair, nearly sending both her and the delicate piece of furniture crashing to the floor. "When you're ready, I'll be outside with the cargo. Don't take too long. I don't want to spend the rest of the night in the village, and there are plenty of other people on these islands willing to pay for what I have."

"You always did have a way of bringing the best price."

"I wonder where I got that from?" Lock snarled over his shoulder as he left the stinking bordello, drawing deep breaths of the hot, but fresh, air outside.

* * * * *

In the jungle behind Lock's home flowed a freshwater cascade. That night, Lock stood naked beneath the fall, his eyes closed. Cool water crashed over his face and body, numbing the discomfort on his back and cleansing away the reek of the bordello. Swimming in the cascade was one of the only real pleasures Lock felt in his life. He made a point to limit his happiness. Contentment bred complacency, and complacency caused death. It made a man lose his drive, desert his skills, and sink into the illusion that life was good.

He stepped out of the water, tugged on cut-off trousers, and walked the pathway home.

His house, like the bordello, contained two floors made of wood and clay. It didn't reek of perfume, pipes, and wine, however, but smelled of the surrounding jungle since he'd ordered his servants to keep all the windows open, except during a storm. He liked the wind. He liked the feeling of freedom that accompanied it, which was why he liked sailing so much. In truth, he felt better at sea than he ever did on land. He'd overheard old sailors talking in the village tavern, heard his own crew when they thought they were alone on deck or below. So many sailors said they hadn't chosen the sea, but the sea had chosen them. It was part of their soul—if pirates had souls. Lock often wondered. What was a soul, anyway? No one could see it or touch it, yet most people believed it existed. Even the bloodiest thieves and cutthroats he'd ever known mentioned their souls when death neared. How many men had he heard call upon gods and goddesses in times of crisis?

Lock climbed the steps to his chamber, tugged off his trousers, and flopped on his bed, not even bothering to pull down the sheets.

Tapping sounded outside his room. Lock's eyes fixed on the slender, pale-skinned maid standing, naked, in his doorway. Lock employed several maids who visited his bed on rotation. The idea of keeping a single mistress had never occurred to him. Fondness for a woman would lead to weakness and weakness led to self-destruction. Relieving sexual tension was enough for him, and he generally preferred the comfort of his own home to the stench of the bordello. At least with his own private stock, he could avoid the diseases running rampant through the whorehouse. He also preferred the whore herself to reap her full reward, rather than handing most of her hard-earned coins over to the madam. Shanna had more than her share of profits from peddling flesh. Lock knew that all too well.

The maid approached, her gaze sweeping Lock's body and focusing on his thick cock and hair-dusted balls beneath. She knelt at the foot of the bed and crawled between his spread legs, her slender fingers massaging his thighs.

"Are you hungry, master?" she asked.

"I could use a bite." Lock's gaze fixed on her as she bent

13

and ran her tongue along his shaft. One of her hands squeezed his sac while the other clasped the base of his cock. Her tongue and lips teased and stroked while he grew bigger and harder, his eyes half-closing as he watched her work.

Lock treated his whores well. He never hit them and tried not to be overly rough when he flung them on their backs and rutted out his pleasure. Many men enjoyed inflicting pain on their sluts, but Lock found no stimulation in sexual abuse. Punishment should be reserved for disobedient crewmen and prisoners, not simple whores doing a night's work.

Lock sighed, his hands gripping the thick wooden headboard as the maid sucked him so deep into her mouth that his cock brushed the back of her throat. She clasped the root of his staff as she sucked and licked until Lock's heart pounded and his hips nearly bucked with impending orgasm.

With a lusty growl, he grasped the maid's shoulders and flung her onto her back. She stared at him, her lips parted, her eyes intent on his. Her head lifted the slightest bit, as if she meant to kiss him, but Lock had no interest in kissing her. He dipped his fingers into the pottery bowl on the table by his bed and removed several reddish leaves. The maid opened her mouth and swallowed the leaves Lock placed on her tongue. All his whores knew he required them to take the herbs to prevent conception. No child of his would grow up as he had, not when he could prevent it. He reached between their bodies, fondling her clit and pussy, making sure she was wet enough to comfortably accept him. His cock slipped into her pussy and he braced his hands on both sides of her head as he thrust, fast and hard. The maid's eyes closed and she clung to him, her arms locked around his neck, her legs squeezing his waist as she ground her hips against his.

Lock plunged into her, making his thrusts longer and slower, then short and fast. His lips slid into a grin as he pushed the panting woman to orgasm. Her hot, wet body pulsed around his engorged cock, and he slammed into her with several rapid thrusts that hurled him into ecstasy.

14

He rolled off her and sprawled flat on his back, staring up at the ceiling as he caught his breath.

After a moment, the woman stood. She gazed at him over her shoulder as she left the room, "Sleep well, master."

Lock nodded slightly. "Close the door."

Lying alone in the moonlit room, Lock considered his earlier thoughts about men and their deities. He still refused to believe in any power greater than himself. *The only entity who can change my fate is myself,* he thought, *and my fate is to sail again the day after next.*

Chapter One
One Month Later

ॐ

Lightning ripped a jagged streak through the sky, disappearing into the rolling black ocean. Thunder was disguised only by the crash of waves as they washed over the deck of the Shana Whore.

Cursing, Lock clung to the mast as another wave completely covered the fast sinking ship. It had taken him years to afford this ship. Now within moments it would be a haven for fish at the bottom of a cold, northern sea.

"She's going down! Get me off!" Karl bellowed from where he'd tied himself to the mast. Unable to free himself, the man clawed at the ropes in panic, his eyes wild as he squinted at Lock through the storm. "Get me off!"

More angry than panicked, Lock's stomach tightened with disgust at his first mate's terror. Whether they were lashed to the boat or out at sea, they were all going to die. Still, his boots skidded on the water-slicked deck as he climbed the short distance toward Karl. Slipping the dagger from the sheath at his waist, Lock slashed the rope, freeing Karl in time for the next wave to wash the man overboard.

Lock smiled, squinting against the rain and seawater blurring his eyes. *Born in violence to die in violence.* At least his life had been consistent.

* * * * *

Lock awoke with stinging eyes, every muscle in his body aching. He first noticed the smell. Heat as powerful as in the tropics but without the warm, cleansing breeze made breathing uncomfortable. The stagnant air reeked of moldy

16

water, rotten scraps, and body odor. There were no scents of a ship, nor was there a gentle rocking motion.

Then he remembered. The Shana Whore had sunk, and Lock had swum for what seemed like hours in the chilly, stormy sea, amazed each time he managed to gasp salty air and swim another stroke, defying nature herself.

He must have washed up on shore, but where?

He detected the sound of others breathing in the dark room, heard their snores and murmurs. He tried sitting up, but found himself bound to a flat wooden platform, bodies close on either side of him. It was then, he realized, his difficulty breathing wasn't necessarily from the heat but from the chain across his chest. He attempted to shift position to relieve some of the heaviness, but he hadn't enough space to move.

Throwing himself upward in his fury, he roused the men beside him who shouted and tried scooting away.

"What the hell is it?" one of them bellowed.

"Don't tell me they started putting animals in with us now?" cried another.

"Hey, guards!" several screamed in unison.

By the time the guards stepped inside, carrying torches, Lock had yanked away several of the chains and sat up. He wound his hands around the chain on his feet and pulled until his palms bled.

The guards, dressed in leather and mail, stared at him for a dumfounded moment before two of them flew at him, their swords drawn.

Lock reached up a shackled hand, grabbed one guard by the throat, and pinned him to the wall beside him. The guard's feet trampled on a prisoner's chest in an attempt to free himself from the choke-hold.

The second guard struck Lock in the back of the head with a sword. Lock dropped the man he was strangling and jerked his elbow backwards, staggering the guard who'd struck him.

Through a gush of blood from his split lips, the guard shouted for reinforcements. Three more guards, two half-dressed from their bedrolls, charged inside, all armed with small wooden clubs. Lock jerked two of the clubs from the guards and swung them with expertise learned from years of studying weapons. Finally, several guards dragged in heavier chains and dropped them over Lock, binding him from shoulder to ankle.

He lay panting and sweat-soaked, rage tearing at his insides.

The guards, their breathing ragged, picked up their weapons and dragged themselves out of the hut, taking the torches with them. Lock had seen enough in the light to realize he was in a long, windowless room containing platforms of prisoners stacked so close together their arms and legs touched.

"Where are we?" Lock demanded.

When no answer came, his fury renewed. He was accustomed to receiving answers to his questions. Then he remembered that he had no idea how far from his original destination he was. Perhaps these people didn't understand him.

"Are you all deaf, or don't you speak my language?"

"I speak it," came a voice from across the room. "And you ain't getting out of here. All you did was make life harder for yourself...until you die, that is."

"Who are those men? Slave traders?" The thought of being sold into slavery made him sick. He's spent too many years being used for his body and would sooner die than live like a slave again.

"Bounty hunters. Might as well be slavers, though."

Bounty hunters. They sought out criminals wanted in any kingdom in the world and collected the rewards on their heads. Lock wondered which kingdom he'd be taken to. He was wanted in countless lands. Pirates were most coveted by bounty hunters. Lock had killed his share of the grubby bastards in the past.

"We'll be stopping in Blue Hollow in the morning," the other prisoner continued. "You know what happens there?"

"Does it matter?"

"You know the agreement the bounty hunters have with the kingdoms in these parts? They can sell us to the highest bidder, if their price exceeds the one on our heads. However the rules are, we receive our stated punishment until someone buys us."

"I'd rather get my punishment."

"Do you know what it is? Maybe slavery would be better."

"I'm sure mine is death, and that is better than slavery."

"But how are you going to die? Is it something easy, like beheading or hanging? Or will it be burning alive, the lash, or disembowelment?"

"Slavery can include all of the above."

"You're either brave or stupid. All I know is, I hope I get bought. My sentence is fifty lashes, unless someone buys me."

Fifty lashes! Lock prayed his sentence would be so light. Fifty lashes he could endure.

"Of course, the bidding only applies if you're not wanted in Begonia."

"What's that?"

"Begonia is the kingdom in control of Blue Hollow, ruled by the Empress Daryn. She favors women and granted the village of Blue Hollow to a group of females. Daryn provides guards for their protection. Many of the guards are female."

Lock snorted. "A useless place. I know there's no price on my head there because I've never been to Begonia or boarded ships from there."

"Then maybe for your sake, no one there will recognize you and you'll catch a woman's fancy. Because I think you're right."

"About?"

"When the torches came in, I got a look at you and I think I know who you are. Lock the White, your sentence in all the kingdoms where you're wanted will surely be death."

Chapter Two

ဢ

"What's going on?" Sparrow looked up from the cart of apples in the marketplace toward the ensemble of guards leading two wagons full of prisoners into Blue Hollow square.

"The bounty hunters have come to peddle slaves," Shea-Ann, Sparrow's closest friend and former nanny, explained. "We missed the bunch they brought last year. Maybe we could take a look at this group before the punishments start."

Sparrow glanced at Shea-Ann. Twenty-four years Sparrow's senior, Shea-Ann had known her since the day she was born. Sparrow had been the third daughter in the royal house of an eastern kingdom overthrown three years ago by commoners. Not that Sparrow blamed them for the uprising. Her brother had been on the throne, and unlike Sparrow, he thrived on cruelty. Taxes were indescribable and punishments brutal. The royal family had been thrust out of power and her brother beheaded. Sparrow, once a princess, now ran a small farm in Blue Hollow, and though at times she missed her creature comforts, she'd never been happier. She was proud to earn her keep through hard work and enjoyed living in a village run by women. Sparrow had never loved life as a princess. She'd always felt guarded, overly-protected, and she disliked watching the damage her brother inflicted while being powerless to stop his greedy rampage. When she left home, Shea-Ann had accompanied her, no longer as a servant, but as a companion. The older woman was a fine healer and midwife, and the people of Blue Hollow demanded her skills as much as they clamored for Sparrow's corn, potatoes, wheat, and milk.

"Why do we need to look at slaves?" Sparrow asked. "We have two farmhands who help us, and the farm isn't so big that I can't handle it on my own when I have to."

"It's a good way to have a look at half-naked men." Shea-Ann's dark slanted eyes gleamed with mischief. The woman was small, scarcely reaching Sparrow's shoulder in height, her body slender and supple, her skin fine and pale. Shea-Ann had always enjoyed escapades with men, even in the palace. "I just don't like to watch the punishments. Such cruelty is usually unnecessary."

Sparrow chose a sack of apples, paid the cart owner, and slung her goods over her shoulder. "All right. We can go look, but do you want to finish shopping first?"

Shea-Ann shook her head. "Always thinking with your stomach instead of your womanhood."

The companions bought fruit, smoked meat, fabric, and wool from several other carts in the marketplace, then brought the merchandise to their wagon.

Together, they wound through the crowd of vendors, women leading horses to the village blacksmith, and children playing in the streets.

As they approached the platform in the center of town, two tall, golden-skinned, black-haired men strutted across the planks, seemingly unhindered by the shackles and chains on their ankles. The hard muscles of their nude, oiled bodies flexed as they struck poses. Raising their arms, they squeezed their fists and their biceps bulged. They turned, revealing corded muscles beneath the smooth skin of their backs and shoulders. Long, sinewy legs stretched into wide stances, their erect cocks saluting their audience as sizeable balls dangled beneath.

Murmurs of approval floated across the crowd of villagers watching the spectacle. Sparrow felt a blush rise in her cheeks as she tore her gaze from the men to glance at Shea-Ann who stared, a satisfied smile on her lips.

"Now this is what I call entertainment," said the older woman.

"I think it's a disgrace," Sparrow muttered, yet she

watched in fascination as another slave—female this time— joined the men. A beaded vest concealed her breasts, and she wore a short leather skirt. Her wrists were manacled, and she bore the brand of murderer on her left bicep. A long, blond braid dangled over her shoulder as she paused in front of the men. One of them approached her from behind. She leaned her back against his muscled chest as he unfastened the ties on her vest so her breasts popped free. He squeezed the globes and rolled the nipples between his fingers while the other man knelt in front of her and lifted her short skirt. He ran a tongue over his lips before covering her clit with his mouth. The woman moaned, arching backwards, lost in the ecstasy of one man's mouth and the other's hands.

"I can't believe this." Sparrow's lip curled with disgust.

"How much for the pair of them?" bellowed a short, gray-haired woman standing close to the platform.

One of the bounty hunters laughed. "Probably more than you could afford!"

"Give us a quote!"

"Fifteen hundred silver pieces for both of them."

"What about just one?" the woman shouted.

"Sorry. They're being sold as a set."

A lithe redheaded woman whom Sparrow recognized as a fur trader waved her hand in the air. "How much for the woman?"

The bounty hunter laughed. "So that's your flavor, is it, Miss? I'll let you have her for two hundred gold pieces."

The fur trader narrowed her eyes. "One hundred."

"Come now! Look at her! She's built for strength and endurance."

Sparrow noted it certainly appeared that way. The blond slave stood between the men, writhing with passion, her hands roaming over the bulging shoulders of the slave lapping her pussy. She tilted her head, biting the earlobe of the man squeezing her breasts and rubbing her nipples with the pads of his thumbs.

"One fifty!" the redheaded fur trader called.

"One seventy five!" the bounty hunter argued.

"All right, one seventy five!"

To the crowd's disappointment, the bounty hunter motioned for the other guards to stop the slaves' love play as he stepped down to settle the bargain with the fur trader.

"What are they doing now?" Sparrow asked Shea-Ann.

Two bounty hunters dragged a tall, blond man to the platform and chained him between two thick, wooden posts.

"Damn," Shea-Ann said. "The punishments are beginning."

"Let's get out of here," Sparrow suggested, but the crowd closed in behind them, pushing them nearer the platform.

One guard stood behind the prisoner whose face tensed with terror. The guard raised his whip and snapped it, slicing the blond's flesh. He gritted his teeth in silence for one more blow, but on the third slice he bellowed with pain.

The bounty hunter in charge of the auction returned to his place on the platform and called out to the crowd, "This man is a horse thief, wanted in the kingdom of Upper Kenna. Unless anyone wishes to speak for him, he will be punished up to fifty lashes!"

The whip hissed and the prisoner screeched.

A woman behind Sparrow said, "I think I'll speak for him. He looks big enough for wood cutting but was screaming like a tortured cat before the third lash fell. He'll be simple to control." The woman's voice rose to a bellow. "I speak for him! I offer ten silver pieces!"

"The Emperor of Upper Kenna will give us twelve!" the guard called back.

"You're going to quibble over two lousy silver pieces when you'll have to drag his arse back to the Kennas, feeding him along the way?"

"A silver piece is a silver piece!"

The whipping guard pulled back his weapon, but the bartering guard held up his hand, signaling a pause in the beating.

"Eleven silver pieces. No more," the woman stated.

"Sold for eleven silver pieces!" The guard shook his fist in the air. "Cut him down, tie him up, and deliver him wherever this woman would like. Bring up the next prisoner!"

A shorter, thicker man with curly red hair was fastened to the posts.

"This man is wanted for highway robbery in Zaltana. He tried to strangle the wagon driver."

Another guard tore the shirt down the prisoner's back. The lash whistled in the air as the bartering continued. "Twenty five lashes is his punishment! Twenty five and the mark of a thief burned on his chest!"

"I was only trying to feed my family!" the redhead screamed as the lashes fell in rapid succession.

"Ten gold pieces!" A middle-aged woman called out. "What's in his pants alone looks like it's worth it!"

"Sold for ten gold pieces!"

"She's right about that," Shea-Ann whispered to Sparrow. "Looks like he has a tree branch in those breeches."

Sparrow raised her eyes to the heavens. "This is the most disgusting display I've seen since my brother was king. I'm going."

"Me too, in another moment."

Ten more slaves were paraded across the scaffold. Most were sentenced to whippings, some were tortured with hot pincers, some branded, and others stretched on a rack set up behind the whipping posts. Many women bought the prisoners out of their punishments, glad for free workers or bed mates, even if they were condemned. Slaves required little more care than animals, and the women of Blue Hollow liked their personal freedom. Some of the prisoners suffered longer than others, particularly the unattractive ones. Some were courageous and refused to scream while others screeched before the first strike landed.

"With all those bloody backs and burned body parts, my business will be flowing," Shea-Ann remarked. "Still, I can't believe some of these men are being bought. There are a few who deserve death."

"I've had enough of this." Sparrow was about to turn away when the next prisoner caught her attention. Though chained and shackled, it still took ten guards to drag him up the steps and hitch him to the poles. Tall and barefoot, he wore only a loincloth. His limbs were long and muscled, his broad chest and back littered with old scars. A shaggy gray and brown beard sprouted from his face, and dark, kinky hair streaked with white dangled over his shoulders and back in matted tendrils. His eyes, the pale blue of bird's eggs, shot defiance and rage but held no hint of fear.

Sparrow heard several women murmur over the man's raw beauty, but no one spoke for him. Strangely, the guard didn't announce the man's punishment or ask for a bid.

A third guard stepped forward, carrying a scourge consisting of several strips of knotted leather. The crowd grew quiet as the punishment began. Sparrow counted twenty-five blows before she whispered to Shea-Ann, "I wonder why they haven't asked for a price on him?"

The smaller woman chuckled. "No one's likely to pay it. If I'm right, that's the pirate Lock the White. He's a devil. Any woman would be a fool to bid for him."

Sparrow glanced at the pirate's slashed back. Blow after blow fell until blood dripped down what was left of his skin, darkening his trousers and staining his boots. Other than a blinking of pale blue eyes and a sheen of sweat on his face and chest, the pirate revealed no sign of pain. Sparrow had lost count of the strikes of the whip, but she knew most men would have shrieked already.

"How much for him?" she shouted, scarcely recognizing her own voice.

Shea-Ann grasped her arm and hissed, "Are you crazy!"

"We cannot take a bid yet," the guard told her.

"Why?"

"He's sentenced to death, but if we sell him, the punishment is reduced to torture until he faints."

Sparrow's brow furrowed as she stared at the pirate's upright posture and stoic expression. He didn't look ready to scream, let alone faint.

Several moments passed before the first signs of pain appeared in the form of blood dripping down the pirate's forearms as he strained against the manacles holding his hands above his head. A second guard joined the beating, his whip wrapping around the pirate's waist, leaving a bloody trail over his stomach and side. He staggered almost to his knees, his arms stretched to the limit above his head. He struggled to right himself amidst the storm of knotted leather, his chest heaving with each ragged breath.

Sparrow's hands balled into fists, her heart pounding in her throat. The guard claimed this man's punishment wasn't death, but if the pirate didn't lose consciousness soon, the severity of the beating would surely cause internal damage.

"If you don't let me bid on him, he's going to be useless!" Sparrow shouted to the guard.

"These orders come from Zaltana. You know how their ruler feels about his word being obeyed. In case you don't know, woman, this is Lock the White, pirate, murderer, thief, and I wouldn't doubt rapist and child molester too, though those crimes have never been mentioned."

The crowd murmured. Several woman turned away from the sight of the pirate's shredded back. Sparrow wondered how he'd managed to stand again beneath the violent onslaught.

"Come on, let's go." Shea-Ann grasped Sparrow's hand and tugged. She jerked away from her friend.

* * * * *

Lock wondered how much longer his legs would support him as he jerked himself upward, using the manacles as leverage. He'd lost count of the blows long ago, and though he was accustomed to pain, he'd never felt anything like this. The guards wielded their weapons well, managing to make their whips land directly in previous cuts until he felt as if the blows were slashing at his very skeleton. He'd meant it when he'd said he'd rather die than be a slave, but with each strike of knotted leather, the idea of being shackled to a mistress became more appealing. When he heard that his punishment would continue until he passed out, he knew he wouldn't live to see the sun set. Lock had never fainted in his life, though there had been more than one time in his childhood when he'd wished for oblivion.

He tried focusing on the horizon, tried separating his mind from his body. Though he felt hot enough to dissolve into the cracks in the bloody platform beneath him, he resisted the urge to shiver, the urge to shriek. If he'd been a praying man, he'd have prayed for unconsciousness.

The beating stopped suddenly, and he was released from the post. He fell forward, managing to catch himself with his hands, agony hotter than the sun shooting up his arms, seeping into his shoulders and what was left of his back. Tears of pain sprang into his eyes, His vision momentarily darkened, but it cleared too quickly. He pushed himself to his feet as guards half-dragged him across the platform toward the rack. Beneath the deadly device, coals were arranged for the fire. The thought of heat against his torn flesh instilled a fear in him he'd never experienced before. His strength returned in a blind rush, and he pulled hard on his bonds, dragging both guards to their knees.

Several more bounty hunters jumped on him, grasping

his chains and hauling him to the rack.

From somewhere in the crowd, he heard a woman's voice bidding on him, and he nearly laughed, giddy from pain and the realization that his nightmare—the one which had inspired him to spend years conditioning himself to torture—had actually come true.

One of the guards approached with a heated blade and carved symbols around both of Lock's arms. To keep from crying out, he bit his lips until he tasted blood, the smell of burning flesh making bile rise in his throat. If he vomited while strapped to the rack, he'd choke to death. *What a humiliating way to die*, he thought.

"How much is Zaltana giving you for him?" the same woman's voice called again.

"More than you can afford, Missy!"

The coals were lit beneath the rack, and as the heat grew, Lock struggled against his bonds. He gasped until his throat felt raw, his heart threatening to explode before the flames actually reached his flesh. The whip fell across his abdomen and he mewled, sickened by the pathetic sound but unable to force it back down his throat. Another whip flicked at his chest, but his limbs were pulled so tightly he couldn't so much as flinch.

Why hadn't he drowned with the rest of his crew? *Because that's how my life has been from the first…*

* * * * *

Sparrow stared in horror at the spectacle on the platform. She wondered how the pirate was still conscious when she felt ready to faint herself. What more could they do, short of killing him? The coals grew hotter, and she saw the first flames springing to life.

"I'll pay for him with jewels from the royal family of RedHorne!" she shouted.

Shea-Ann's jaw dropped. "You can't do that! It's all you

29

have left from…"

Sparrow shot her a look that would have stopped a charging war horse in its tracks.

"That family was unseated years ago. How did you come by such jewels?" The bartering guard sounded suspicious.

"She was a RedHorne Princess!" one of the villagers called to him.

"I want to see the jewels, then," the guard said.

"Stop damaging him first." Sparrow stepped forward. "As it is, I'm already paying for destroyed merchandise."

The guard motioned for the flames to be doused and the torture to stop.

Sparrow approached the scaffold, unfastening the pouch on her hip. Though crime was uncommon in Blue Hollow, she'd always feared a random thief and the loss of the only ties left to her family, so when she ventured out for the day, she kept her jewels with her.

As she climbed the steps to the scaffold, she caught the reek of blood and smoke and nearly gagged. She glanced at the pirate. His eyes were unfocused with pain, his body slick with blood and sweat. She knew he'd committed terrible acts, but couldn't help feeling pity for his suffering. If they'd wanted him to pay for his crimes, why couldn't they have simply killed him and gotten it over with?

Sparrow turned her attention to the guard, extending her hand, her mother's ruby and sapphire necklace resting across her palm.

The guard snatched the bauble, inspecting it closely.

"Nice," he said. "Very nice. Zaltana is willing to pay two thousand gold pieces for him. As beautiful as these jewels are, they're not worth quite that much. Nearly, but not quite."

"If you don't bargain with me, you'll still have to travel to Zaltana to collect payment. That's quite a distance, and you know how dangerous it is for strangers to cross Zaltanian land."

The guard pondered her words then nodded, his gloved hand closing over the necklace. "He's yours. Where would you like us to take him?"

"My farm several miles north of here."

He glanced at the group of guards. "Do what she says."

The guards unchained the pirate from the rack and hauled him to his feet. Disoriented, he took two unsteady steps before one of the bounty hunters kicked him down the scaffold stairs, dispersing the crowd. Lock landed with a grunt on his stomach. He braced his hands against the packed dirt, the muscles in his big arms straining as he attempted to raise himself. A second guard approached with a pail of water that had been heating beside the coals. He threw it on the pirate's mutilated back. The shriek of agony that sprang from Lock the White's throat made Sparrow shiver.

"So he is human after all," the bartering guard muttered.

Sparrow flung the man a vicious look before walking from the scaffold. The guards dragged Lock to his feet, wary of the pirate though he was far too weak to fight them again. Beneath his dark skin, his face was as pale as the streaks in his hair and beard. His eyelids flickered rapidly, and she wondered if he was fighting for consciousness or oblivion.

"This is going to be a disaster," Shea-Ann said from beside Sparrow. The small woman folded her arms across her chest and shook her head. "I cannot believe what you've done."

"Don't tell me you didn't feel a little sorry for him."

"I feel sorry for the people he's hurt, too, but somehow I doubt he has any regrets. You, better than anyone, should know that."

Sparrow's chest tightened. Shea-Ann was right. Sparrow knew first hand the damage a man like the pirate could visit on decent people, such as herself. By rights she should have reveled in his pain and destruction, but her fury was reserved for one man alone. Lock the White had nothing to do with her—until the moment his stubborn strength had touched an unexplored part of her spirit and driven her to this unthinkable deed.

"One more thing, Missy." The guard Sparrow had paid approached her with a wicked smile. "You are aware of Empress Daryn's law?"

"What law?" Sparrow lifted an eyebrow. In truth, she'd always avoided the slave trade and knew nothing of the laws surrounding it.

"Anyone who purchases a prisoner wanted for murder agrees that should he escape, she will take his punishment for him."

"Death?" Sparrow felt a little sick.

The guard shook his head. "No. It would never be death. Empress Daryn isn't unnecessarily cruel. You must take his lesser punishment, the one used during bartering."

"Tortured until I faint?"

"That's the one, Missy." The guard smiled brightly. "Nice doing business with you."

The bounty hunters cleared the remainder of prisoners back to the wagons, but Sparrow remained planted at the bottom of the scaffold.

Shea-Ann clicked her tongue. "Now you've done it! That's what you get for having such a soft heart. Compassion has always been your worst fault."

"You should talk! You're the healer. I'm just a farmer."

"A farmer who has responsibility for Lock the White, the worst pirate to ever sail out of the Archipelago of SothSea!"

Chapter Three

ஐ

Sparrow opened the door of her farmhouse, a structure containing one spacious room and a small loft above. Behind her, Shea-Ann muttered under her breath about the foolishness of young women, but Sparrow refused to argue with her until later. At the moment, she had other things to think about.

"Where do you want 'em?" asked one of the guards who dragged Lock toward the house.

"Drop him against that trunk." Shea-Ann pointed to the simple oak trunk at the foot of Sparrow's bed. She glanced at the former princess. "We can see to his front side first, then lay him down. He certainly won't be on his back any time soon."

The guards hurled Lock to his knees, his stomach slamming against the edge of the trunk. He uttered a soft moan and leaned against the wooden surface, his head buried in his arms.

"Good luck to you, girl," one of the bounty hunters said to Sparrow. "You'll be needing it."

"Take my advice and never take these off," the other guard motioned towards Lock's shackles, "or else he'll be out of here like a shooting arrow and will most likely cut your throat before he goes."

Sparrow offered a nervous giggle. "Then I guess it will save me Empress Daryn's punishment."

The first guard shook his head. "I like your spirit, girl. I hope what you did for him today doesn't lash back in your pretty face."

"Oh, it will." Shea-Ann tossed a disgusted glance at her

young friend as she gathered her healing supplies. "The likes of him respect the whip more than kindness."

"I thought you were against me keeping him?" Sparrow snapped at her friend. "Why are you helping?"

"I'm a healer," Shea-Ann retorted. "I'm doing my job. Besides, someone has to watch out for you."

The guards offered to install a base for Lock's manacles strong enough to keep him from escaping.

"We've had practice with this," the guards told her. "He's strong as a team of oxen. Nearly escaped twice before we got here, but we know what holds him now."

"I'd be grateful for your help," Sparrow said.

"Where would you like to keep him? The barn?"

Sparrow shook her head and pointed to an empty corner of the room. "That will be fine for now."

"In the house?"

"Just do what she tells you." Shea-Ann waved her hand, but muttered under her breath. "The girl is daft. If he's staying here, I'm finding a room in the village."

While the guards worked, Sparrow assisted Shea-Ann. Sparrow washed the pirate's burned arms, marveling at the thickness of his biceps. She was considered a muscular woman, strong from working her farm, but his arms were easily three times her size, about as big as the blacksmith's they'd visited in Begonia last year, except Lock's limbs were much longer.

When she'd finished bandaging his arms, Shea-Ann said, "Move him so I can see to his front. I want to hurry up and get to his back—not that there's much skin left."

Sparrow nudged the pirate, surprised to find him still awake, but she doubted anyone could sleep with that much pain.

"Move back," she told him, both hands clutching one of his arms. He did as she suggested, closing his eyes tightly and

34

swallowing hard as the motion must have been excruciating. He shivered in spite of the warm summer day.

Sparrow noticed the slightest expression of sympathy in Shea-Ann's dark eyes. "As soon as we find you a permanent position, I'll give you something for the pain."

If the pirate heard her, he didn't acknowledge her words. Shea-Ann worked quickly, leaving Sparrow to apply bandages while she walked to the round wooden table in the center of the room and prepared a sleeping potion.

"Think you can get to the bed?" Sparrow asked Lock.

"Drink this first." Shea-Ann held a mug to his lips. "Tastes lousy, but you won't wake up until morning."

He swallowed the pungent mixture, and after a moment's hesitation, stood and stumbled to the bed, one hand braced against Sparrow's shoulder.

Damn, he's heavy, she thought, relieved when he dropped stomach-down on the mattress.

"What a mess," Shea-Ann said as she set to work on the pirate's back. "You're going to need new bedclothes."

Sparrow glanced at the blood staining her blankets and shrugged. There was nothing she could do about it now.

"Move his hair," Shea-Ann ordered.

As gently as she could, Sparrow pulled his long hair away from his back. Blood had pasted the two-toned mass to his flesh, and he nearly jumped off the bed at the first sweep of her hand. Sparrow felt sick. She doubted she could have ever been a healer like Shea-Ann. She reached into her waist pouch and removed a carved wooden clip to pin Lock's hair on top of his head so it wouldn't slip into the raw mass of his shoulders and back. Several strands of hair clung to his forehead, and she brushed them away, thinking that if he was clean and healthy, he'd be very handsome, bush-like beard and all.

His eyes opened halfway, and she was struck again by their odd blue color.

"Hurts to breathe," he murmured in a SothSea language, but Sparrow understood. Before her family had been stripped of power, she'd spent her days studying with many fine teachers and had mastered ten languages. The pirate's dialect was unusual, but she could communicate with him.

"What did he say?" Shea-Ann asked, her eyes fixed on her work.

"He said it hurts to breathe."

Shea-Ann laughed humorlessly. "I don't doubt it. Tell him that potion will work soon and he won't feel a thing."

Sparrow translated, and even as she spoke, the pirate's eyes slipped shut and his strained breathing became regular. Sparrow's entire body relaxed, and she realized she'd been holding every muscle tense since the village square.

"I don't like how you're looking at him," Shea-Ann said.

"What do you mean?"

"I've known you since the day you were born, Sparrow. In fact, I was there. Don't get any ideas about this slave. He might be harmless now, but he is evil. Believe me. There's not a pirate from the Archipelago who has a decent bone in his body, and this one is the worst of the lot."

"I don't feel anything." Sparrow nodded toward the bloody meat that was his back. "Look at him."

"You're remembering what you saw *before* they set to work on him. All those long, sinewy limbs. Those thighs. I haven't seen a buttocks this tight since I was a girl."

"Shea-Ann, it sounds to me like you're the one whose thoughts are straying."

"I'm being honest. He has the look of a breeding bull if ever I saw one—at least he did. Those bounty hunters have made a wreck of him. If he doesn't die of infection, it will be a miracle, and these scars are not going to be at all attractive."

"He has a lot of scars." Sparrow glanced over the untouched skin of his arms and some old, white marks interspersed with the bloody ones on his ribs.

"I'm not surprised. They're all rough, those pirates. Scum. Worse than scum."

"I think you've made your point, Shea-Ann."

"I hope so. If he lives, I hope you know enough to fear him and never, never risk his escape."

Sparrow glanced at the pirate's large body sprawled on her bed, remembered the expression of utter hatred in his eyes when he'd been dragged to the scaffold, and felt her stomach knot again. No, she wasn't stupid. She definitely knew enough to fear him.

Chapter Four

ဢ

Lock awoke to a streak of sunlight across his face. He attempted to move, but his back was on fire and the rest of his body ached like he'd fought a White Island yak. Across the room, the young woman from the day before sat at a round wooden table, shelling peas. She wore baggy trousers belted with a strip of leather and worn brown boots. A vest left her rounded arms and shoulders bare, her muscles moving sensuously in the light shining in through the room's single window. Her long, light brown hair hung in a braid down her back. Her rose-colored mouth was small and delicate, her nose straight, and her forehead high and smooth. Even from where he lay, he noted the thickness of her dark lashes. Somewhere in his fuzzy brain, he realized she was pretty, but he was in too much pain to really care what she looked like. All he knew was that she'd *bought* him.

Her gaze fixed on him, and she offered a smile. *Go ahead and gloat, you little bitch,* he thought. *Wait until I can get up again.*

She dropped the peas and approached the bed. Her eyes were darker blue than his, wide-set, and beautifully shaped. A light spray of freckles decorated her nose and full cheeks.

"I'd say good morning, but I don't think there's anything good about it for you right now," she said.

Hearing her speak his own language surprised him. He thought she'd spoken it the night before, but after he'd been brought up to the scaffold, the rest of the day was hazy.

"Are you hungry?" she asked.

Food was the last thing on his mind. The thought of movement made him sick, but he needed to piss, and his mouth and throat were so dry he nearly choked when he tried swallowing.

"I have salve for your back." She washed her hands in a basin by the bed, dried them, and reached for a pot of strong-scented, slimy-looking paste.

He drew a sharp breath at her first touch, then managed to relax a bit. The salve was very cool, and though it didn't take away the pain, it made the thought of moving slightly less daunting. Still, when he sat up, he bit his cheek to keep from groaning.

She washed her hands and reached for a chamber pot. Humiliated by the thought of her tending his bodily functions, he nearly refused, but he hadn't a choice.

She must have noted the rage in his eyes because she said, "We all have to do it."

"Don't patronize me."

The woman raised an eyebrow. "You have some attitude for a man in your condition."

"You bought my attitude."

"Guess I did." She ripped the chamber pot from him and disappeared outside, leaving him to fix his own loincloth. He finished the task and sat on the edge of the bed, too numb to move. The whole situation was so incredibly degrading, and he was in too much pain to do a thing about it. He didn't dare risk an escape attempt. He knew he didn't have the strength to break the chains, and even if he did, he doubted he'd make it past the front door. No, he'd have to wait.

The woman returned with a bucket of fresh water. She brought him a full mug and he accepted it, willing himself not to flinch at the motion. When he drank, even swallowing hurt. He almost wished for that old witch's potion from the night before.

"You should eat something."

He shook his head.

"Maybe after you clean up."

He stared at the basin of water. He felt disgusting, not having washed since his ship had crashed, but the thought of moving any more than he had to was far from appealing.

"I'll help you." She dampened a cloth in the basin.

With a snarl, he snatched the cloth from her and began washing slowly, every movement excruciating.

"You know being this stubborn is what got you into trouble yesterday," she said, watching him.

"You don't even know me."

"I know if you weren't stubborn you'd have passed out long before they got you to the rack."

He nearly shivered at the memory. "It has nothing to do with stubbornness. Some people just faint easily."

"You call that easily?" She reached for another cloth and finished helping him wash. This time he didn't protest. All he wanted was to lie back down and not move until he had to pee again.

"I want to change those bandages." She nodded toward his arms.

She walked across the room and filled a bowl from a pot simmering over the fireplace.

"Eat this." She placed the stew on his knee. The aroma of boiled vegetables and meat made him realize he was a little hungry, and he had to sit up while she worked on his arms.

She unraveled one of his bandages. He glanced at the symbols branded into this flesh and asked, "What does it say?"

"This arm is for thief," she told him. "The other one says murderer."

At least his flesh would carry no lies.

By the time she'd finished cleaning his arms and applying fresh bandages, he'd managed to empty half the bowl.

"Do you need help lying down again?" she asked.

He shot her another annoyed look and lay on his stomach. He'd been sitting up so long that the salve had dried on his oozing flesh, and movement was almost as agonizing as when he'd first awakened. He closed his eyes tightly, his cheek resting against a pillow that smelled faintly of wild flowers. After a moment, he realized his hair—the only part of him that didn't hurt—was being stroked with a gentleness he'd never experienced. *How can anything feel good enough to rival the pain in my back?*

He opened his eyes and found himself staring into the woman's large, soft ones.

"As your slave, do you expect me to put up with your touch?" he said in his most frigid voice.

The caress stopped instantly, and without a word she returned to the table and continued shelling peas.

When he closed his eyes, he wondered why he could still feel her hand on his hair.

* * * * *

"That's what I get for trading my mother's necklace for the son-of-a-bitch," Sparrow muttered to her cow, Daphne. Seated on a milking stool, she squeezed the cow's udder, listening to the rhythm of the milk as it hit the bucket.

"Sparrow, I'm back!" Shea-Ann stepped into the barn, looking weary. She'd been gone all night and part of the morning caring for other newly-bought slaves. "I'm going to get some sleep. How's the pirate?"

"Flippant."

"Excuse me?"

"He was arguing with me all morning."

"He has the strength to argue?"

"Evidently. It's as if he's furious because I saved his life."

"I told you." Shea-Ann shook her head. "He's going to be nothing but trouble. Do you want to ride to Begonia and see if

41

the bounty hunters will take him back before it's too late?"

Sparrow's stomach twisted at the thought of what they'd do to him. He might be rude and ungrateful, but any further punishment in his condition would kill him, and she had no desire to see him dead, though she wondered why not.

Shea-Ann left Sparrow alone to finish her chores and reflect on the pirate lying in her bed. *Her bed!* She'd slept wrapped in blankets by the fire, and he had the nerve to speak to her with contempt!

She stalked to the house with the bucket of milk and slammed it on the table, the white liquid sloshing onto her hands. She glared at the pirate only to realize he was staring at her.

"Don't you ever sleep?" she demanded.

"Switch places with me and see how well you sleep." He sounded tired.

"If it wasn't for me, you'd be dead."

"Did I ask you to buy me?"

She shook her head. Evidently he wasn't tired enough to keep from arguing.

"I wish I'd never stepped into the village yesterday," she muttered.

"I wish I hadn't either."

Her lips flicked upward in a smile. "I'm sure that's true."

He lifted his arm and reached for the mug of water by the bed. His hand curved around it for a second before he dropped his arm, his breathing shallow.

"Would you like a drink?" She couldn't keep the sarcasm from her voice. His manner made her furious. To her, there was no shame in admitting weakness, but he'd rather deny his own limitations rather than ask for help. Such behavior made no sense.

"No. I wanted to rearrange the table."

Sparrow bit her lip to keep from laughing out loud. She

would not allow his sense of humor to get to her. She was surprised he even had a sense of humor. His expression was so incredibly hard, and she didn't think of criminals as having charms and preferences the same as other people.

"Here." She took the mug from him. He raised his head to sip.

She sat close enough to feel the heat of his flesh and brushed his forehead with her knuckles. "I just want to see if you have a fever," she explained.

"She said I did." He motioned with his eyes toward Shea-Ann who slept on a second bed closer to the fire.

Sparrow placed the mug aside and changed the water in the basin by his bed. She dipped a cloth in the fresh water and placed it on the portion of his brow unconcealed by the pillow. She muttered, "I don't want you to croak in my bed."

"So you have a specific place you want me to croak in?" he murmured. She knew by the sound of his voice he was drifting to sleep.

"I'll let you know when I think of it," Sparrow replied, gazing at the sharpness of his cheekbones, the shape of his nose, and the fullness of his lower lip. She shook her head and walked to the fire, stirring the pot of stew. The pirate was arrogant, rude, and ungrateful. He was a filthy, oozing body lying helpless in her bed. What was it she found attractive about him? Perhaps Shea-Ann was right. She kept remembering how he looked when he'd been dragged up the scaffold. All that untamed male power. Even now, his body exuded strength in every curve and plane of his muscles and each expression in his pale blue eyes. That morning when she'd brought him the chamber pot, she'd seen his respectable equipment. All his parts, both soft and hard, were large and thick. Evidently torture hadn't shrunk either his attitude or his masculinity.

He obviously didn't like her at all, but he was her slave. She wondered if she could think of a way to use his body...

No. Sparrow chastised herself. *That would be rape, and she was no rapist. But,* she reflected, *there's more than one way to plant a field.*

Chapter Five

ξ○

Lock lost track of how long he lay like a useless sack of grain, moving only to wash, eat, and use the chamber pot. Eventually the leaping flames on his back turned to smoldering heat and he was able to move without feeling physically ill.

Both Sparrow and the older healer, Shea-Ann, kept careful watch over him. The healer was a monotonous bitch, always droning on about how vile Lock was and how Sparrow had wasted the family jewels.

"Don't you ever shut up?" Lock snarled at Shea-Ann one evening when the healer was delving into gossip she'd heard regarding one of Lock's past raids. Though he spoke with Sparrow in his own language, he understood theirs and when the mood took him, he argued with Shea-Ann.

"All of it's true! You sank a ship of a hundred men."

"One hundred fifty, and it wasn't the first, I assure you."

"And proud of it, too, aren't you?" Shea-Ann snarled. "Sparrow, I can't believe this scum in our house!"

"It's not by my choice, hag," Lock hissed.

"You shut your mouth, or I'll take a horsewhip to you myself!" The healer paused in stirring the pot of stew and pointed the ladle at Lock.

"It would be my pleasure!" the pirate spat.

"Stop it, both of you!" Sparrow bellowed. "You make my head ache."

"Among other things?" Lock tossed her a lewd glance.

Sparrow blushed to the roots of her hair. The woman was unusually innocent and didn't hide her desire for him well. He was experienced enough in the ways of lust to know when someone wanted him.

"You're disgusting," Sparrow snarled at him, her blue eyes flashing. "Not only are you horribly scarred, but you stink."

"Forgive me if I've neglected to visit the palace bath, My Queen." He bowed his head in a mock gesture of respect. She was right, however. He needed a full washing. His own smell was starting to make him sick.

The argument must have made her think as well, because the next day when Shea-Ann left for her rounds in the village, Sparrow dragged the wooden tub near the bed and filled it with water.

"Do you want me to go while you undress?" she began, but by the time she'd finished, he'd unfastened the ties on his loincloth and slid it off. Since his feet were shackled, the cloth was the only clothing that allowed him to undress without removing his chains. He wondered what the hell Sparrow was going to do when winter came. He certainly wasn't about to freeze his balls off because she was afraid he'd nab the first opportunity to run away – even if he would.

Her gaze swept him from head to foot, then fixed on his cock. He had to admit his apparatus was something to be proud of, even when not erect. However something about the pretty little bitch filled him with more desire than he wanted to admit, and since he'd started feeling like his old self, just looking at her was enough to make him hard.

Lock noted her scarlet cheeks with satisfaction. He curled his fist around his steely rod and pumped it twice, winking at Sparrow. "How about feeling your first cock, girl? I'm more than willing to let you have a few strokes."

Sparrow's expression tensed and she fired him an enraged look. "I would rather eat rotten goat's cheese with rat droppings in it."

Lock chuckled and stepped into the tub. With his back

46

still far from healed, the water hurt, but not mercilessly as when the bounty hunter had doused him with hot water after being tossed off the scaffold. He shook his head clear of that memory. That had been sheer, blinding agony.

Sparrow cast him another glance before yanking the blankets off the bed and bringing them outside to air.

Lock reached for the cake of soap beside the tub and washed. He tugged on the chain still attached to his shackled feet. It was a very strong, thick chain. He'd need some sort of weapon to break it, but he'd consider that later, after he was fully recovered. He tried wetting his matted, itchy hair. If he'd had access to a knife, he'd have cut it off days ago. When it was clean, it wasn't bad, but dirty, the long, heavy mass was driving him to madness.

Sparrow returned and picked up a bucket of water heating by the fire. She dumped it over his head, leaving the bucket over his face and whacking the top of it.

Lock ripped it from his head and threw it across the room, the motion pulling the healing flesh of his shoulders and back. He gritted his teeth at her gloating expression.

Lathering the soap in his hands, he reached up and washed his hair. After a moment, he dropped his arms, his back throbbing.

"I'll do it." Sparrow stepped behind him. He jerked away from her touch, but she said, "I want you clean if you're staying here."

"Why don't you cut it off?"

"I'm not bringing any kind of blade near you. Do I look stupid?"

"You acted stupid when you bartered for me."

"Why are you so mean?" she asked, rubbing her hands with the soap and digging her fingers into his hair. She massaged his scalp and he resisted the urge to close his eyes. Her small hands were strong, her touch most pleasant. He bent his head forward. As her thumbs rubbed his nape in a circular motion, his eyes did close. Too soon, she finished the shampoo by dumping more water over his head and washing away the soap. His back stung, but it had almost been worth the massage. It had definitely been worth the opportunity to wash.

He was about to stand, but she touched his hair again.

"What's wrong?" Lock tilted his face to stare up at her. "No lice, is there?"

She giggled. "No. I'm surprised you're concerned about it."

"I'm a pirate, not a pig."

"Could have fooled me."

"You have a sharp tongue for an innocent little girl." Lock grasped her wrist and tugged her to the side of the tub.

"Let me go!"

"I'm the one who's chained."

"I'll bite your cock off if you try anything on me!"

Lock didn't loosen his grip, but used his thumb to gently stroke the inside of her wrist. "Sounds interesting. Damn, your skin is soft."

She stared into his eyes, attraction mixed with fury. "Probably because you're accustomed to leather-skinned prostitutes!"

"Right, but I've had my share of princesses, too." His hand moved to the hollow of her elbow and he reached for her other wrist. When she didn't try pulling away, he nearly smiled. She might be easier to manipulate into setting him free than he'd thought. Her attraction to him was obvious, even in his hideous state, and she must have been curious about the sexual games he'd wager she knew little about.

"No princess worth her crown would sully her skin with the likes of you!"

"You'd be surprised how eager royals are to claw the trousers off a genuine SothSea pirate."

"Well not me!"

Lock shrugged. "Well you're no longer a royal, are you? You're a farm girl."

"And proud of it! How about you? Have you ever done anything in your life you're proud of?"

Lock had no answer for her, so he guided her arms around his neck as he sat straighter in the tub. She stiffened, but didn't protest.

His gaze held hers as his palms splayed against her back. For a small woman, her muscles were hard, her body trim. He felt his cock leap beneath the warm water. He nearly smiled when she leaned a bit closer. Slowly, so as not to startle her, he brushed his mouth against hers. Her eyes slipped shut at the first touch of their lips. Her hands threaded in the hair at his nape, and Lock's eyes closed as he deepened the kiss. His tongue traced the delicate shape of her lips, then parted them gently. Her warm, moist tongue met his, mimicking his strokes. She tasted of apples and cinnamon. So sweet and sultry.

Lock's heartbeat quickened, and his arms tightened around her in spite of how the skin on his back stretched painfully. She tasted so delicious, he felt like dragging her in the tub with him and plunging his cock deep into her soft little body.

One of his hands slid up her back. He cradled her head in his palm as he tasted every corner of her mouth.

"That's it, girl," he whispered against her lips. He cupped one of her breasts, his thumb circling her hard nipple through her billowy shirt.

"Lock—"

His mouth covered hers again before she finished speaking. He slipped his hand beneath her shirt and kneaded first one breast, then the other. Stiff little nipples scraped his callused palms, and she pulled away.

"That's enough!" she snapped, her face flushed pink and her breasts rising and falling with each labored breath.

"Not for me." He stood and stepped out of the tub, his nude, dripping body looming above her.

She strode across the room and flung a towel at his chest. Grinning, he caught it.

"Don't think that will ever happen again!" she snapped.

"You think it won't?"

"I know it won't!"

"So why didn't you stop me sooner?"

"Because—"

"You want me. Even shredded up like I am, you want me between your legs, girl."

Sparrow's mouth hung open then she laughed long and loud. "Just like a man! The only reason I kissed you was because I've never seen a man like you up close before."

"So it was curiosity, was it?" he teased. The woman was full of shit. He'd felt her lust in her kiss, in her touch, and most of all in her pebble-hard nipples that begged for his caresses.

"Yes. Now it's satisfied. You were no different than any other man."

"I suppose you've had many to compare me to?" Lock said as he fastened a fresh loincloth she'd bought for him in the village the day before.

"I'm taking my bed back," she told him flatly, ignoring his question.

"You want me in it?"

"Don't flatter yourself!"

He grinned and silently sat on the blankets close to the fire while she shorted the chains on his feet.

"How long do you really think I'll stay in chains like this?" he asked.

"You don't have a choice. You're mine now."

"I'll never be yours. I belong to myself."

"Not anymore."

"You smug little piece of dung." The woman was really beginning to irritate him! "Remember, you're not a princess anymore."

"And you're not a pirate."

He smiled, a wicked twist of the lips. "I'll always be a pirate. You're going to learn that the hard way, little girl."

Neither of them spoke again as she drained the tub and left for the barn.

* * * * *

"What makes a man that nasty?" Sparrow patted Daphne's brown neck as the cow grazed in the field behind the barn. "Wish you had the answers, girl. Wish somebody had the answers. You'd think saving the man from torture would earn me a little gratitude."

Sparrow gazed at the setting sun as she led Daphne back to the barn for the night. When she'd rescued Lock she hadn't done it because she'd wanted his thanks or because she'd wanted a slave. She'd felt sorry for him. That was all. It was his attitude that made her question her actions, and now that he was growing strong, what was she going to do with him? She'd wager he'd never act the part of a slave, and she didn't like the idea of keeping a man chained to her wall like a dog.

She smiled, remembering how he'd looked before he'd been tortured. He was so tall and big with all that wild two-colored hair and eyes that looked like a demon's. Most likely he'd be more apt to frighten off thieves than a guard dog.

Sparrow knew the pirate's attitude shouldn't have surprised her. He was no different than most of the men she'd known in her life. Her brother had been a wretch, completely selfish and amused by the suffering of his subjects. Her father had been little better, and then there had been *the fiend*. The man who'd haunted Sparrow's sleep and twisted her gut every time she thought of him. Sparrow hated few people, but this man she would kill on sight, though she hoped she'd never see him again.

When her family had been overthrown, she'd left with her younger sister, Thea. Both women had been protected all their lives and were naive of the world outside the palace. No lessons from books or stories from teachers could provide the experience of dwelling in the real world. In spite of their fear and apprehension, Sparrow and Thea had looked forward to the adventures their new life offered. They planned to settle, perhaps raise horses. Thea had always loved horses. Together they'd made so many plans that would never come to pass...

Once Sparrow deposited Daphne to the barn and checked the rest of her animals, she walked to the house. She opened the door to the sound of Shea-Ann screeching, "If you don't stop that vile tongue from wagging, I'll rip it out!"

"And stir it up in one of your witch's brews?" Lock smiled, his teeth gleaming through his beard. Shea-Ann's fury always seemed to put him in a good mood.

"I'm not a witch, you ignorant scum! Healing is an art and a respected profession, but I shouldn't expect you to have the intelligence to understand that." Shea-Ann raised the wooden spoon she was using to stir the dinner cooking on the pot over the fire. Just before she flung it at Lock, Sparrow grasped her wrist.

"Do you realize you both fight constantly?"

"Not my fault," Shea-Ann and Lock said in unison.

"Looks like you're strong enough to start pulling your weight around here." Sparrow approached Lock, standing just shy of his reach.

He raised the chain in front of his face, his pale eyes staring at the links. "Good. Anything is better than being locked up in here."

"What do you think we should do with him?" Sparrow stood with Shea-Ann by the fire. She took a spoonful of the stew and swallowed.

"He's your property."

"I'm sure I can think of something for him to do."

"Hey! You can talk to me," Lock snapped.

Shea-Ann continued speaking of the pirate as if he wasn't in the room. "We can't let him out of this house, you know that. As soon as we try to unchain him, he'll be off."

"Even if you gave him a sleeping potion, he's rather heavy to move," Sparrow reflected. "Not that I couldn't do it."

"Either of you two bitches tries to give me another sleeping potion and you'll regret it!"

"Such a strong man," Shea-Ann said. "Pity we can't use him for the farm work."

"No, that's impossible. Too risky."

"And he's not healed enough for it now," Shea-Ann added. "I know! He can do the washing up."

Lock stood, nearly yanking his chain from the wall. "Not on your lives! I'm not doing the washing up."

"Oh," Sparrow raised an eyebrow, "not man enough for it?"

"Come over here, girl, and I'll show you what a man is."

Sparrow swallowed and glanced back into the stew pot. His offer was almost too tempting. She said, "It's settled then. From now on you'll do the dishes and the wash."

"Nothing's settled!"

"You haven't got much of a choice, *boy*." Shea-Ann looked down her nose at Lock.

"I'm nobody's boy!" he snarled, the mere annoyance in his eyes turning to pure rage.

"I was alive before you were a happy whistle on your father's lips!"

"Shea-Ann, that's enough," Sparrow said softly. "He's doing the washing up and there's no more need to discuss it."

"Over my dead body!"

Shea-Ann turned her spoon on Lock again. "It would

have been had it not been for My Lady!"

"Your *lady*? Your *lady*? I forget I'm in the presence of a *princess*." Lock extended a long arm as far as his chains would allow. "Come, Princess, and let me kiss the hem of your trousers."

"You love to be hateful, don't you?" Sparrow shook her head at him. "Why? Life is such a short gift, I can't imagine wasting so much time being miserable."

"Life is the underside of a slimy rock, and we're the slugs who suck upon it."

"Marvelous conversation for before dinner," Shea-Ann said. "Just get used to your place. I do the cooking and bring in what goods I can from healing, Sparrow does the wood cutting and farm work, and you do the washing up."

"If she does all that, she doesn't need a male slave." Lock jerked his head in Sparrow's direction. "And I can see why she's got no husband. She's got all the femininity of a he-goat."

Sparrow's eyes hazed red with fury. She clenched her fists and stomped toward Lock. "I have news for you, I had my share of proposals when my family was in power! I was engaged to a prince!"

"And where is he now that you're common?"

"I might be a commoner, but I'm not *nearly* as common as you!"

"Can't argue with that." He snatched her wrist before she realized what was happening. She tried pulling away, but he held her fast and placed a kiss on the back of her hand. "I wonder, Princess, did you give him an early taste of the royal wedding night?"

"Let go of me!" She tugged harder.

Shea-Ann whacked him over the head with the shaggy end of a broom. "Unhand her, you murdering scum!"

Lock released her, smiling wickedly, his gaze still fixed on Sparrow's. "No, Princess, I don't believe he did. I'm truly honored. I've never met an actual virgin before."

"That's it! No supper for you!" Shea-Ann raised the broom again, but this time Lock caught it before it landed and jerked it from the older woman's hands as she shouted, "Didn't your mother ever teach you any manners?"

Lock chuckled. He leaned back against the wall, a smile still lingering on his lips.

"And whether you eat or not, you're still doing the washing up." The healer shrugged.

Lock reverted to his own language as he flung a few choice words in Shea-Ann's direction.

"What did he say?" Shea-Ann glanced at Sparrow.

"You don't want to know." Sparrow curled her lip, not having heard such language since the time she and her younger sister had run off to the docks on the outskirts of the royal city. "Trust me."

Chapter Six

ಐ

"This is absolutely disgusting!" Shea-Ann muttered, staring at the mound of filthy dishes and smelly laundry piled around Lock's corner of the room.

"I don't know how he can stand it." Sparrow wrinkled her nose, glancing at the pirate who slept soundly, wrapped in a blanket on the floor amidst pots full of stagnant water, plates encrusted with meat scraps, Shea-Ann's bloody aprons from her rounds, and Sparrow's filthy woolen socks she used when chopping wood.

"Something has to be done about it. We can't go on like this or else we'll get rats."

"I hope they bite him right on his rear end. Speaking of his rear end..." Sparrow approached Lock and nudged him in the buttocks with her boot. When he didn't move, she pulled back her foot to kick him harder, but he caught her ankle and tugged. She landed on her back amidst a pile of dirty laundry.

"Listen to me, I want this mess cleaned up!" Sparrow glared at him, kicking her foot in an attempt to free herself from his grasp. She clenched her teeth in fury. He was the strongest man she'd ever met! She kicked him with her other foot, catching him across the face. He dragged her closer and kissed her.

Sparrow struggled, her heart pounding. His beard was rough on her face, and she tasted blood on his lips where she'd kicked him. She pushed his shoulders, but his grasp was firm. His tongue traced her lips, and she shivered, though from anything but disgust. She wanted to cling to him. As when he'd kissed her in the bath, she'd wanted to surrender completely to the warm, muscled body that held her so close, but she couldn't. If she gave in to a man like him, he'd view it as weakness...or cheapness, and she was neither a milksop nor a whore.

Again the broom crashed down on Lock's head. "Let her go, you animal! Get those vile lips off My Lady! The gods know what kind of diseases you have, you SothSea swine!"

"I haven't got any diseases, witch!" Lock released Sparrow, and she leapt away as he leered at her and added, "Anymore."

"That's it!" Sparrow suddenly forgot her desire as she spat into the air and wiped her mouth on the back of her hand. She pointed at Lock and bellowed, "You clean this mess up and do it before I get back from the field tonight!"

"I think we should get rid of him," Shea-Ann stated, her eyes serious. "He obviously can't be trusted. I told you from the first this would be a disaster. We should give him back to the bounty hunters, tell them to keep your necklace and get what they can for him from Zaltana."

Sparrow glanced at Lock. His pale eyes held hers, goading her. She wondered if he felt any fear at all about returning to the bounty hunters and their torture. He must have. Why did she care? He made it plain that he was dangerous, that he had no regard for her at all, even after what she did for him. Shea-Ann was right. She should rid herself of him and let their house get back to normal.

"No," she replied, "I bought him. He belongs to me."

Shea-Ann stepped close to Sparrow and whispered, "Are you sure about that?"

* * * * *

When Sparrow returned from the field that night, she was surprised to find the dishes washed and laundry ready to be hung outside. Shea-Ann had yet to return from the village, and Lock sat on the floor, shaking his foot, his arms folded across his chest.

"Do you have any idea how boring it is sitting here day after day?"

"Is that why you did the washing up, or is it because you're afraid I might send you back to the bounty hunters?"

"Get one thing straight, Sparrow," his eyes held hers with a hardness that made her shiver, "I'm not afraid of you, them, or anybody. Whatever my fate is, I'll face it because I haven't got a choice. Neither do you."

"You really think if you hadn't made different decisions your life wouldn't be better?"

"I made the best decisions I could for myself."

"By becoming a pirate?"

"How can you still be so naive? Your Knights of the Ruby Order: Lock was taken from you. You were a princess and now you're shoveling dung and chopping wood. Life is about survival. We do what we can to make it from one day to the next."

"I think it can be more than that." She dragged a chair closer to him and straddled it. "Do you know what I dream about?"

"Do I look like I care?"

"What do you dream about?"

Lock lowered his eyes. He didn't remember his dreams very often, but when he did, they usually came true, like the nightmare about being tortured in the village square. He knew she wasn't referring to sleep dreams, though, but dreams one had about what they'd like to happen in their lives.

"I don't have any," Lock stated.

"You must. Everybody has dreams and desires. You're a pirate. Maybe you imagined yourself becoming the greatest thief in the world. Not a very respectable dream, but it's still a dream."

He raised an eyebrow. "I never wanted that."

"Than maybe you dreamed of having hair that's all one

color," she teased.

"Very funny."

"I'll get dinner." Sparrow stood and filled two bowls with stew. "Looks like Shea-Ann is going to be late."

"Then we'll finally have a peaceful meal." He winked. "Looks like I did have a dream after all."

Sparrow couldn't control her smile. When he was this amiable, she could actually like him. She said, "Shea-Ann is very loyal and protective of people she cares about. You two will get used to each other."

"I wouldn't wager on it," he muttered.

They ate for several moments in silence before he said, "I cleaned it because I couldn't take the smell anymore."

"Neither could I, and I was tired of buying new things at the market. I couldn't afford anymore."

"And you call me stubborn."

She was about to retort when Shea-Ann stepped into the house, grumbling about the girl in the marketplace trying to cheat her out of a portion of shrimp.

"Good evening to you, too," Sparrow teased her old friend.

"It certainly could be worse." Shea-Ann smiled, her anger about the shrimp subsiding. "I delivered a big baby girl for Myra the shoemaker."

"The entire village was starting to wonder if she'd ever have that baby," Sparrow replied. "How many weeks late was she?"

"A bit over two, but well worth the wait. The baby's a beauty."

"What did she call her?"

"Lenora."

"Nice name." Sparrow carried two bowls of stew to the table. "If I ever have a daughter, I'm going to call her Thea."

"Thea?" Lock snorted. "What kind of a stupid name is that?"

Sparrow turned and flung one of the bowls so quickly he scarcely had time to raise his arm in defense. The bowl cracked against his forearm, drowning him with hot soup. Several beans clung to his hair, a thin piece of onion dangled over his left eyebrow, but Sparrow was too furious to appreciate how funny he looked. She stomped out of the house, slamming the door behind her.

* * * * *

"Crazy." Lock scowled and wiped the stew from his face and hair. "Women are all crazy. All that over a stupid name."

"It was her sister's name, you ignorant yak!" Shea-Ann curled her lip at him.

"So her sister has an ugly name."

"Her sister is dead. Defiled and killed by scum like you!"

Lock couldn't explain the odd feeling that settled in his chest. Why should he care about Sparrow or any member of her family? He said, "I'm no rapist."

The healer made a skeptical sound.

"I'm not!"

"Well I'm proud of you!" Shea-Ann tossed him a disgusted glance. "At least it's one foul crime you didn't commit—or so you claim!"

She followed Sparrow outside, leaving Lock alone with his thoughts.

"Seems like Sparrow's a bigger fool than I first thought. Her sister was murdered, but she takes me under her roof. She's just looking for trouble."

Shea-Ann's accusation—one he knew the rest of the village shared—galled him. Yes, he was a thief, a murderer, a mercenary when the work paid enough, but he was *not* a rapist. To him, defilement was the worst kind of crime.

Nothing made one feel as filthy as the unwelcome body of another devouring one's own.

The door opened, and the women stepped inside. Neither so much as looked at him as they sat down to eat. When they'd finished, Shea-Ann jerked her thumb in his direction, "What about him."

Sparrow's large eyes fixed on Lock. He bit the rude comment on the tip of his tongue, uncertain of why he restrained himself. He told himself she wasn't worth arguing with, and a night without food wouldn't bother him. He'd gone days without food when he'd been lost at sea.

She brought him stew, bread, and water.

"I'm going to the barn for a while," Sparrow told Shea-Ann.

The healer yawned. "I'm going to sleep. See you tomorrow."

Sparrow waited until Shea-Ann slipped into bed before taking the lantern, leaving the house in darkness, save the glow of the remaining embers in the fire.

Lock sat with his back against the wall, his arms folded across his chest. If he was in the Archipelago, he'd be lying in his own bed with the windows open around him. The salty sea air would blow through the house, and he'd drift off to the sound of gulls. Or maybe he wouldn't be in the house at all. Some nights he spent on the beach. He'd build a fire in the sand just below the shadow of the cliff overhanging the western beach. He'd watch the black waves licking the glistening shore.

The door opened, and Sparrow stepped in, her lantern glowing. She sat by the fire, tugging a shawl around her.

"Did she look like you?" The words slipped from Lock's lips before he fully decided whether he wanted to speak or not.

Sparrow's head snapped over her shoulder. "You're still up?"

"So did she?"

"Who?"

"Who do you think? Your sister."

"Why do you care?"

He shrugged.

Sparrow turned back to the fire.

Lock moved as close to the hearth as his chains would allow. While the nights weren't cold, they were much cooler than in the Archipelago. Sparrow had bought Lock an ankle-length tunic in the village so he could use it for warmth without removing his chains. At that moment, however, it wasn't cold that pressed him closer to the flames. The unfamiliar pang of regret about his earlier insult regarding her sister made him want to set things right with her. Damn the soft little bitch to hell! Why did she move him?

"She was younger than me," Sparrow murmured, "but people always said we looked alike."

Lock stared at the gentle curve of her cheek, the way the firelight danced across her freckled nose, and the emotions gleaming in her blue eyes. "She must have been pretty."

"Thank you," Sparrow whispered, turning to him. Her gaze fixed on his and her lips parted as she drew a sharp breath.

Lock's pulse quickened when he remembered the kisses they'd shared only a short time ago. *Never again*, she'd said.

Sparrow's hands rested in her lap. He covered them with one of his own.

"What do you want?" she asked, her expression wary.

His hand slid to her elbow then gently grasped her upper arm as he tugged her to him. Her eyes fixed on his mouth as he edged closer, as if to kiss her. Instead, his lips hovered over her cheek and forehead. He kissed her temple then her earlobe which he took between his teeth and nibbled until she squirmed, a giggle bubbling in her throat. It was a fresh sound of genuine pleasure, completely different from the husky laughter and throaty groans of the women he was accustomed to.

Lock pulled her onto the floor, wrapping his arms around her as he ran the tip of his tongue over her ear, then nuzzled her throat.

"Your beard tickles!" She wiggled in his arms. Her knee brushed his cock and Lock's arms tightened around her as their lips met. His tongue slipped into her mouth, slid over her teeth and tasted her every soft, warm nook. She uttered a contented sound as her hands splayed across his back, pressing him closer. Lock was glad he'd healed enough not to wince at her touch. Why didn't she clutch his chest, or better yet the swelling, pulsing cock trapped between them?

From across the room, Shea-Ann murmured in her sleep.

Sparrow jerked in his arms and pushed at his shoulders as she whispered fiercely, "Let me go!"

"What are you worried about?" he asked against her lips.

"Just do it!"

"Not until—"

"Sparrow?" Shea-Ann called in a sleepy voice. "What's wrong?"

"Nothing, Shea-Ann!" Sparrow replied. Lock credited her with keeping a steady voice as he licked her neck and kneaded her breasts. "I'm going to bed in a minute!"

When Lock began unfastening the ties on her shirt, Sparrow's hand cracked across his face hard. He dropped his hands from her shirt and chuckled.

"What's going on over there?" Shea-Ann demanded, sounding much less sleepy this time.

"I said nothing!" Sparrow's snapped then said more calmly, "Goodnight, Shea-Ann."

The healer grumbled to herself as Sparrow dimmed the lantern on the table and crawled into bed. She cast a glance in

Lock's direction before snuggling beneath her blanket, and he grinned. The girl was loaded with passion, and Lock was an expert at using sensuality to his advantage. One way or another, he'd gain his freedom, and maybe get a taste of the delectable little princess as well.

* * * * *

The following evening, Sparrow returned to the house at dusk. As always, her eyes immediately focused on Lock's corner of the room. The dishes and laundry had been done, and he was sprawled on his side, his head resting on one arm, his eyes closed. Sparrow felt her lips tug upward in a smile. When asleep, with those pale eyes shut and not flashing fury and contempt, he was rather cute. His skin was smooth for a man who spent his life outdoors, his cheekbones beautifully sculpted. She knew the soft, delicious feeling of his parted lips against hers and she resisted the urge to kiss him.

Sparrow, you're losing your mind! The man is making you into a love fiend! All you can think about, all you dream about at night, is that rotten pirate's gorgeous, hulking body!

Her thoughts scattered as Shea-Ann burst into the house followed by another older woman with dark hair and eyes.

Lock snapped awake, squinting at the three women.

"What's wrong?" Sparrow asked her old nanny.

"Sparrow, this is my sister. She traveled here to tell me our grandmother has died. The family would like me to return home to settle some affairs, but I told her I didn't want to leave you alone right now due to our situation." Shea-Ann glared in Lock's direction.

"I'm so sorry," Sparrow said to Shea-Ann's sister. "How sad for your family. It's not a problem for Shea-Ann to go home with you. I have everything under control here."

"I doubt that," Shea-Ann said.

Sparrow embraced her old nanny. "He's chained up, and I have no problem running this farm on my own. He even cleaned up. See."

Shea-Ann glanced around the clean house. "I hate to leave you, but it's important for me to go home."

"Go. Really."

"I could be gone for a couple of months. It will take time to sail there, then there are the family affairs to see to…"

Sparrow shook her head. "Please, don't worry. When will you be leaving?"

Shea-Ann's sister spoke in a soft voice. "In the morning. I'm sorry to arrive with such bad news."

"Not at all. Both of you sit down and I'll bring you something to eat. Lock and I will get along just fine while you're gone, won't we?" Sparrow glanced at the pirate and tingled with uncertainty when she saw the strange, half-smile on his lips.

When he spoke, his voice was uncharacteristically soft and polite. "I'm certain we will."

He ran the tip of his tongue over his top lip, and Sparrow shivered. How could she live alone with Lock and *not* give in to the incredible desire to kiss him again – or perhaps do something even more regrettable?

* * * * *

The next morning, after seeing Shea-Ann and her sister to the edge of the farm, Sparrow walked back to the house, already missing her nanny, but with a giddy feeling deep in her gut. She knew Lock was tied up, and no matter what he said, he couldn't escape or hurt her. Still, now that the pathetic weakness due to the torture had worn off, something about him terrified her. Maybe it was her own desire she feared. How could she find a pirate—a thief and a murderer— attractive? She might be a farmer, but she was still of royal blood. She had been raised as a princess: educated, cultured, taught right from wrong. Lock was her opposite in every way. Not that she doubted his intelligence. He was well versed in languages and his piercing eyes reflected a quick mind, but he was a criminal. He cared nothing for justice or the law. He was rough, arrogant, and possessed a tongue vile enough to sour a vulture's stomach. What was it about him that made her legs weak and her heartbeat quicken? She wondered how such a man could excite her, how any man could excite her after what had happened to Thea. Perhaps she was still naive, but when Sparrow looked into the pirate's eyes, she didn't see the coldness that had shone in the eyes of *the fiend*. Lock had a soul and a heart. She felt it.

"So, we're alone." Lock leered at her as soon as she stepped into the house. "This worked out well for you, didn't it, girl?"

"The last person I want to be alone with is you, but circumstances can't be helped."

He tossed her a roguish grin as he washed dishes from the morning meal. "I think you like a man in your kitchen, washing your undergarments and feeling those plump little breasts of yours."

"Not only are you completely wrong, but why must you be so rude?"

"I've been on my best behavior, *Princess*."

"I don't have time to argue with you. I've got a farm to run." Sparrow took her hat from the table and left the house, slamming the door behind her.

She spent the day caring for her animals, two pigs, two horses — usually three, but Shea-Ann had taken hers — several chickens, a goat, and Daphne. Sparrow liked animals, but she admitted to a special fondness for Daphne. There was something sweet and soothing about the cow's large, dark eyes, and Sparrow couldn't help thinking of her almost as a pet.

Sparrow usually enjoyed working her farm. At times it was difficult with just her and Shea-Ann, but her life was her own. When she'd been a princess, everything had been planned for her, and Sparrow's heart had always been independent.

When she reached the garden, the two girls Sparrow hired from the village were already weeding. The girls were sisters, Ginny, age eight, and Emerald, fifteen. They were nice children from a decent family, and their banter often reminded Sparrow of her relationship with her own sisters. She hadn't seen much of her remaining family members since their banishment, but she'd heard both her other younger and older sister had married and had several children. Only Sparrow remained alone. Not that she felt she was really *alone*. After all, she had Shea-Ann.

"Sparrow," Emerald brushed wild red hair from her dirt-stained face and offered a toothy smile, "we heard you bought a man."

Sparrow sighed. "I'm afraid it's true."

"Some of the women in the village said he was a pirate, that he's seven feet tall and has hair like a warlock."

Ginny wrinkled her freckled nose and said, "Yuck."

"He's not quite seven feet tall," Sparrow couldn't restrain her amused smile. The warlock's hair she couldn't argue with.

"They say he was whipped and racked, and he didn't even scream."

Sparrow's smile faded. In spite of how much Lock irritated her, she still felt sick whenever she thought of how much he'd suffered.

"Our aunt was at the village that day," Emerald continued. "She said he was handsome — before the whipping."

"He's still handsome," Sparrow spoke before she thought.

"Can I see him?"

Ginny looked at her older sister as if she'd sprouted a second head. "What do you want to see a man for? Ma says men are mean, stupid, and dirty. She says pigs make better company."

"When you get older, you'll understand," Emerald said. "Can I see him, Sparrow?"

Sparrow looked hesitant. "I don't think that's a good idea. He's dangerous."

"Where is he?"

"Chained in the house. Look, when you girls finish weeding, I have to get money for you, so you can look at him from the doorway."

Emerald beamed, and Ginny shook her head. "I still say yuck."

The girls worked almost each day until late morning. Sparrow and Shea-Ann paid them a weekly fee, and usually provided them with a meal before sending them home. When they'd finished their work that morning, they followed Sparrow back to the house.

She opened the door, and Lock's pale eyes riveted to her from where he'd been sitting on the floor.

"I have children with me, so try to behave yourself," she told him.

Emerald and Ginny lingered shyly in the doorway while Sparrow opened the trunk at the foot of her bed.

"He *does* have hair like a warlock," Ginny said to Emerald in a loud whisper. Emerald motioned for the girl to keep quiet. They stepped over the threshold and approached Lock.

Sparrow leapt between them. "Stop there! Don't get any closer to him. That's as far as his chains reach."

The girls jumped back, their eyes wide.

"I don't believe this," Lock muttered. "I'm not going to hurt a couple of children."

"I wouldn't put anything past you to get your freedom," Sparrow said.

"Maybe you're not as dumb as you look," he told her.

"You don't smell," Ginny said to Lock.

"I don't *smell*? What's that supposed to mean?"

"Ma says pirates stink like dead fish. That's why she tells us to stay away from the docks, because pirates will steal us and make us stay on their ships forever. She says they'll make us eat octopus guts. Ma says pirates have no teeth."

"Ma's a real sweetheart, ain't she?" Lock sneered. He growled and gnashed his teeth like a wolf, causing the girls to leap back even further. "I have plenty of teeth."

"Don't you have anything better to do than frighten helpless children?" Sparrow snapped. She approached the girls and paid them with coins from her purse, then offered them a basket of apples and berries. "Don't be afraid. He's chained up and can't get out without the key, and I keep that."

The girls' huge eyes fixed on Lock as he stood and rattled his chains. Sparrow's stomach clenched at the sight of him, so tall, his muscles flexing and his two-toned hair flying around him.

"I want Ma!" Ginny screamed and flew out the door.

"He *is* seven feet tall!" Emerald breathed, terror and fascination in her young eyes before she lifted her skirts and raced after her sister.

Lock dropped back onto the floor, a pleased smile on his lips.

"I can't believe you just did that." Sparrow placed her hands on her hips. "That little girl will most likely have nightmares for a year."

"Ah!" Lock waved his hand. "That's probably the most fun she's had in her life. Nothing like a good scare every now and then."

"You really are a pirate," Sparrow hissed before trudging back to the barn.

She was shoveling out the stable when three of the women from the village stepped inside.

"Good afternoon, Sparrow," said a chubby woman of late middle age who Sparrow knew to be a fisherwoman.

Another of the women, the local blacksmith, a tall, muscular blond, added, "We took a ride out here to have a look at your man."

"Excuse me?" Sparrow stopped shoveling and stared at them.

The last woman, whom Sparrow recognized as a seamstress, giggled. "Emerald and young Ginny said he's something to see, of course I'd take Emerald's description as more apt. Ginny made him out to be a combination of a wizard and a wild boar."

"The girls did say he was a giant." The blacksmith winked. "I saw him from a distance during the whipping, but I wouldn't mind a closer look."

"You rode all the way out here to look at my slave?"

"None of us were fool enough to buy him, with his reputation, but we'd still like to have a look," the oldest woman said.

"He's a person," Sparrow said. "You can't just look at him like so much horseflesh."

"Why not?" asked the seamstress. "Do you think men don't display their female slaves? It just so happens, in our village we have the power."

The blacksmith smiled. "That's why I love it here. Never got along in my home village."

"Just one little look, Sparrow. There are others who've been talking about coming up here to get a look at Lock the White. He has quite a reputation, you know."

"He's a rotten criminal, and I think he's gotten just what he deserves," the seamstress said. "If you ask me, most men should be in chains."

"So how about it, Sparrow? Give us a look?"

Sparrow was about to adamantly refuse, knowing how

much Lock would hate being gawked at like a slave on display. *How much he'd hate it…*

"All right," she said. "But just for a minute."

The women followed her to the house. When they stepped inside, Lock, clad only in his loincloth, scrubbed dishes in a basin of water. He glanced at them.

The women stared then burst into laughter.

"Just like all men should be!" The blacksmith clapped Sparrow on the back. "Barefoot and working in the kitchen!"

"What the hell's this?" Lock demanded, his pale eyes sweeping each of the women.

"They wanted to have a look at you." Sparrow tossed him a gloating smile and folded her arms across her chest.

"Not bad." The seamstress took a few steps closer, but still remained a safe distance away from Lock as he stood, towering above the group, his fists clenched almost as tightly as his teeth. "Strong lines. Stunning height. Pity about his back, though."

"And he's big." The fisherwoman giggled, her plump cheeks stained pink. "Biggest man I've ever seen in these parts."

"What am I, a horse?" Lock snarled. "Get these bitches out of here!"

"Need to teach him some manners." The blacksmith glanced over her shoulder at Sparrow. "But at least he speaks our language."

"You'll have to train him to do more than the washing up," the seamstress said. "Once he's tamed, you can move him to the barn and let him do the heavy work."

"That hair is rather pretty," the fisherwoman looked thoughtful. "If you cut it off, it would fetch a good price from the wig maker. Odd color, though, she might take off for that. You can keep letting it grow, cutting it off, and making a profit, just like you do with sheep."

71

"You're all daft. Every last one of you." Lock bellowed, "Get out!"

"Why are men so loud?" The seamstress winced. "My sixth husband was loud up until the day he died."

"Six husbands?" Lock curled his lip. "What were you, poisoning them until you found one you liked?"

"I sort of like his voice." The blacksmith's eyes raked Lock from head to foot. "Deep and powerful. And he has a fine body—save his back, of course. I'd bed him down so long as he kept a shirt on."

"I wonder if other parts of him are as big as the rest?" The fisherwoman blushed again. "He looks like he's toting a log beneath that loincloth."

Lock smiled humorlessly and said, "Why don't we find out?" He jerked off his loincloth and flung it aside. In spite of the scars marking his flesh, the women stared at his body like cats ogling a bowl of cream. From his broad, sculpted shoulders to his long, muscular legs, he was pure, raw male, and his long, thick, semi-erect cock and huge balls dangling beneath paid tribute to that fact.

"Merciful goddess," the fisherwoman murmured, touching a hand to her breast.

"If he wasn't such a killer, he'd have been worth the price you paid for him," the seamstress breathed.

The blacksmith stared at his cock and said, "More."

Sparrow knew her face was bright red as she turned toward the door and held it open for her guests. "I think that's quite enough. You asked to see him, so now you've seen."

"You know, Sparrow, I don't think we'll be able to keep the other women away," the blacksmith said. "Not after the description I plan on giving them."

"You should charge a fee to look at him," the seamstress suggested. "The novelty will wear off eventually, but until then, you could make a little profit."

"I will not charge women to look at him! Do I look like a flesh peddler? Now I'll ask you all to leave and tell everyone else not to bother coming."

"Tell the others if they want a look at me, Sparrow usually gets home around dusk!" Lock called to the retreating women. "But I don't want to miss supper, so be waiting when she gets here. Ten at a time in the house. The others form a line outside. One…no two silver pieces a head. That sounds fair, doesn't it, girl?" He wiggled his eyebrows in Sparrow's direction. "I'm worth a good two hundred a look, but I don't think this pathetic village has that kind of wealth lying around."

The women, still chatting among themselves, left the house. Sparrow slammed the door behind them and glared at Lock. "Do you have even a shred of self-respect? And put that loincloth back on! Preferably your tunic, too!"

He laughed. "What's the harm in looking? You thought bringing them here to gawk at me would annoy me? I've had worse than that in my day. Bring them in. Make yourself some money. Nice to know women are willing to pay just to have a look. Not that I blame them."

He didn't touch the loincloth, but sat on the floor, his back braced against the wall and his arms folded behind his head, making his large biceps bulge. His cock appeared even bigger than before as it stood up in a kinky bush of brown and white pubic hair. That, along with his broad, hairy chest and his taut abdomen made Sparrow's mouth dry.

"What about you?" he asked in a husky voice, his eyes sweeping her from head to toe. "You already paid top dollar for me. Want to try your goods?"

Sparrow licked her dry lips. That suggestion was almost too tempting, but if he didn't have any pride, at least *she* did.

"I have to get back to work," she muttered.

"There's always tonight!" he called as she closed the door behind her.

Chapter Seven

ಹ

Lock stared at the door and cursed. Who did the little bitch think she was? Dragging women and children in and out of the house all day to gawk at him!

He'd known by the smug look on her pretty face that she'd brought the women just to annoy him. Little did she know he'd endured far worse in his life. If those women wanted to pay to see him, fine. Debasing himself had been a way of life for him since the day he'd been born.

Don't you have any self-respect? she'd asked. He'd earned the fear of other men. He'd fought to make himself the most terrifying pirate in the SothSeas. Where he came from, that was as close to respect as a man could get.

When Sparrow and the women had entered the house, he hadn't cared one way or the other about the villagers. It was the look on Sparrow's face when she gazed at him, the way her trousers clung to her legs, and the way the open neck of her billowy shirt revealed the firm, plump curve of her breasts that made him want to bed her down like no woman he'd ever met before. Just looking at her and envisioning the look of discovery in her innocent eyes when he took her stirred his flaccid organ enough to provide the pesky village women with a decent show. He hadn't been watching for their reactions, though. Only Sparrow's. She'd blushed the loveliest shade of red and looked at his cock like she wanted to devour it. He had no doubts about her sexual inexperience – not that she wasn't an absolute pleasure to kiss and fondle—but he knew once she got the first real taste of hard rutting, she'd be wilder than any SothSea whore. Still, he knew the former princess would only share her wiles with a single man. She was decent, of that he was certain. She was too good for him, but he wanted her anyway, and he wanted his freedom more. By the time he was through, he'd have both his freedom and a taste of the dethroned princess to take with him as a memory.

He was already formulating a plan. Sparrow had told the children she kept his key on her. All he had to do was lure her close enough again and this time take what he wanted...in every way.

* * * * *

Sparrow walked slowly to the house, dragging a sled of firewood behind her. Winter would be coming in a few short months, and she'd been chopping extra wood in preparation for the frigid season. She felt a little weary as she parked the sled outside of the house and stepped in, looking forward to a hot meal and a good night's sleep.

All afternoon, her mind had been filled with the vision of Lock naked. When he'd been ill, she and Shea-Ann had seen him nude many times. They'd had to help him do everything, since he was too weak and in too much pain to do much for himself. Though she'd found him attractive even through the worst of times, it had been next to impossible to become aroused over a man whose back was like a slab of raw meat. He healed remarkably fast, however, and the whipping seemed so long ago. He was almost completely healed and exuded power like she'd never imagined. She wondered what it would feel like to have his big, naked body claim hers. She'd always imagined her first time to be with a gentle man, one who loved her and whom she loved. Now she was having lusty thoughts about a rugged, hateful pirate, and she couldn't help herself.

As she stepped into the house, her gaze riveted to Lock's corner of the room. She'd expected him to greet her with one of his snide remarks, but to her surprise he was asleep on his blankets. At the fireplace, she stirred the pot of stew and filled two bowls. She was about to place Lock's within distance of his reach when she noticed a mug of water had spilled all over the floor by his head.

Muttering, she placed the bowls on the table, took up a rag, and squatted beside him to clean up the water.

She screamed as his arms locked around her, pinning her own to her sides. She struggled, kicking him violently, but his legs wrapped around her and he held her in a grapple hold.

"Let go of me!" she bellowed, her heart pounding. Blinded by sheer terror of what he might do, she continued fighting, though she was unable to move a limb.

"Where's the key, princess?" he said close to her ear, his beard rough against her face.

"No! I'll never let you go!"

"I'm nobody's slave! You're going to give me that key one way or the other!"

"Never!"

"That fond of me, are you?" He gloated, shaking her hard. "Give it to me!"

Sparrow had never been so frightened in her life. His body was like unbendable metal, his hold almost painful. She saw fire in his demonic blue eyes and wondered if he meant to kill her. It served her right for taking him into her house. Everyone had warned her that he was a murdering thief. Suddenly she remembered the law the bounty hunter had told her of. If he escaped, she'd receive his punishment!

"Lock, listen to me! If you run away, I have to take your punishment. That's the law here."

He loosened his grip only enough to spin her so that she faced him. His eyes were so hard, so furious, and so full of...He pressed her closer, and she felt his hard cock against her belly.

"What are you talking about?" he demanded.

"If you escape and word gets out, I have to take your punishment because I was responsible for you."

He hesitated, studying her face. "Do you think I care?"

"Yes," she whispered, praying that if she acted as though she believed he was capable of human emotions, he would start to believe it himself. "I think you do."

His lip curled slightly and she saw his chest rise and fall with agitated breathing. He snarled through clenched teeth, his fingers bruising her arms. "Give me the key or I'll kill you."

"I'd rather have you kill me quickly than have them torture me!"

"What makes you think I'll do it quick?" He stood, dragging her to her feet and thrusting her against the wall. He pinned his body against hers, his broad, warm chest crushing her breasts, his steely thighs trapping her legs. He rubbed his cock against her crotch. Sparrow shivered. He buried his face in her neck, his tongue licking her flesh, his teeth nipping, his beard tickling. Sparrow closed her eyes and felt every bit of strength leave her legs.

The man was a beast! He was ravaging her, or so he thought. The sensations of his body and lips were like nothing Sparrow had ever experienced. His earlier kisses had been gentle, almost tender, but these were filled with such forbidden passion that she felt as if she was drowning in desire. He released his hold on her arms and ran his hands over her hips, up her ribs, and finally cupped her breasts. A warm globe in each hand, he squeezed gently. His thumbs caressed her nipples through her rough cotton shirt, and Sparrow gasped. Her hands gripped his back hard, and she felt his sharp intake of breath. Remembering his still-healing flesh, she nearly drew back, but why should she? He was using his body to punish her, why shouldn't she do her best to punish him?

She dug her fingers deeper into the newly healed skin, and he groaned. He dropped to his knees and unraveled the ties of her shirt, licking her flesh as it was bared. His mouth captured one pert nipple. He sucked hard, his beard rough against her tender flesh. A guttural moan erupted from the depths of Sparrow's soul. His tongue laved the nipple while he kneaded her other breast.

She felt as if she was melting, but somewhere in the back of her mind, she remembered the reason behind this sensual scene. He wanted the key and was going to search every part of her to find it. She reached beneath the waist of her trousers, removed the key, and flung it.

Lock's head snapped over his shoulder and he stared, open mouthed, at the key glistening in the corner of the room. Sparrow took the opportunity to leap out of the way. He caught her ankle, but she kicked him and scrambled out of his reach.

"You bitch!" he raged, his eyes shooting blue fire. His chest rose and fell in his fury. Sparrow trembled both from arousal and terror. He pointed at her. "You better pray I don't get out of here, girl! You better pray! I'll make the bounty hunters look like Knights of the Ruby Order for what I have planned for you!"

Sparrow sat for a moment, panting, her eyes fixed on Lock's. Suddenly she wasn't hungry anymore. She lay on her bed, wrapped herself in her blankets, and wished she'd never made the mistake of saving his life.

* * * * *

"Wake up, bitch!"

Sparrow jumped from the bed, her heart pounding and her eyes frantic. She'd lain awake for most of the night, more unsettled by Lock's attack than she wanted to admit. It seemed like she'd finally drifted off when his bellow roused her.

"It's about time." Lock stood, his arms folded across his chest. "I thought you died in that bed—and without ever having had a man in it."

Sparrow poured water into a basin and washed, her stomach grumbling with hunger. She'd been too upset all night to get up and eat. Now she was ravenous.

"Have you lost your tongue?" Lock continued. "What

does a man have to do to get some food around here?"

"He has to keep silent!" Sparrow snapped, furious at him for disrupting her life. She'd been happy before she'd met him.

"Starting to get to you, aren't I, Princess? Just think, I'm yours forever, unless you set me free."

"You know I can't do that."

"Oh, yes. You not only paid for me but took my punishment as well. I'm not sure I believe you about that part of the trade."

"Why would I lie?"

"Thought you'd play on my sympathy, but surprise, girl. SothSea pirates don't have sympathy."

Sparrow stared at him, but in spite of her anger, she remembered his hesitation the night before when she'd told him why she wouldn't free him. For the briefest moment, she'd seen confusion in his demonic eyes. Maybe he didn't even realize it, but he *did* feel something for her.

"I don't think that's true," Sparrow told him.

"To me, mercy is a waste of time. If I felt, Princess, I'd have been dead by now."

"And if I didn't feel, you'd be dead!"

"What do you want from me? Do you want me to kiss that tight little ass of yours because you made me a slave? Come here and pull down those trousers. I'll do it." He flung her a hateful look. "Give you some excitement."

"Why do you always have to be so vicious? Is that the only way you can stomach your own lousy life? What made you more angry, Lock, that I outsmarted you last night or that you're starting to feel something for me?"

"Feel for you?" He laughed. "Look at you! Muscle-bound little runt."

Sparrow pointed a finger at him and roared, "*You're* ridiculing *my* looks? That's rich. You're an oversized, ignorant, arrogant, ugly, murdering thief!"

"What do you mean ugly?"

Sparrow stopped suddenly and drew a calming breath. "I know what you're doing. You're trying to force me into giving you the key. I'm sorry, but I don't relish the thought of being tortured until I faint."

They stared at each other for a moment, and he sat, running a hand through his hair. "I'm not keen on that part of it, either."

She smiled softly. "I knew you had some decency in there somewhere."

"What is wrong with you?" He glared at her, pointing to one of his branded arms, then the other. "It's spelled out for you. Murderer. Thief. You know it. Everyone knows it. Stop trying to make me into something I'm not, and both of us will be a lot happier!"

"Why are you so afraid of being something other than a pirate?"

"You mean like a slave? I don't think so, Princess. Not everyone can come down in the world as easy as you."

"Come down?" She laughed humorlessly. "I think a slave would be a step up from a pirate."

He snarled. "I'm not surprised."

Sparrow took several steps closer so that she stood just out of his reach yet could see the fine lines in the corners of his eyes and the thickness of his lashes. "When you were a boy, didn't you ever dream of being anything but a pirate?"

"There you go with dreams again. They mean nothing. I could dream every night of ramming your fresh young body until we both pass out, but it doesn't mean it's going to happen."

Sparrow stared into his eyes for a long moment. In spite of his vulgarity, his words aroused her more than she wanted to admit.

"Like that idea, do you, girl?" His smile was more sensual

than leering.

Sparrow walked across the room to prepare the morning meal. She could take him when he was taunting her, but the idea of actually making love with him was more than she could handle. If she hadn't been so terrified of his strength and his temper, she might have freed him just long enough to bed him.

She slid his bowl of food toward him with the broom handle, fearful of getting too close lest he try assaulting her again.

"I won't be back until tonight," she told him before she left. "After I'm finished with the farm work, I have to make a trip to the village. I'll be home around dusk."

"You have to give me something to do while I'm here. I'm losing my mind. I forgot what sunlight looks like."

Sparrow glanced over her shoulder and sighed.

"Want to shell some peas?"

His eyes widened in feigned excitement. "Oh can I really, Mistress? I didn't faint from the lash, but I don't think I can endure the excitement of shelling peas."

"Fine. Then sit there all day."

She opened the door and he hissed, "Give me the damned peas!"

Unable to control her smile, Sparrow did as he asked.

* * * * *

Sparrow squinted at the crowd of women gathered outside her home. There were tall women, fat women, skinny women, old women, and young women. There were women with dogs on leashes, women selling food and ale out of wagons. The sound of wind instruments and drums echoed over the hillside.

"What in the name of the twin Goddesses is happening here?" Sparrow murmured as she fought her way through the crowd to the front door which, to her dismay, was ajar. A row of tall, burly brunettes whom Sparrow recognized as triplets who farmed on the opposite side of the village, blocked her entrance. At collective wail of laughter from the ladies closest to the door, Sparrow stood on tiptoe and stared over two of the triplets' shoulders.

Her jaw dropped as she noticed Lock standing as close to the entrance as his chains would allow. Naked, he flexed his biceps and winked at several of the women. Two girls played flutes while an older women -their mother—beat on two tall drums. Usually the mother and daughters played their instruments at village gatherings, but today they'd found a better reason to entertain. Lock danced to the rhythm of the drums, gyrating his hips in a manner so suggestive that Sparrow felt herself blushing as she watched his cock and balls bounce with his every movement. His hands and arms flowed to the sound of the flute, and his sensual mouth wore a smile that was as sarcastic as it was inviting. Sparrow's favorite frying pan, filled with gold, copper, and silver coins, lay at his feet.

The music stopped, and Lock stood, his hands on his hips, his kinky hair grabbing at his broad shoulders, several strands brushing his lean chest. One of his hands cupped his balls and his other curled around his cock, pumping the shaft. It swelled even more. Giggles and lusty murmurs swept through the crowd.

Lock wiggled his eyebrows and sang, "Me first mate drank a barrel 'o rum before we slipped into dock. He fell over his feet, the drink had 'em beat, and a crack in the wharf ate his cock."

"That's enough!" Sparrow snarled, shoving her way past the triplets and standing in front of Lock. "Everybody out of my house! Out!"

"Sparrow, we were just having a bit of fun!" someone shouted.

"Come on, Sparrow! Just a little longer. We'll pay!"

"No!" Sparrow picked up the frying pan and flung the contents at the crowd. The women leapt back, and the ones inside fled.

"And don't *ever come back*!" Sparrow bellowed after the dispersing crowd. She slammed the door shut and glared at Lock. "Are you crazy?"

He shrugged. "Looks like they accepted my invitation from the other day."

"Who are you to extend any invitations to *my* house?"

"I can't believe you were fool enough to throw away that money. The pan was almost full to the top. Another hour or so, and you wouldn't have had to farm for the rest of the year."

"What is wrong with you? Is profit all you care about, that you'll sell yourself even when you don't have to?"

"I'm a slave!"

Sparrow tossed her hands skyward and began preparing dinner. "Put on your clothes!"

"It's a warm night and I'd rather have it blowin' in the breeze."

"Well *I* wouldn't!"

"You're a liar."

Sparrow's jaw tensed and she spun, pointing a wooden spoon at him. "My life is not so pathetic that I get my pleasure from watching a filthy pig like you grabbing his own privates!"

He winked. "I sailed around the wild blue sea looking for a woman of lust. On one sunny shore I met with a whore, and devoured her golden tanned bust."

"Stop saying those disgusting rhymes!" Sparrow hissed.

"Outside the brothel beneath the sky blue, I handed the madam a coin for a screw —"

"I said stop!"

Lock sat against the wall chuckling. "Forgive me,

Princess. I'm just a rotten sea-dog and have forgotten about your sweet virgin ears."

"Why must you make everything so difficult?"

A broad smile flashed across his handsome face as he chimed, "I heard about old Madeline, whose pussy and tits were so damn fine…"

Sparrow clenched her teeth and tried her best to ignore him. She'd begun to realize that Lock, like a child, would continue pursuing the forbidden. He'd soon tire of taunting her — or run out of limericks. Either way, Sparrow would win.

* * * * *

Sparrow guided her wagon toward her barn as the sun set in the clear summer sky. The day had been uncomfortably hot, and the night would apparently be little better. After working around the farm, she'd hitched one of the horses to the wagon and driven to the village for some goods. Due to the heat, she kept her horse to a slow pace and enjoyed the peaceful landscape of rolling hills and distant woods.

At the barn, she unhitched the shaggy-maned chestnut mare and unloaded her supplies. With a sack of wheat slung over her shoulder, she made her way to the house.

Sparrow dumped the sack in a corner of the room and brushed sweat from her forehead. "It's hot out there."

"You want hot? Go to the Archipelago," Lock said.

Sparrow noticed he'd again discarded his tunic and wore only his loincloth, revealing the length of his steely legs. She gazed at the hard lines of his chest and abdomen. His hair dangled down his back in a thick braid, loose at the end since he had nothing to tie it with. She thought what a pity it was for such a fine-looking man to be stuck in a room. If she didn't devise a way to allow him some exercise, he'd loose that gorgeous body of his.

"Are you hungry?" Sparrow asked. "I bought some loaves of bread in the village, and —"

She stopped mid-sentence as the door burst open and two men, both dressed in dirty, sweat-stained shirts and trousers and each armed with a dagger, stood in the doorway.

* * * * *

Lock glared at the two men who strode into the house. Both were tall and thickly built, one with lanky blond hair, the other with balding black. When the black-haired one leered in Sparrow's direction, Lock noted he was missing two front teeth.

The blond advanced on Sparrow who grasped the closest weapon—the broom- and rammed the wooden end into her attacker's gut. He gasped as the blow landed, but recouped quickly and jerked the broom from her hand, dragging her toward him.

"Saw you leaving the village alone, lassie." The blond licked Sparrow's ear and she flinched with disgust. Lock's heart pounded with rage. If he was free of his chains, he'd have ripped out the man's tongue!

"Looks like she ain't alone," the black-haired man glanced in Lock's direction. "That's one big man she's got chained to the wall. Maybe she ain't as sweet as she looks."

"Let me go!" Sparrow rammed her elbow into her captor's gut and stomped on his foot with her booted heel.

He gasped in pain, loosening his hold. She reached for the broom again. The blond lunged at her, his dagger drawn, and grasped her even harder, one arm around her waist while his other hand pressed the blade to her throat.

"Move again, lassie, and I'll cut your throat."

Lock clenched his teeth and lunged, blind rage making him momentarily forget he was bound. He nearly fell as the chains tightened.

"Nice, doggie," the black-haired man sneered in Lock's direction.

85

"See if she's got anything worth taking in this dung heap," the blond called to his companion. "I'm going to entertain myself before I go."

He flung Sparrow so hard on the bed that Lock saw her teeth jar, still she kicked at her attacker as he approached. He raised his dagger. "Keep it up, lassie, and I'll cut you up from your toes to your ears!"

Sparrow's eyes met Lock's briefly, and the fear in her expression made his stomach twist in a manner he'd never experienced—not even during his torture. If only she could throw him the key! *Damn the key*, he thought, grasping the chains, curling them around his hands. He pulled with every bit of strength he could muster. The bounty hunters had done their job well, and the chains were firmly rooted in the ground. Lock continued pulling, every muscle in his body feeling as if it had burst into flames. Sweat ran into his eyes, and the chains cut into his palms, making them slick with blood. He felt the metal pulling loose.

"Hey! What the hell are you doing?" The black-haired man shouted. He leapt on Lock's back, his dagger drawn. Lock jerked his arm backwards, and the man crashed into the wall, blacking out as the back of his head struck wood.

Across the room, the blond was too busy fighting with Sparrow to notice his friend's mishap. Lock grasped the chains again, and with one supreme effort, tore them from the ground. Without losing a second, he dove across the room, wrapped the chains still dangling from his manacles around the blond's throat, and squeezed.

The blond dropped his knife and clawed at Lock's hands in an attempt to free himself. The man's body flapped like a fish in Lock's deadly embrace, but he was unable to make a sound as his breath was completely cut off. Lock waited until the man lay limp in his grasp before snapping his neck to ensure death.

He picked up the fallen dagger, walked to the other unconscious thief, and rammed the blade through his heart.

Lock stood, panting, his hands bloody and stinging, and turned to Sparrow. She sat on her bed, knees drawn up to her chest, tears streaking her face, her eyes fixed on him with terror. He had the oddest urge to take her in his arms and soothe her. As he stepped closer, she leapt off the bed, backing away from him.

"Goddess help me," she whispered.

"There is no goddess!" Lock snapped, wondering why her fear of him affected him so much. He had to get away from her, away from this mad village ruled by women where men were kept chained like animals. He needed to get back to SothSea where no one cared about anyone but himself, and the women didn't have innocent eyes and a sense of honor. "Now give me the key!"

Sparrow stood as if frozen. With a growl, Lock dragged her to him and reached into the waistband of her pants where he knew she kept the key. She punched him hard in the stomach, but he scarcely felt the blow. When she grasped handfuls of his hair and pulled, he gritted his teeth. *That* he felt.

He found the key and shoved her aside as he unlocked his bonds. He tugged the boots off one of the dead thieves and dragged them on, slipping the key into it before he pulled on his tunic. As he strode through the open door, he forced himself not to look back. He knew if he looked, if he saw the frantic expression in her beautiful blue eyes, he might do something stupid, like kiss her again. If he did that, then he'd have to make love with her, and if he made love with her, he knew he'd never, never let her go.

At a steady pace, Lock headed for the distant woods. The clear night and full moon made traveling easy. Though he wasn't quite sure where he was headed, he knew he could live in the forest until he made a decision about the best way to catch a ship back to the Archipelago.

And while I'm on my way to freedom, Sparrow will be tortured for the sole crime of showing me compassion. He remembered all too clearly the agony of the lash, the strain of the rack that threatened to tear his arms and legs from the rest of his body. Sometimes when he closed his eyes, he could still smell the burning coals beneath his ravaged back, could smell his flesh burning as the knife carved symbols into his arms. *Thief. Murderer.*

Afterward, when his life had been an endless cycle of pain—pain when he breathed and moved, during wakefulness and sleep—Sparrow had been his only relief. Sparrow and even that old witch Shea-Ann with her salve and potions. It had been Sparrow, however, who faithfully applied the salve to his back. When his fever had climbed, it had been Sparrow who had sat with him day and night, bathing him with cool water and seeing to his most personal needs. He'd blamed his physical weakness for the strange feeling in his stomach whenever she touched him, but as he grew stronger, the feeling remained, eating at him from the inside like a fanged worm trapped in his gut. She made him feel things he'd never felt, like warmth and good humor. She was making him soft, and though he wanted to get as far from her as possible, part of him wanted to bury himself in her, body and spirit.

She'd been the only person in his entire life to ever show him a shred of kindness, and he'd left her with two dead bodies and the possibility of torture.

He thought of how her skin had felt when he'd fondled her. She was a strong woman, her hands callused from hard work, but the flesh of her round, warm breasts and sleek abdomen, as well as the rest of her body was soft as the belly of a baby animal. The idea of that tender skin being cut by the lash made him wince.

He glanced around, realizing he was partway into the wood, the trees dark, spiky silhouettes around him. He stopped, squeezing his hands into fists, feeling the hot sticky blood on his palms from when he'd broken free of the chains.

"Damn the crazy bitch!" he hissed through clenched teeth as he turned abruptly, stalking out of the woods and back over the fields toward Sparrow's farm. "I think her insanity has infected me."

Chapter Eight

❧

Sparrow sat on the edge of her bed for a moment, her arms wrapped tightly around her body, tears dripping down her face. What in the name of the twin goddesses was she going to do? She had two dead bodies in her house, and Lock was gone.

If he escapes, you get tortured until you faint.

"No way." Sparrow suddenly regained her self-control, wiped her eyes with her palms, and began packing her few belongings into a large sack. She'd set all her animals free, take one of the horses, and be gone by sunrise. She'd go to Shea-Ann's village and tell her friend what had happened. Maybe she could even settle there and start a new life. Maybe—

Her eyes shot up from where she knelt, unloading the trunk at the foot of her bed. Lock strode through the door, his pale eyes brilliant with a barrage of emotions: anger, confusion, and something else Sparrow dared not hope for.

"You came back." She stood but didn't take a step closer to him.

His lip curled. "Can't have them taking the lash to you now, can we, girl?"

"I knew you cared. I knew it." She crossed the room and flung her arms around his waist, resting her cheek against his chest. His skin was damp with sweat, roughened by a dusting of hair, the muscles beneath hard. She felt his heart beating against her face, and she closed her eyes. *He came back!*

Sparrow felt Lock's arms encircle her, holding her close for several long, wonderful moments before he grasped her shoulders and pushed her away.

"I'll get rid of these carcasses." He glanced at the thieves' bodies. "You clean this place up. No one will ever know what happened."

"Your hands." Sparrow grasped his wrists, her fingers reaching a little more than halfway around their thickness. She tugged him toward the table.

He pulled away. "We don't have time to waste."

"Those cuts are deep and dirty. Do you want another infection?"

He must have realized the sense of her words, because he sat quietly at the table while she cleaned and bandaged his hands. She kept her eyes focused on her work until she'd finished. When she looked up, she found him staring at her with an intensity that nearly stole her breath. He didn't speak, however, but stood, slung one of the bodies over his shoulder, grasped the other by the leg, and hauled them outside. Sparrow grabbed two buckets, and as she went to fill them in the well, saw Lock stacking the corpses on the sled she used to tote wood. He ripped open two empty sacks she used for storage and covered the bodies before he dragged them off and disappeared behind a hill in the distance.

Feeling a little sick, Sparrow cleaned the blood from her floor and arranged several chairs that had toppled over during the skirmish. Afterward, she lit a second lantern to brighten the room and started a pot of stew over the fire. The meal was nearly finished when Lock returned.

"What did you do with them?" she asked.

"Don't worry. They won't be found."

"You probably have plenty of experience getting rid of bodies."

"Yes, and I have no qualms about getting rid of a third tonight, if you get my meaning," he sneered.

"You didn't come back to kill me," she stated. For the first time since she'd brought him into her house, she had no fear of him killing her.

His eyes swept her from head to foot, and his jaw tightened before he kicked out a chair and sat at the table while she brought over the dinner.

Lock ate slowly, silently, his eyes studying Sparrow until she squirmed in her seat.

"What?" she demanded.

"Just thinking about what I can do about this problem."

"What problem? You came back so I wouldn't get punished. It proves you care enough about me to give up your freedom."

"Give up my freedom?" Lock laughed. "I was starting to think you were swifter than you looked. I told you before, Princess, I'm no slave."

"What are we going to do then? If you don't run away, I won't have to keep you chained up anymore."

"And *you* call *me* arrogant."

"I'm not trying to be arrogant. You can live here."

"Or you could come with me."

"With you?"

"Why not? You could live at my house in the SothSeas. That way when I return from sailing, I'll have a wench warming my bed and not have to bother with the whores."

"The *whores*?"

"Do I look celibate to you, girl?"

"I thought you might have had someone..."

"Can't be bothered with one wench thinking she owns me—or so I thought. Looks like my taste might be changing." He grasped her hand across the table. She tried pulling away, but he held her fast and continued, "Once I teach you a few things, I wager you'll be better entertainment than any whore."

Sparrow's mouth opened several times, but she couldn't find the words to properly combat such an insult. Finally, she said, "You filthy, repulsive, vile, obnoxious—" Her words were silenced by his lips as he kissed her deeply, using his foot to drag her chair closer to his. One of his hands cupped the back of her head while the other grasped her waist and hauled her out of the chair and onto his lap. Overpowered by his strength, Sparrow could do nothing but straddle his legs and pray that she wouldn't humiliate herself by giving in to the desire coursing through her entire body.

His tongue traced her lips, slipped into her mouth and sought hers. Her fists opened against his back, and she slid her palms over taut muscle. He gently bit her lower lip. She shivered and mimicked his action, dragging a soft moan from his throat. The sound made her heartbeat quicken. Knowing he was as affected by their closeness as she gave her a feeling of power. Apparently Lock was attracted to "muscle-bound runts."

He stood, both hands grasping her buttocks while his mouth continued plundering hers. Instinctively, Sparrow locked her legs around his waist. She buried her hands in his thick, two-toned hair and licked the roof of his mouth.

Lock crossed the room in two steps and lowered her to the bed. He lifted her shirt over her head, threw it aside, and shed his tunic. Sparrow's eyes opened halfway, unable to resist looking at his exquisite body. For a man of his size and height, he was lean, with little extra flesh, only thick bones and hard muscle. His bandaged hands caressed her breasts, his fingertips stroking her nipples until his touch became a thrilling torment of pain and pleasure. Her breath became ragged, and she was lost in sensation. She closed her eyes and murmured his name as she felt him slip off her boots and trousers.

No man had ever seen her naked. She'd always been modest, but at that moment, nothing mattered except savoring every touch, every kiss, every caress he bestowed upon her lust-driven body. She gasped when his finger slipped into her wet pussy and gathered moisture that he used to stroke her clit. Sparrow panted as that marvelous finger quickened. Her nub felt so sensitive his touch almost hurt, and she felt ready to explode from need.

Suddenly his body covered hers, and her eyes flew open. His hair-roughened leg slid between hers, and she felt his cock—hard as a metal pike beneath silken flesh—pressing against her crotch. She stared at him, surprised by the softness in his pale blue eyes. His lips were parted, his breath nearly as ragged at hers.

He kissed her hard, as if he could absorb her very soul. His mouth trailed down her throat and fastened on the rosy spike of one nipple. Her gasp was almost a sob as he licked and sucked while his hand kneaded the soft circle of her other breast. She clutched his shoulders and locked her legs around his waist as he shifted into her, slow and smooth, giving her time to accept his length and girth.

The sensation of him deep inside her pussy momentarily broke her reverie. Her eyes snapped open. Again, she was dragged beneath the blue surface of his eyes. As he moved slowly, gently within her, she felt like she'd been possessed by the wildest creature on earth, tamed only for her.

She closed her eyes as pleasure crept back into her body and blocked her mind of all thoughts except reaching the plateau toward which he was driving them.

She clung to him, and his voice was a ragged command in her ear as he said, "Harder, Princess. Hold me as hard as you can."

She clutched his slick flesh. Her own body felt like she'd been thrust into an inferno as his thrusts became shorter and faster, his cock seeming to fill her more completely than she'd ever dreamed possible. She exploded in a climax that made the world go black. She could no longer see, only feel. She heard his cry of fulfillment as he rammed into her quivering body, then stiffened and pulsed, his every muscle tense before he collapsed atop her.

He rolled onto his side and dragged her to his chest, one leg draped over both of hers, his chin resting on top of her head.

Sparrow closed her eyes and snuggled close to him, a smile on her lips.

"Don't fall asleep on me, girl." She felt the rumble of laughter in his chest. "We've only just begun."

Sparrow's belly tightened. What had started out as the worst night of her life had suddenly become the best.

* * * * *

Sparrow awoke with a smile on her lips that faded when she opened her eyes and realized she was on the floor. No, she was actually *chained* to the floor.

She noticed Lock seated at the table, eating his morning meal and staring at her with none of the tenderness she'd seen in his eyes the night before. He wore only trousers and boots, his torso bare, the key to the shackles dangling from a piece of rope around his neck.

"What the hell is this?" she demanded, shaking the chains binding her feet.

"I found a solution to our problem."

"What?"

"From now on, Sparrow, this is my farm. You're my slave."

"This is ridiculous! Get these chains off me!"

He smiled, leaning back in his chair and watching her struggle against her bonds.

"You won't get away with this!" Sparrow snarled.

"Of course I will. Those two girls who work for you left to visit relatives with their mother. They won't be back for weeks. No one else ever comes to this farm. It's just us, Princess."

"Lock, think about this," she pleaded, torn between fury

and pain. "I know you care about me. You're just doing this for spite. After last night, you can't possibly —"

"Last night was a release both of us have wanted for months. Nothing more."

Sparrow stared at him, wondering if he saw how his words lacerated her. Last night had been more than a sexual game to her. She cared for him, and she knew that beneath his icy barrier, he cared for her, too.

"Lock —"

"Just call me master." He stood, tossing her a hateful smile before leaving the house.

"Wait!" she shouted. "Damn you, Lock! Listen to me!"

Halfway out the door, he glanced over his shoulder.

"Make sure you take care of my animals," she said. "Don't forget to milk my cow, and be nice to her!"

"Be nice to a cow?"

Sparrow poked her finger so hard in his direction her chains rattled. "Just do what I tell you!"

"You're hardly in the position to be making demands."

"Listen to me, you bastard! This farm is all I have! Have you ever worked a farm in your life? Do you know what you're doing out there?"

He looked disgusted. "I can't believe what I'm hearing. It's a farm. How hard can it be to run?"

"Just milk the cow before you do anything."

He stepped back inside, his arms folded across his chest as he stalked her, standing just shy of her grasp. "Like that cow, do you?"

Sparrow paused, her eyes on his. He'd do anything to spite her. She knew it. Even after what they'd shared last night, even after she'd saved his life. It was her initial act of kindness that seemed to infuriate him the most.

"Why are you so angry with me for helping you?" she

asked.

"By keeping me chained like an animal? Fine help you were."

"You know what I mean, Lock."

"Maybe this experience will teach you to *mind your own business.*"

This time when he left, he didn't return in spite of her call for him to come back.

Sparrow grasped the chains and pulled, getting nothing for her effort except sore hands, but even Lock had difficulty ripping the chains from the floor. She was still amazed he'd been able to do it. She wondered why he hadn't done it before. Perhaps even he hadn't realized he'd had the ability. She'd never seen anyone as furious as he'd been at the thieves, and she knew at times anger accentuated strength.

After the first hour of sitting on the floor staring around the room, she began to understand the extent of Lock's boredom.

By the time he returned to the house at dusk, she was actually grateful to have someone to talk to. She noted he looked hot and dirty, but that didn't stop him from tossing her a roguish grin.

"I hope you haven't ruined my farm." She stood, tapping her foot. "Did you feed the chickens and the pigs? I hope you let the horses out in the field, and you better have milked Daphne."

"*Daphne?* You named the cow *Daphne?*"

"What's so funny."

"That's a stupid name for a cow. Perhaps I shouldn't say that. You didn't name her after another relative, did you?"

Sparrow wondered if he saw how his words wounded her, but what could she expect from the cold, ignorant son-of-a-bitch?

"Did you do what I told you?" she demanded.

He ignored her and began ladling into bowls the stew that had been cooking all day over the fire. He brought her one with a chunk of bread.

She glanced at the food with disgust. "You cooked that stew, so I'm not about to eat it. What do you know about cooking?"

"Starve then." He placed the food at her feet and sat at the table, positioning his seat so he could stare at her. Sparrow wished she could wipe the gloating expression from his face.

After a moment she sat on the floor and began eating, hoping she wouldn't gag on the first bite. To her surprise, it tasted good. Better than her own cooking, she hated to admit.

"Where did you learn to cook like this?" she demanded.

"I was a cook after I was a cabin boy."

"Who taught you sailing? Your father?"

Lock laughed. "Your guess is as good as mine about who he was."

Sparrow was momentarily taken aback. When she spoke, it was with disbelief. "You're holding a helpless woman captive when your own mother was attacked? You must really make her proud."

He sprang across the room and grasped her shoulders, pinning her to the wall. He leaned his face so close to hers that their noses almost brushed and she could see rage smoldering beneath the surface of his pale eyes. "My mother is a madam who loaned me to any pig with a coin until I was old enough to get away from that demon's den!"

Just when Sparrow thought he couldn't shock her any more, he managed to do or say something worse. This time, however, her disgust wasn't directed at him. What sort of a life did he have? No wonder he thought being a pirate was an acceptable choice. Anything must have been better than the abuse he spoke of.

She murmured, "I'm sorry. I didn't know."

"There's a lot you didn't know when you bought me, girl. Now you're just starting to realize and regret it."

"I don't regret it. I did the decent thing. It's not my fault you can't accept kindness from anybody."

"You live in a fantasy!" He shook her before turning away and pacing the room. He ran a hand through his hair. "You took a pirate into your home."

"Then why can't you let me into your heart? I think I have gotten there a little."

"A heart pumps blood, Sparrow. That's all. It has nothing to do with feelings. You're looking for a lover. You won't find one here."

"I already have."

He laughed. "What will it take for you to understand exactly what I am? Isn't it enough that I have you chained in your own home?"

"I have you chained!" She pointed in his face. "You're so afraid you might feel for me that you have to treat me like this."

"Crazy. She's absolutely mad," he said to the air as he sat down and finished his meal.

When they finished eating, he filled a basin with water and dragged it to her.

"You can do the washing up," he said. "That's your job around here. I run the farm, you do the wash."

"Fine." Sparrow began washing the dishes, willing herself to remain calm when she wished she could clobber him with her empty soup bowl. "I'm not so stubborn that I'll sit in a filthy mess just to spite you."

"Glad you feel that way." He removed his shirt, stained with dirt and sweat, and tossed it in her face. She flung it aside, glaring at him. His trousers and socks followed. Sparrow was too furious to give his gorgeous body more than a cursory glance.

She picked up a wooden spoon from the basin and hurled it at his back when he turned away. His head snapped over his shoulder just as she flung her bowl. He raised his hand in time to thrust it aside and took a step toward her, dodging another bowl and two mugs.

"Stay away from me unless you plan on unchaining me!" she hissed.

"I don't think so." He caught her wrists and tugged her to his naked body.

She rammed her knee upward, aiming between his legs, but he shifted and she struck his hip instead.

"That was just vicious," he said, pinning her to the wall. "I have to think of a fitting punishment for my little slave."

She struggled, but his hold was unbreakable. He kissed her neck, and Sparrow's body tingled. Damn him!

"Stop it!" she snarled.

His response was a kiss so deep and long she thought she might faint. She felt her body surrendering, but she refused to let him see how much he affected her. She said, "The only way you'll ever sleep with me again is if you take me by force."

"I don't think I'll be forcing anything, Princess." One of his hands moved to her breast and caressed her through her shirt.

She felt her heartbeat quicken at his touch. "I want love. I won't ever give myself to a man who mistreats me like this."

"A little late for that."

"You had me once, Lock, and the memory had better last you a lifetime, unless you are the rapist the bounty hunters assumed you were."

He turned from her quickly, dragged on another pair of trousers and headed for the door.

"Where are you going?" she called.

"Swimming."

He slammed the door behind him, leaving Sparrow alone

and aching with desire.

Chapter Nine

ಔ

The sun had set completely by the time Lock reached the lake two hills away from Sparrow's farm.

He yanked off his trousers and waded into the moonlit water. Never in his life had he imagined anyone irritating him as much as Sparrow. The woman lived in a dream! She kept insisting he possessed redeeming qualities when he was a thief and a murderer. Last night when he'd returned to the house, she'd thrown herself into his arms like he was a long lost lover instead of a returning slave. What bothered him most was that once she'd clung to him, he hadn't wanted to let her go. He'd known, as soon as he'd stepped into the house he was going to bed her. He hadn't abandoned his freedom simply to keep her out of danger. He wanted payment for all those months of being chained to the floor. He wanted satisfaction for the desire he'd felt since his health had returned. All those weeks of looking at Sparrow, listening to her soft, pleasant voice, catching the aroma of the floral-scented soap she bathed with had driven him mad with lust. That small taste of her when he'd tried to steal the key had aroused him more than he realized, and now that he'd made love with her, his appetite for her had increased to the point of starvation. If he'd been a different sort of man, he would have taken her by force. Lock was many things, but he was not a rapist. He'd spent too many years abused by others to do the same to somebody else. Murder he could commit and accept. Murder only sent a person out of this hellish world. Rape was an attempt to rob a person's dignity, and as big a thief as Lock was, a person's body was the one thing he would not steal.

He dove until he touched the lake's rocky bottom then surfaced and floated on his back, gazing up at the starry sky.

She'd enjoyed last night, of that he was certain. He'd made love with her in every position and manner imaginable. For a woman who'd never been with a man, she caught on fast. A couple of times he thought her stamina would outlast his, but he'd never been so excited by any woman and he'd even managed to impress himself with his longevity. Afterward, Sparrow had fallen into such a deep, contented sleep, she hadn't even stirred when he carried her to the floor and chained her down.

She'd looked so pretty and sweet while asleep he'd almost changed his mind about shackling her. They could have spent every night in her bed—or in his if he took her back to the SothSeas. She'd been completely giving of herself. She'd touched him with more gentleness than he'd ever felt and whispered endearments no one had ever spoken in his presence. Her lust had been intoxicating, but her affection had threatened to steal his essence and make him hers forever. Lock belonged to no one but himself. He wasn't about to give one small female control over him that even whip-wielding bounty-hunters hadn't been able to take.

He swam to shore and sat on the grass. Sparrow might have refused his advances tonight, but eventually he'd wear her down. No woman so lusty could control her urges indefinitely, and after last night, he knew exactly what made her scream.

After several moments, Lock made his way back to the farm, pausing to look over the garden. Farming was almost as difficult as running a ship properly. It was hot, dirty work that required strength and patience. Part of him respected Sparrow for how well she did on her own. When he'd finished the farm work, he'd cut enough wood to last through the winter and stacked it behind the house, though he wondered why he'd bothered. He and Sparrow would be at the Archipelago long before winter. Of course he'd have to assign a couple of eunuchs to guard her while he was at sea. He couldn't risk having a lady unprotected on SeaSpider Island.

He at least wanted to wait for that witch Shea-Ann to return so he could have the pleasure of gagging her annoying mouth and chaining her next to Sparrow for a few days. When he and the princess left, he might not even untie Shea-Ann. He shook his head, his smile fading. He couldn't do that, or else Sparrow might really never bed him again.

By the time he returned to the house, Sparrow was asleep on her blankets, her delicate lips parted, one hand cushioning her cheek. The dishes and laundry were washed and piled neatly beside the basin. He collected the laundry and hung it on a line outside then leaned against the wall and stared at Sparrow for a long time before flopping on the bed and gazing at the ceiling. He remembered the feeling of her body against his, her soft breasts rubbing against his chest. His cock swelled just thinking about it.

Damn the little bitch! She was supposed to be the one suffering and there he lay alone with a body scarred beyond repair and an erection so hard he could have used it to fight a duel.

Sparrow made a soft sound in her sleep, and he glanced at her. Maybe now that she was sleepy, she'd be easier to convince. He dropped one foot to the floor, then changed his mind. He was not about to beg sexual favors from a woman he had chained up.

He couldn't believe he was having such difficulty. He'd spent enough years as a whore that he should have been able to seduce anyone.

Still gazing at her, he drifted to sleep.

* * * * *

The next morning, Lock arose before Sparrow. He left her food and fresh water before attending the farm work.

"I've known bitches in my life, but she's the worst. Why? That damned sweetness. She makes it impossible to hate her completely," Lock said as he squeezed Daphne's udder, filling a pail. He paused and curled his lip. "Now she's got me talking to a cow. I really have to think about getting out of here before I lose what's left of my mind."

When he finished milking Daphne, he turned her out in the field along with the horses. It was then he noticed the fence which kept the pigs and chickens was damaged. He decided to mend it before beginning any of the more time-consuming work.

He retrieved Sparrow's box of tools from the barn and set to work. As soon as he stepped over the fence, one of the pigs, a fat grayish male, approached, grunting.

"What do you want?" Lock snapped, choosing a hammer and placing the rest of the tools aside. No sooner had he stood when his legs were knocked out from under him. He landed on his back in the mud, the pig staring at him from a short distance away.

"I'm going love eating you when slaughter time comes." Lock sat up. When he rose, the pig took a step closer. Lock and the pig stared at each other. Lock put one foot forward, and the pig took two more steps, looking ready to charge.

"This is crazy." Lock stood to his full height and the pig galloped toward him.

Lock dove over the fence and the pig dropped onto the mud, grunting with contentment.

I'll be damned if I let a pig tell me where I can and cannot go. Again he stepped over the fence and picked up the hammer. The pig charged, but this time Lock jumped on top of it, straddling the fat, muddy back and gripping the small, flopping ears. The pig fought worse than a wild stallion he'd tamed in his youth.

"Son of a swine!" Lock's legs tightened around the pig's slippery sides. He slid backwards off the pig, splashing in the mud and scattering the chickens. Lock pushed himself onto his elbows and blew at a chicken feather stuck to the tip of his muddy nose. He brushed it away and raised himself to a squat, facing down the pig for the second time.

When the animal attacked, he caught it in an unbreakable hold, clinging to the dirty body, half running, half dragging, until the pig finally tired.

Panting, Lock picked up the hammer and pointed it at the swine. "If your mistress is as easy to break, I'll be a happy man."

He suddenly heard Sparrow shouting for him from the house. Thinking more thieves might have broken in while he'd been fighting with the pig, he bounded over the fence, raced across the yard and burst into the house.

Sparrow stood, her hands on her hips, her eyes sweeping over him and demanded, "What in the name of the Goddess is going on out there?"

* * * * *

Sparrow stared at Lock, torn between disgust and laughter. From head to boot, he was completely covered in mud. He looked like he'd swum in it, and from the sound of his shouting and the pig's squealing, she wondered if he'd done just that.

"What kind of a pervert are you?" she demanded. "What were you doing with my pigs?"

He pointed a finger at her, his eyes blazing. "Not what you're thinking girl, even though the pigs would probably be more accommodating than you!"

"It didn't seem that way two nights ago!" she snapped. "You seemed to thoroughly enjoy yourself at my expense!"

"And I suppose you nearly squeezed me to death with your legs just because you wanted the exercise?"

Sparrow felt heat rise in her face. If she hadn't been chained, she would have clawed his beautiful blue eyes out. "It would take a deep sea octopus to squeeze you to death, you oversized lout!"

"Why did you call me in here? I have work to do on my farm."

"This is *my* farm! You're *my* slave! And I didn't buy you to ruin my hard work!"

"I'm trying to repair your damned fence and that devil's swine thinks he owns the run out there!"

"Giving you trouble, is he?"

"Like everything else on this bloody farm. I've made up my mind we're going to the Archipelago."

"This is my home! I'm not going anywhere."

"So you're rather stay and be tortured?"

"All I know is that I'm not going anywhere with you, least of all to the Archipelago where I'll have to suffer as your love slave!"

"Suffer? Those sure as hell weren't moans of pain I was hearing the other night."

"You're a boor!" Sparrow's fists clenched so tightly her hands ached. He made her angrier than she'd ever been in her entire life. Still, she forced herself to feign calmness as she said, "I suppose it's not your fault. How would someone of your ill breeding know how to treat a lady?"

"Still think you're a princess?" He stepped across the room and yanked her into his arms, his muddy lips covering hers.

Sparrow punched his shoulders, but he grasped her arms and forced them to her sides. She felt mud drenching her clothes. His were plastered to his body with the grimy brown liquid. In spite of the smell of pigs and dirt, Sparrow couldn't help thinking the sensation of his slippery skin and hard muscles was incredibly arousing. He loosened his hold and she shoved him as hard as she could, frustrated that she didn't move him a bit. He smiled, his teeth gleaming against his muddy face, grabbed a change of clothes, and headed for the door.

107

"You make sure you go swimming again before you come home!" she bellowed after him. "Filthy pig!"

Sparrow did her best to clean her own soiled body with the leftover dishwater, but she had no fresh clothes to wear, and soon the mud dried to a hard shell on her tunic.

"Damn him," she muttered, glancing at the dirty garment. It was the only dress she had. There wasn't much use for dresses while working a farm, but she kept one for village gatherings. Now it was going to be filthy and tattered from use, as Lock gave no sign of providing her with fresh clothes. She'd have to ask for them. The other night, when they'd slept together, she thought she was falling in love with him. Now she almost hated him. Almost. Why couldn't she hate him completely? What was it about him that lured her like a cat to cream?

When he came home that evening, he was clean, his hair damp from swimming.

He stepped halfway across the room and paused, wrinkling his nose. "Smells like a pigpen in here."

Sparrow felt anger twist her stomach and she said, "I wonder why? Look what you did to my dress!"

He approached, his arms folded across his chest, and studied her with a shrewd expression she had come to know all too well. "We can't have you reeking, can we, Princess? How about a bath and a change of clothes?"

Sparrow hesitated. "I don't trust you, Lock."

Ignoring her, he began carrying in buckets of water, heating them, and filling the tub. She watched the tub with longing eyes, more cautious than ever about his sudden kindness.

When the bath was ready, he opened the trunk at the foot of her bed and searched through her bag of soaps. He sniffed one cake which she knew to be rose-scented and asked, "This one?"

Sparrow shrugged, wishing to appear indifferent though

it was her favorite.

"You'll have to unchain me so I can take off this dress and bathe," she said.

He laughed. "Just like you unchained me and gave me privacy?"

"What do you care about privacy?"

"That's beside the point."

She placed her hands on her hips. "How am I suppose to bathe, then?"

He took up a cooking knife, and approached.

"No!" she screamed. She hadn't been so fearful of him in days, but she'd been a fool to think he—the worst pirate of the SothSeas—could ever change. He still had the heart of a murderer, not matter what she might have felt for him. "Lock, no! You don't want to kill me!"

"Kill you?" He raised an eyebrow and shook his head. She kicked at him, but he caught her foot. She clutched a handful of his beard and pulled hard, but he grasped her arms and wrenched them behind her back, holding them with one hand while he used the other to slice off her dress.

"You bastard!" He had no respect for her at all! None! She willed herself not to shed tears of rage and frustration.

Lock threw the knife aside and picked her up. Sparrow's arms looped instinctively around his neck. Her heart pounded with rage and desire. The sensation of her naked curves pressed against his hard body made her insides riot. Lock dropped her in the warm water, and tossed her the soap. Then he dragged a chair in front of the tub and straddled it backwards, his eyes fixed on her. "Better wash before it cools, girl, because you're not getting out of there until you're clean."

"I hate you!" she seethed. "I hate the sight of you! I wish you were dead!"

He smiled. "That's more like it."

"If I didn't hate you so much, I'd pity you! You're

pathetic! Blaming the whole world because you're scum! Not all women are your mother, Lock, and not all men are bounty hunters!"

His smile faded as he stood, kicking the chair aside. "If you're not going to clean yourself, looks like I'll have to do it!"

"Touch me and I'll rip out those demon's eyes of yours!"

"You can have fun trying."

He squatted behind her, one arm snaking around her shoulders, holding her arms immobile while he used his free hand to search for the soap in the heated water. He felt beneath her breasts and stroked her belly, circling her navel with the tip of his finger. "It's not here."

He cupped her buttocks and squeezed, then gently prodded the soft flesh between her bottom cheeks. Except for her pounding heart and agitated breathing, Sparrow remained stock still as his finger poked the tight little hole and slipped partway in. "Not there. Where is that elusive soap, Princess?"

"You're an animal!" she snarled as the finger slipped out and his hand dipped between her legs while he nipped her ear.

His palm slipped over her inner thigh as he found the scented bar and ran it over her belly. He soaped her breasts, paying careful attention to her nipples. His touch was incredibly gentle. As he washed her skin, his lips and tongue traced her shoulder and the shape of her ear.

Sparrow felt herself weakening in his grasp. She wondered if he'd stop if she told him too. She was almost afraid to find out. If he didn't, then her worst fear would be confirmed: he was capable of rape. If he did, then his carnal ministrations would stop and she'd be left again with unfulfilled passion. *That's crazy, Sparrow!* If he was a rapist, he wouldn't bother fondling her. His touch was clearly intended to arouse, an inclination no rapist would have.

"What is it, Princess?" he whispered against her ear, his beard tickling her neck. "You want to wash yourself instead of having me do it?"

"And if I did?" She felt something cold against her back and remembered the key he kept around his neck. If she could only steal it back without him noticing. Perhaps she could engross him so deeply in pleasures of the flesh that he wouldn't know or care if she took the key. Damn! The pirate's lecherous ways had infected her. The means of her plan seemed even more satisfying to her than the end!

"If that's what you want, as long as you're clean." Lock dropped the soap and began moving away.

"Wait!" She turned, grasping his wrist and tugging him closer. He squatted beside the tub and she kissed him, her tongue circling his mouth and parting his lips. "You have such a marvelous mouth, Lock."

He glanced at her warily, but she tilted her face to his again, and his mouth covered hers. When he broke the kiss, Sparrow felt his reluctance and her stomach fluttered, both from the knowledge that she was luring him and from the lust he inspired in her. Lock moved from the back of the tub and again found the soap beneath the warm water. He lathered his hands and ran them over her shoulders, under her arms, across her breasts. Sparrow tugged off his open shirt and tossed it aside, splaying her wet hands across his chest. Leaning forward, she circled his nipple with the tip of her tongue, tentative at first. He sighed, murmuring her name. Sparrow's fingers gripped his ribs while she used the flat of her tongue to lave his nipple then taste every inch of his hard, hair-roughened chest. By the twin goddesses, she could touch him all night! However she had a more important agenda than attaining personal pleasure. She traced the rope around his neck, pressed the key to his breastbone then, to avoid suspicion, continued her caresses.

* * * * *

Lock resisted the urge to moan with pleasure as Sparrow licked and nipped his entire chest. The woman was like a volcano in her passion, still and seemingly harmless at first,

111

then explosive. Actually she had *him* about ready to explode. His heart pounded and his cock felt ready to burst through his trousers. Sparrow rose to her knees so she could better explore him. One of her small hands strayed down his belly then she gripped his cock.

"That's it, girl," he murmured. "You know what I want."

"Oh yes, Lock," she murmured between the kisses she sprinkled over his ribs. "Since we've made love, I feel I know you so much better."

"I knew you wouldn't be able to get enough of it once you got a taste." He stopped speaking and drew a deep breath, releasing it slowly as she tugged down his trousers. Lock stood and kicked them aside, noting the lusty gleam in her eyes as her gaze swept his cock and balls then lingered over his heavily-muscled legs.

"Come closer," she whispered.

He stepped nearer.

Sparrow gazed up at him, water misting her face and streaking her firm, beautiful breasts. "I've heard stories about men liking women to —"

"To what?" he pressed, licking his lips which had suddenly gone dry. With her kneeling in the tub and him standing, she was almost facing his cock directly. He hoped she was contemplating what he thought she was contemplating.

"I couldn't." She blushed suddenly and sank back into the tub.

"Say it, girl! I guarantee it'll be nothing I haven't heard – or done – before."

"Then I guess it wouldn't be as pleasing for you as I thought, for me to —"

"To what?" Lock tried to keep the agitation from his voice. The image of her soft, delicate lips fastened around his cock was enough to make him pole hard. His rod already stood out stiff and aching, an invitation for her sweet lips and moist tongue.

She gazed at him, the sultry look in her usually innocent eyes making his head spin. "To use my mouth on your..." She reached out and trailed a fingertip down the length of his cock.

"It'd please me."

"Even if I've never had experience in doing such a thing?"

"Oh, girl, that's one thing I can teach you well."

Sparrow smiled and rested her hands on his hips as he stepped nearer. Her mouth hovered so close to his cock he could feel her breath fanning the sensitive skin. For a moment he thought she might change her mind, then she buried her lips in his pubic hair and kissed his length from root to head. The tip of her tongue traced delicate shapes along the underside.

Lock's fingers sifted through her hair and his buttocks tensed as she gripped it with strong fingers, kneading the tight globes while she licked every inch of his cock. Her lips fondled his balls before she took his cock head into her mouth. She paused, and he groaned, "Don't stop. Suck."

She drew him deeper, sucking and swirling her tongue over the head and up the shaft. Her fingers prodded between his bottom cheeks as he'd done to her, pressing against the ring of muscle.

Sparrow drew back slowly and gazed up at him. "How was that?"

In reply, Lock grasped her arms and dragged her to his chest as his mouth devoured hers. Sparrow moaned and writhed against him, slipping one of her hands between them and curling her fingers around the key dangling from his neck.

Lock froze and pulled away from her, his teeth gritted with rage. The bitch had played him with the wiles of a seasoned whore! His hand clamped over hers that still held the key. "Drop it."

Her blue eyes opened wide. "But, Lock—"

"I know what you're after. Don't even think about it, Sparrow. This key is mine, just as you are."

"I'm not yours!"

He glanced at her hard nipples and kiss-bruised lips and said with a smile, "Aren't you? I don't think a woman who sucked my cock with such feeling belongs to anyone *but* me. Finish your bath and I'll get you a towel and fresh clothes... Come to think of it, I'll just bring you the towel. I like you naked."

"If you don't bring me clothes, Lock, you will regret it," she spoke through clenched teeth.

His eyes swept her firm, round breasts and sleekly muscled arms and belly. He didn't think he could get any harder than he'd been moments ago, but the idea of her chained there naked all night made him feel like a steel pike. He said, "I'm sure I will, but it's a risk I'll have to take."

Chapter Ten

❧

"Give me some clothes!" Sparrow sang at the top of her voice.

The house had been dark for hours, the lanterns long burned-out. Lock lay on his stomach, a pillow clutched over his head to drown out the bitch's incessant screeching.

"Clothes. Clothes. I want clothes!" she chanted.

Lock jumped out of the bed. "Will you shut up!"

"Not until you clothe me." Sparrow began singing a folk song and Lock was mystified that such a beautiful woman could have such a terrible voice. Sparrow began adding her own verses, "Bring me some clothes! I'm cold to my toes!"

"It's sweltering in here!" he snapped.

"Not when you're naked."

"Get under the blankets."

"No. I want clothes!"

Lock trudged to her corner of the room and grasped her shoulders, holding her so they were nose to nose. He hissed through clenched teeth, "Shut your mouth or I will cut out your tongue!"

"No you won't. I'm through being intimidated by you, Lock," she told him and slid her arms around his neck, pressing her naked breasts to his bare chest. The sensation nearly made Lock groan. She squirmed closer, and Lock began to feel as if he had a permanent erection. She whispered in his ear, "I want something to wear. I can sing all night and sleep all day while you have to tend the farm tomorrow."

"I don't have to."

"Of course you do! It's your farm now, remember? If someone doesn't take care of it, you'll have nothing. So, what will it be?"

"I don't give a damn about this farm. I can take you out of here any time I want."

"And no matter where you go, Lock, I can sing all night!"

She began humming, and he kissed her, his hands roaming over her back and buttocks. She slapped his wrists. "None of that! I won't make love with you while I'm tied up."

"You'll sleep with me whenever I tell you. If I choose to respect your wishes—"

"Respect? Hah! You don't even know the meaning of the word. Now give me some clothes!"

He sighed deeply, took one of his shirts, and tossed it to her.

"Getting soft, are you?" she asked as she slipped the shirt over her head. It hung past her knees, and she settled into the blankets. "Goodnight, Lock."

He growled in response and returned to the bed. To his annoyance, touching her had aroused him so much he was unable to sleep for nearly an hour.

* * * * *

Sparrow smiled to herself as she finished cleaning the dishes and stretched out on her blankets. Lock had awakened her before he'd left, and she knew he'd done it for spite about her behavior the night before.

Now she prepared to catch up on the sleep she'd missed. She closed her eyes and remembered the feeling of his body against hers, the way he'd run the soap over her. He was spiteful and arrogant, but he wasn't as vicious as he pretended to be—at least not with her. She knew his reputation and wasn't foolish enough to believe he wasn't guilty of the crimes he was accused of, but she did know that even though he chained her up, he still felt something for her. It was just a matter of which of them would come around first and admit there was more than lust between them.

Sparrow guessed it was noon when Lock returned to the house carrying a bag of meat scraps that he added to the stew.

"Did you go hunting?" she asked.

He wiped his hands, stained with bloody juice, and glanced at her. "I'd intended to, but I realized there was no need. You have a farm full of animals waiting for slaughter."

She stared at him. "You killed one of my animals? Which one?"

He shrugged. "Just the cow."

Sparrow felt her belly drop to the floor. "You killed Daphne?"

"Why not? She's an animal, isn't she? Or should I say *was.*"

Sparrow's vision blackened with rage, and she ran as far as the chains would allow, her hands stretching toward him like claws. "You bastard! You killed my cow!"

"For the next few days we'll have Daphne stew, Daphne pie, Daphne…"

Sparrow thought she might be sick. Daphne! She hadn't just been another farm animal, she'd been Sparrow's favorite. Daphne with her dark brown eyes and sweet face. Any feeling she had left for Lock dissolved with the tears that streamed down her face. She turned from him, lay on her blankets, and cried.

"All this over a bloody cow?" he snapped.

"Go to hell!" she sobbed.

She felt his hand on her shoulder and she jerked away.

"I didn't kill the damn cow," he said. "I'm cooking a rabbit."

"You're a liar! It's my cow. You are the most unfeeling son-of-a-bitch I've ever known! You'd do anything to get back at me for saving your life. Shea-Ann warned me not to buy you, but no, I wouldn't listen. I felt sorry for you. What a fool!"

"Will you stop crying?"

She ignored him and continued sobbing, releasing the sadness and frustration she'd repressed since she'd brought the bastard into her house.

Moments later, she felt something blowing on her, then something bristly brushed her face. She glanced up and could have laughed with happiness.

"Daphne!" She hugged the cow's thick neck, not even caring about the muddy tracks leading across her rope carpet.

* * * * *

Lock leaned against the wall and stared at Sparrow hugging the cow and speaking to it with more affection than his own mother had ever spoken to him. Sparrow's hands gently stroked the animal's neck and she actually kissed the ugly beast's face.

Was it possible to be jealous of a cow? Evidently, because he was. Of course, she'd tried being kind to him, but he'd have none of it. The more she attempted to reach him, the worse he'd treat her. Maybe she'd been right. Maybe he was hesitant to explore any feelings for her, because if he allowed such a woman to infiltrate his life, he'd have to change—something he wasn't sure he was ready to do.

"I told you I didn't kill her," Lock said.

"So you've proven it." Sparrow wiped her eyes and gave Daphne a final affectionate pat. She glared at Lock. "Now get this cow out of my house. There's mud all over the place."

He guided the cow back to the field, and when he returned, Sparrow was still crying softly, facing the wall. He never imagined a woman's tears over a stupid cow could affect him, but before he could stop himself, he was on his knees beside her, smoothing hair from her hot, tear-streaked face.

"Now what's wrong?" he asked.

"What's wrong? You have me chained up in my own house. You treat me worse than a whore."

"I do not."

"Maybe not according to the way you're used to living!"

A smile played around his lips. She had a point.

"If you hate me so much, Lock, why don't you just leave? You can't really care whether or not they punish me for your escape."

"I don't hate you."

"Then I'd hate to see how you'd treat me if you did."

"That's true."

She shot him a scathing look, her eyes glistening, her face flushed and nose red from crying. He used his sleeve to dry her face before he brushed a chaste kiss across her lips.

"I shouldn't have said I killed the stupid cow."

She shrugged, gaining back her self-control. "At least you didn't really do it."

He stared at her for a long moment before lifting the key from around his neck and removing her shackles. His hand clamped gently over one of her feet, his thumb stroking the arch.

She jerked backward, unable to control a smile. "That tickles."

His hand slid up her leg, dipped beneath the shirt, and stroked her inner thigh. He moved closer, one hand clasping her nape and drawing her nearer for a lingering kiss.

"I want you," he said, his voice husky.

She shook her head. "Then what? The shackles again?"

"No. No more chains for either of us."

"I'd be a fool to trust you."

"Yes, you would." He stroked her cheek with his knuckles before he took her face in his hands and kissed her, his tongue slipping between her lips and stroking hers, stealing her breath.

Lock heard her soft sigh and his heartbeat quickened. She held him close, her palms splayed across his back, her tongue slashing his. He lifted her into his arms and carried her to the bed.

Lock gazed down at her face, the thick lashes framing her blue eyes, the hint of freckles across her pert nose and full cheeks, and the alluring shape of her moist lips. His fingers tangled with hers, gently pressing her hands to the mattress as he kissed her. His mouth opened on hers, and she mimicked the gesture. Their tongues met, stroking and teasing. Lock closed his eyes, surrendering completely to the sensations of his sweet fallen princess.

Sparrow tugged her hands from his grip and slipped her arms around his neck, threading her fingers through his hair. Lock traced her hairline with his lips. He pressed tender kisses to her temples and the tip of her nose. Bedding a woman with love in his heart was such a new experience that each time he and Sparrow shared pleasures of the flesh, he almost felt like a novice. His heart pounded and his insides trembled with the most genuine pleasure he'd ever experienced.

"Oh, Lock," she breathed when he licked her ear and nuzzled her neck.

He unfastened the ties on her shirt, parting the front and baring her breasts. Leaning forward, he captured one nipple between his teeth, nibbling carefully while teasing with the very tip of his tongue. He slipped his hand beneath the shirt and stroked her hip. His thumb parted the soft curls of pubic hair partially hiding her clit and caressed the nub. She sighed, wiggling against his hand as it slid between her legs, his palm covering her clit while his fingers traced her pussy. Dipping two fingers inside her slit, he gathered moisture and circled her clit.

Lock tugged off her shirt and rolled her onto her stomach.

"What are you doing?" She tried glancing at him, but he lifted her hair over her shoulder and kissed her nape before moving his lips down her spine to the crack of her bottom cheeks. He kissed each round globe, marveling at the smoothness of her skin. Placing one hand under her belly, he lifted her slightly and licked the ultra sensitive flesh between her pussy and sphincter.

"Lock!" Her sharp tone was tainted by a giggle. "Don't do that!"

"You don't like it?"

"No, I like it, but—"

"Then shut up and enjoy it, Princess." He continued licking, feeling her stomach and buttocks clench with pleasure. Flipping her onto her back, he covered her clit with his mouth and ran the tip of his tongue down each side. She gasped and clutched handfuls of his hair. Lock grinned before thrusting his tongue into her pussy and exploring as far as he could reach before returning to her clit and lapping.

"Oh, goddess, I can't stand this!" Sparrow moaned.

With closed eyes, Lock continued lapping and thrusting, enjoying her cries and the squirming of her hips and bottom that he cupped and held steady.

"Oh, oh, oh!!" Sparrow's voice rose in pitch with each word as his tongue fixed on her clit, stroking fast and steady until she exploded. Lock shoved his tongue inside her again, feeling her pulse and quiver. Arousing her hardened his cock to bursting. He covered her body, still jerking in the final throes of her climax, and thrust into her hot, drenched pussy.

"Lock, please!" she panted, clinging to him as he began thrusting, driving her back to the peak almost before she'd completely descended.

"That's it, girl! Tell me what you want!"

"Don't stop! Don't!"

"I don't think I could even if I wanted to," he gasped, speeding up his thrusts. Never in his life had he desired a woman so much. He kissed her, his heart throbbing madly as his tongue slipped in and out of her mouth in time with his ramming cock. He tore his lips away to draw sips of air.

"You need me?" There was a hint of triumph in her breathless voice.

Need her? At that moment he felt he'd rather die than leave her quaking, heating body. In spite of his almost blinding desire, something stopped him from admitting such need for anyone.

"Do you need me?" she asked again, her hands sliding down his back and clutching his buttocks, her fingers sinking between the globes and pressing, stroking, penetrating.

"Hell and damnation, girl!" he groaned. Her fingers pushed harder and his thrusts became as wild as the slamming of his heart. With a cry of passion, she convulsed, her pussy squeezing his cock, her hands fierce on his ass.

She moaned, "Do yo—"

"Fuck, I need you!" he shouted as his climax stole what was left of his stubborn self-control. "I need you!"

Lock collapsed on top of her, feeling the slick heat of their skins and their hearts slamming in union. Rolling onto his side, he held her close to his chest.

Though he couldn't see her face, he sensed her smile. "You know, I'm afraid to fall asleep with you. I'll probably wake up tied again."

"No. Never again," he admitted. He didn't want her as a servant. To his dismay, he preferred her as a partner. "But I won't live as a slave, Sparrow."

She turned and faced him, her eyes serious. "I know that. I don't want you to, but there's no other way for us here."

"We don't have to stay here."

"Would you take me even if I didn't want to go with you?"

"Yes."

"Because you want me in your bed or because you don't want me tortured?"

"Both."

To his surprise, she smiled and looped her arms around his neck. "I'll go with you, but on two conditions. We have to wait for Shea-Ann to come back. I don't want her to worry."

"She'll worry no matter what. You're with me."

"But if she knows it's what I want, she'll respect that."

"What's the second condition?"

"I want you to acknowledge any children we might have."

Her insinuation sparked his anger. "I've never had any children. You're the first woman I've ever bedded without ensuring that. If I didn't have any intention of acknowledging our children, I would have been more careful. No son or daughter of mine is going to grow up like I did."

Sparrow smiled and slipped on top of him, her knees smooth against his sides. "I knew you had integrity somewhere in there."

"Way down deep. I mean *way* down, Princess. Try not to forget it." He wasn't sure why he still felt the need to warn her. Being his woman wouldn't be easy for her. She was so honest and decent. He'd have to make an attempt to live up to her expectations, but he had the feeling he was going to fall miserably short. His spirit was far too wild.

* * * * *

Sparrow smiled as she set the table for dinner. After she and Lock had made love, she'd walked around the farm to see what needed to be done since her absence and was pleased to find he'd kept up with the daily work as well as completed many of the repairs she'd been procrastinating.

She was prepared to help him in the fields, but he told her to return to the house.

"I have to do something with myself until that old witch comes back," he said. "You take care of the house. I'll take care of the farm."

Sparrow felt a peculiar thrill at his words. It was if they were a married couple. Married. Even if they wanted to marry, it would have to wait until they left Begonia. Lock was a slave in this land, and marriage between him and Sparrow would not be acknowledged.

Not that he'd asked her to marry him, anyway, she thought, her smile fading. And did she want to marry him, a pirate? Of course she did. Why else would she have consented to leave Begonia with him? She knew by losing her heart to him, she'd also lost her mind. Only a crazy woman would bind herself to Lock the White.

As dusk rolled in and Lock still hadn't returned, Sparrow began to worry. Had she been a fool to trust him again? Perhaps he'd taken off and left her to face the bounty hunters.

She sighed with relief when he stepped through the door. He reached for her before she could speak and kissed her. She melted against him, her fingers clutching his sweat-damped shirt.

"I'm going swimming," he said. "Want to come?"

Sparrow nodded, grasping a blanket from the foot of the bed.

Together they walked across the moonlit hills to the lake.

"It's a warm night," she said. "I love summertime."

"You'd like SothSea weather. It's always hot."

At the lake, Sparrow watched as Lock undressed and strode into the water, swimming to the middle.

He brushed wet hair from his eyes and called, "Aren't you coming?"

She glanced around the field.

"We're alone, Princess."

She slipped off her clothes, feeling conspicuous. She'd

never walked around naked outside before, but she liked the feeling of freedom. She waded in and swam to meet him. His arms slid around her, and she felt cool droplets of water on his lips when he kissed her.

"You must like the water," she said, "spending your life at sea and all."

"I love the water. Lakes are nice enough, but I love the ocean. Have you ever been to sea, Sparrow?"

"No."

"There's no feeling like it. The smell of salt, the sharpness of the wind, the deck beneath your feet. Sometimes when I'm out there, I feel like I never want to dock."

His arms slid up her back, and her breasts pressed to his chest beneath the dark water. She smiled, touching her lips to his cool, wet throat. "I'm starting to love the water, too."

"Are you, girl?" His voice rumbled close to her ear. He turned her so he could nuzzle her neck, fondle her breasts, and stroke her clit at the same time.

She moaned and leaned against him, allowing him to support her completely. The sensations of his big, callused hands and his soft lips tenderly tugging the flesh of her ear and neck were so pleasurable, she wanted them to last all night.

"Come here." He tugged her toward a smooth, flat stone in a shallow part of the lake. Lock sat on it, his legs outstretched but slightly bent, and beckoned her closer. "Get on top of me and put my cock in you."

Sparrow grinned, her eyes gleaming, as she did as he asked. Positioning herself on top of him, she swallowed his hard cock with her pussy. He supported her waist, his thumbs gently stroking her hips. Water lapped their skin like hundreds of soft caresses.

"I like looking at you," he told her.

The sensation of his body, the sound of his voice, and the expression of lust in his pale eyes made her feel giddy inside.

Sparrow took his face in her hands and touched every inch of it. Her fingers smoothed his forehead and traced his eyebrows. She caressed his cheekbones and stroked the length of his nose. All the while, their hips rocked in a motion both calming and stimulating.

"Oh, Lock," she whispered, her fingertips outlining his mouth. His tongue snaked out and licked between her fingers before he captured one with his lips and sucked it gently.

As their bodies heated and their movements became more demanding, Sparrow clung to his neck, leaning back and closing her eyes. His hands gripped her waist and hips harder. Sparrow exploded, moaning and crying his name. With a groan of fulfilled passion, Lock erupted inside her as waves soothed them from every direction. Afterward, they lay on the blanket she'd brought. Sparrow curled against his chest as they gazed at the sky.

"Do you think I'll like your island?" she asked.

"Parts of it. I don't want to stay there, though. We'll take my belongings, buy another ship, and move somewhere else."

"Why?"

"I don't want you living in the Archipelago with all those cutthroats. Even with guards on you."

"Guards?" She sat up, a hand on his chest. "What are you talking about?"

"While I'm at sea, it wouldn't be safe for you otherwise."

"So you're not going to stop pirating?"

He narrowed his eyes. "I haven't decided what I'm going to do yet."

"Couldn't I travel with you? If I learned how to run a farm, I can learn how to sail."

"We have time to discuss all this. Right now I want to go back to the house, eat supper, and fuck you till you can't walk."

Sparrow's stomach danced as she tugged on her clothes.

He was right. They could discuss his redemption later.

* * * * *

"I have to go to the village for supplies," Sparrow remarked the following morning at breakfast.

"I'll go with you."

"Lock, as long as you're living here, when we're seen in public, you have to wear a slave band."

His lip curled. "What?"

"It's the law. I'm sorry."

He muttered a curse in his own language, but she understood every word.

"You're the one who said you'd stay until Shea-Ann comes back," she told him.

"Fine."

Sparrow opened the trunk at the foot of her bed and removed a metal band. She approached Lock and snapped it around his thick bicep, glad she'd chosen the right size. She'd bought it the same day she'd bought him, and she'd hoped he'd live to wear it. Now she hoped for a time when they could walk together as a free couple.

He glanced at the band with disgust.

"I can't control you," she said. "I can only ask you to keep your promise."

"And play the part of your slave?"

She trailed a finger across his chest. "Is that really so bad?"

"I suppose we'll find out."

* * * * *

Every eye in the village followed Sparrow and Lock as they walked through the marketplace. At first she felt conspicuous, then began to enjoy the attention. Lock was a breathtaking sight, so tall, long-limbed, and packed with sculpted muscle. He wore trousers, boots, and a leather vest that left his big arms and broad shoulders exposed, the slave band glistening around one thick biceps. His brown and white hair was pinned back from his face with a plain silver clip and hung in a kinky mass halfway down his back. He walked two steps behind Sparrow, appearing every bit the tamed servant, and Sparrow relished the envy in the eyes of nearly every woman who saw them together.

She paused at a fruit cart and bought a sack of apples which she gave to Lock to carry, then a sack of wheat which he slung over his other shoulder.

When they passed the fish cart, the fisherwoman stood talking with the tall blacksmith, two of the women who'd "inspected" Lock several days ago.

"So, Sparrow, you got your man to behave?" The blacksmith offered a toothy smile. Her arms folded beneath her small breasts, which appeared more like a man's pectorals. She stepped closer to Lock, her gaze sweeping him.

"How long has he been unchained?" The fisherwoman stared hard at the couple from beneath her fuzzy white eyebrows. "Several cottages were robbed a few days ago."

"It wasn't him," Sparrow snapped.

"He is a pirate," the blacksmith said.

"I know it wasn't him because two nights ago thieves followed me home, and if it hadn't been for Lock, I'd have been robbed, raped, and probably murdered."

"He protected you?"

Sparrow gazed at Lock, resisting the urge to kiss him in front of the entire village. "He's very loyal."

The blacksmith said, "Now that he's tamed, you could fetch a high price for him at the palace in Begonia."

"I'm not selling."

The blacksmith and the fisherwoman exchanged glances

and smiled at Sparrow.

"Perhaps you use him for more than farm work." The blacksmith's eyes fixed on the enticing bulge in Lock's trousers. Sparrow knew she was remembering the sight of him naked, and jealousy burned in her gut. "I can understand why you wouldn't want to sell him if that's the case. He's young and strong, and he looks like he's loaded with stamina. How about loaning him out? I'll shoe all your horses for free if you let me bed him."

Lock glanced at the blacksmith from head to foot and said, "Tell her to throw in either a blindfold or an aphrodisiac because that's the only way a man could get hard facing her."

The blacksmith's fists clenched and if Sparrow hadn't stepped between her and Lock, she probably would have hit him.

The fisherwoman glared at him and told Sparrow, "You should cut out his foul tongue!"

"No," Sparrow smiled as she and Lock continued on their way, "his tongue is one of his greatest assets. And he's also not for sale or for rent."

"Good luck to you!" snarled the blacksmith. "I wouldn't really have paid for that scarred freak, anyway! I just thought I'd do you a favor and free you of him for a couple of hours!"

"A couple of hours?" Lock muttered to Sparrow. "She could probably kill a White Island yak after five minutes."

Sparrow ran a fingertip across his belly. "You might say that about me after tonight. That little trick you taught me with the leather belt and the flower petals, I want to practice more."

He laughed. "I knew you'd like that one. I won't tell you where I learned it, though."

"Somehow I don't think I'd like to hear."

"And I'm wise enough to know it." He dumped the sacks in their wagon. "Anything else while we're here?"

"No. I just want to go home so we can practice."

"There's work to do first. Wouldn't want to neglect your farm."

Sparrow smiled. At least now it was back to being *her* farm.

"Everybody look out!" a man's voice shouted before five horses tore through the village square.

Lock grasped Sparrow in one arm and hoisted her onto the wagon beside him before she was trampled.

She pointed to the group of horses and the man following them on his own chestnut mount. "He comes here sometimes to sell horses. That's where we got ours."

"He's a jackass." Lock glared in the man's direction, but his eyes drifted to a big-boned white stallion who had just kicked over the fisherwoman's cart. The animal's eyes were wild, its dirt-stained coat damp with sweat.

Shaking her fist, the fisherwoman bellowed, "Damn men! Every time they come to the village, they ruin something!"

"Sorry, old woman." The horseman nodded in her direction, lassoed the stallion, and whipped him hard across the flanks. The horse bucked, nearly kicking several passers by.

Sparrow noted the horse's sleek coat was marked with old scars. Apparently, the horseman used his whip often.

"You can't tame anything that way." Sparrow shook her head as the man continued beating the horse and bellowing curses. Lock stepped from the wagon. "Where are you going? Lock!"

She hurried after him.

The horseman raised his whip, and Lock jerked it from his hand.

"Who the hell are you?" The horseman snarled at Lock. "Give me that whip back!"

Lock glanced at the well several paces to his left. He tossed the whip down the deep, dark hole.

"Son-of-a-bitch!" the horseman's teeth clenched with fury, and he slid his foot from the stirrup to kick Lock in the face.

Lock caught his foot and yanked him from the saddle. The man landed with a grunt on his back.

"I'll beat you within an inch of your life! I'll..." The man spat a mouthful of dirt, climbed to his feet, and paused in his speech as he found himself at eye-level with Lock's broad chest. He craned his neck to look into the pirate's face with its animal-like bone structure and demonic eyes. "I'll be on my way. I don't have time for this, but the guards in Begonia will hear about it. A man can't even sell his goods without being attacked..."

"Please, Sir." Sparrow stepped forward. She placed a hand on Lock's chest. "He didn't mean anything. He has an aversion to whips."

"I wonder why," the blacksmith gloated, and Lock shot her a furious look. Sparrow's heartbeat quickened. If she didn't get him out of the village and back to the farm, who knew what else might happen?

"He's my responsibility," Sparrow continued. "I'll pay for the damages."

The horseman's eyes focused on Sparrow's money pouch from which she counted several coins.

"Well, I suppose for a beautiful woman I can be lenient." The man rubbed his stubbled jaw. "Let's say five silver pieces and call it even."

"That's robbery!" Lock bellowed.

"Will you shut up?" Sparrow hissed through clenched teeth.

Lock threw up his hands in disgust and walked away while Sparrow paid the horseman.

After he'd pocketed the money, the man glanced over his shoulder and noticed Lock stroking the stallion's neck. Though trembling, the horse seemed calmer beneath the pirate's touch. Sparrow almost smiled. He and the horse were so similar, both spirited, handsome, battle-scarred…

"Get your hands off that animal, slave!" the horseman bellowed. "He's going to the slaughterhouse from here. No one's got any use for a horse that can't be trained."

"Maybe *you* can't train him," Lock said.

"Others have tried."

"With a whip?"

"It usually works," the horseman glanced at one of Lock's scarred shoulders, "as you must know."

Lock took a step toward the man, and Sparrow said quickly, "How much for the horse?"

"Missy, you don't want him."

"Yes, I do."

"She has a way with wild things." The blacksmith winked in Sparrow's direction.

"I don't know…"

"You're here to make a profit, aren't you?" Sparrow placed a hand on her hip. "So how much?"

* * * * *

"That's the last time I take you to the village." Sparrow glanced at Lock from the corner of her eye as she drove the wagon toward the farm. "You're far too expensive."

Lock looked over his shoulder at the while stallion prancing behind the wagon. After paying the trader, he and Sparrow had taken the horse to the blacksmith's stables where they'd cleaned him and tended his injuries. Several times the stallion tried nipping and kicking, but such behavior was understandable after the abuse he'd suffered. With proper handling, Lock was certain the beautiful horse would be well mannered and trainable. The idea of taming and riding him was almost as thrilling as the thought of sailing again.

He turned his gaze back to Sparrow and brushed a tendril

of hair behind her ear. He wasn't exactly sure how to express what he felt for her or why she apparently felt so much for him. "Why are you so nice to me?"

"What?" she giggled.

"Why?"

"I like you."

"What's to like? I haven't treated you very well since I've known you."

"I think you've probably treated me better than you've ever treated anyone."

"Is it that obvious?"

Sparrow stopped the wagon and kissed him. He slid his arms around her and murmured, "I guess so."

Lock picked up the reins, and as they continued home, wondered if he was capable of love after all.

Chapter Eleven

ல

At the farm, Sparrow cooked and did the wash while Lock worked the field and tended the livestock.

It was late afternoon when she began hanging laundry on the lines behind the house. She saw Lock and the stallion in the fenced off portion of field where Daphne usually grazed. As she pinned up towels, undergarments, and shirts, she watched Lock's attempts at taming the horse. The animal was wary from years of abuse and used its fierce temper and strength to defend itself. Again Sparrow was struck by the similarities between pirate and stallion.

She was a bit surprised by Lock's patience. She held her breath the first time he attempted to mount the horse bareback. The animal threw him, and he landed hard.

"Will you be careful!" Sparrow shouted to him.

He stood, winked at her, and raised a finger to his lips. The stallion grew agitated from the sound of her voice, and Sparrow scolded herself. If he was going to gain the white beast's trust, she shouldn't interfere.

She watched the battle between horse and man for as long as she could stand seeing Lock thrown to the grass.

"Crazy," she muttered. "He'd going to knock his brains out—at least what brains he has."

She walked back to the house and continued with her chores, trying to forget about Lock until dusk fell when she stepped outside to call him for dinner.

She smiled when she saw him on the stallion's back, riding the perimeter of the fence. Horse and rider were both tall and beautiful, the horse's white coat blending with the white streaks in Lock's hair.

She approached the fence and spoke quietly, "Good job."

Lock stopped the horse with a gentle tug on the reins. He patted the animal's muscular neck. "Took a while, but as you said, I'm stubborn."

"Just ask the pig."

He laughed. "I'll start him with the saddle gradually."

"Yes," she nodded toward his crotch, "that can't be good for important parts of you."

"That's why we have knees, girl." He gripped the horse's sides, then tossed her a roguish grin. "But if you still think it's damaged and want to massage it later…"

"In your dreams."

"Each and every night."

"Supper's nearly ready, so you better cool him down and put him to bed for the night," she said and turned back to the house, giddy as she thought about the dessert to come once they were in *their* bed. She'd probably end up giving the incorrigible demon that risqué massage after all.

Inside, Sparrow brought stew, bread, and cooked apples to the table while Lock washed in a basin of water and changed his shirt.

They sat together and began eating.

"It seemed to bother you when that blacksmith made an offer for me."

"Wouldn't it bother you if someone offered money for my body?"

"When I got through with him, he'd never have to think about bedding a woman again." Lock ripped a chunk of bread from the loaf and took a bite, his pale eyes gleaming. "I'd geld him just for the suggestion."

Sparrow squirmed in her seat, a thrill coursing through her. She never realized how exciting it was to have a man willing—and well able—to protect her. "And if that blond-haired gladiator had laid a hand on you, I'd have torn her breasts off."

Lock threw the bread aside, finished what he was chewing and dragged her chair closer to his. He licked her lips, glossy from the stew, and kissed her. Sparrow locked her arms around his neck and straddled his lap.

"This is the only stallion I want to ride," she whispered against his lips. Her hands slid beneath his shirt, her fingertips tracing his ribs and clutching his hair-roughened pectorals.

Lock stood, lifting her onto the table and shoving aside the bread and bowls of food. He tugged off her shirt and pushed her onto her back, his mouth devouring her breasts, his hands caressing her belly and hips. He tugged her trousers down to her ankles, and as he dropped his own, she kicked hers aside and wrapped her legs around his waist. She sighed as his cock plunged deep inside her, his hands splayed across her back. Raising her enough to capture one nipple between his lips, he sucked hard and nibbled the tip.

"Goddess have mercy," she said breathlessly, closing her eyes and clutching handfuls of his thick, kinky hair.

His lips traveled over her breasts and throat.

"Look at me," he commanded, his voice raw with passion. Sparrow's eyes opened halfway and she gazed into his pale blue ones. He slowed his movements and traced her lips with his thumb. "How do you like it, Princess?"

"Any way you want to give it," was her breathless reply.

"You must have a preference."

Sparrow's eyes opened fully as she considered his question and the sensations flooding her body. "Rough. I want it rough."

He smiled wickedly and pushed her down, his body pounding into hers. He reached across the table for the soft, cooked apples and smeared the warm fruit over her nipples. He licked them clean while she gasped his name and clawed at his shoulders, completely lost in sensation.

He grasped her wrists and pinned her hands above her head. When he kissed her, he tasted of apples. She licked his tongue, her body straining against his, aching for fulfillment only he could give.

Just when she thought she was going to shatter into a thousand pieces, his movements slowed. Her eyes flew open.

"I want to hear you." He brushed the tip of her nose with his and fastened his mouth to hers. He nipped her lips and raised his head, her eyes gleaming with lust. "I want to hear how much you want me."

"I want you!"

He laughed, offering a couple of taunting thrusts. He sucked one nipple, then the other until her high-pitched cry sounded throughout the room.

Sparrow felt laughter rumble in his chest. "That's what I want, Princess. Tell me you need me."

Sparrow heard the teasing edge to his voice and knew he was throwing her own words back at her.

"Say it!" he ordered, using one of his hands to continue holding both of hers while he stroked her clit with the other, his finger keeping time with his thrusting cock.

"I need you!" she cried.

He drove into her so hard and fast that the heavy oak table shook.

"You're going to break my furniture!" she gasped, then shrieked with pleasure as his teeth gently chewed one nipple, his tongue lapping the pebble-hard peak. She struggled to free her hands from his grasp, wanting nothing more than to cling to him as her body erupted beneath his carnal onslaught.

She shouted his name and he released her wrists, his arms closing around her and crushing her to his chest. She clutched him so tightly her arms and legs ached, but she didn't care. All she felt was waves of throbbing ecstasy. His climax forced her back onto the table, and for a long moment, she lay beneath him, both catching their breath amidst a table full of half-eaten food.

She laughed. "That was the best meal I've had in a long time."

"That was the first course."

Her eyes widened slightly as he swept her into his arms and carried her to the bed.

* * * * *

The night's heat awoke Sparrow. Though she lay on top of the bedcovers, her skin felt hot and sticky. She reached for Lock, but found the bed empty beside her. A breeze blew through the window at the far corner of the room. She slipped out of bed, hoping the wind might cool her.

Even the wind's too warm, she thought, stepping closer to the window. She caught sight of Lock in the middle of the moonlit field, the white stallion grazing in the distance behind him.

She slipped on her boots and a thin cotton shift and went to join him.

As she approached, she saw he was moving across the field with the grace of a big cat, performing kicks, blocks, and strikes. Though she knew he was practicing fighting, his motions reminded her of a dance. She vaguely remembered taking a trip with her father years ago. They'd visited a kingdom in the North where they'd watched several Knights of the Ruby Order perform an exhibition of their fighting techniques. The Knights were healers and warriors, and such performances were rare, since they lived by strict vows and a stern code of ethics. The Northern King had been a friend of their leader, however, and the Knights had agreed to the exhibition as a favor. Watching Lock made her think of the Knights. His practice looked so similar to theirs.

She sat on the fence and stared at him, her eyes devouring his lean, muscled torso glistening with perspiration. She gazed at his long, powerful legs as they shifted in low stances or kicked at various levels — at times above his own head.

Finally he stopped and glanced at her, wiping damp hair from his forehead.

"Where did you learn how to do that?" she asked.

He approached, his breathing returning to normal, and stood in front of her, a hand braced on the fence post on either side of her legs. She watched the pulse beating in the hollow of his sweat-sheened throat and glanced at the sleekness of his body. Sliding her hands over his chest, she reveled in the feeling of his hot, wet skin.

"Years ago I was first mate on a ship called The Bloody Morning. She sank off the coast of an island to the east. Only four of us survived, and we were forced to live there until we could find a way off. We were told ships scarcely docked there. There were six huts on the whole damn island, girl. Six. Twenty people lived there, six of them children. They'd moved away from their homeland."

"Why?"

"To live in peace. At first we didn't understand their language, but later I learned to speak it. They were members of a house of warriors who served a great lord. Tired of bloodshed, they left and settled on the island. They appeared to have nothing, but in one of the huts, an old man had a hoard of armor and weapons that would fetch a very high price off the island. Two of the members of our crew attempted to steal the old man's belongings, not that they could go anywhere once they took them. The old man's nephew caught them, and they pulled a knife on him. I'd never seen anyone fight like that boy. He used his body like weapon. He had the speed and strength of the wind."

"What happened to the thieves?"

"He killed them both."

"You didn't try to steal from them, I hope?"

Lock wrinkled his nose. "Do I look daft? I wanted to learn their fighting style. I figured I had nothing else to do on that island. I didn't know how long I'd be there, but if it was long enough, I'd master their technique. I was bigger than any of them, and knew once I could fight like them, I'd have the advantage. When the time came for me to leave, I could take the armor and weapons, and they could do nothing about it."

"So you used them?" Sparrow wondered if her disappointment shone in her eyes. At times she could forget he was a pirate, a thief, a killer.

"I used them. For three years I lived on that island. The only other man left from The Bloody Morning had been injured when we sank, and he died of a fever soon after we washed ashore. I lived with those people, worked with them. We survived mostly by fishing, but also did some farming."

"Which is why you didn't make a complete mess of my farm while I was tied up."

He winked at her. "You've done well, Sparrow. I can see why you're proud."

She smiled, pleased by his words, and said, "Finish your story."

"When I wasn't doing my share of the work, I practiced. Practiced every day until my arms and legs felt as heavy as steel. I wanted to know everything those masters knew — all at once, of course."

She chuckled. "Looks like you did pretty well."

"I learned everything they had to teach. Then a ship docked, and I was ready to go back to my life."

"As a pirate?"

"It was all I knew."

"But they showed you an honest life."

"I didn't see it that way at the time. I took what I'd learned as another way to make myself unbeatable. In a way, it did. Since then, I've never been beaten in a fight — until those bounty hunters got their hands on me."

"So you stole the weapons and armor when you left the

island?"

He sighed, his eyes fixed on hers. "No. I didn't."

"Why?"

"I..." He shook his head. "I don't know. The time came, and I just didn't want to do it anymore."

"Because you felt loyalty to them for all they'd done for you."

"Maybe. I don't know."

"You've always had a heart, Lock." She slid her arms around his neck and touched her nose to his.

"I don't think I have a heart like you mean."

"If you didn't have a heart, we wouldn't be together right now. You feel for me. Admit it."

"If I could feel for anyone, it would be for you, but I don't think I'm capable."

"Of course you are."

"I've lived like an animal, Sparrow. Surviving day by day, There's almost nothing I haven't done for money."

"Much of that wasn't your fault."

"Maybe, but most of it was."

"I don't care about your past, Lock. I care about now and the future."

Lock caressed her face. "Whatever happened to that prince you were supposed to marry?"

"You were right." Sparrow lowered her eyes. "He didn't want a commoner."

"That fool's loss is my gain."

He kissed her, and Sparrow clung to him, knowing the pirate had completely stolen her heart. Her grip tightened around his neck as he lifted her off the fence and carried her to the lake.

Placing her on the grass, Lock kissed her before undressing and wading into the water. Sparrow discarded her clothes and followed him, watching as he ducked beneath the surface and rose, shaking out his thick mass of kinky hair. She swam to him and slipped her arms around his waist. He glanced at her and grinned, but continued washing, scrubbing his underarms and using both hands to cleanse his cock and balls beneath the water's surface.

"I have plans for us tonight, girl," he winked.

"What plans?" she asked as she also began a thorough scrubbing. For some reason, she sensed his plans had nothing to do with a night out in the village.

"I think you'll enjoy the evening, if you get my meaning."

"Really? I can hardly wait."

Lock strode towards her, placing a smacking kiss on her mouth before he left the water and gathered their clothing. She approached, and he handed her their garments before sweeping her into his arms and carrying her back to the house.

"Keeping toting me around this place and I'll get spoiled."

"You should be spoiled."

Sparrow rubbed her nose against his and smiled. "I'm not meant for spoiling. I had that kind of life as a princess."

"Depends on the kind of spoiling we're talking about, girl. I'm no royal, that's for damn sure, but I know a few things about keeping women happy."

"I want to be more than just a woman to you!"

"You're not just *a* woman. You're *my* woman. Not because you're a slave or a whore, but because we're inside each other now."

Back at the house, Lock placed Sparrow on the bed and took the clothes still clutched in her hands. Tossing the pile aside, he stretched out near her, facing her feet.

"What are you doing?" she grinned.

"Something you'll like as much as I do." He dragged her closer and buried his face in her crotch, running his tongue

142

over her clit. "Take my cock, Sparrow. Do what you did that day in the tub."

Sparrow's pulse quickened, both from the sensation of his mouth on her clit and the idea of simultaneously doing the same to his cock.

She edged closer and clasped the root of his staff as she licked it from top to bottom. Her tongue swirled around the head, and she took him partway into her mouth, sucking hard and quick. Lock groaned as he lapped her clit and plunged his tongue into her pussy.

Sparrow uttered a helpless sound, continuing to lick, suck, and nip his cock. It swelled beneath her ministrations. Knowing she pleasured him while he pleasured her excited her so much that within moments she erupted in orgasm. Even as she shook, throbbed, and panted, she continued licking his cock.

Lock's tongue and lips never ceased their movements. He explored the delicate folds of moist flesh, sucked on her hard little nub, and flattened his tongue against the flesh between her pussy and bottom hole. A second orgasm built inside Sparrow. This time when she climaxed, she momentarily tore her mouth from his cock as her breath came in pleasured sobs.

He continued devouring her. Sparrow's legs trembled and her clit ached with desire. Surely no one could live through this kind of pleasure? Yet she felt as if she was cheating him – and herself. She grasped his balls and laved his cock head, trailing her tongue along the underside. She buried her lips at the base and lapped the kinky hair as well as his balls. An anguished sound broke from Lock's throat, still he continued pleasuring her. His tongue swirled inside her while his finger circled her clit.

Sparrow came again, whimpering with desire, though this time she refused to give up on him. She laved and mouthed his cock until her orgasm waned, then she drew him deep into her mouth, as if gulping his shaft.

"Ahh!" Lock groaned, his entire body tense.

Sparrow withdrew his cock partway and tried the short quick sucking motions on his cock head. His hips thrust towards her, and she grasped his rock-hard buttocks as he came so long and hard she wondered if he'd ever stop.

Finally both sprawled, limp and fulfilled, on the bed. The last thing she felt before tumbling into sleep was Lock's hand grasping her foot and his lips pressing to the arch.

* * * * *

Since Lock had agreed to act as Sparrow's slave until Shea-Ann returned, he expected the coming weeks to stretch endlessly, but to his surprise, days passed with unprecedented swiftness. Had it not been for the arm band, he might have even forgotten he was—in the eyes of the village—Sparrow's property. They spent their days working the farm and caring for the house and nights making love, swimming in the lake or riding the white stallion across the countryside.

With Lock's diligent training and patience, the stallion had learned to trust him and obeyed his every command. He and Sparrow spent days arguing over the horse's name, and finally decided on Sea Storm.

With the approaching fall, the nights grew cooler, and one evening after supper, Lock and Sparrow donned cloaks, mounted Sea Storm, and rode to the edge of the woods. Lock smiled as he nudged the stallion to a canter. Sparrow clung to his waist. He loved the feeling of her body so close to his, reminding him of what was to come later that evening.

By the trees, he slowed the horse, and they plodded along the forest's edge.

"It's a beautiful night," Sparrow said, tugging out a leaf that had blown into Lock's hair. "It'll snow in a few months."

"We'll most likely be gone by then."

Sparrow's eyes clouded. "I keep forgetting we won't be staying here."

"I hate to take you from a home you love, Sparrow, but I can't spend the rest of my life pretending to be a slave."

"I don't want you to. I said I'd follow you anywhere, Lock, and I meant it."

"It's getting cloudy. Feels like a storm." Lock glanced skyward. "Let's go home."

Sparrow grinned, her hands sliding over his thighs. "I like that idea."

"I know what your plan is, girl. You'll wear me out so I won't be able to travel," he teased.

"So lacking in stamina, are you?"

He glanced over his shoulder, flinging her a look of carnal challenge. "When it comes to some things, I can outdistance this horse."

She laughed and dropped her hand to his crotch. "And some parts of you almost outweigh him."

He glanced between his legs and said, "I wouldn't go that far, girl. Almost, though."

She playfully swatted him in the back of the head. Just as a frosty rain started to fall, they turned Sea Storm back toward the house.

By the time they arrived at home, all three were soaked. While Lock brought the stallion to the barn to settle him for the night, Sparrow returned to the house.

When Lock finally stepped inside and shook off his half-frozen cloak, Sparrow had a fire leaping in the hearth and was awaiting him beneath the bedcovers.

She sat up, the blankets falling from her bare breasts, and smiled at him. "Come here and let me warm you up."

He shed his wet clothes and slid beneath the blankets.

She shivered as his body covered hers, and she teased, "To think I just got warm!"

"I can get you warm," he captured one of her nipples in his mouth and lapped it, then pulled back, "unless you'd rather sleep alone?"

Sparrow wrapped her arms and legs around him. "Don't even *think* about leaving this bed!"

"Not right now," he nipped her shoulder and slid a hand between her silky thighs, cupping her crotch and rubbing gently, "but it might get a little dull for the whole night."

Before she could speak, his mouth covered hers and he kissed her as if he could draw her very essence inside him so they would never part.

He rolled onto his side and propped his cheek on his hand, gazing down at her. The fingertips of his free hand danced over her flesh, tracing every inch of her shoulders, breasts, and belly. He outlined each rib, stroked the thatch of dark, coiled hairs between her legs, and explored her soft, moist core.

She sighed, watching him through half-closed eyes. She trusted him implicitly, he could see it in her expression, in the way she opened her body and spirit to him. No one had ever trusted him like that, nor had he ever trusted anyone—until now.

"I love looking at you," he said, his touch making her writhe. Her eyes slipped shut and she uttered a soft, kittenish sound that made his pulse race.

Suddenly the kitten became a tigress, and she pounced on him, her thighs clasping his waist, her fingers gripping his shoulders.

"Goddess, I want you, Lock!"

"I'm yours, Princess!" He grasped her waist as she rode him hard, her breasts bouncing and her thighs clasping his hips as her wet pussy clenched his cock.

He willed his body into submission as he watched her tremble above him, her breasts thrust forward and her head thrown back. She melted onto his chest, and he felt her giggle.

"You're a little animal." He grasped her shoulders and kissed her.

She purred, curling her fist around his cock and squeezing. "I think I like this weapon. How's about forcing me to walk the plank, Captain?"

"I've done it before, girl. Off the plank and into the deep green sea."

She shrieked and laughed as he jerked her into his arms and stood, carrying her across the room and dropping her on the table.

"Not here again, Lock!" she complained, but clutched his shoulders as he pressed her onto her back and ravaged her breasts. He rubbed his cheek against the soft, warm flesh, took one of her nipples between his teeth and tickled it with his tongue until she moaned. He teased her other breast while he entered her with a swift, hard thrust. She gave a cry of raw pleasure and raked her nails down his arms.

Lock closed his eyes and pinned her hands on either side of her head as he lunged fast and hard into her straining body. He felt the beginning of an incredible climax and lost all reason, until something hard and bristly cracked him over his head.

"Get off her, you SothSea swine!"

Lock's eyes snapped open, and he glanced over his shoulder in time for the straw end of a broom to crack him across the face.

Shea-Ann stood, poised to do battle, her eyes gleaming with anger in her rounded face.

"Shea-Ann!" Sparrow drew her knees up to her waist and tried to hide her full breasts with both hands.

The nanny drew back the broom, but this time Lock ripped it from her grasp and flung it across the room. "Are you mad, hag?"

"How dare you attack My Lady when she saved your worthless life! I will rip you apart with my bare hands!" Shea-Ann flew at him. He caught her and twisted her arms behind her back, restraining her as gently as possible. He felt like breaking the old witch's arms, but knew Sparrow would hate him for it.

"Sparrow, run while you can!" the nanny screamed.

"Shea-Ann, will you calm yourself!" Sparrow ordered, retrieving one of Lock's shirts and tugging it over her head. "He didn't attack me!"

"He didn't?" Shea-Ann stopped struggling and stared at Sparrow in disbelief.

"We have much to talk about," Sparrow told her.

"I dare say! Let me go, you big oaf!"

Cursing in his own language, Lock released the older woman who spun, rubbing her arms, and glared at him.

"What's he doing unchained? And why was he... He didn't force you?" Shea-Ann asked weakly.

"No." Sparrow stood beside Lock and took his hand.

"Don't tell me the two of you..."

"Are together as man and woman," Sparrow finished.

The nanny slapped a hand to her forehead and moaned. "Goddess help us! Where did I fail?"

Lock raised his eyes to heaven and reached for his trousers. He dragged them on along with a shirt, not bothering to fasten the ties.

"Shea-Ann, so much has happened since you left. I have things to tell you." Sparrow pulled out a chair, and Shea-Ann dropped into it. Sparrow continued, "I'll make tea and we can talk."

Lock glanced at Sparrow as she boiled water and fixed the mugs, then he turned back at Shea-Ann. If looks could kill, he'd have been dust. He couldn't help the broad smile that spread across his face.

"I suppose you think it's going to be an easy life for you, living as a kept man?" the nanny snapped. "All you need to do is please her with that breeder bull's body of yours!"

"Shea-Ann!" Sparrow said.

"I'll never be a kept man," Lock said, all traces of humor disappearing with the old woman's accusation. He'd spent his childhood as the worst kind of slave and any implication that he would enjoy peddling his flesh made his temper boil. "I agreed to stay here until you returned because Sparrow has feelings for you. We'll be moving on, and I'll make a life for her."

"What kind of life can you give her? She already has a good, honest life. You're nothing but a pirate!"

Lock's teeth clenched. How he'd love to wring Shea-Ann's scrawny neck! What bothered him most was she was right. He'd always lived the life of a criminal, and Sparrow was a good woman. How could he possibly change into a respectable mate for her? How could he provide for her in the manner she deserved, and if they should have children, how could he set an example for them? No child of his would lead the life he had.

"Is it true? Are you going away with him, Sparrow?"

Sparrow approached the table and took Shea-Ann's hand. "I want to go with him."

"Why?"

"Because," Sparrow glanced at Lock, "I love him."

Lock's heart pounded, and he stood, heading for the door. He needed air.

A whipping and the rack hadn't made him feel faint, but the responsibility that accompanied Sparrow's words was more than he could tolerate.

"You say you love him and he goes walking?" Shea-Ann said. "Sparrow, don't ruin your life with the likes of him..."

The remainder of the old witch's words were cut off as Lock stepped into the windy autumn night.

149

Chapter Twelve

ॐ

"Sparrow, I need an explanation!" Shea-Ann stood and paced the room. "Do you have any idea what you're doing? He's a pirate!"

"I know what he is." Sparrow's anger bristled. Her sudden confession regarding her love for Lock had tossed her off balance. She hadn't intended to blurt it out, but it was the only honest answer to Shea-Ann's question. She did love him.

"How can you love him?"

"It's not hard, once you get to know him. Will you calm yourself and listen to me?"

"I'm listening!"

For the next several moments, Sparrow explained the events of the past weeks. She told Shea-Ann how Lock had rescued her from the thieves, escaped, and returned.

"I still don't trust him." Shea-Ann folded her arms across her chest. "But I admit that maybe way down—I mean way, way down—inside, he might have some redeeming quality. He must feel something for you to have come back."

Sparrow glanced toward the door. "I think he loves me."

Shea-Ann laughed. "You're losing your mind. A man like that's not capable of love. See how he reacted when you mentioned the word?"

"He doesn't trust easily, and he has reason." Sparrow thought about Lock's mother. Surely a person should be able to trust his own mother. From the moment he was born, Lock had no one to trust. She didn't condone his actions, but at least she could understand them.

"Sparrow, even if he does have some sense of loyalty to

you doesn't mean it's enough to change his ways. He's too old. His path is already chosen."

Sparrow met her friend's eyes. "Don't you believe a person can change if he wants to?"

"Do you really think he wants to?"

"I don't know. Only Lock can answer that question."

"For your sake, I hope he does want to change. If not, then I pity you, Sparrow. The man is dangerous. And what are his intentions toward you? You've been sleeping together. What if there's a child?"

"Lock wouldn't abandon his children."

Shea-Ann snorted. "He probably has children scattered all over the Archipelago and beyond."

"He doesn't. He said he's been careful, that he doesn't want any child of his to live the life he has."

"And you believe him?"

"Yes."

"You're too naive for your own good!"

"I'm not asking for your approval, Shea-Ann. We waited so I could talk to you because I think of you as my family."

Shea-Ann embraced Sparrow tightly. "I think of you as a daughter. I want you to be happy. I pray this man wants the same. If you love him, I suppose he can't be completely horrible."

"I'm going to find him," Sparrow said. "Why don't you get some rest? You must have had a difficult journey."

Sparrow slipped on her cloak and left the house. She found Lock sitting on the fence, staring at the forest across the field. The wind blew strong and cold, but the rain had stopped. Sparrow tugged the cloak tighter around her and sat beside Lock.

"Why did you leave?" she asked.

"I thought you wanted to talk with the witch alone."

Sparrow smiled. "Would you at least try to get along with her?"

"Only if she never touches a broom again."

"Do you have anything to say to me?"

He shook his head.

Sparrow's stomach lurched. What had she expected, for him to say he loved her back? She knew he wouldn't say it, but she'd wished.

He reached out and stroked her hair.

"There's a gathering in the village tomorrow," she said. "I thought we could go."

"If you want."

She hopped off the fence and stood between his legs, a hand on each thigh. "Do you want to go the barn and finish what we started?"

"The barn? You're as wanton as they come."

She slid her arms around his neck. "Only because you've corrupted me."

An odd look crossed his face, but was gone so quickly it might not have been.

He stood and pulled her close, his mouth searching hers. She giggled, tugged away from him, and ran toward the barn. He caught her with several long strides and swept her into his arms.

Inside the barn, he placed her on her feet. He licked and kissed the side of her neck, sucking gently until she writhed. Sparrow covered her hands with his as they cupped her breasts. His thumbs brushed her nipples and she uttered a contented sigh. Lock undressed her, tossing her clothes into a pile of hay. Squatting in front of her nude body, he grasped her hips and pressed his face to the thatch of hair between her legs. His tongue tickled her clit before he turned her around, slapped her buttocks and nudged her towards a trunk beside Sea Storm's stall.

"Face the trunk on your knees," he ordered, discarding his clothes and dropping them beside hers.

Sparrow glanced over her shoulder at him, her belly fluttering. Whenever he ordered her into a particular position, she knew indescribable joy would soon follow. There seemed to be nothing Lock didn't know about pleasures of the flesh, not that she was one to judge. Prior to meeting him, she'd done no more than kiss a man.

She dropped to her knees, her forearms braced on top of the trunk. Glancing over her shoulder, she watched as Lock approached and knelt behind her. One of his arms snaked around her waist, and he held her close. His cock brushed her buttocks, and she waited, her heart pounding, for him to penetrate. Instead he covered her back with kisses while his free hand reached around her and caressed her belly. He brushed her clit with his thumb. Anticipation and excitement already had her wet for him, but she knew from experience he never took her quickly, but made certain she was well prepared. Gathering moisture from her pussy, he explored her soft folds and rubbed her clit. One of his fingers slipped inside her and gently caressed the top of her pussy. Sparrow moaned softly. She felt his chest rumble with laughter as he continued stroking her. His tongue ran down her spine, and he moved slightly, licking her lower back just above the parting of her bottom cheeks.

"Oh Lock, please," she murmured.

He growled, his body covering hers. His cock entered her before he began leisurely thrusts while his arms stretched over hers. Their fingers entwined and Sparrow wiggled her hips in pleasure. Within moments, she learned his rhythm. It felt so wonderful being claimed by him, on her knees in a barn, with the wind howling outside.

"Lock! Oh, by the goddess!" she cried as an orgasm washed over her.

"I'm here, girl!"

"Oh!" she moaned, another climax building deep inside her.

This time when she came, she heard Lock's ragged breath as his thrusts came faster and harder.

He panted, his voice jerky with lust, "That...old...bitch better not...hit me with...a broom again!"

With a growl of pleasure he came, his body surging into hers.

His cheek dropped to her back, his beard rough against her flesh as they sat, limp and panting until he finally moved. Tugging her against his chest, he kissed her hair.

"I suppose we should go back to the house," Sparrow murmured.

Lock grunted in reply and gathered their clothes.

Sparrow loved Shea-Ann, but she had to admit feeling a little disappointed that she and Lock no longer had the entire farm to themselves.

* * * * *

Sparrow stirred and snuggled closer to Lock. She opened her eyes and saw that it was dark, probably close to midnight.

Part of her was still disappointed that he hadn't admitted feeling any love for her. He'd said he wasn't capable of love, but Sparrow didn't believe it. He just had little experience caring for someone. His past had convinced him he couldn't feel affection, but the future with her promised a new way of life for him—and her.

Lock turned in his sleep, his arm tightening around her, his head buried in her shoulder. No man who touched her like he did was incapable of love.

* * * * *

Sparrow sat astride Sea Storm, Lock behind her, holding the reins. Every now and then, she'd feel his arms tighten around her, and she glanced back at him and smiled. Beside them, Shea-Ann's horse plodded. The healer kept glancing at Sparrow and the pirate as if she still couldn't believe they were a pair.

The village gathering happened every autumn, and Sparrow looked forward to it. The market was open all day and there was music, dancing, games, feasts, and horse races.

"This will be a good day to haggle for new cloth," Shea-Ann said. "I want to make some dresses for us, seeing how your only good one was ruined."

Sparrow glanced at Lock and he shrugged. Neither of them had mentioned *how* the dress had been ruined. It was one of their secrets.

The sound of flutes, laughter, and conversation grew louder as they neared the village square and dismounted. For a fee, the blacksmith would board horses for the day, so Shea-Ann and Sparrow paid for their mounts, then headed for the village.

"I'm going shopping," Shea-Ann said, "then I have rounds to make. I'll meet you later."

"Good riddance," Lock muttered under his breath, and Sparrow poked him with her elbow.

"SothSea swine," Shea-Ann said.

"Shriveled witch."

"Murdering yak!"

"Buzzard!"

"That's enough!" Sparrow snapped. "Both of you! You're acting worse than children! Shea-Ann, go about your business, and Lock, close your mouth!"

Flinging one last goading look at the pirate, Shea-Ann disappeared in the crowded marketplace.

"It's a wonder you're as sweet as you are seeing how she raised you," Lock said to Sparrow.

"You think I'm sweet?"

His teeth gleamed against his beard as he smiled and continued walking. Sparrow fell into step beside him, and they chatted about the farm when a voice interrupted them.

"So you've given him the liberty to walk alongside you?" the fisherwoman called from her cart.

"How I treat my slave is my business," Sparrow told her. "Got any squid?"

The woman winked and beckoned her closer. "The best you'll taste in these parts."

Sparrow and Lock approached the cart and selected several pieces of squid. They brought the slippery meat across to one of the community fires in the square to cook it.

"My favorite breakfast," Lock said, taking a bite of a dangling squid leg.

"I know." Sparrow wrinkled her nose. "It's really not the first thing I'd reach for in the morning, but I thought I'd indulge you this once."

"This once? Seems you've been doing that for weeks."

"What's a little squid for all you've done for the farm? It's never looked so good. All the repairs are made, and we're stocked for the winter. At least we'll be leaving Shea-Ann prepared."

"You don't want to leave, do you?"

Sparrow looked down at her hands. "I'll miss it here, but I know you can't stay."

"Won't stay," he murmured. "For what you've done for me, I should stay to make you happy, but I won't lie to you, Sparrow. It would last for a while, but I cannot live as a slave."

"You'd end up resenting me. I know that."

"And if we go, will you end up resenting me? Be honest."

She sighed. "Maybe a little, but I've had to uproot before. I'm sure wherever we settle, I'll be happy, as long as I'm with you. Besides, if we do have children, I wouldn't want them to see you as my slave. It wouldn't be right."

"I've been thinking about where we can go when we leave here. We could go further south. Once we're out of Begonia and I'm free, we could settle on the coast. I'll work as a fisherman."

"A fisherman?"

"I need to be at sea, Sparrow. I miss it."

If she looked hard enough, she could almost see the ocean in his blue eyes. The sea was part of him, and wherever they went, he needed it, just as she needed him.

"Will you be happy as a fisherman?"

"It'll be better than not being at sea. Once I earn enough, I can build a bigger ship and take up trading. Honest trade, this time."

"You're serious about this?"

"I've never been more serious about anything in my life."

She stared at him. The life he described sounded so good to her, but what would it be like for him? He was so wild, so passionate about everything. How happy could he be living as a fisherman, waiting for the chance to sail again? She wanted him to discard his criminal ways, but she didn't want to kill his spirit.

"What's going on there?" He nodded toward a gathering of women, men, and horses.

"It's just a race. Exciting to watch. I always wanted to enter, but my horses aren't fast enough."

"Even Sea Storm?"

She laughed. "He'd probably win."

Lock stood and squinted at the horses lined up facing the field outside of the village. "No doubt he would win, but not with me riding. I'm too big."

"You couldn't ride him, anyway, Lock. It's for women only."

"What are all those men doing there?"

157

"They're slaves. They belong to the women entering the race. The winner gets to bed the one of her choice. She also collects prizes donated by the vendors."

Lock noticed the ensemble of men, most tall, young, and muscular, all wearing arm bands like his.

"Enter," Lock said.

"What?"

"You said you always wanted to race. Get Sea Storm and enter."

"That would mean I have to put you up as a prize along with the others. Never."

"Even if you lose—which you won't—it's nothing I haven't done before."

"It's a risk I'm not willing to take."

The *idea* of any other woman sleeping with Lock made Sparrow burn with rage.

Together, they joined the crowd waiting for the race to begin. Sparrow stared at the women mounted on tall, sleek horses, and her heart pounded. She'd always loved riding, and when she'd lived in the palace, had owned many fine, fast horses. Though she often rode Sea Storm at the farm, the thought of racing across the field and jumping fences while the rest of the village watched made her tingle. It had been so long...

"We have one more entry!" Shea-Ann shouted, and Sparrow's eyes widened as the nanny strode up to the contestants, Lock behind her leading Sea Storm.

The blacksmith laughed and patted the neck of her big-boned black stallion. "You plan on riding, old woman? I thought you were a healer."

"That doesn't mean I'm a bad rider!" Shea-Ann approached Sea-Storm and attempted to mount the towering stallion.

Sparrow cursed softly. Was Shea-Ann losing her mind?

The woman could just about ride her gentle, chubby mare.

"Shea-Ann, what are you doing?" Sparrow demanded, shoving her way through the crowd.

"You wouldn't ride," Lock said. "Shea-Ann was more than willing to put me up as a prize."

Sparrow glared at her old nanny who shrugged. "Would you prefer to ride?"

"I'm not entering."

A voice shouted, "Ready...Set...Off!"

"You see, it's too late..." Sparrow's sentence was cut off by her shriek of surprise as Lock tossed her onto Sea-Storm's back and slapped the stallion's rump hard.

* * * * *

Lock watched as the white stallion bolted, galloping after the flanks of the other horses.

"Are you mad!" Shea-Ann whacked Lock on the arm. "You could have gotten her killed!"

Lock smiled. "Sparrow will love it! Look at them. They've almost caught the others."

Shea-Ann's face was tense with fury. "I almost hope she loses and you have to bed someone like the blacksmith!"

Lock's smile faded as he squinted at the muscular blacksmith and her stallion several lengths ahead of the others. If she did win, Lock hoped she'd been insulted enough by his comments weeks ago to never pick him. Knowing the big, blond bitch, she'd choose him for spite.

Win, Sparrow, he thought to himself. *Don't mess this up, damn it!*

Lock clenched his fists, his heart throbbing madly as Sea Storm and Sparrow leapt ahead of the others, the white's nose at the black's hindquarters.

The blacksmith began beating her horse with a switch,

and the animal leapt. Sparrow never touched Sea Storm but her body moved with his in an attempt to make the run as easy as possible for him. She was small and light in spite of her muscular build, much less burden than the thickly built blacksmith. Lock had trained Sea Storm well without breaking his spirit, and the stallion's competitive nature surged with his speeding legs. Again he inched up on the black. Nose to nose they sailed over a fence in the center of the field.

Lock was aware of the crowd shouting and cheering around him, but his main focus was on the race. That night, he'd either be returning home with the Sparrow or screwing the damn blacksmith. He'd have to close his eyes and think of Sparrow to even attempt entering that beast-woman's body. He thought of how she smelled like horses and five-month old sweat. She was too much like the gnarled pirates who pawed him as a boy.

The black and white stallions were still neck-to-neck as they reached the homestretch. The others were several lengths behind them with no hope of catching the leaders. Suddenly Sea-Storm bounded ahead of the slowing black. Lock saw Sparrow smiling even as the wind and horse's mane lashed her face.

Shea-Ann screamed her approval along with the rest of the crowd as Sparrow rode to victory.

She slowed Sea-Storm and hugged the stallion's sweaty neck. "Good boy!"

The blacksmith sat astride her blowing mount, glaring in Lock's direction. He winked at her, but refrained from approaching Sparrow and Sea Storm. He remained in line with the other slaves.

A slim, redheaded woman approached Sparrow and said, "Congratulations. That's a fine, fast horse you have. You've won the first prize, two new blankets from the seamstress's shop, a pair of boots from the cobbler, two sacks of apples, and the slave of your choice for tonight."

Smiling, Sparrow glanced at Lock and dismounted while Shea-Ann held Sea Storm. She looked so beautiful, her cheeks flushed from the ride, her face sprinkled with perspiration and streaked with dirt. He stood straighter, towering over the other slaves, as he waited for her to claim him.

Sparrow walked past him, and his brow furrowed as he stared after her. She started at the far end of the line, glancing over the slaves, pausing in front of some. She took particular interest in a man nearly as tall as Lock, smooth shaven, with short black hair.

I knew it! He thought, his pulse throbbing. *She doesn't like the beard after all!*

Sparrow moved to the next man, then the next. She paused in front of a yellow-haired slave, extremely muscular, but far too short by Lock's standards. Still, he had another smooth face.

I'm shaving the wretched thing off! Lock thought. *And this is all my own fault. She was innocent. I corrupted her. Now I'm going to pay for it.* The thought of her with another man was unbearable!

The yellow-haired slave gave Sparrow an inviting smile, and Lock thought of ways to kill him.

She moved past the man and continued down the line, stopping in front of Lock. She rested her hand against his chest, and he wondered if she felt his pounding heart.

"I guess I'll take this one."

"But you have him every night!" Someone called from the crowd. "Try another, Sparrow!"

"No." She slid her hand under Lock's vest and ran her nails over his ribs. That single touch made his cock leap in his trousers. She smiled. "I'm attached to this one."

"That wasn't funny," Lock said.

"Had you worried, did I?"

"I hope you two plan on staying in the barn again," Shea-

Ann said as Lock took Sea Storm from her, "because I have no intention of sleeping in a bed beside you if you plan on humping all night."

"That's why we want to settle elsewhere," Lock told her. "Why don't you try finding yourself someone to hump, if any man will have you."

"It would be the ride of his life, boy!" Shea-Ann hissed.

"Are you two ever going to get along?" Sparrow sighed.

"Not bloody likely," Lock and Shea-Ann replied in unison. They exchanged an annoyed look.

"I have to go back to my work," Shea-Ann said, poking a finger at Lock. "And don't be bothering me anymore with nonsense."

The healer headed back to the village square, leaving Lock and Sparrow to cool down Sea Storm with a walk over the meadows.

* * * * *

In the village square, Sparrow and Lock brought Sea Storm to the stable, rubbed him down, and left him to rest while they collected the prizes from the race. The fisherwoman allowed Sparrow to leave her winnings at her cart until the gathering ended.

Once they'd stacked the blankets, boots, and fruit next to a barrel of oysters, the couple bought a jug of cider from one of the carts and sat under a tree to drink it. Sparrow uncorked the jug and took a long swallow, then passed it to Lock. She noted his eyes strayed to a group of children playing tag, and he smiled.

"This is a nice place for children to grow up," he said. "Not like SeaSpider Island."

"Maybe if your mother hadn't treated you so badly."

He shrugged and took another drink. "More than likely her mother treated her the same. Life in the Archipelago is like trying to swim with chains on your feet. No matter how you struggle, you're going to sink."

"Then maybe it's good you're not there anymore."

"Maybe. I know it's good because I found you." He placed a hand to the back of her neck and kissed her.

"Not even waiting until tonight, Sparrow?" the blacksmith called as she strode toward them and dropped onto the grass. "Can't say I blame you. It's a wonder you're able to keep up with your farm work. He looks like he could keep a woman busy all night."

"If you want a man so badly, why don't you find one of your own?"

"Can't be bothered with that." The blacksmith waved her hand. "Then you have to feed and clothe them. But, I suppose I could get plenty of work out of the right man. In my bed all night and in my stable all day...Might wear him out fast, though. Are you sure you don't want to rent this one for a night? I wouldn't let him get away. I've got some good, strong chains in my stable. He'd be a sight, bound to my wall."

Sparrow stood. "Come with me, Lock."

The blacksmith chuckled. "I think he liked my idea, Sparrow. I saw a glimmer in those demon eyes."

"He always looks that way when he's plotting someone's death," Sparrow said, grasping Lock's wrist and walking back to the village.

"That woman is disgusting!" Sparrow said.

He smirked. "She wants my body. Can't blame her for that."

"And you are incorrigible! I don't want any woman getting your body except me!"

"Then why don't we go home and you can collect your prize before the hag—I mean Shea-Ann—finishes her rounds?"

Sparrow glanced at him, the cider making her head pleasantly dizzy. She noted he didn't seem affected in the least, but the Goddess knew what he must have drank on that pirate ship of his.

"Why not?" she said. "Few more sips of this, and I'll bed you right here."

He slipped the jug from her hand. "A few more sips of that, and you'll be too drunk to enjoy me."

"You arrogant bull!" she snarled, grasping the front of his shirt. She bit his lower lip and licked it. "Don't ever change, Lock."

As they collected their belongings and Sea-Storm from the square, the sound of singing and music echoed through the village. The scent of bonfires and cooking food wafted on the air. Still, Sparrow couldn't wait to get home and make love with Lock.

While he saddled Sea-Storm and placed half the supplies on him, leaving the other half for Shea-Ann's mount, Sparrow leaned against a stall, her eyes raking his long legs and muscled arms. She approached, stumbled into the horse, and giggled.

"Good thing you didn't drink that stuff before the race." Lock hoisted her onto the stallion and mounted behind her, taking the reins. "You'd have gotten yourself killed for sure."

"You're the one who flung me on the horse and forced me into the race!"

"And you had a great time, didn't you?"

She glanced over her shoulder at him and wrinkled her nose as she smiled. "Yes, but I'm going to have a better time tonight."

He shook his head, and though he didn't smile, she saw laughter in his eyes. "If you don't fall into a drunken stupor before then. You didn't even drink that much, Sparrow."

"I'm not drunk!" She reached behind her and grasped his cock.

"Stop that, before we both fall off."

She gave him a squeeze. "Maybe I'm a little fuzzy-headed."

"A little?"

"Um," she leaned against him, her eyes slipping shut as the horse plodded toward home. She lazily stroked Sea Storm's neck. "He's such a good horse, Lock. You did wonderfully training him."

"You're the one who bought him from that sorry excuse for a horse trader."

"The man was a vicious fool," Sparrow murmured, nearly asleep.

The last thing she remembered was Lock lifting her from Sea Storm and tucking her into bed.

Chapter Thirteen

ॐ

Sparrow awoke to a hand shaking her shoulder. She blinked, still a bit groggy from the cider, and focused on Lock.

"Get up, girl. Bad storm's coming."

Sparrow's eyes opened wide and she glanced at Shea-Ann who was tossing food into a bag. The older woman glanced at Sparrow. "Better listen to him. The winds are almost powerful enough to knock you off your feet. We have to get to the cave. Lock's already brought the animals except for Sea Storm and my horse."

Sparrow was on her feet before Shea-Ann finished talking. She rushed to the window and glanced out at the dark, churning sky. "By the Goddess, we haven't had such a storm in years."

"Let's go," Lock ordered, taking the bag from Shea-Ann and heading for the door. Sparrow dragged on her boots and cloak and followed Lock outside. The force of the wind nearly took her breath as she squinted against the icy rain and mounted Sea Storm. They hurried across the field to the caves that many villagers used during emergencies. She noticed some people disappearing into the mossy entrances, and she, Lock, Shea-Ann, and their horses stepped into the cave they'd claimed as their own. Farm animals scattered nervously about the torch lit inside while outside the storm howled.

"Going to be a long night." Lock squeezed out his wet hair. "I'll be surprised if there's anything left to go home to once this ends."

"We've been through storms before," Shea-Ann said. "Surely it won't be that bad."

"I hope not, but I've seen storms in every part of the

world. This won't be good. You'd best prepare those remedies of yours, old woman. After this, I'm sure your skills will be needed."

"I pray you're wrong," Sparrow murmured.

"So do I," Lock admitted.

Sparrow lay on a blanket beside Lock, her cheek resting against his chest. Even with the comfort of his arm around her, she still jumped at the ferocious claps of thunder. Strong winds blew rain through the mouth of the cave, causing the animals to press closer to them. Shea-Ann lay beside them, wrapped in blankets, but Sparrow saw that she didn't sleep any better than the rest of the cave's inhabitants.

By morning, Sparrow drifted into a light sleep. She awoke as Lock disentangled himself from her and walked outside.

Sparrow and Shea-Ann followed.

"Goddess help us," Sparrow murmured, her eyes sweeping the torn countryside. In the distance, uprooted trees scattered across the rain-soaked fields. Slowly, people emerged from the surrounding caves, all staring at the results of the storm.

"I wonder if there's anything left of our house and the village?" Sparrow asked.

"Looks like you were right," Shea-Ann said to Lock.

He didn't speak, but began gathering the animals.

When they returned home, both the house and the barn were destroyed, roofs ripped apart, walls fallen in.

"This will take weeks to rebuild," Sparrow said as they stepped through the rubble.

Sparrow's two young farm hands raced across the field.

"Shea-Ann, we need you in the village. People were injured during the storm," Emerald panted.

"I'll get my supplies," Shea-Ann said.

"How bad is the damage in the village?" Sparrow asked the girls.

167

"There's nothing left. Someone went to Begonia for help, but they're unable to send any. The city is damaged as well, sections of the palace included. There's no one to help us rebuild."

"We'll do it ourselves," Sparrow said. "We've always done for ourselves."

"We haven't many builders," Emerald said.

"We haven't *any* builders," said Shea-Ann, who had returned with her bag of healing supplies. She mounted her horse.

"I'll go to the village with you." Lock reached for Sea Storm. "I've had experience building. Storms like this are common in the Archipelago."

"But you're leaving." Shea-Ann cast him a bitter look. "You and Sparrow."

"We can't leave with the village like this." Sparrow met Lock's eyes. "We can't."

"We won't." He glanced at the young village girls. "Can you two ride bareback?"

The children nodded, and he helped them onto Sparrow's farm horse then he mounted Sea-Storm.

"Maybe if you help them in the village, they'll help us out here," Sparrow said, slipping onto Sea Storm and holding Lock's waist. "You can't go to town alone. You're still considered a slave."

As the girls had said, the village was almost completely destroyed. Only a couple of cottages and the blacksmith shop still stood.

"This is hopeless!" Sparrow heard someone say as she dismounted.

"We'll never rebuild before winter." The fisher woman approached Sparrow and Shea-Ann. "Even my boat sunk in the dock."

Lock strode through the debris. "We need to get

168

organized. You!" He pointed to a group of male slaves standing with their mistresses. "Start sorting through this dung heap and see what wood is salvageable. You women bring us tools and wagons which weren't ruined."

The villagers stared at Lock with contempt.

"You're a slave! Who are you do be giving orders?" a woman shouted.

"He's about the only person here who's had experience with this sort of thing!" Shea-Ann bellowed. "Slave or not, if he can get this village on its feet before winter, then I suggest we all listen to him!"

The villagers murmured among themselves, but carried out Lock's orders.

He glanced at Shea-Ann and winked. "Thank you, witch."

"My pleasure, yak. Now, I best get to work. There are many injuries to tend."

Sparrow shook her head. "I can't understand you two."

"I think the witch and I understand each other," Lock observed as he walked through the village, instructing slaves and freewomen alike. He turned to Sparrow. "Our wagon is still intact. Take one of the horses and bring it here."

Before she left, she stood on tiptoe and kissed him. "I think you're wonderful."

He scowled, but his eyes reflected his pleasure. "Enough of that. There's work to do, girl."

As Sparrow hurried to her horse, she glanced over her shoulder at Lock. He stood, so tall and strong, his kinky two-tone hair snapping in the autumn wind, as he shouted orders. Sparrow glimpsed the powerful ship's Captain he must have been. Again she wondered if he'd be happy living a simple life with her.

* * * * *

Sparrow paused in sawing wood and used her hand to

shield her eyes from the sun as she stared at Lock who helped raise the walls of a new cottage. Several of the slaves as well as the blacksmith were helping, yet no matter who Lock stood with, he was noticeable. His height, his build, his hair, everything about him exuded pure masculine beauty.

Sparrow resumed sawing then loaded the wood into a wagon which Shea-Ann drove across the square.

It had only been three days since the storm, but already the village had improved, with most of the results due to Lock. He was a natural leader, and the people followed him, slave band on his arm and all. His knowledge about building as well as his dedication greatly impressed Sparrow, and his diligence inspired a group of people who, days ago, had nearly succumbed to hopelessness.

At dusk, Sparrow stood by the well in the center of town and rolled her aching shoulders. She felt a hand on the back of her neck and glanced at Lock. She smiled, relaxing as his fingers massaged her sore back.

"I think everything is going well," she remarked.

He glanced around the darkening village, at the random fires with people lounging around them, tired after another day of hard work. "Not a bad crew. I'd have most of them on any vessel of mine."

She laughed. "We're not at sea, Captain."

"It'll be a while before anyone will call me that again."

She looked at him and took his hand. She noticed a long cut running from the back of his wrist between his two middle fingers. Wetting her sleeve, she cleaned off the blood, then raised his hand to her lips and kissed it.

He took her face in his hands, her thumbs caressing her soft cheeks, and whispered, "You've done something to me, girl."

"I haven't done anything."

"Before you, I never cared about anything. I never thought I could."

"You weren't given the chance. Your own mother —"

"I don't want to talk about her. She doesn't exist anymore."

"Why don't we go to sleep? You must be tired. I don't think you've slept at all since the storm."

"There's too much to do."

Sparrow took his hand and tugged him to one of the fires where Shea-Ann and several women slept. Sparrow spread a blanket on the ground. She lay with her head on Lock's chest, one hand entangled in his hair.

"Lock?" she whispered. When he didn't reply, she shifted her face to look at him and smiled. He was already asleep. She kissed him lightly, so as not to wake him and said, "I love you."

* * * * *

About a week after the storm, Sparrow and Shea-Ann were feeding the chickens behind their newly-built barn while Lock chopped firewood nearby. Sparrow cast longing glances at his bare, dirt-streaked chest, perspiration gleaming beneath the mat of curling dark hair.

"I can't believe the village is almost back to normal," Shea-Ann said. "The Yak did well."

"You weren't bad yourself, witch," Lock called, splitting a log and tossing the pieces into a nearby pile.

"If it weren't for you, I'm not sure what we'd have done," Sparrow told him.

"You'd have managed. You did well before I got here, and would do just as well without me."

"True," Sparrow tossed him a coquettish look, "but I'd miss you none the less."

"So when you take her away, what are your intentions, boy?" Shea-Ann demanded.

Lock stopped his ax in mid-swing and approached the

women. "How's that your business?"

"I think of Sparrow as a daughter. She is my business. She's expressed her love for you, but I've yet to hear you admit the same."

Lock gave a humorless laugh and turned back to the chopping block.

"Walking away again, are you?" Shea-Ann taunted.

"Shea-Ann, what's between me and Lock is our concern, no one else's," Sparrow said, not wanting to exclude her old nanny, but feeling she must defend Lock. She understood his hesitation to admit love for anyone or anything.

"I know I should keep my place, Sparrow, but before you make a mistake, I want you to think carefully. Does he want to use you until the novelty wears off? What will he do about any offspring? What sort of future will you have?"

"Do you think I'd dump her off without a care?" Lock's pale eyes gleamed with fury as he stalked back to the nanny, his hands gripping the ax a bit too tightly for Sparrow's taste.

Shea-Ann must have felt the same, for she stepped back several paces, but kept her gaze fixed on the pirate as she said, "All I know is Sparrow saved your skin and has fallen in love with you. She's given up everything for you, and you haven't even mentioned standing by her except to drag her with you when you go."

Lock's gaze darted from Shea-Ann to Sparrow, his expression torn between anger and desperation. "I can't very well leave her here. You know what the sentence will be if the law in Begonia discovers I've gone."

"So at least you can feel guilt!" the old healer snapped.

"Shea-Ann!" Sparrow said. "Keep silent!"

"I don't feel guilt!"

Sparrow held his eyes. "You don't?"

"No."

"Then what do you feel?" Shea-Ann asked in a softer

tone.

"I'm taking her because I want her with me."

"So you don't care a bit for her, only for yourself." Shea-Ann shook her head. "Typical man. Not even a mention of marrying her."

"I don't need you to suggest marriage to Sparrow, hag! You think I haven't wanted to marry her for months?"

Sparrow's eyes widened, and she felt her own anger rising. "Then why haven't you asked?"

"Because he doesn't think he's good enough for you," Shea-Ann murmured. "That's it, isn't it?"

"Will you be quiet?" Sparrow and Lock shouted at the healer in unison.

Sparrow looked at him, her heart pounding. "Is that true?"

He took so long to speak that Sparrow thought he was going to ignore her question completely. Finally he said, "Isn't it?"

"So you'd rather take me with you as a mistress than propose? You want me to possibly bear your children but not your name?" Sparrow wasn't sure which was more powerful, her anger or her pain.

"Marriage is a great commitment. I'll stand by any children we have. If we marry, what if you suddenly realize you've chosen the wrong man? I'm not meant for marriage. Look at me, Sparrow. I'm a pirate."

"*Were* a pirate."

"There's nothing I haven't seen and little I haven't done. Is that what you want to be shackled to?"

"I love you," Sparrow said. "To me, that's all that matters. Do you love me, Lock?"

He drew a deep breath and opened his free hand helplessly. "I don't know."

"You don't..." Sparrow couldn't finish speaking. Her

heart ripped.

"I've never loved anything or anybody. What if I can't?"

"When you escaped all those months ago," Shea-Ann asked, "why did you come back?"

"You started this, witch!" Lock hissed through clenched teeth and pointed the ax at Shea-Ann.

"Why did you come back?" Sparrow asked. "Is it because you thought I might have more of my mother's jewels left? Is it because you wanted to bed me? Why?"

He laughed. "Jewels. If money was what I wanted, all I had to do was find a way back to the Archipelago. I have more money buried there than you can *imagine*, even when you were a princess. As for the bedding, I wanted you, but it's not why I came back. I came back because I couldn't stand the thought of you being punished for my crimes. I couldn't bear the sight of those thieves pawing you. I came back because I didn't want to imagine living the rest of my life without seeing you again. Is that enough?"

"It's enough for me." Shea-Ann's face flushed and she touched a hand to her breast. "And you say you're not sure you can love?"

Sparrow stepped close to Lock and splayed her hands across his chest as she looked into his eyes. She felt his heart pounding beneath her palms and noted his wild expression. He dropped the ax, grasped her upper arms and demanded, "If I asked for your hand, what would you say?"

"Ask and find out."

"Will you be my wife?"

"Yes."

He searched her face before kissing her deeply. Sparrow felt her knees weaken as his tongue traced the shape of her mouth and his arms pressed her so close that her breasts flattened against his chest.

"I'll be going to the square for a few hours," Shea-Ann

said from behind them. "I've done enough damage here."

Lock broke the kiss and spoke to the healer without taking his eyes from Sparrow. "You'd better stay late."

Shea-Ann's voice rippled with humor. "I'll gather my things and stay the night."

"Good idea," Lock said. Sparrow shrieked with delight as he swept her into his arms and carried her to the house.

Playfully, Lock flung her on the bed. He tugged off his trousers and kicked them aside before pouring water from a pitcher into a bowl and taking a cloth. He began washing.

Sparrow undressed slowly, and Lock's gaze riveted to her. He paused in washing as she slid off her boots and trousers, then tugged her shirt over her head. Unwinding her hair from its braid, she used her fingers to comb it over her shoulder as she stared at him with seductive eyes.

She stood and approached him, taking the damp cloth from his hand and dipping it into the water, her gaze never leaving his. She ran the cloth over his sweaty, dirt-stained chest and down his muscled abdomen.

Standing on tiptoe, she tilted her face up to his and whispered against his lips, "Raise your arms."

A grin tugged at his lips as he did what she asked. Sparrow wet the cloth again and ran it over first one, beautifully shaped, hair-dusted armpit, then the other. She cleaned a bleeding scratch on his left bicep and washed his other arm.

With infinite tenderness, Sparrow began washing his cock that was already hard from anticipation. When she was finished, she tossed the cloth aside and sank to her knees, cupping as much of his balls as she could fit into one hand. She licked every inch of his cock then took the head into her mouth and teased it with the tip of her tongue. One hand squeezed his sac while her other held the base of his cock.

"Sparrow," he sighed, his hands threading through her hair and caressing her shoulders.

She felt the tension in his big body and nearly smiled. He was so strong, so gorgeous, and he was all hers!

Suddenly he picked her up and brought her to the bed. Parting her thighs, he used both hands to raise her buttocks high. "Put your legs around my neck."

She did as he asked, moaning with pleasure as he licked her clit, swirled his tongue in her pussy, and tickled the flesh nearest her bottom hole. Sparrow's legs tightened around him and somewhere in the midst of passion, she hoped she wasn't choking him.

Lock's hands gripped her buttocks tightly. One of his fingers prodded her sphincter as his tongue fastened on her clit, licking and sucking until she cried out and convulsed in orgasm.

He continued with his ministrations until the last delightful contraction rippled through her. Releasing her slowly, he rolled her onto her stomach and entered her from behind. His hands gripped her wrists, pinning them above her head as he thrust. Sparrow groaned, her passion rekindling.

Lock licked the back of her neck and nipped her earlobe as his body surged into hers. The first pulsations of her orgasm seemed to undo his control, and he lunged into her hard and fast, joining her in bliss.

Sparrow lay beneath him, her heart pounding. "Lock," she murmured, "you're crushing me."

He moved instantly, dragging her to his chest and murmuring a lethargic apology.

"That was so damn good, girl," he said after a moment.

"Seems to get better every time." She gazed at him and smiled.

He kissed her brow. "I like keeping you happy."

There was no doubt about it. Sparrow was happier than she'd ever been in her life.

Chapter Fourteen

ഇ

"I can hardly wait to marry you." Sparrow kissed Lock's chest. They lay entwined in her bed, gazing at the fire in the hearth across the room. "I only wish there was some way we could marry right here. It would be such a nice place to live. We're right on the coast, so you could have a ship for fishing and trade, and I could keep the farm."

"There's no point in talking about it. You know the law in Begonia says you can't marry a slave. We have no choice but to go."

"The village is still getting on its feet, and I don't want to leave until I know everything is all right. Shea-Ann—"

"I think it's a good idea that we wait. Give you a chance to change your mind."

She raised her head on her elbow and narrowed her eyes at him. "I will *not* change my mind!"

"I always thought you were a little crazy." He winked and slipped from the bed to stoke the fire.

Sparrow's eyes fixed on his naked form, firelight licking his flesh, creating shadows against his long, muscled frame.

"I want to ride to the city tomorrow," Sparrow said.

"Why?"

"There are some women I know in the palace council. I want to make sure there's no legal way we can marry here."

He turned to her and winked. "That's what I like about you, girl. You never give up."

"If I'd given up, we'd never be together."

He walked toward her, his kinky two-toned hair grabbing

177

at his shoulders, his cock awakening as his eyes fixed on hers.

"We should get some sleep." She moistened her lips. "We'll have to leave early to get to the city. I don't even know how easy it will be to get to the palace. I know the storm damaged them, too."

"I'm ready to do damage." He loomed over her, his mouth brushing hers. "Right here and now."

"We really should…"

Other than moans of pleasure, she fell silent as his lips moved down her throat to her breasts. *Change my mind? How can he even suggest such a thing?*

Her last coherent thought before she surrendered to sensation was she hoped there was some buried law that would allow them to marry.

* * * * *

"It's a pirate ship!" Ginny screamed, her short legs pumping as fast as they could as she rushed toward Lock and Sparrow who had just arrived in the village square.

"What?" Sparrow raised herself in Sea Storm's saddle, doing her best to look over Lock's mass of hair toward the shoreline.

"It's true." Emerald jogged up behind her sister, panting. "Docked this morning. They haven't done anything, though. They claim to be stopping off for fresh water."

"You're sure it's a pirate ship?" Lock asked the girls.

Ginny lifted her chin. "Ma said so. She said it's the end of the world."

"Ma again," Lock muttered, kicking Sea Storm to a canter.

When they arrived at the dock, a group of villagers stood, staring at a ship that Lock recognized as the Lady Fire. The Captain—if someone hadn't killed him already—was nearly as infamous and feared as Lock.

"Do you think it is pirates?" Sparrow asked, her arms

tightening around his waist.

"It is. Captain's name is Rino." Lock dismounted. "Wait here."

Sparrow nudged Sea Storm forward, and Lock glared at her. "Are you deaf, girl?"

"You can't go anywhere without me. You're still a slave, remember? If those villagers see you approaching that ship, they'll think you're one of them."

He raised an eyebrow. "I am one of them."

"You want to go with them?"

He held her eyes. "No."

"I'm still going with you."

Together, they approached the ship. Several pirates stood on shore looking ready for a hunt. They carried bows and arrows and kept glancing toward the woods. One of them noticed Lock and nudged the man nearest him. Conversation stopped, and they stared in Lock's direction.

"If it ain't Lock the White!" A voice bellowed from the ship. A tall, big-boned redhead swung down to shore, his boots landing with a splash in the shallow water. He laughed as he approached, his green eyes glistening in the sunlight. "We all thought you were dead."

"I was hoping *you* were."

"Better to be dead than be wearing that." The Captain nodded towards Lock's slave band. Then he looked at Sparrow who stood by Lock, one hand touching his forearm in an almost protective gesture. "Or maybe you've found the privileges of slavery outweigh the humiliation."

"What are you doing here, Rino?"

"We've been at sea a few months. Need some water. Do a little hunting." Rino folded his arms across his broad chest draped in a loose shirt of black silk. He glanced at Sparrow. "Want to sell him, missy? I'll pay you more than he's worth."

"He's not for sale."

"Too bad. I'd love to see you spit shining my deck, Lock."

"The ocean would sooner dry up. So you don't intend to stay?"

"Only a night or two. Nothing here worth staying for. This village is dung heap."

Lock silently thanked any gods who might exist that the repairs from the storm still weren't complete. Rino's raids were devastating, and he hated the thought of taking on his entire crew alone, which is what he'd do before he allowed the sea swine to touch a hair on Sparrow's head.

"If you want a lift back to the Archipelago, I can still use a cabin boy," Rino told Lock.

Lock growled deep in his throat, resisting the urge to choke the life out of Rino. He turned back to the village.

"By the bloody goddess of SothSea!" Rino chimed. "What the hell happened to your back? Looks like you were almost whipped to death. I'd have love to have been there just to hear Lock the White scream for his life."

Lock continued walking, but Sparrow glanced over her shoulder and said, "Then you'd have been badly disappointed."

The villagers gathered around Lock and Sparrow as they distanced themselves from the ship.

"Are they going to attack?" someone asked. "Should we notify the guard from the city, not that they'd come to help us in a hurry."

Lock shook his head. "They'll be going. There's nothing of profit for them here. Just stay out of their way, if you can. They've been known to take slaves."

The villagers dispersed, and Sparrow glanced at him. "Do they really?"

"Of course. Many pirates do."

"Did you?"

"Slaves are too expensive to keep. I prefer cargo that

doesn't eat, drink, and shit."

"Tactfully put as always."

Lock winked at her before they mounted Sea Storm, passed through the square, and headed for the city of Begonia.

* * * * *

Though small, Begonia was considered one of the loveliest port cities on the Western Continent. As Sparrow and Lock reached the crest of the hill, the sun bleached palace loomed in the distance, a long, rectangular building of white brick and marble.

"Unusual looking palace," Lock said.

"It's nothing like the one I came from."

"It's a fine tribute to men."

Sparrow wrinkled her nose. "To men?"

"What do you think of when you look at it, girl?"

She stared at the structure, tall, sword-like. She almost blushed. "Honestly, Lock. Is your mind always in your trousers?"

He glanced over his shoulder and winked. "So it reminds you of me, too, does it?"

She playfully slapped his shoulder as they continued toward the city.

The palace had withstood the storm, except for some minimal damage, but the city wall was ruined and dozens of workers scattered around it, making repairs. At the gate, the guards questioned Lock and Sparrow briefly and allowed them to pass.

Inside, some of the houses had been destroyed, but many still stood, and the market was open for business, as busy as Sparrow remembered. They dismounted Sea Storm, and Sparrow paid a boy to stable him for the morning.

"Let's have a look around the market before going to the

palace," Sparrow suggested. "It's so much better than the one in the village."

"Best markets in the world are in the Kennas."

"I've heard about the Kennas but have never been there."

"Once we're out of here and I have another ship, I'll take you there."

Sparrow entwined her fingers with his and smiled. "I'd like that. I speak their language."

"You speak mine, too. How many do you speak?"

"Ten. It was my favorite area of study. I was training to be an ambassador when my family was overthrown."

"Never thought I'd be marrying a woman with royal blood," he muttered. "But I guess you never thought you'd be marrying a pirate, either."

"Reformed pirate."

He tossed her a look she didn't quite understand, so she chose to ignore it. Nothing was going to ruin their day. Even if she didn't receive her desired answer from the women at the palace, they could still enjoy the visit to the city.

"What pretty bracelets." Sparrow's gaze swept a cart full of wide silver bangles carved with symbols.

The vendor, a skinny man with matted black braids picked up one of the bracelets and offered it to Sparrow for closer inspection. "Imported from the Isle of Sole made by the tribe of Six Stars. The tribe is dying out and these trinkets are very rare. Worth twenty coins a piece."

Lock glanced over Sparrow's shoulder at the bracelets and said, "Those aren't from Sole and no member of Six Stars would create such messy work. Symbols are wrong, too. Twenty coins? Ain't worth two."

The man glared at Lock, his teeth clenched. "So a slave is supposed to be an expert on jewels?"

"I've been to Sole over a dozen times. I'll wager you've never so much as seen the coast."

Sparrow returned the bracelet and tugged Lock away from the cart before he and the vender erupted into a full-blown argument.

"I should take you shopping more often," she said.

"Most vendors are bigger thieves than I ever was. Made by Six Stars. Do I look like a jackass?" Lock raised his voice and glanced over his shoulder at the vendor who shook his fist in the pirate's direction.

"Would you try to behave yourself at least for the rest of the morning?" Sparrow lifted her eyes skyward.

"What did I do?"

His pale eyes looked so genuinely confused that she couldn't resist smiling. "Come on, Lock. The palace entrance is just around the corner and..."

Sparrow stopped speaking suddenly and stared several feet away at a man seated on a black gelding. Tall, with a body of solid muscle and a face that looked as if it had been carved from a mountainside, Sparrow would never forget him. Eyes of such dark brown they appeared black riveted to her. Four white scars ran down his left cheek, and Sparrow remembered how he'd sustained the marks. Her heart pounded so hard her chest ached, and she forgot everything except the desire to see him dead.

"Son-of-a-bitch!" Sparrow shrieked and raced at the worst fiend she'd ever known.

* * * * *

Lock stared at Sparrow for a stunned moment before chasing after her. Had the woman gone completely mad after all?

He saw her pull a dagger from her belt before she flew at a large man—rough-looking even by Lock's standards—on horseback.

Lock grasped her waist before she reached her mark, just

in time to protect her from the powerful kick of a booted foot. The man's kick caught Lock in the shoulder and knocked him onto the dirt so hard he grunted with the force of landing. He was glad he'd knocked Sparrow aside. The kick would have caused her serious injury. Lock felt like he'd been slammed by a horse. A guard who happened to be bartering at a nearby stall, held Sparrow who struggled in his grasp and bellowed, "Murdering bastard!"

Lock pushed himself to his feet. The man on horseback glanced at him and smiled wickedly.

"What is going on here?" a feminine voice called.

A blond woman in burgundy robes approached Sparrow and the guard.

"Sparrow?" The woman looked surprised. "What's wrong?"

"Him!" Sparrow glared at the man on horseback. "Arrest him! He's a rapist and a murderer!"

"He's also the Empress's favorite gladiator."

Sparrow snapped, "I don't care who he is, Monique! I know *what* he is!"

The woman motioned for the gladiator to go. As soon as he'd left the area, Monique ordered the guard to release Sparrow.

"Are you sure, My Lady?" asked the guard, struggling to hold Sparrow who fought with all her strength.

Monique nodded.

The guard dropped his hands from Sparrow and she snarled, "He is a criminal!"

"Sparrow, I told you his position in the city. You know I could have let you be arrested for this disturbance, but you're my friend, so I won't report it."

"Some friend! That *gladiator* is the animal who killed my sister!"

Monique's eyes widened. "So he's the one...I'm so sorry,

Sparrow. No wonder why you're upset."

"Upset isn't the word!"

"I'm afraid Miska's the Empress's favorite, so there's nothing I can do to help you find justice. He's been given all the privileges of a gladiator. You know how respected they are in the city."

"Respect! That bastard killed Thea! I'm going to kill him myself!" Sparrow ran in the direction Miska had ridden.

Lock caught her and held her close,

"Let me go!" She tried to push away. "I'm going to kill him, Lock, and no one will stop me!"

"Sparrow, he'd destroy you in seconds."

"Not before I cut off his balls!"

Lock felt his stomach tighten. He'd never seen Sparrow so furious. Not that he blamed her, but for her to fight Miska would end in disaster. One look in the man's eyes and Lock knew he had no soul. He'd reminded Lock of himself—or rather how he used to be before meeting Sparrow.

"Let me go!"

He tightened his grip, feeling her trembling against him. Finally she stopped struggling and looked up at him, tears glistening in her beautiful eyes. "You don't know what he did to her, Lock. I want him dead."

"I won't let you do it."

"You have no right!"

"If you attack him, he'll kill you, and I couldn't bear it." He grasped her shoulders and shook her gently. "I've never had anything like what we share. Don't take it away from me."

Sparrow's anger faded and she touched his face, the pain in her eyes lacerating him worse than a whip's cut. She nodded.

Monique approached and touched Sparrow's arm. "I am sorry."

Sparrow shook her head and blinked tears from her eyes. "Doesn't matter. I came here on more important business. Monique, I need your help. Lock and I want to marry."

The blond glanced at the band on Lock's arm. "But he's your slave. You can't marry a slave in Begonia."

"I know, but I was hoping there might be some law…"

"None that I now of, and I've been on the council most of my life, but I can look in the scrolls again. Would you like to come with me to the palace?"

"Yes. Please."

"This way." Monique motioned for them to follow her through the narrow streets of the marketplace, past the well in the spacious square, and finally to the gate of the tall, white palace itself.

* * * * *

In the company of Monique, Sparrow and Lock were allowed to enter the palace through the main hall. At one time, Sparrow would have been shown the respect of a princess regardless of whether she visited the palace with a council member or alone. Since her family's fall, she was treated as a commoner, even though she retained acquaintanceships with both council members and the Empress of Begonia herself.

Two guards dressed in silver armor opened the double doors at the palace entrance, and Monique led them into the hall, a vast square marble room. Blue and white tapestries hung from the high ceilings, and finely-woven rugs scattered across the floor. An oak table stood in the center of the room, reaching almost from wall to wall. On a raised marble platform on the far wall stood two silver thrones, side by side.

Sparrow experienced a feeling of familiarity as she looked at the hall. She remembered her life as a princess clearly, though at times it seemed so long ago. Once, she never would have imagined working a farm or sharing her bed with a man who was rough as a rock face, who had never put on airs. At least when Lock said he loved her, seldom as that may be, she believed him. Unlike ladies and gentlemen of the court, he didn't bother with love lies. He didn't try to pretend he was someone he wasn't, and she knew in spite of his faults, she was far happier with him than she ever would have been with the prince to whom she'd been betrothed.

"Now," Monique paused and glanced at Lock, "I suppose you want him to join us?"

"If possible."

Monique sighed. "Slaves aren't usually allowed in the archives, but I'll make an exception, considering your unique relationship with this one."

"Thank you for small favors," Lock muttered.

Sparrow poked her elbow into his stomach. "Will you be quiet? This is a palace, not a tavern!"

Monique lifted her chin and glanced away from Lock.

"Forgive me," Lock spoke with quiet reserve though his eyes flashed anger at Sparrow, "My Lady."

Monique led them to the nearest door that opened to a narrow corridor with a winding staircase leading to the top of the palace. They stopped at a second floor hallway and entered the archive, a vast room with shelves on all four walls containing innumerable scrolls and leather bound books. Long wooden ladders hung from the ceiling so the volumes on the highest shelves could be reached. Several oak tables, lit by metal lanterns carved into the shape of dragons, stood in the center of the carpeted floor. Two ladies dressed in robes similar to Monique's sat at the tables. They looked up from their scrolls and glanced at Lock with curiosity.

Sparrow knew them both, and they nodded at her in greeting before returning to their work.

"Follow me." Monique walked across the room and stood by the light of a round window in between several shelves. "This section involves the laws of marriage. Over there," she pointed to a higher shelf, "regards slavery. I know you don't understand the legal intricacies of our ways, but you can help me look through the books to find something that might pertain to your situation."

Sparrow sighed as she stared at the rows of books in each section. It might take longer than she expected.

"Is it permissible for me to help?" Lock asked.

Monique and Sparrow turned to him. Sparrow noted the surprise on the woman's face and she felt a bit taken aback herself. Lock's voice had sounded so soft and polite she wondered if she'd taken the right man with her.

"He can read?" Monique raised an eyebrow.

Sparrow met Lock's eyes and he offered her a smug grin. She said, "Of course he can read."

Monique's brow furrowed. "A slave really shouldn't be allowed to touch our books, but...I suppose there's no harm in it, especially seeing how long it could take to read these volumes."

They each chose a book and sat at an empty table where they spent hours searching for any law that might allow Sparrow and Lock to marry in Begonia.

"Slaves are meant to stay slaves. That's all there is to it." Monique closed the book in front of her and rubbed her eyes. "Why do you have to marry him, anyway? Can't you just keep him as he is? Give a man too much power and he'll tread on you."

"I'm a little tired of being spoken of like an object." Lock folded his arms across his chest.

Monique continued as if Lock didn't exist. "If it's lust you feel, Sparrow, it will fade."

"Why does everyone think I'm in lust?"

"Look at him." Monique pointed at Lock. "Quite a piece of man flesh, if I do say so. Tall, strong, good lines."

"Do you want to check his teeth while you're at it?" Sparrow's voice dripped with disgust.

Monique didn't seem to notice. "If you want me to."

"Nobody's checking my teeth!" Lock stood and Monique leapt.

"Is he dangerous?" The woman's wide eyes turned to Sparrow.

"Not if you know how to handle him. Lock, will you sit down and stop scaring people."

"All I did was stand up!"

"Sparrow, if he can't control himself, he'll have to wait in the slave quarters."

"Sparrow! So nice to see you again!"

Sparrow glanced over her shoulder toward Empress Daryn who approached, followed by two slight, chestnut-haired male slaves. The men wore ankle-length white tunics open at the chest, their long hair bound at their napes with golden bands. They walked six paces behind their leader, their hands folded in front of them, their eyes cast toward the floor.

Sparrow saw Lock's lip curl with disgust, and she placed a warning hand on his arm as she bowed to Daryn. "So nice to see you again as well. Monique was helping me search through the law books."

"She wishes to marry this slave." Monique pointed at Lock.

"Marry? A slave? My dear, have you finally lost your mind along with your Knights of the Ruby Order: Lock?" The Empress's gaze swept Lock. "Lovely, though a bit too tall. He might make a decent gladiator."

"He really wouldn't." Sparrow wrinkled her nose. "He doesn't have the proper training. He cares for my pigs."

Lock opened his mouth to speak, but Sparrow elbowed him again as Daryn burst into laughter. "Pigs? I'm sure that's not *all* he does for you Sparrow. Remember, you won't have to bother marrying him. Just order him to perform for you. It's so much better than binding yourself legally to a man."

"But I'd like to marry and have children." Sparrow tried to keep her temper in check.

"Then find yourself a free man. There's no law that allows slaves to marry in Begonia…or maybe there is." Daryn narrowed her eyes and stroked her chin with a red-tipped finger. "Each year, there's a competition in my private harem."

"What kind of competition?" Lock asked.

The Empress smiled at Sparrow, ignoring Lock. "The competitors are all male slaves, mostly my own, though others are welcome to enter, with the permission of their mistresses."

"What kind of competition?" Lock asked again.

"Most women don't allow their slaves to enter because they generally end up losing them."

"What kind of competition?" Sparrow asked.

"The slaves perform for me."

"I did use the same language as Sparrow, didn't I?" Lock spoke sarcastically.

"Perform?" Sparrow asked.

"Yes. Whatever talents they might have. Some sing, some dance, some provide a demonstration with weapons. The one I find most interesting wins. He can have anything he desires. Most of them choose their freedom. If this man of yours really wants to marry you as well, and if he wins, he can request his freedom and you can marry. However, I wouldn't wager on him staying with you once he's free. Most likely he's just using your innocence, Sparrow."

"So if Lock competes and wins, you'll grant his freedom?"

"If he wants it."

Sparrow gazed at Lock. She couldn't decide what he felt from his expression. At times he drove her to insanity!

"Oh, and if your slave wins, you get fifty gold pieces. Just a bit of compensation for the woman who loses a laborer."

"Well, you've found your law." Monique sighed. She bid Sparrow good-bye and bowed to Daryn before leaving.

"Sparrow, I was just on my way to the games. Since you're here, why don't you come watch my gladiators? My favorite, Miska, is fighting today."

Sparrow's stomach tightened. For a few brief hours she'd been so absorbed in the law books that she'd forgotten about Miska. The sound of his name, the memory of what he'd done, sickened her. "No. I'd rather not. We should be going home now."

"I'd like to watch," Lock said.

Again, Daryn looked right through him and conversed with Sparrow. "Pity. Perhaps next time?"

"I'd like to watch," Lock repeated, a bit louder.

Sparrow stared at him. He knew how much she hated Miska. "Why?"

"I'm curious about the sport." He held her eyes. "Please."

Please? Again, Lock was acting completely out of character. Watching the gladiators seemed to be quite important to him.

"All right," Sparrow said to Daryn. "We'll watch. Lock can come with us, can't he?"

"If you like, your slave may accompany you."

The Empress led the way out of the palace, her slender men behind her, a living extension of her dress's blue velvet train.

Lock muttered curses in his own language under his breath, and Sparrow whispered, "Will you behave before you get yourself thrown into the dungeon! I don't know why you want to see these games, Lock. You know how much I hate that man!"

He touched her hair gently. "I have my reasons. I'm not doing this to hurt you, Sparrow. Believe me."

She sighed. Maybe Miska would be slaughtered during the games, then they'd be worth watching after all.

191

Chapter Fifteen

&

Lock tried his best to ignore the looks of anger and hurt Sparrow flung at him as they followed Daryn through the palace halls. He knew she hated the thought of seeing Miska again, but Lock wanted to measure the man's fighting skill. If his plan worked, Sparrow would have, without danger to herself, the revenge she so desired. Outside, a carriage waited. The Empress invited Sparrow to ride inside with her while Lock followed on foot along with the two effeminate servants.

Sparrow's got more muscle than they do, he thought with disgust. Even when out of the Empress's presence, the men walked with their gazes cast down, their expressions impassive.

"So what are these games like?" Lock asked.

The slave closest to him replied in scarcely a whisper.

"What's that?" Lock spoke louder.

"Shhh!" The other man shot Lock a furious look. "Do you want to get us punished?"

Lock raised an eyebrow and lowered his voice to a mock whisper, "So what are these games like?"

"Any man can compete in the games, even slaves if their mistresses allow," the first said. "It's the Empress's favorite kind of entertainment, other than making love."

"Brawling and sex. Wonder if she's related to my mother?" Lock muttered.

The slave continued, "The winners of the games earn prizes. A skilled gladiator can become very wealthy."

"So Miska must be rich?"

"Miska is the Empress's most revered fighter. No one has

192

beaten him since he arrived a year ago."

"So anyone can challenge him, then?"

"No. That would only waste his time. A fighter begins in the lower ranks and works his way up."

Lock's brow furrowed. "That could take a while."

"Is your mistress interested in sending you to the games? Is that why you're asking so many questions?"

"I don't think that's what she has in mind."

"Pity." The slave's large, dark eyes raked Lock from head to foot, lingering over the crotch of his soft leather pants. "You look like you'd do well. Will you be staying at the palace? You could share my room in the slave quarters."

The slightest smile touched Lock's lips as he glanced away. "I'm too old and wise for you, boy."

"Will you both be silent!" The second slave snapped. "The Empress will—"

"You be silent!" Lock's admirer glared at his companion. "He was simply asking a question. It's only common courtesy to answer."

"Would you show him the same courtesy if he looked like a pantry rat instead of a breeding bull?"

"Quiet, both of you!" Lock raised his eyes to heaven.

"There's the ring," the slaves chimed.

Lock stared at the square stone building on the cliff at the edge of the city.

Outside, several horses stood fastened to posts, stable boys tending them. Men and women mingled and entered the building through two wide wooden doors held open by guards dressed in red silks and chain mail with swords at their hips.

The carriage stopped, and the two slender slaves hurried to assist their Empress down the steps. One of them—the annoying one who kept motioning for silence—offered Sparrow his hand, but Lock bumped him with his hip, sending him stumbling into the mud by the carriage wheel. Lock extended his own hand to Sparrow.

Her mouth opened in shock as she glanced at the little servant who pushed himself to his feet, brushing dirt from his white tunic and firing an enraged look at Lock.

The Empress glanced over her shoulder at the slave. "Theodore, will you stop being so clumsy! Pay more attention to Namir. See how nicely he carries himself?"

The other slave looked down his nose at his companion and offered Lock an enticing smile. Lock curled his lip, *Can't wait to get out of this crazy city and back in the ocean where there's sanity. Typhoons and tidal waves, but sanity.*

The Empress strolled to the entrance, her slaves behind her.

"Lock, why did you do that?" Sparrow whispered as they followed Daryn.

"You should have tried walking with those two. They could make a monk turn murderer."

Sparrow tilted her head. "I think they're kind of cute. They look like little matching candlesticks."

"One of them offered to share his bed with me if we stayed at the palace."

"Why is it that everyone wants to bed you down?"

"It's my masculine prowess. I've got virility flowing out of my arse..."

"Stop it!" She half giggled, half hissed. The man was incorrigible. "I still don't know why you wanted to come here."

"I'll explain in good time."

They stepped inside the building and found themselves in a narrow corridor with a stairway leading upward. Namir stood at the landing, beckoning them. At the top, they found themselves in a balcony running along the perimeter of the building, several feet above the vast room below. A single row of chairs lined the balcony, all filled with onlookers—lords and ladies judging by their dress. The room below had a dirt floor, one tiny section separated by iron bars that created a cage in front of an oak door. Two guards, heavily armored and carrying spears, stood inside.

Sparrow sat beside the Empress, Lock, Theodore, and Namir behind them.

"The gladiators enter through there," Namir whispered, pointing to the guarded door.

Theodore raised a finger to his lips, pretended to stamp his foot, and cast a worried glance at the Empress.

Namir looked disgusted but fell silent.

At a cheer from the crowd, Lock focused his complete attention on the room below. A burly blond flung open the door and rushed to the center of the floor. A tall, muscular, dark-skinned man followed. Both wore leather trousers, metal chest plates, arm bands, and helmets. They attacked each other, the blond aiming his fist at the darker man's face, the darker one dodging the blows and kicking his opponent in the stomach, knocking him onto his back. The blond leapt to his feet as the dark man kicked again, his heel smashing downward. For several moments, the men traded blows until the dark one wrestled his heavyset match to the dirt. The sound of snapping bone followed by the blond's bellow of pain echoed through the arena. The lords and ladies cheered.

Sloppy fighting, Lock thought, *very sloppy. If they're all like this, no wonder Miska is the favorite.*

The next match was little better than the first, but with the third, the fighting became cleaner, more intricate. The later warriors performed unique moves with accuracy, strength, and speed. Lock took a step closer to the edge of the balcony as his interest rose. Namir touched his arm.

Lock glanced at the young slave who shook his head and whispered, "Stay here."

Lock nodded, shrugging his hand off. The men fighting

below were worthy entertainment. Their movements reminded Lock of the skills he'd learned from the clan when he'd been shipwrecked. Still, Lock knew by watching he'd have beaten every man in the Empress's arena.

Below, two fighters, a redhead and a man with a black beard, grappled in the bloody dirt. Suddenly the redhead snapped the bearded man's neck. He dropped the body and staggered to his feet, blood streaking his face so it looked as red as his hair. The crowd roared, and he stumbled from the arena while the guards cleared away the body. Several servant boys hurried to rake the bloody dirt in preparation for the next fight.

"This is the last of the day," the Empress said to Sparrow. "Miska is my favorite warrior. He's fighting a gladiator owned by one of my cousins. She thinks her man will win, but she's been saying that for the past six months. Miska has killed more than a dozen of her slaves. You'd think she'd just give up and admit I've found the greatest warrior on the continent, perhaps the world."

Lock felt his skin prickle. *We'll see about that...*

A tall, thickly muscled warrior, his head shaved to reveal a tattooed scalp, strode into the arena. He wore a leather skirt and a metal breastplate. Knee-high leather boots covered his feet, and he carried a short, double-edged sword. Lock's interest piqued. Thus far, none of the gladiators had carried weapons.

A shout of animal fury echoed throughout the building as Miska charged through the door directly at his opponent. The favored gladiator's long red hair snapped behind him, his face a mask of fury as he skillfully swung his great sword. Blow upon blow struck his opponent, but the tattooed man blocked and countered with strength and agility. Miska whirled, the blade grazing his opponent's face, drawing blood from his cheek.

Lock felt his fists clench at the speed and power of the blows. He glanced at Sparrow, noticed the tension on her face, and felt guilty for asking her to come. Still, he had to know the extent of Miska's skill.

The fight lasted longer than the others, and even the crowd was uncharacteristically quiet as they stared in fascination at the men. Their muscled arms glistened with sweat and their grunts and battle cries filled the arena. The tattooed one showed the first signs of tiring while Miska appeared fresh as when he'd first stepped into the ring. He pressed his advantage, raining teeth-jarring blows until he knocked the sword from the tattooed man's hand. A collective gasp sounded from the crowd as Miska spun, slashing his sword across his opponent's throat. The gladiator collapsed, his head half severed from his shoulders, blood pooling beneath his body.

Sparrow dropped to her seat, her hand gripping the wooden edge of the balcony.

The Empress turned to her with a smile. "Exciting, isn't it?"

"I have to go," Sparrow said.

"Wait! Will your man be entering my competition?"

Sparrow glanced at Lock, her face pale. He resisted the urge to hold her and said, "I can perform for her."

"Yes. He'll enter." Sparrow bowed to Daryn and hurried down the steps, Lock behind her.

Chapter Sixteen

ॐ

"Sparrow!"

Sparrow glanced at Lock, realizing for the first time he'd been speaking to her. She couldn't keep her mind off Miska. How he'd looked in the arena—so savage and overpowering—just as she remembered him when he'd murdered Thea.

"I said do you have money? We have to stop by the market before we go. I need something to wear in the competition."

"Lock, what exactly do you plan to do in the competition? The only songs I've ever heard you sing are those awful rhymes."

"I'm going to dance."

"Dance?" Sparrow wrinkled her nose. "Not like you did at the house for those women?"

"I was just playing then. Every Archipelago whore learns the Daggers of Desire from the time he can walk."

"Lock, you're not—"

"Do you want me to win this or not?"

"Do you really think you can?" Sparrow couldn't disguise her hope. If he won his freedom, it would be like a dream.

"If I didn't think I could win, I wouldn't suggest entering. Now, I have to find some clothes."

"What kind of clothes?"

He smiled, and as they entered the market, she was almost sorry she'd asked.

* * * * *

"But I want to watch this." Sparrow placed her hands on her hips as she stared at Lock who stood in the center of the barn. Tools and animals had been pushed into corners or sent out to pasture while he practiced for the Empress's competition.

A muslin cloak draped Lock's tall frame, his face concealed by a veil-like hood that left only his pale eyes visible. The muslin was for practice, since during the dance Lock would slash his clothing with daggers. For the competition, they had bought yards of sheer black and blue silk. Sparrow had nearly choked on the price, but Lock insisted the costume must be right for the dance to be effective. To Sparrow's curiosity, they'd also bought a tight-fitting black loincloth and several strips of leather.

"For the last time, no."

"Why not?"

"Leave us alone!" Shea-Ann shooed Sparrow with a wave of her hand. "I'm dying to see a yak dance."

Sparrow glared at Lock and pointed at her old nanny. "Why does *she* get to watch?"

"Because I might be rusty and I need someone to tell me how the movements look."

"I could tell you."

"He's probably afraid you'll change your mind about the competition if you watch," Shea-Ann said. "I can only imagine what this slab of sea scum is going to do."

"You'd better watch closely, hag, because what you're about to see is probably better than any rutting you've ever had."

Shea-Ann cast him a look that said she didn't quite believe him.

"Lock!"

"Sparrow, will you just go sew the leather to the loincloth like I showed you? And that silk needs to be hemmed."

"I am not a seamstress!"

"Do you want me to win or don't you?"

"I want to watch you dance!"

"You'll see me at the competition!"

"What are you trying to hide from me?"

Shea-Ann stood, grasped Sparrow's arm, and tugged her to the door. "Will you let us get on with this? I have remedies to mix."

Reluctantly, Sparrow left the barn, muttering all the way back to the house where she sat by the fire, hemming the silk.

"This would make such a beautiful dress." She touched soft fabric, the same pale blue as Lock's eyes.

Why wouldn't he allow her to watch? How bad could it be, to watch a man dance with daggers? *The Daggers of Desire...*

A couple of hours passed, and Sparrow, her fingers aching from the needle, placed the material aside. They had several weeks before the competition, and she could work on the rest of the silk as well as the leather loincloth over the next few days. She stirred the stew in the pot over the fire and prepared the table for dinner.

Shea-Ann burst into the house, fanning her flushed face with her hand. "That boy has a certain charm, Sparrow, much as I hate to admit it."

"So how did he look? What was the dance like?"

"It was...He is...Unless the Empress is dead, he's sure to win."

Sparrow's belly churned with curiosity. "Then he performs well?"

"Dear, if he's anything in bed like he is doing that dance, I'm surprised you can even get up in the morning."

"Shea-Ann!"

"Forgive me, but it's true. The yak has talent."

"Where is he now?"

"Went for a swim. He should be back soon."

Sparrow stirred the pot again, and when she turned back from the fire, noticed Shea-Ann lifting her skirt above her ankles and dancing across the room with a hip motion that was nothing short of scandalous.

"Shea-Ann!"

The old woman stopped, blushing. "Sorry. That dance is compelling. Not that I can do it like the yak, but when I was young..."

"You probably could have out-danced half the whores of the Archipelago." Lock stepped into the room and winked at Shea-Ann. Barefoot, he wore only his trousers, the slashed muslin and daggers in one hand. His hair hung in wet ringlets down his back, and river water streaked his face and torso. Sparrow's gaze swept him. She wished it was already after dinner and they were cuddled in bed.

"Shea-Ann said you should win."

"I intend to win, and when I do, I'm going to give you the one thing you want most in the world."

"Modest, aren't you?" Sparrow smiled at him. "Sit down. It's time to eat."

Sparrow filled their bowls while Lock divided a loaf of bread among them. Over dinner, they discussed the farm, the problems Shea-Ann had faced healing that day, and the preparation for Lock's competition.

"I can't believe it's this late." Shea-Ann yawned. "All that time I spent in the barn watching this man with his wiles when I should have been tending my herbs. Now I have all those mixtures, powders, and teas to prepare."

"Teach me what to do, and I'll help," Lock offered.

Shea-Ann lifted an eyebrow. "Something's wrong between us, yak. Why are we getting on so well?"

"You're attitude's improving." Lock popped a slice of apple into his mouth and winked.

"My attitude? You're the one with—"

"Do you want to show me how to mix those witch brews of yours?"

"As I've told you before, healing is a respected art."

"I respect it enough. You saved my life, and I do know a bit about it, you know. Mostly emergency skills learned in the field."

"That's all the well and good, but a true healer knows more than simple stitching and bone-setting."

"There's not many healers to learn from in the Archipelago. A few, most of them who know little more than I do."

"It takes time and dedication, but I think you could learn."

"Don't think it's for me." Lock shook a tendril of hair from his eyes. "I'm more of a fighter than a healer."

"You can be both. Look at the Knights of the Ruby Order."

Lock snorted with laughter. "They're like holy men. I couldn't be any Knight."

"I have to agree with you there," Shea-Ann admitted, but stroked her chin as she glanced at him. "You'd look good in the uniform, though."

"Or out of it." Sparrow tossed Lock a coquettish look.

"Enough of that!" Shea-Ann waved her hand. "Either he's going to help me or make love with you."

"Help her." Sparrow began clearing the table. "We can play later."

Lock stood and dragged her roughly to his chest, his beard tickling her face as he kissed her. "I'll hold you to it."

* * * * *

"How long have you been a healer?" Lock asked Shea-Ann as he packaged dried herbs while she prepared mixtures.

"I've trained since I was a girl. My grandmother taught me."

"You must miss her."

Shea-Ann glanced at him. "Surprised you'd consider such a thing. Yes, I've missed her since I left my village years ago. Now that she's gone, I think of her often. Family is good to have."

"I wouldn't know."

"You've got Sparrow."

"I still don't know how that happened."

Lock focused on his work, carefully separating the herbs into even piles, as Shea-Ann had instructed.

"I guess you have me, too, yak," the older woman muttered.

He smiled. "That's about the most decent thing you've said since I came here."

"I still worry about Sparrow with you."

"I'd never hurt her."

"Not intentionally. Just remember, it's a lady you're with—one who still doesn't really see the pirate in you."

"Sparrow knows what I am."

"She's too busy looking at what you are to remember what you were, and between you and me, Lock, the pirate will always be a part of you, won't he?"

"The pirate knew how to repair your village."

"And he also knows how to destroy it, doesn't he?"

"I don't understand you, old woman. I thought you wanted me to marry Sparrow."

"She loves you, and I know you love her as much as you can love anybody. I think you have potential, but a man doesn't change overnight. You were born and raised in the Archipelago."

"I've always been honest about myself, with you and with

Sparrow. I want to make her happy. I might not know how to do it all the time."

Lock held the healer's gaze. Whenever she droned on about him and Sparrow, he wanted to tell her to mind her own business, but she did speak the truth. He knew about Sparrow's purity and his own uncleanliness. Just that morning, what had she told him? *This is a palace, not a tavern!* She'd assumed his sarcastic attitude had been a result of his ignorance. She'd even been surprised he could read. Why shouldn't she have been? Few in the Archipelago, particularly pirates, could read. He'd learned during his travels because he believed knowledge was power.

Even learning about herbs from Shea-Ann interested him. Not that he could be a healer, any more than he could be a Knight, but if the old woman taught, he'd listen. When pirating, he'd always felt his greatest cargo was the knowledge he gathered from the people and cultures he met along the way. He missed the sea and longed for the day he could sail again, this time with Sparrow beside him.

* * * * *

Sparrow's eyes opened halfway as she felt Lock's weight on the bed beside her. She rolled toward him as he wrapped his arms around her and buried his face in her neck.

"Is it morning?" she murmured.

"A couple of hours till dawn."

"You and Shea-Ann have been up all night?"

"There was a lot of work to do. I told her I'd help her more tomorrow."

"She tried to make a healer out of me. I'd rather slop the pigs."

He smiled and kissed her hair.

With a contented sigh, she snuggled closer to his warmth and slept.

* * * * *

Lock awoke just before dawn and reached for Sparrow, but she had already left to begin her chores. He guessed she was in the barn milking Daphne. Glancing down at his morning erection, Lock smiled. Maybe they could enjoy a few moments together before Shea-Ann was up and about.

Lock left the house and washed in the river before joining Sparrow in the barn. He approached silently, a grin on his lips as he watched her seated on the milking stool, talking to Daphne as she worked her udder.

Lock had nearly reached her when the cow gave him away, lifting her great head in his direction and making that annoying cow-sound.

Sparrow spun, looking a bit startled before she smiled. "Good morning."

"It can be." He winked, standing behind her so his cock brushed her back.

"Umm, Lock," she murmured, leaning into him, "I have to finish with this cow first."

"I can finish," he knelt beside her, kissing her cheek. "She likes me."

"I don't blame her," Sparrow purred. "You really know how to pull on a girl's udder."

Lock chuckled as she stood and gave him the stool. Though he tried keeping his eyes on his work, it proved difficult when Sparrow positioned herself in plain view and removed all her clothes.

"Do you like watching?" Sparrow asked.

"Hell, yes."

She smiled, stroking her breasts. She cupped them in her palms and ran her thumbs over her nipples until they stood out like pebbles. Still using one hand to stroke her breasts, she dipped the other between her legs and explored herself. She inserted two fingers into her pussy and tugged them away, gleaming. Using the moisture, she circled her clit slowly.

Lock's heart pounded and he tried to control his breathing as he continued milking the cow. Several times he missed the bucket and squirted milk across his chest, but he didn't waste time wiping it. The faster he finished, the faster he'd be buried inside Sparrow's tempting body.

Sparrow leaned against the stall, her breath quickening and her breasts and neck flushed an enticing shade of pink as her climax neared. She stopped just before pushing herself over and gazed at him with longing. "Are you almost done?"

"I'm done." Lock stood, nearly toppling over the bucket and stool. He reached her in two strides and pressed her closer to the stall, his mouth devouring hers.

"Shea-Ann will be up soon," Sparrow said, grasping his cock in her hand and guiding it into her sopping pussy.

Lock sighed, his eyes slipping shut as he flexed his knees and pumped slowly, savoring every moment inside her slick, warm pussy.

"Come on, Lock!" she panted, gripping his buttocks tightly. "I can't wait!"

He covered her mouth with his, their tongues slashing one another's as he drove, fast and hard, into her trembling body. She was so ready it took only a few strokes to send her into orgasm, and he joined her as soon as he felt the first ripples of her climax.

"Sparrow!" Shea-Ann called from the house.

"Just in time," Lock panted as he and Sparrow disentangled their bodies and pulled on their clothes. "At least she doesn't club me with a broom anymore."

Sparrow laughed as they exchanged a kiss before beginning their day.

* * * * *

"You know, I'm actually glad you'll be staying in

Begonia," Shea-Ann said to Lock as she and Sparrow made the final adjustments on his costume. "You're learning fast and are a great help with my herbs. You're not a bad assistant on my rounds, either."

"You've been using up all his time." Sparrow cast her old nanny a look from the corner of her eye. "When he's not on the farm, he's with you. I'm beginning to wonder which one of us he should marry."

"You didn't wonder that last night." Lock grinned.

"I'm too old for him," Shea-Ann teased. "Maybe if I was a decade or so younger, you'd have competition from me."

"The skills she teaches will come in handy at sea," Lock said.

"I hope I like the sea." Sparrow adjusted the silk on Lock's shoulders.

"So do I." He took a step backward and shook out his sleeves. "What do you think?"

"You look like a god." Sparrow's eyes swept his tall frame draped in black and blue silk. The fabric covered his face except for his eyes that seemed even more brilliant next to the silk. Sparrow's belly tightened at the thought of what the robe hid. The leather loincloth scarcely concealed Lock's male attributes. Strips of leather had been sewn to the belt and dangled to his knees, made to flow as he moved. Sparrow had seen how little the leather left to the imagination.

"The competition is tomorrow afternoon, so we'd better leave early," Sparrow said. "You can dress there. Monique said the baths in the Empress's harem will be at your disposal, and I can help you with the body paint."

"I wish I could see the competition!" Shea-Ann pouted. "But I can't go. A couple of the women in the village are about to deliver any time now."

"You've already seen him dance," Sparrow said.

"Still, I'd like to be there when he wins."

"I hope he wins."

"I don't see how he can lose."

"I just want it to be over." Sparrow slid her arms around Lock's waist and rested her cheek against his silk-covered chest.

"Well, take off that costume and we'll get you packed for tomorrow." Shea-Ann reached for a leather bag.

Sparrow took the clothes from Lock as he undressed and tugged on his trousers, shirt, and boots.

"I'm riding to the lake for a swim. Anyone want to come?"

"I will," Sparrow said and glanced at Shea-Ann.

"You two go ahead. And don't wear him out too much Sparrow. He has to compete tomorrow."

Sparrow slid her hand into Lock's as they left the house. She smiled at him, lust in her eyes. "I'll make sure he gets a good night's sleep."

His hand slipped down her back and pinched her buttocks. She uttered a short yelp and, laughing, sprinted toward the stable.

They rode Sea Storm bareback to the lake where they turned him loose in the field. Lock removed all his clothes while Sparrow undressed to her shift. She took a step toward the water, but he grasped her wrist and dragged her to his chest.

She tilted her face up to his. "You know, I just realized I never thanked you."

"For what?"

"For stopping me from attacking Miska two weeks ago. It was stupid of me. I just felt so furious when I saw him. I felt Thea's death all over again."

Lock's mouth brushed hers with a comforting kiss. It was pleasant and loving, but she wanted to forget about Miska. If anyone could make her forget, it was Lock. She slid her arms around his neck and traced his mouth with her tongue. His lips parted. He devoured her, sweeping her into his arms and walking to the lake.

Giggling, she shivered as the cool water touched her skin.

"Cold?" He nipped her ear. "This water is perfect."

"Honestly, Lock, sometimes I think you were born in the water, you love it so much."

"There's nothing like it. Soft, strong, soothing, and rough. The essence of beauty. Just like you."

Sparrow smiled. Sometimes her rugged pirate said the sweetest things.

Suddenly he disappeared beneath the surface. She searched for him in the moonlit lake, then shrieked and giggled as a hand grasped her ankle and tugged. Suddenly she was in his arms again. This time when he kissed her, he left no opportunity for words or wandering thoughts. She could only feel the sensation of his lips against hers, the rough, wet touch of his hands on her arms and back as he slipped the sleeves of her shift down her shoulders and bared her breasts to his hungry mouth.

She gasped, his tongue warm on her nipple compared to the chilly night water. She wove her fingers through his thick, wet hair and closed her eyes, leaning into the cushion of water.

He kissed her again, his hands molding her breasts, his fingertips slipping over her ribs and across her hips. He stroked her inner thighs and cupped her sex until she clung to him, using one hand to guide his cock into her pussy.

She wrapped her legs around his waist and he grasped her buttocks, her hands and hips moving in a sensual rhythm.

"I love you," she whispered, her lips roaming over his neck, licking away droplets of cool water. She used her tongue to trace the shape of his ear. A groan of desire rumbled in his chest, and he took several steps toward the shore. He pushed her onto her back in the shallow water, his mouth covering hers in a fierce kiss. She grasped the back of his head, never wanting his lips to leave hers. Bracing a hand on each side of her head, he clutched the mud and smooth rocks beneath the water as his hips thrust frantically. Sparrow squeezed her eyes shut. Her nipples, hard peaks from the touch of water combined with rising passion, scraped Lock's chest. Her body arched upward, meeting his, joining his rhythm, until they both burst into a shattering climax.

Sparrow lay beneath him, feeling their pounding hearts slow. Only when she'd regained her breath and opened her eyes did she realize fat drops of cold rain pelted them, mingling with the river water.

He wrinkled his nose. "It's raining."

"So that's what they call those big drops pouring from the sky."

"Mockery doesn't sound good from you." He playfully nipped her nose before he stood, grasping her hands and tugging her to her feet.

"I forgot. It's reserved only for you and Shea-Ann."

"Oh no." He waved his hand, smiling as they stepped out of the lake and reached for their clothes. "Don't try to say I'm like the witch."

"She's starting to think of you as an assistant, and you seem to be learning a lot from her. Come on, Lock, admit it. You like Shea-Ann."

He tilted his face skyward, squinting against the raindrops. "Maybe a little. But don't let *her* know that."

"Race you home."

He laughed. "You with those short little legs."

"You weren't complaining about my legs when they were around your waist a few minutes ago."

"I didn't say they weren't nice and strong."

"Lock!" She shoved him and bolted toward the house, glancing once over her shoulder. He followed at a slow jog, waving to her and smiling.

Brat! He's such a brat! Sparrow thought, torn between irritation and good humor. She quickened her pace, planning to lock him out when she reached the house, but seconds later she shrieked as he lifted her and half-tossed her in the air. Lock ran to the house, Sparrow snug in his arms.

"Sometimes I really hate you!" She giggled against his lips as he kissed her, placing her on her feet. She leaned against the door, her arms around his neck.

Suddenly the door opened and they both stumbled in, catching themselves before they fell on the rug.

"Would you look at the both of you!" Shea-Ann snapped. "Acting like that in front of the house! At least have the decency to go in the barn!"

"Where are you going?" Sparrow glanced at the leather bag slung over her friend's shoulder.

"I'm spending the night in the village. With a couple of those women ready to deliver at any time, I'm better off sleeping there than having to ride off in the middle of the night."

"Do you need help?" Lock asked.

"No. You've been up almost every night helping me, but tonight get a good rest so you'll win tomorrow. Good luck, yak."

"Thank you, hag."

"Sparrow," Shea-Ann hugged her, "everything will be fine."

"I know it will."

"Come on," Lock said to Shea-Ann. "I'll saddle your horse for you."

Shea-Ann's eyebrow lifted and she watched Lock walk across the grass. "If I didn't know better, I'd say the pirate's taken a liking to me."

"I think you like him a bit yourself."

Shea-Ann winked at Sparrow and said, "But don't let him

211

know about it. See you when you get back. And *don't worry.* You'll be married before you know."

Sparrow drew a deep breath and released it as her friend joined Lock in the barn. Shea-Ann was right. The Empress was already attracted to Lock, and with his seductive performance, he was certain to win. When he did, he'd ask for his freedom and they could truly get on with their lives.

* * * * *

The ship lurched in violent water. Waves drenched the deck, stinging Lock's eyes as he bellowed for Sparrow.

He heard her shriek and pushed his way past sailors who did their best to keep their footing on the slippery deck. An enormous wave washed over the ship. Lock grasped the wooden rail, managing to keep his footing while others tumbled overboard and disappeared into the dark, churning water.

"Sparrow!" he hollered, his throat aching.

Behind a fallen mast, he saw her pinned beneath a hulking male body. Her hand grasped a loose slab of wood, and she struck it across her attacker's face. He dropped to one side, but as she crawled across the slippery deck he caught her ankle and hauled her roughly into his embrace.

Lock dove, catching the mast as the ship tilted, and leapt at the dark figure, pain flaring across his ribs...

* * * * *

"Lock!" Sparrow's hands shook him, and he leapt awake, his heart pounding so violently his chest ached.

His vision cleared. *The farmhouse.* There was no ship. Not yet. Nor would there be.

"Gods," he murmured, wiping sweat from his eyes.

"Must have been a horrible nightmare. Are you all right?" She rubbed his back.

"Nightmare." *More like a vision.* By now he knew the

difference. He lay back down, wrapping his arms around her as she settled against his chest. He uttered a shaky laugh. "You don't get sea sick, do you, girl?"

"I don't know. I told you I've never been to sea. I suppose we'll find out when you take me."

"I changed my mind about that."

"Why?"

"It's no place for you. You'd hate it."

"But you told me I'd love it."

"I've been away from it for a time, so I've glorified it. Unless you're used to it, the rocking of the ship makes most people vomit. And it reeks. Stinks like salt and fish."

"Lock!" She giggled sleepily. "You love the sea."

"Did I ever tell you what happens when you run aground? Sometimes you get stuck on an island with cannibals."

"Cannibals?"

"Happened to me once. They damn near skewered my balls."

"Not much of a meal."

"Hey!" He lifted his head, staring at her.

"Just teasing, but at least it got you back to reality." She giggled and kissed him. "Go back to sleep, Lock. It was just a bad dream."

He hoped she was right, but his stomach tightened. He already knew his dreams were cursed.

Chapter Seventeen

ຕ

Lock broke the surface of the warm pool and hoisted himself to the edge, wiping rivulets of water from his eyes. He glanced around the bathing chamber in the lower levels of the palace of Begonia. Slaves washed in the snake-shaped pool filled by a natural hot spring. Others slept on the smooth rock floor scattered with soft rope carpets. Most prepared for the contest, each hoping to win his freedom. Many of the slaves belonged to the Empress, but a few—like Lock—had been given permission from other mistresses to enter. Sparrow was the only mistress—and the only female—in the chamber. Lock glanced over his shoulder to where she stood by a stone table preparing body paint and smoothing creases from his costume.

He approached, and she looked at him, her face tense.

He smiled as he stepped into the tight loincloth sewn with long strips of leather that hung to his knees and exposed almost every inch of him when he moved. "By the look on your face, you'd think you were the one competing."

"Aren't you nervous at all?"

"What for?"

"What for? This is important!"

"I can only do my best."

"Come here." She tugged him between her knees as she perched on the stone table and reached for a wide-tooth bone comb to disentangle his kinky hair. "It's going to take the rest of the morning for all this hair to dry."

"Competition starts late this afternoon." He closed his eyes and bent his head forward as she discarded the comb and massaged sandalwood-scented oil into his nape and shoulders. "That feels good."

"Smells good, too."

"Are you saying I stink otherwise?"

She giggled and kissed his cheek. "No. I..."

Several nearby slaves cast them nosy glances. Lock knew they were unaccustomed to open affection between slaves and mistresses. Most likely they even disapproved of it.

"What are you looking at?" Lock growled, causing them to turn away. Most of the slaves were similar in appearance to Theodore and Namir. A few were tall and well-muscled, but most of the larger, rougher ones either worked as laborers or were placed as gladiators. None present seemed willing to provoke a SothSea pirate.

"I hate this," Sparrow whispered. "I really do. I can't wait until we can live normally. Lie on the table so I can do the paint."

She hopped to her feet as he lay on his back.

She picked up a pot of black paint, dipped in a fine, soft brush, and touched it to his belly. His stomach jerked against the first contact of cold paint on warm skin. The hard muscles tightened before he released a long breath and lay still.

To create the illusion of male perfection, he needed to disguise the scars left from the whip. His back would be covered by silk, but his bare chest and stomach were marked with several long scars. Sparrow accented the lines with black paint and added several more, creating images of thorny branches across Lock's abdomen and chest. He closed his eyes as she worked, his thoughts churning with flashes of the previous night's vision, the approaching competition, and what would come after.

As much as he loved the sea, he knew he couldn't take Sparrow there. Not after the nightmare. It had been so real that he could see, smell, and feel every part of it—just like he had during the dream about being tortured in the village square.

And there had been other dreams over the years, ones that meant little but nevertheless came true.

"All right. I'm finished."

Lock opened his eyes and glanced down at his torso. Thorny branches scattered the lean muscles of his chest and abdomen.

"Good," he said, tying his hair at his nape with a strip of leather. "I'll finish getting ready, then we can go for a walk outside."

"Anything to get out of here." Sparrow glanced at the slaves, several of whom watched her and Lock from the corners of their eyes.

Lock filled a basin with water and stood in front of a tall mirror at the back of the chamber as he shaved. The wiry, brown and white hair fell away, revealing a smooth, oval jaw and several fine lines on the corners of his mouth. Completely exposed, his lower lip looked even fuller and softer.

When he finally turned to her, she stared at him, her eyes wide.

"Goodness." She stepped forward and took his face in her hands, running a fingertip over his jaw line. "You look almost like a boy."

"Some boy."

"You're not at all frightening anymore."

"Anymore? I don't know if I'm being praised or insulted."

She ran her knuckles across his smooth cheek. "I think you're very handsome."

"That's more like it." He lifted her onto the table, stepped between her legs, and kissed her.

"Lock, they're watching us."

"They have been since we arrived. Let's give them something to stare at."

"Let's go for that walk you promised me."

He reached for the silk, draped one length of it over his body and hung the second piece over his shoulder. He picked up the leather sheaths containing the two polished daggers he'd be dancing with and followed her out of the bath chamber, up the winding corridors to the main hall, and out to the courtyard where they'd wait until the competition began.

* * * * *

Sparrow sat beside four other slave owners on a bench cushioned in red velvet. Beside them, on a raised platform, Daryn lounged on an onyx chair, her eyes fixed on the slave singing in the center of the marble chamber. To the Empress's left side, a group of men and women dressed in embroidered trousers and vests played music on drums, pipes, and stringed instruments, providing background for the entertaining slaves. Dozens of chandeliers filled with white candles lit the chamber. The floor had been emptied, leaving space for the slaves who lined the walls, awaiting their turn to perform.

Sparrow stared across the room at Lock who sat close to the double doors at the end of the hall. Draped in blue and black silk from the top of his head to his feet covered with shoes of thin leather, even his face was hidden, leaving only his pale blue eyes exposed. Those eyes met Sparrow's and he winked. If she hadn't been so nervous, she would have smiled.

The singer struck a particularly high note, and Sparrow's attention jerked back to him. *He's good*, she thought. So had the acrobat been talented, and the man who performed a sword exhibition. She'd never seen Lock dance and prayed he was as skilled as Shea-Ann said. He had some tough competition—men who spent years in the harem living only to perfect their talents and please the Empress. Lock was a pirate, his time dedicated to running a ship and fighting. He might have learned some skills from the SothSea whores, but would it be enough to entice the Empress into granting his freedom?

The singer finished and bowed deeply to the Empress who offered him a nod of approval. He cleared the floor and took his place along the wall. A tall, slender blond wearing sheer black pantaloons knelt in the center of the floor. Sparrow noted he was extremely well-proportioned, and the Empress as well as the mistresses and several other slaves watched him with approving eyes. His hair hung like silk down his back, and his face was almost feminine in its beauty. The music began, and the slave moved his arms and hips in a sensual motion before swirling gracefully to his feet and dancing around the chamber.

Damn it, Sparrow thought as she watched the slave, fascinated by his performance. She glanced at the Empress and noted the smile on her face as her eyes caressed the handsome slave's form while he spun and stretched, his long, slender limbs moving like plants flowing in crystalline water.

Lock can't compete with that. He's gorgeous but has too many rough edges. Everyone likes this slave's grace...

The dancer ended his performance in a lunge, his arms stretched above his head, his hands positioned like eagle's wings. A light mist of perspiration covered smooth, hairless flesh over hard muscle. The Empress applauded and everyone joined in. She motioned for the slave to continue.

Sparrow noticed that a few times, when she particularly enjoyed a slave, she asked him for a second performance.

The blond smiled graciously and danced again while Sparrow cast her gaze to Lock. He watched the dancer with interest, but his pale eyes revealed no emotion. Sparrow wondered if he knew how slight his chance of winning over the blond.

When the dancer finished, he melted against the wall with the others, and Lock — the last competitor — walked to the center of the floor, his silk robes brushing the ground. He stood motionless, and as the music began, his arms outstretched, his hands open, palms up. His shoulders and arms moved slowly, sensually, an invitation for lust. His blue eyes shone like jewels against the silk, and he turned, his robes sweeping across the floor, flowing on the air as he spun, his hands disappearing in a swirl of blue and black. The music's pace increased, and as he spun, his arms pointed straight overhead, silver blades glistening in the candlelight. He lowered his arms, blades flashing, and tossed them high, catching them and twirling again. One of the silk robes fell to his feet, slashed by the blade, the movement itself imperceptible to the eye. With his long arms now exposed, the thick muscles rippled visibly as he spun the blades. One dagger drew circles overhead with the other flickering to his waist, causing several more yards of silk to float to the ground, baring his legs. The loincloth fit his lean waist and bulging cock like a second skin, and the strips of black leather parted with each of his stances, revealing the hard, curved muscles of his thighs and calves. When he spun, his bare buttocks was completely exposed, each cheek a tight, round globe of smooth flesh.

Sparrow swallowed, her mouth dry. She realized her hands were trembling and could scarcely believe watching a body she knew so intimately could make her heart pound. The blond dancer had been good, but his performance was *nothing* compared to this!

Lock's dance was graceful and rough at the same time. His every movement promised dangerous, delicious sex, the fulfillment of every animalistic dream. He turned the daggers inward, blades hidden against his wrists, and lifted the edges of the last piece of silk concealing his face, back, and shoulders. As his long legs swallowed the space between the center of the floor and the throne, the silk billowed behind him like a demonic cloud. He dropped to his knees, his legs spread wide, his leather-covered cock dangling between the gaps of black leather. He arched his back, the top of his head nearly touching the floor as his blue eyes slipped shut and the daggers flickered towards his temples, slicing away the last of the silk, revealing his smooth-shaven face with its chiseled cheekbones, beautiful nose, and sensual mouth. He wore a black vest, cut to expose his front and conceal his back. His back still arched sensually, revealing the taut muscles of his abdomen and the breadth of his muscled chest, his hands touched the floor behind his head, his fingers grasping the pool of blue silk.

Sparrow wanted to look at the Empress and the others in the room to see if they were as enthralled as she in what was surely the best performance of the day, but she couldn't tear her eyes from Lock.

He straightened his back in a fluid motion and stood, his hips thrust forward in a suggestive manner that made Sparrow's pulse pound. His brown and white hair hung wildly down his back and over his shoulders as he continued dancing, his hips gyrating, his daggers slicing air. As the speed of the music increased, his motions followed until he was a blur of silver blades, two-toned hair, and glistening flesh.

The music stopped suddenly, and he dropped to the ground at the Empress's feet, his knees tucked beneath him, his torso bowed with his arms stretched overhead, his face to the floor in a completely submissive position. Spirals of his long hair clung to the sweat-beaded muscles of his arms and shoulders. The damp silk vest hugged his broad back and lean waist.

Sparrow realized the room had fallen into complete silence, and she glanced around, noting all eyes were fixed on Lock. Beside Sparrow, one of the mistresses fanned herself with her hand while the others stared, mouths slightly open. The slaves' faces were frozen as they sensed their own defeat.

The Empress drew a deep breath and ordered, "Look up."

Lock slowly raised himself, but remained kneeling, eyes cast respectfully to the base of Daryn's throne.

Oh, he's smart, Sparrow thought to herself. *He knows enough to suck on her toes and not get too cocky.*

"Continue," Daryn ordered, motioning with her hand.

Lock stood and took his place as the music began.

For an hour, Lock danced for the Empress. Sparrow was completely shocked by this new side of her lover. Lock knew many dances and performed them with mystical beauty and precision, almost like one who *enjoyed* it.

By the time the last song ended, the Empress had moved from her throne to sit at the edge of the platform, close to the floor and to Lock. He knelt with his back to her, so close she could reach out and touch him. Again he arched backwards, his blue eyes finally fixed on her. His fingertips touched the hem of her gown. The music ceased, and he turned, on his hands and knees in front of her, his pale eyes meeting hers through ringlets of sweat-soaked hair. The tip of his tongue traced lips that curved upward in the slightest yet most inviting smile.

The Empress reached out and took his chin in her hand. Sparrow's stomach tightened with jealousy and anticipation as Daryn spoke, her lips hovering over Lock's. "Tell me what you want. I'll give you anything in my power."

Lock's smile faded and the alluring expression in his eyes turned hard. "I want Miska in the ring."

Sparrow felt her heart stop beating. *No! His freedom! He's supposed to ask for his freedom!*

The Empress laughed. "You want to die?"

"I want Miska in the ring," Lock repeated.

Daryn returned to her throne, her elbows resting on the edge, her fingers creating a peak on which she rested her chin. "Done. There are games planned for the morning. You'll fight Miska then. Tonight, you and your mistress will remain here. Everyone, the competition is over for this year. You may go."

Slaves and mistresses alike bowed and cleared the chamber.

Numb, Sparrow was unable to stand. She stared at Lock as he approached her, the torn silks slung over his arm. He brushed hair from his face and dropped to the ground beside her, still catching his breath from his performance.

"I haven't had so much fun in a long time," he commented and began stretching his legs.

"How could you?" Sparrow hissed, all her emotions

returning in a rush. She grasped his shoulders, her fingers biting into muscle. "You were supposed to ask for your freedom so we could get married!"

"Sparrow, we can get married anywhere. This is one sure chance to give Miska what he deserves."

"Who gives a damn about Miska!"

"I thought you hated him?"

"I hate him as much as I love you."

"Then I'll kill him for you."

"Kill him for me?" Her fingers loosened and she slipped her arms around his neck. "I don't want you to fight him."

"Too late."

"No, we can go to Daryn and say you changed your mind. We can—"

"Do you still believe Miska deserves to die for what he did to your sister?"

"Yes!"

"Then I'm not going to Daryn." He stood. "Come. I'd like to get a good rest tonight."

"Lock!" She clung to his arm. "What if he kills you?"

"Then there's a lot of people who think I deserve to die."

"I don't believe this." Sparrow covered her face with her hands. "This is a nightmare."

"I don't plan on losing, girl. Why do you think I asked to see him fight before? I wanted to know if I could beat him."

"And?"

"And I won't lie to you and say it will be easy, but yes. I can beat him." He touched her cheek and kissed her . "I will beat him, Sparrow."

I hope so, she thought. *If you don't, then Miska really will have taken from me everything I've ever loved.*

Chapter Eighteen

Sparrow and Lock returned to her room where a warm bath and meal awaited them.

"If you're still mad at me, why don't I just spend the night in the slave quarters?" Lock dropped the ripped silks and sheathed daggers in a heap on the floor and removed the loincloth. Naked, he reached for an apple from the bowl on the table.

Sparrow's eyes raked him. "And you'd probably jaunt down there unclothed, too."

"What's that supposed to mean?"

"It means I have never in my entire life seen such a disgusting display as your so-called dance!"

"It was fine with you when you thought I was bartering for my freedom."

"Seems like you'd rather fight a gladiator than marry me."

Lock raised his eyes to heaven and swallowed the piece of apple he was chewing. "Unbelievable. I'm going to give you what you want most in the world—I danced my ass off to get it—and you're still not satisfied!"

"I told you, I don't care about Miska! I don't want you to die!" Sparrow turned away, but not before Lock noticed tears glistening in her eyes. He stepped across the room and placed his hands on her shoulders. She shrugged him off. "Don't touch me!"

Ignoring her, he tugged her into his arms. Her cheek was soft against his chest. Her arms slid around his waist and squeezed. "I'm afraid you'll be hurt, Lock. I don't want to see you suffer again. When you were tortured in the square it nearly broke my heart, and I wasn't even in love with you then."

Lock held her closer and rested his cheek against the top of her head. Her words troubled him. Though he'd grown accustomed to their relationship, the realization of the depth of her feelings for him was a great responsibility. He never imagined anyone caring so much about him, and he hated knowing his actions affected her so.

"Think of it this way, Sparrow, Thea probably wasn't the only person he brutalized. She probably wasn't the last. Someone has to stop him."

"It doesn't have to be you!"

"Will you trust me?" He tilted her face to his and kissed her. "I really need a bath."

Sparrow glanced over her shoulder at the tub. "It's big enough for two. Want company?"

He picked her up and walked toward the tub.

"Wait!" she giggled. "Take off my dress first!"

He placed her on the edge of the tub and tugged her dress over her head, tossing it aside as they slipped into the warm water. Lock ducked under and wet his hair.

"Let me get behind you and I'll wash it," Sparrow said. She lathered his hair with floral-scented soap and massaged his scalp, her fingers sliding through kinky tendrils. "I love your hair."

Lock closed his eyes and leaned against her, enjoying the feel of her breasts against his back. "I remember the first time you washed it."

"You were so irritated because you could hardly do it yourself."

"I was irritated because of how I felt about you."

She rubbed her cheek against his. "You liked me then? I thought you hated me."

He moved swiftly, dragging her from behind him so her chest pressed to his, their legs entangled in the water. "I never hated you. I always liked you too much. Nobody ever treated me like you do. I didn't know how to deal with it."

"You don't have any problem now." She smiled, covering his mouth with hers.

He closed his eyes and buried his hands in her hair as their tongues fenced.

A knock sounded on the chamber door and before Sparrow could answer, two servants stepped inside.

"Don't you wait for an invitation?" Lock snapped, reaching for a towel to cover Sparrow.

"Pardon," one of the servants said, "but by order of the Empress, we've come to retrieve you."

Lock and Sparrow exchanged looks.

"What does she want him for?" Sparrow demanded.

"She wants him in her chamber. Come now."

"I don't want you in her chamber!" Sparrow whispered.

Lock shrugged. "She's the Empress. If she wants me, you know I have to go."

"And you love it, don't you?" Sparrow sounded furious.

He stepped out of the tub and reached for his trousers and shirt. Sparrow, the damp towel wrapped around her mid-section, watched as he dressed.

"I never should have let you talk me into allowing you to enter the competition! You'll sell your body for anything!"

His eyes met hers with a harshness that nearly stole her breath. "What do you expect from a SothSea whore and a pirate to boot?"

He left her glaring after him as he followed the servants to the Empress's chamber. Sparrow was right, of course. There was little he hadn't done or wouldn't do to get what he wanted. He also knew Sparrow spoke in anger. He didn't blame her. If she had been ordered to some Emperor's chamber for sex, he probably would have killed the man himself and ended up with a death sentence. Still, her words wounded him in a manner he'd never expected. He thought by challenging Miska, he was giving Sparrow the opportunity for the revenge she so wanted. He'd seen her rage in the city square when she'd tried to attack the gladiator. Lock was certain she wanted Miska dead more than she wanted marriage. Never, never would he understand women—at least not a woman like Sparrow. The Empress was much easier to read. He'd guessed that if he won the competition she'd want to sleep with him, if he hadn't asked for his freedom. When he'd been helping Shea-Ann with her herbs, he'd asked her for one to put someone to sleep. Shea-Ann, never completely trusting him, wanted to know why. He'd told her his suspicions regarding the Empress. Shea-Ann had provided him with a potion that, when mixed with the Empress's food or drink, would send her to sleep for an entire night.

Outside the Empress's chamber, the guards knocked.

"Send him in."

One guard opened the door and stepped aside for Lock to pass. The door closed behind him, and he glanced around a carpeted marble room. An enormous tub took up one wall, an even larger bed stood against the other. A round table laden with fruit, bread, cheese, and wine stood in the center of the room.

The Empress lay on the bed amidst black velvet pillows and red satin sheets. Her long hair hung down her shoulders in gleaming chestnut tendrils. She wore a loincloth of black beads. Her large, slightly sagging cranberry-tipped breasts were bare. Though not an ugly woman, Lock found her by no means attractive, and since meeting Sparrow, the idea of bedding anyone but her was unappealing to him. Still, he knew better than to reveal his feelings to the Empress.

"Come." The Empress beckoned Lock with a finger. He walked to the bed and crawled toward her. His hands roamed over her body as he smiled seductively. The Empress grasped handfuls of his hair, still damp from the bath, and pulled hard until his mouth hovered over hers.

"I know why you told Sparrow you'd marry her. Being a husband is better than being a slave—unless you're slave to the right woman."

"Dare I hope you're the right woman, Empress?"

She chuckled deep in her throat, closing her eyes as Lock's mouth swept down her neck. Her hands slid beneath his shirt, her pointed nails digging so hard into his flesh that he wondered if she drew blood. He forced himself to keep his disgust from his face. She had all the finesse of the pirates who'd paid for his body during his boyhood.

"I'd love some of your wine," he murmured against her lips.

"Of course. How selfish of me. You must be starving and thirsty after that lovely performance. Too bad you've already bathed. We could have had so much fun in my tub."

"We still can." Lock rolled out of the bed and approached the table. He glanced over his shoulder, noting the Empress still lay on the bed. With his back to her, he slipped Shea-Ann's potion from his trousers and emptied it into a wine glass. "I could spend my life in the water."

"You could spend the rest of your life in me." The Empress slid off the bed and approached Lock, her hands roaming over his waist. She grasped his cock, squeezing hard. Lock forced a smile, pretended to sip from the wine glass, and offered it to her.

The Empress ignored the wine, but Lock held the glass to her mouth and said, "Drink it and let me lick your beautiful mouth clean."

"You are a jewel," she purred, taking a long drink from the glass.

Lock swept her into his arms and carried her to the bed, running his tongue over her full lips, closing his eyes and trying to pretend it was Sparrow he kissed.

"If Miska doesn't destroy you in the ring tomorrow, I might consider making you mine," Daryn said. "Would you like that?"

Lock only smiled and kissed her again. *The woman is a complete bitch. Sparrow is supposedly her friend. She knows Sparrow and I want to marry, but she'll use her power to take what she wants anyway. Not only that, Sparrow didn't even bother telling her what Miska had done since she knew Daryn wouldn't punish her best gladiator. I'd rather mate with an eel.*

The Empress clung to Lock, thrusting her body against his while he closed his eyes and tolerated her touch. It had been years since he'd played the part of the whore, since he'd lain with someone against his will. Just a few more moments, and the potion should work...

Daryn's arms slipped from him, and she muttered something about feeling sleepy before she fell into unconsciousness, her legs still entwined with Lock's. His lip curling, he disentangled himself from the Empress. He walked to the table, took a sip of wine from the bottle and sloshed it around in his mouth, hoping to wipe away her taste.

He opened the door, and the guards outside raised their swords.

One of them said, "The Empress told us you'd be spending the night."

"She ordered me out. She's asleep. See for yourself."

The guard peered inside, saw Daryn sleeping peacefully on the bed, and nodded. "Be on your way."

Lock walked to Sparrow's room. She'd probably be more furious with him than ever, but he hoped to warm her up. He needed to spend the night in her arms. Not that he planned on losing to Miska, but plans didn't *always* work out.

* * * * *

Sparrow lay on her bed facing the ceiling, unable to sleep for the enraged thoughts twisting her mind. She hated Daryn for sleeping with the man she loved. She hated Lock for selling himself for any price, and most of all she hated herself because no matter how bad he was for her, she couldn't control her feelings for him.

"That's what you get for falling in love with a pirate!" She clenched her teeth so hard so wondered how they didn't crack. While rage and jealousy twisted her insides, he made love with an Empress! Sparrow imagined the sort of bed Daryn had. Years ago in her own palace, Sparrow had a big, beautiful bed covered with silk and satin sheets. Why would he want rough wool and muslin in a farmer's bed when he could have fine fabric, wealth, the best any slave could ask for?

"Slave!" Sparrow sat up, pressing her hands to her temples. "He's not a slave at all. Not really." But that afternoon, when he'd danced, she'd forgotten what he was. He'd become a symbol of sexuality, a rare jewel for sale to the highest bidder, and who could bid higher than an Empress?

He's worse than a slave! He's a pirate! Everyone knows he'll do anything for money!

A tapping on the door roused her from her angry thoughts.

"Who is it?" she demanded.

"Me."

If possible, Sparrow's stomach tightened even more. *Lock!* He was done with the Empress and had come slithering back to her.

"Go to the slave quarters!"

"I'm not going to the slave quarters!"

"You'll do what I tell you or I'll have you whip…" She stopped, the words sticking in her throat. No matter how furious she was, she couldn't threaten him with that.

Suddenly the door burst in, the lock clattering to the floor. Sparrow sat up, her hands clutching her pounding chest. Lock slammed what was left of the door behind him and strode toward her, his pale eyes glowing like a demon's, his jaw clenched.

"You'll have me *what*?"

"Nothing," she muttered, then pointed at him. "Get out of here! I don't want to see you."

He stopped and offered a deep, mocking bow. "Forgive me, My Lady. I was under the impression you wanted me in your bed every night for the rest of our lives. I guess I was mistaken."

"Huh! A lot you care! You're in there pleasuring that bitch—"

Lock glanced over his shoulder and snapped, "Will you be quiet? Do you want to get yourself executed for treason?"

"Bitch!" Sparrow repeated. "That raw-boned, painted, ugly—"

Lock dove on top of her, his body pressing hers into the sheets, one large hand clamped over her mouth. "Are you crazy, girl?"

She struggled beneath him, but he was too strong. Her teeth found the flesh of his palm, and she bit. *Hard.*

He let loose a string of curses, but held her fast. "I'll let you up if you promise to lower that loud mouth of yours!"

Sparrow nodded, her heart racing with anger and—to her dismay—arousal.

Lock's hand moved from her mouth to her neck. He kissed her, not roughly as his blazing expression would have led her to believe, but tenderly. His lips brushed her temple, and she jerked away, wishing she could hate him.

"How dare you come here after being with *her*? You stink like her perfume. You have her lip paint on your face!"

Lock wrinkled his nose and rubbed his face with his hands. "Is it gone? That woman is worse than an octopus."

"As if you didn't have a fine time bedding an Empress!"

"She certainly wouldn't have been the first, if I'd bedded her at all!"

"You're a liar!"

"Why do you think I came back so fast?"

"Don't tell me she let you go. I saw how she looked at you, like she wanted to devour every inch of you—not that I blamed her."

He smiled. "So you liked the dance after all?"

"Only if it had been for me."

Lock's fingers sifted through her hair. "I didn't sleep with her, Sparrow. I couldn't wait to get back to you. Shea-Ann gave me a potion to mix with her wine. She'll be asleep until morning and when she wakes won't remember a thing. For all she knows, we fucked the whole night."

"Must you always be so crude?"

He lowered his head to her breast and loosened the ties of her nightshirt with his teeth. "Let's find out."

Sparrow threaded her fingers through his hair, closing her eyes. "I don't want to share you with any other woman, Lock."

"There is no other woman for me."

Sparrow shifted position so Lock could remove her clothes. When she lay naked, he gently covered her eyes with his hand. "Close them."

She did as he asked, her belly tense with anticipation.

"Relax," he whispered against her lips as he massaged her temples. His caress trailed across her jaw then his fingertips stroked her throat, moving to her collarbones and shoulders. Long, soft touches traveled down one of her arms from biceps to wrist. His thumb massaged her palm and he gently rubbed the length of each finger before beginning the same ministrations on her other arm and hand.

Sparrow's entire body relaxed as contented pleasure enfolded her like a warm embrace. She sighed as Lock's kisses covered every inch of her breasts, leaving only her nipples untouched and yearning. Finally he took one peak between his lips and flicked his tongue over it until his caress was almost painful. Then he moved to her opposite nipple, paying it the same attention.

Sighing, Sparrow's toes curled with desire as his lips trailed beneath her breasts and covered her abdomen. He ran his tongue down the joining of her hips and thighs and along the edge of her pubic hair. His large, callused hands tenderly gripped her thighs, rubbing down to her knees which he kissed. He caressed her shins, calves, and ankles then kissed the arch of each of her feet. Burying his face between her legs, he lapped her clit and ran his tongue down her pussy lips.

"Oh, Lock," she panted, "I love you. I love you so much."

His hands slipped beneath her buttocks and kneaded as he sucked her clit and poked his tongue into her pussy. He licked her soft, heated folds of flesh and used the tip of his tongue to tease her perineum.

Sparrow gripped his hair, her eyes closed tightly as his marvelous tongue thrust her into orgasm. She moaned and writhed helplessly beneath his onslaught. All the while his lips and tongue never ceased their lusty motions. Finally she lay still, except for the rise and fall of her breasts as her breathing returned to normal.

Her pleasure was tainted by one horrible thought. If Miska killed him tomorrow, she doubted she could bear it.

* * * * *

"So you really like to dance?" Sparrow nestled against Lock's side, taking one of his hands in hers and studying the texture of his skin and the shape of his long fingers.

"I love it."

"I never would have imagined."

"Like I said, my mother made me learn when I was young."

"Your mother should have been whipped for what she

did to you."

"Forget about her. Like I said before. She's dead to me."

"But you can still love to dance, even after what you went through?"

"I do it in private, for myself. This afternoon was the first time I performed in public since I was twelve. From now on, it's just for you."

Sparrow smiled, her body tingling again. She draped her leg across Lock's, her foot running up his hair-roughened calf. "I look forward to it. But we have a problem, Lock. What are we going to do about getting married?"

"We'll move on when you're ready."

"I knew it! You only wanted to do this so you could go back to sea."

"No. I said I'm not taking you to sea."

"But I want to—"

"We'll talk about it tomorrow." He kissed the top of her head. "Right now I need some sleep. I want to be sharp when I meet Miska."

Sparrow nodded, her smile fading. He didn't even have to add he wanted to be sharp or else Miska would destroy him.

* * * * *

Sparrow wrapped her arms tightly around her body as she huddled in one corner of the cage in the Empress's ring. Guards stood at attention around the perimeter of the cage, and the sounds of chatting and laughter wafted from the balcony where Daryn, Lords and Ladies, and their servants awaited the beginning of the games. Slaves, little more than slender boys dressed in simple muslin tunics, filled the ring, raking the dirt floor smooth.

Sparrow stared at her booted feet, fighting waves of nausea as she shivered slightly in spite of the warmth of the ring. Sunlight poured in through the open roof, and the day was dreadfully humid. Even in her thin tunic, heat prickled along her spine. She hadn't slept at all the night before, but had watched Lock, studied every line of his face as he rested so easily she wondered if he'd ever felt nervous about anything in his life.

He might die today, Sparrow thought then closed her eyes and shook her head. She couldn't think that way. She wouldn't.

She sighed as the slaves filed past her, carrying rakes, their tanned faces misted with sweat. The cage was sheltered by overhanging stone and, other than the balcony, was probably the coolest area in the ring. For some reason he wouldn't disclose, Lock had insisted she watch from the cage, and Daryn had agreed. The Empress hadn't mentioned the previous evening, and Sparrow guessed she didn't want to admit her lack of memory due to Shea-Ann's potion. Sparrow wished her old friend were with her. She could have used her company as she awaited Lock's fight.

"Keep back," one of the guards told Sparrow as he lifted his sword.

The first two fighters rushed through the open doors at the back of the cage. In the ring, they attacked one another, dirt flying, their grunts, bellows, and panting breath filling the structure. Sparrow watched them without really seeing the fight. Her mind churned with thoughts of Lock and Miska. Since Thea's death, she'd never felt such desolation and terror.

The first fight ended without a kill, and the second passed just as quickly. Sparrow watched the slaves return with their rakes, smoothing the dirt and clearing away bloodstains.

The guards suddenly tensed, their weapons drawn. They stood so close together Sparrow had to stand on her toes and search for an empty space between their shoulders to see Lock. Dressed in calf-high boots and brown leather pants, his chest protected by a chain mail vest, he swept through the doors. Metal cuffs wrapped around his forearms. He held a short, straight sword comfortably in his right hand. His long hair hung in a tight braid down his back, and not a muscle moved in his face as his pale gaze fixed on the cage doors. Sparrow doubted he saw her. She knew he was aware of nothing but the coming of Miska.

A deep battle cry erupted from the inner wall. Sparrow jumped, her nerves already frayed to the breaking point. She felt the ground shake as Miska, wearing a knee-length leather skirt and metal plates on his chest and back, stormed through the door and out of the cage, directly toward Lock.

* * * * *

Lock's grip tightened on his sword as he watched Miska soaring toward him, his red hair flying behind him, his teeth bared and eyes gleaming. The first blow of metal on metal jarred Lock to the bone. Miska was as powerful as he appeared. Nearly as tall as Lock and even more thickly built, Miska had certainly earned his reputation in the ring. As Lock blocked blow upon blow, he searched for an opening, but the gladiator's defense proved just as good as his attack. It had been several months since Lock had fought an opponent. When he was at sea, fights occurred often, and though he'd practiced fighting diligently and kept in peak physical condition with riding, swimming, dancing, and wood chopping, nothing compared with a live opponent. Still, once fighting was in the blood, it seldom left, and within moments, Lock was reading Miska's motions through his eyes and sensing each of the gladiator's blows almost before they landed.

The men broke, circling each other, their chests heaving from the force of their attack combined with the oppressive heat. Miska's teeth gleamed as he sneered, "The Empress said you wanted to fight me."

"No, I want to kill you."

"Is it because I kicked you on your ass in the square a few weeks ago?"

"I'm honored you remember." Lock's voice dripped sarcasm.

"Most men would remember Lock the White. You have a reputation. Killing you will be good for my status in the ring." Miska licked his thick lips. "And when I'm through here, I'm asking the Empress to give me that woman of yours. I like her kind. Small, innocent looking. Tell me, pirate, does she like it rough? She better."

Lock's teeth ground, but he forced himself to remain calm. Miska wanted to enrage him, wanted him to fight foolishly. Still, the gladiator's words worried Lock. He hadn't considered the danger Sparrow might be in when he'd asked to fight Miska. If he lost, she'd be alone and unprotected against the same animal who brutalized her sister.

"You'll never find out, Miska."

Simultaneously, the men attacked. Their blades locked. He stared into the gladiator's furious green eyes, thought of Sparrow's sister at the mercy of this man strong enough to become the Empress's favorite gladiator, and hated him. Long ago, he'd been the victim of such pigs. Even worse, Miska had hurt Sparrow.

Lock's foot shot out in a kick powerful enough to hurl Miska almost to his knees. He struck an overhead blow before the gladiator could fully recover, still the man blocked it, his own kick smashing Lock's ribs.

With a snarl of pure animal fury, Miska doubled his attack, raining blows upon Lock from every direction. The man was very skilled. Whoever had taught him to fight had done well. Lock spun and blocked an overhead blow. Blades locked, and Miska's sword flew from his hand. Lock thrust his weapon, but Miska caught his arm at the wrist and snapped backward. Lock lost his blade and crashed to his back. The landing knocked the wind from him, every bone in his body protesting the attack. Miska dove at him, but Lock flipped to his feet and kicked Miska in the back of the head. The gladiator crashed face first in the dirt. Lock leapt on him from behind, his arms tightening around Miska's thick neck. The gladiator's fingers bit into Lock's forearms. Lock grunted in pain as he felt flesh tearing, Miska's nails practically hitting bone. One of the gladiator's hands reached up, grasped a handful of Lock's hair, and yanked so hard the white and brown tendrils tore out at the root. He felt blood mingling with the sweat running down his neck as he glanced at the bloody mass of hair dropping from the gladiator's hand. Miska stood, lifting Lock's feet from the ground as he ran backwards into the ring's stone wall.

He's strong as a White Island Yak, Lock thought, feeling his vision blacken as Miska repeatedly rammed backwards into the wall, striking Lock's head each time. Again Lock struck against the stone. At the same time, Miska's elbow rammed backwards. Pain flared up Lock's side as he felt his ribs crack, the sound echoing across the ring. His hold loosened on Miska who tore away, falling to his knees and coughing as he attempted to regain his breath. Lock, one arm holding his throbbing side, kicked the gladiator in the face. Miska noticed the blow coming and moved slightly. Though he avoided the full impact, blood still spurted from his broken nose. His foot struck out at Lock who caught his leg and stomped his groin.

Miska hollered in pain, clutching his balls. Lock dropped to his knees behind the gladiator, wrapped one arm around his neck, and punched him in the temple. Miska's head lolled to the side, his eyes unfocused. Lock grasped him by the arm and dragged him across the ring, pausing only to pick up one of the discarded blades. His ribs aching with each ragged breath, the back of his head and forearms stinging as blood oozed from torn flesh, he approached the cage.

Blinking sweat from his eyes, he searched for Sparrow who pushed her way past the guards. She stared at him, her face pale and her eyes wide. To ensure the gladiator's immobility, Lock rammed his knee into Miska's back, and the semi-conscious man groaned. Lock flung him at Sparrow's feet and offered her the blade.

"He's yours."

* * * * *

Sparrow stared at Lock, her heart pounding. As she'd watched him fight, part of her soul had felt every blow. She just wanted the damn match to end. Several times she thought Miska might win. He was so powerful, so skilled. To Sparrow, since the day he'd murdered Thea, he'd been a symbol of fear and pure evil. She thought the one thing she wanted most was revenge, but if the price of revenge was Lock's pain—or worse, his life—she didn't want any part of it. Miska was evil and Thea was dead. Nothing would bring her back, least of all Lock's death.

"He's yours," Lock repeated, his words roughly spoken through gasps of air. Blood and dirt caked his face, and the artery running along the side of his neck pounded beneath sweat-sheened flesh. Sparrow noted one of his arms still pressed against his side. Though his features were calmly assembled, his eyes gleamed with excitement tinged with pain.

Miska was finally hers, but at what price?

The gladiator's eyes blinked rapidly as he fought for consciousness.

Sparrow glanced from the sword, to Miska, to Lock. She shook her head and turned away.

She stared at the rock wall as she heard the sound of metal slicing flesh followed by a gurgling sound. The crowd shrieked, boos mingling with cheers. She heard a body drop and knew Lock had finished Miska. She walked into the darkness of the inner wall.

No sooner had she stepped into the labyrinth-like corridors when Sparrow nearly crashed into a broad chest covered in black silk, a circle of red thorns embroidered around a ruby over the wearer's heart. She looked into the face of a tall man with chestnut hair. A second man, blond, wearing an identical uniform, stood beside him. Their tunics were recognized in almost every part of the world. Knights of the Ruby Order.

"Excuse me, Sirs," Sparrow murmured.

"No, excuse us," said the chestnut-haired Knight. Both bowed their heads and stepped aside for her to pass.

"Sparrow!" Lock called.

She turned to him. He glanced at the Knights.

"We've come for Miska's body," said the blond Knight. "Though we don't advocate killing, you've done us a service."

Lock nodded at them but focused his attention on Sparrow. "You're still angry."

She took a step closer to him and wiped blood running from the corner of his torn mouth. "You're hurt. Let me help you get cleaned up."

"Allow us to assist you," the dark-haired Knight said. "I'm Sir Erik. This is Sir Warrant. We're of the Ruby Order—"

"We know who you are," Lock told them.

"Knights are respected healers," Sparrow said. "We'd be glad for your help."

"I'll see to Miska's body," Warrant said.

Erik nodded and motioned for Lock and Sparrow to follow him to one of the small, empty chambers running along both sides of the corridor.

Lock sat on the ground while the Knight knelt beside him, removing a leather bag from his shoulder and searching through his healing supplies. He glanced at Sparrow. "I could use some water."

"I'll get it." She met Lock's eyes before leaving the chamber.

* * * * *

"Let me help you get this off," Erik lifted the mail vest from Lock and tossed it aside. Lock winced in pain as he raised

239

his arms to remove the sweat-soaked shirt beneath. The Knight examined his side. "I knew these ribs had to be broken. You took a few hard blows out there."

"Hardly noticed." Lock attempted to chuckle at his joke, but the motion hurt.

The Knight felt Lock's ribs and removed a bandage from his bag. "Miska was a very well-trained fighter. Warrant and I were surprised you beat him. Your skill is impressive."

"Why were you looking for Miska?"

"It's a sad and guilt-ridden story for our Order. Several years ago, he came to us and asked to join our ranks. Becoming a Knight is not a simple task. Candidates are chosen carefully and training is grueling. We all must perfect both fighting and healing arts. We cannot accept payment for either, but the skills we learn are priceless. We have some of the best healers and masters of the fighting arts in the world among our men. Trainees are instructed in the best ways we can offer. When Miska arrived, we questioned him, tested him, and he was allowed to join as a Trainee. He fulfilled his duties, took his shifts, and learned the healing arts, but it was fighting that most interested him. No one considered this particularly unusual. Each Knight has his own special interests and skills. Some are completely dedicated to healing and learn only basic fighting while others do the opposite. Others lean more toward scholarly tasks or engineering."

"Sounds like a hard life but a good one."

"It is. Becoming a Knight was the best decision I ever made. Most of us feel that way, and few leave the Order. None have ever left on Miska's terms. He learned all he could from some of our best instructors in the fighting arts. While stationed for his training, we discovered he'd attacked a family and brutalized their daughter. He stole their money and a horse and left. We've been chasing him ever since. A criminal with skills learned in our Order is too dangerous to roam free. It sickens me to think of the crimes he's committed since he left us."

I know about some, Lock thought. Perhaps if they'd caught Miska sooner, Sparrow's sister would still be alive. "I knew I was right to kill him."

Sir Erik's eyes met Lock's, and Lock was almost taken aback by the Knight's expression. The man's large gray eyes were wise, strong, and kind. They held no innocence yet none of the wickedness Lock knew tainted his own soul.

"Killing is not always the answer to everything, but in this case I agree. The Order has never before made such a mistake in choosing a Trainee, and we hope it never happens again. We found no indication of his violent past, and he never spoke of it."

"Is that something you'd expect a would-be Knight to tell you?" Lock scoffed, slowly pulling his shirt on. With the bandage in place, his ribs felt a little better.

"Yes."

"Then you'd be hard up for Trainees. I imagine you are, anyway. Only decent, perfect men could join you."

Erik laughed. "I'm afraid you have an unrealistic view of us. We don't look for perfection, just for men who strive to do their best for themselves and their fellows. Miska's past wouldn't have necessarily condemned him with us, but his lack of honesty did. Each man has faults, but he must admit them. It's not always easy. Admitting I'm wrong has always been a problem for me."

"Few of us like to admit when we're wrong." Lock thought about the expression on Sparrow's face when he'd thrust Miska at her feet. He'd been so certain she wanted revenge. He'd nearly gotten himself killed to give her what she wanted, but he'd obviously been far from the truth.

Sparrow stepped inside carrying a bucket of water and several pieces of cloth. Her gaze met Lock's. "Are you all right?"

"Fine."

Sparrow knelt beside Erik and handed him a cloth that he

dipped in water. He unraveled the braid and bathed the back of Lock's neck where Miska had ripped out a chunk of hair. The Knight stitched the flesh before he began sewing Lock's torn forearms. Lock watched carefully, asking questions about healing techniques and mentally comparing them with what he'd learned from Shea-Ann.

"You have an interest in healing?" Sir Erik asked.

"I do."

Sparrow met Lock's eyes. "I'd rather have you pursue that than some of the other things you've done lately."

A smile played around Sir Erik's lips. "Smart woman. Well, that's about all I can do for you."

"Thank you for your help." Lock extended his hand to Erik who grasped it firmly.

"If you ever decide to pursue that interest in healing, you might want to visit our Order. A man with your fighting skill would have a good chance at becoming a trainee."

Lock laughed. "I thought you didn't want any other indecent choices?"

"I don't think you would be a wrong choice."

"How can you make that judgment?"

"Just a feeling."

"Were you one of the people who helped choose Miska?" Lock smirked.

"No," Erik's probing eyes held Lock's, "I wasn't. Good luck to you both."

"Thank you, Sir," Sparrow replied before the Knight left.

Dipping a fresh cloth in the water, she began cleaning the blood and dirt from Lock's face, one of her hands touching his chin. He longed for her to touch him with affection instead of simply out of necessity.

"I wish you hadn't done this," she said.

"I'm glad I did."

Sparrow's jaw stiffened.

"Why are you constantly angry with me? I gave you what I thought you wanted."

"Well you were wrong."

"Obviously." He caught her hand before she could continue cleaning his face. "I want to get out of here and go home."

"Don't you think you should rest for a while? I know you're hurt."

He strode out of the chamber without replying, fury twisting his stomach. It was madness to be angry with her, but he couldn't help it. He had this crazy fantasy that she'd have been grateful for what he'd done. He'd imagined her throwing her arms around his neck and kissing him. For what? Killing a man, even if the man had murdered her sister?

Outside, Sea Storm awaited them. They had ridden the horse to the ring that morning, and Namir had graciously volunteered to care for him during the games.

The slender slave smiled, his eyes gleaming, when he saw Lock.

I bet he'd have been appreciative, Lock thought. *Too bad he ain't Sparrow.*

"You won!" Namir said. "I knew you would."

"Yeah," Lock muttered, his voice tinged with sarcasm. His ribs smarted, arms and scalp stung, and the rest of him felt like one big ache. "I won."

"Thank you, Namir." Sparrow took Sea-Storm's reins and mounted.

"I'll look forward to your next visit to the city," Namir said to the couple, though his gaze remained fixed on Lock.

Lock mounted behind Sparrow and they turned towards home.

Chapter Nineteen

By the time they reached the farm several hours later, Lock's ribs hurt so much he could scarcely wait to dismount and fall into bed. When Sea-Storm moved any faster than a walk, every strike of his hooves on dirt jarred Lock to the bone. His head hurt from the repeated slamming against the wall as well as the missing chunk of his scalp. And worst of all, during the entire ride, Sparrow had said no more than five words.

They stopped in front of the house, and Sparrow dismounted first, Lock moving slowly, careful not to show any sign of discomfort.

"I'll see to the horse." Sparrow glanced at him. "You look awful."

"I feel great." He flung her a mocking smile and stepped into the house while she walked Sea-Storm to the barn.

"By the Goddess, what happened?" Shea-Ann's brow furrowed as Lock entered the house. She left the table where she'd been preparing herbs and approached him. "Where's Sparrow? Were you attacked?"

"Sparrow's fine. We weren't attacked, and it's a long story."

"I want to hear everything. Come sit down. What's wrong with your side?"

"Broken ribs."

"You rode all the way from the city with broken ribs? Are you crazy?"

Lock lowered himself to the bed, resting his head against the pillow and closing his eyes. "Don't you start shouting at me, too. Sparrow's done enough of that to last me the next ten years."

"Did you win your freedom?"

"If I tell you will you spare me the reprimand?"

Shea-Ann approached with salve for his cuts. "I can't make any promises, but you better start talking, yak."

Lock wasn't sure why, but he was actually grateful to tell someone his side of the story—even if that someone was Shea-Ann.

By the time he finished speaking, Shea-Ann had applied the salve as well as checked his ribs. She stood beside the bed, her hands folded beneath her breasts, and said, "Just like a man."

"What's that supposed to mean?"

"You thought by killing Miska—and I'm glad you did, the brutal bastard—it would please Sparrow. You thought she wanted revenge more than she wanted you."

"It seemed that way. If I'd been in her place—"

"You'd like to see Sparrow risk her life?"

"That's different."

"No, it's not." Shea-Ann placed a hand on his knee. "Lock, a woman prefers a live lover over a dead enemy."

"I wish…"

"What?"

He shook his head, closing his eyes. "Doesn't matter."

No matter what he thought or what he wanted, Sparrow was still furious. At that moment, he was too tired to care.

* * * * *

After Sparrow settled Sea-Storm in the barn, she hauled a bucket of water from the well and headed for the house. Shea-Ann met her halfway.

"Good. I was going to get some water," the old nanny said. "Are you all right? Lock told me everything."

"I don't know what I feel," Sparrow murmured. "I thought he was going to ask for his freedom. I thought he wanted to marry me, that he loved me."

Shea-Ann placed her hands on her hips. "You don't honestly expect me to believe that you don't think he loves you?"

"I don't understand him."

"He wanted to kill that bastard because he loves you. Yes, he made a stupid decision. Yes, he was trying to flaunt his masculinity, but underneath it all, he did it for you."

"I know. Shea-Ann, when he fought, if anything had happened to him, I don't know what I'd have done."

"You should have made him stay in the city at least another day. The ride home with those broken ribs wasn't a good idea. He could have pierced a lung."

"Broken ribs?" Sparrow's eyes widened. "He didn't say anything about broken ribs."

"Broken ribs, half his scalp torn out, all those gashes." Shea-Ann shook her head. "Such stupidity, and all for a woman who doesn't care in the first place."

"Of course I care! If I didn't care, I wouldn't be so angry!"

"Life is so strange," Shea-Ann observed. "When he first came here, I remember you trying to offer him comfort he refused. Now he looks to me like a man in need of a gentle touch and you're in no mind to give it. Oh well. I always said a pirate doesn't deserve kindness."

Shea-Ann walked toward the barn. Sparrow glanced over her shoulder at her friend. She knew what Shea-Ann was trying to do, and it worked. She was right. Though Lock hadn't expressed his love for her in the manner she'd expected, he loved her nonetheless.

In the house, Sparrow filled a wooden bowl with water. She took a soft cloth and moistened it then sat on the edge of the bed. Lock's eyes were closed, his breathing even. She noticed some of his color had returned. When he'd dismounted earlier, his face had been pale as wax. *Mine probably would have been, too, if I'd ridden that far with broken ribs.*

His shirt draped over a nearby chair, and she noted the bandages that swathed his middle. The broken skin on the corner of his mouth still oozed blood and had swelled slightly. Sparrow took the damp cloth and touched it to the swelling.

His eyes flickered open and stared into hers. "The horse all right?"

"He's fine," Sparrow said.

"Are you all right?"

She nodded, her free hand stroking his cheek. Beardless, his blue eyes calm from sleep, he looked uncharacteristically vulnerable. "Why didn't you tell me your ribs are broken? You shouldn't have ridden."

"I wanted to get out of that city. I never want to see it again."

"I love you." She touched her lips to his forehead. She kissed his eyelids then his mouth, gently, avoiding the cut.

He tugged her onto the bed beside him, one arm wrapped around her waist. She closed her eyes and rested her cheek against his bare chest, her fingers lightly tracing his bandaged ribs.

"Thank you for what you did today," she said. "But I'm no killer. Not even for Miska."

"I'm glad. My Sparrow isn't a killer, even for revenge." His voice was soft. "I thought it would make you happy. I was wrong, and I'm sorry."

"You thought you were giving me what I wanted most, but I only want you, Lock."

"Still?"

"Always." She kissed his cheek and took his hand, entwining her fingers with his as they drifted to sleep.

* * * * *

When Sparrow awoke, it was late afternoon. There was work to do, and she was sleeping in the middle of the day! She rubbed her eyes and slipped from Lock's arms, careful not to wake him, and splashed water on her face before stepping outside. Shea-Ann stood in front of the house, scattering seed to chickens.

"At least that damn pirate ship will be setting sail today," Shea-Ann told her. "We're all sick of looking at that nasty ark in our waters."

"Rino's ship?" Sparrow curled her lip as she remembered the pirate. She knew Lock didn't like him at all, and she could understand why. He was sarcastic, obnoxious, and arrogant. She smiled. *Funny Lock should hate a man so like himself.* But at least Lock had a heart beneath all his rough edges.

"They haven't stolen anything and I'm surprised."

"What's to steal?" Sparrow glanced around. "The village is still undergoing repairs from the storm, and it's not as if we're wealthy. If they want to steal, they'd have to go to Begonia, and I don't think Rino is interested in fighting the Empress's army. *I* wouldn't mind fighting her myself."

"You should speak softly when voicing such thoughts," Shea-Ann warned.

"I'd say it about any woman who tried to bed Lock."

"Oh, yes. We both thought that might happen. He used the potion, did he?"

"Yes, but that doesn't make me feel much better. Shea-Ann, you should have seen how he danced."

"Magnificent, wasn't he?"

"Yes, but I wanted to kill everyone in the room. They way they looked at him, the way he enticed them—"

"All the wiles of a SothSea whore." Shea-Ann smiled. "As much as the yak can irritate me, he's stunning in a loincloth."

"Shea-Ann!"

"It's true. And as much as I know you hated seeing him in

the ring, he did the world a favor by killing Miska."

"I know. I just don't like seeing him hurt."

"Truth be told, I'm not keen on it, either. There's something endearing about the yak."

"Lock will be glad to know Rino's ship is leaving. I guess there's rivalry between them."

"What do you want? The Archipelago is full of cutthroats and thieves. If it hadn't been for a whipping that nearly killed him, being taken into slavery and meeting you, he would have continued on as horrible as the rest of them."

"Maybe." Sparrow cast her eyes downward, thinking of the fight with Miska, of the way he'd debased himself for the Empress. "I don't know."

"Sparrow," Shea-Ann placed aside the feed bucket and touched her friend's shoulder, "I know by now the two of you have a unique relationship, but in spite of the affection you have for each other, he's still wild. You'll never completely tame him."

"I don't want to."

Shea-Ann raised an eyebrow.

"Well maybe I want to a little," Sparrow admitted. "I don't want him tame, I just want him safe. I want him to know an honest life can be even more rewarding than being a pirate. You know we met some Knights of the Ruby Order."

"Lock told me."

"It sounds crazy, but I could picture him in one of those tunics."

"The yak? A Knight?" Shea-Ann snorted with laughter then looked thoughtful. "He does have an interest in healing, if he has the stamina to truly study it. And he is a great fighter. If he could stay honest... Those Knights take serious vows. They also enter the front lines of battle to fight and heal. Theirs is not a life without danger."

"I didn't say he was going to become one. I just said he'd

look good in the tunic." Sparrow glanced over her shoulder at the sound of thundering hooves and murmured, "By the goddess..."

Shea-Ann raised a hand against the sunlight, squinting at the approaching riders. "Palace guards, and they're coming this way."

Sparrow's stomach tightened with fear as she guessed what they wanted.

Six guards dressed in the red uniforms of Begonia, mounted on white mares, surrounded Sparrow and Shea-Ann.

"The Empress has sent us to retrieve your slave. She wants him at the palace to replace the gladiator he killed," said one of the guards, the leader according to the gold crescent embroidered on his chest.

"He's wounded and can't travel," Shea-Ann replied.

"He left the city fast enough."

"I'm a healer, and I tell you he can't be moved."

Three of the guards dismounted and strode toward the house. Sparrow ran ahead of them. "You can't take him!"

"We do whatever our Empress orders. Get out of the way, or we'll arrest you." The guard shoved Sparrow aside and stepped into the house. She forced her way past them and stood in front of Lock as he sat up, all traces of sleep vanishing from his face.

"What's this?" he demanded.

"The Empress wants you back at the palace as a gladiator," Sparrow said.

"Do as you're told, slave, or we'll take you in chains."

To Sparrow's surprise, Lock sighed and appeared resigned as he stepped forward. As he walked by the guards toward the door, he kicked backwards, his foot striking one of the guards in the stomach and knocking him into the man behind him. While the third guard drew his blade and shouted for his companions outside, Sparrow picked up the chair by the bed and smashed it over the nearest guard's head. Lock had already wrestled the first guard's blade from his hand and knocked him unconscious. The guard he'd kicked leapt to his feet. His sword clashed with Lock's stolen one just as the three guards rushed through the door, their swords drawn. Two of them joined the man Lock was fighting while the third charged at Sparrow. She leapt over the bed and grabbed a burning log from the fire, rolling aside as the guard's blade smashed against the stone mantle, just missing her head.

Lock kicked the guard who'd attacked Sparrow face first into a wall as he continued fighting the remaining two guards. Sparrow tossed the flaming wood at the men, distracting them while Lock killed one and struck the other unconscious.

Shea-Ann hurried to Sparrow. "Are you all right?"

"I'm fine." Sparrow stepped over one of the bodies toward Lock. His shoulder had been cut by one of the guard's blades, and blood dripped down his arm to the floor.

Immediately Shea-Ann bid him to sit while she cleaned and stitched the injury.

"You have to leave right away," the healer said.

"I can't leave Sparrow. You know what the law states will happen to her."

"I'm going with you," Sparrow said.

"We'll never get away in time. I can't ride fast for very long. Daryn will send more guards and they'll catch us. Damn it! I don't care about myself, but why did I have to put you in danger?"

"The ship," Sparrow said, meeting Shea-Ann's eyes. The healer looked worried, but nodded in agreement.

"What ship?" Lock demanded.

"Rino's pirate ship is setting sail this afternoon. Lock, you can talk to him and get us passage on it."

"Absolutely not," Lock stated.

Sparrow grasped his arm. "It's the only way."

"I can't take you to sea. I told you that."

"Why can't you take me?"

"Remember those dreams I told you about? The ones that come true? I had one about you at sea. There was a storm. Someone was attacking you."

"That doesn't mean it will happen on Rino's ship," Sparrow said, though fear crept down her spine. When Lock had told her about his dreams, she'd been skeptical, not wanting to believe he might possess the power to see into the future. The idea that one of his visions might involve her was more unsettling than she wanted to admit.

"I'm going back to the city," Lock said.

"And do what?" Shea-Ann placed her hands on her hips.

"Whatever the Empress wants. If I have to go back to the ring—"

"No!" Sparrow grasped his arm, her fingers biting into the hard curve of his biceps. "If you go there, I'll attack her myself! Do you want me to be executed for murdering the Empress?"

Lock's startled eyes met hers. "You said you're not a killer."

"I would be if it meant your life." Sparrow's own words shocked her. She would sooner kill Daryn and risk her own life than see Lock as a gladiator.

"We have no time for this foolishness!" Shea-Ann snapped. "These guards will awaken soon. You have to get on board that pirate ship."

"What about you?" Sparrow embraced her friend. "You might be punished if we go."

Shea-Ann shook her head. "I'll say Lock went crazy, took you, threatened me, and escaped. By law, he's your responsibility, not mine. As long as they believe I was forced, I'll be in no danger. Yak, go saddle your horse. I'll help Sparrow pack a few things. You both have to leave right away."

Lock held Sparrow's gaze before he headed for the barn.

Sparrow tossed some of their belongings into a leather bag while Shea-Ann packed food and simple healing supplies. "Lock knows what to do with them."

"I'll miss you, Shea-Ann." Sparrow embraced her old nanny tightly.

Shea-Ann kissed her cheek. "Take care of yourself, Sparrow. I know Lock loves you, but be careful of him. Years of wickedness can't be wiped out in a few months."

"We love each other," Sparrow said. "It'll be enough. It'll have to be."

* * * * *

"I knew it all along, Lock the White!" Rino laughed from where he leaned against the rail of the Lady Fire. "You'd never last as a slave. So now you come crawling to me for passage."

Lock resisted the urge to climb on board and strangle the life from Rino. The man's smug expression and mocking tone twisted his stomach, but boarding the Lady Fire was the only way to escape the Empress's guards. It was the only way for Lock and Sparrow to start a life together. His dream might not even happen. If they could make it to a safe shore, then Sparrow would never have to set foot on another ship again.

"I'll work for passage for me, Sparrow, and this horse."

Rino whistled. "Haven't much room for a horse, but I know you'll do the work of three strong men, and we could use that woman of yours, too. My last cook died of a fever shortly before we landed here."

Lock glanced at Sparrow who murmured, "It's fine with me. We have to hurry."

"When are you sailing?"

"Now."

"Give us permission to board, and you've got yourself a

cook and a crewman."

"Lock, can you handle that kind of work with your ribs?" she whispered.

"There's nothing wrong with me," Lock snapped, though he kept his voice low. "Whatever you do, girl, don't let him know I'm not up to par. He can't be trusted in any way."

Lock noted the concerned look in her eyes, but she nodded and followed him and Sea Storm on board. She glanced over her shoulder toward the hills. Though she couldn't see her farm from the dock, her thoughts were with Shea-Ann. She hoped one day she'd see her old nanny again.

On the deck, Rino approached, his straight red hair hanging down his shoulders like blood, his expression smug as he folded his arms across his chest and said, "Whoever thought you'd be working on my vessel—and bringing me such a lovely cook to boot."

Rino stepped closer to Sparrow, touching her shoulder with a long, grubby index finger.

Lock's stomach tightened and his hands clenched Sea Storm's reins so tightly the leather cut into his palm. He stepped between Sparrow and Rino.

"You better get that mean that look off your face," the Captain's green eyes fixed on Lock's. "This is *my* vessel."

"This is your vessel," Lock's words were even in spite of the rage threatening to boil him from the inside out, "but the woman is *mine*. We understand each other?"

After a moment, Rino smiled easily. "Has she gelded you, Lock? Don't worry about it. There's a world full of women. I don't need to steal yours. One of my men will show you where to keep the horse and bring the woman to the galley."

"My name is Sparrow."

Rino ignored her and turned away. "You're really going to earn your keep, Lock. Every pirate in the Archipelago would love to be me at this moment, having Lock the White scrubbing his deck."

"I hate him," Sparrow whispered to Lock.

"I won't let anything happen to you. I promise. I'll kill him first."

"Don't start talking mutiny already. All we have to do is make it to the next port, right?"

"The next port," he said. With his luck, the next port would be a month away.

Chapter Twenty

ဢ

Lock clenched his teeth as he hoisted the anchor, his ribs screaming against the motion. When he finished, he joined several other crewmen in clearing space for the barrels of wine expected at the next port.

Rino approached, nodding at the blood seeping through Lock's sleeve. "Wounded, are you?"

"Scratch." Lock tied a fast, secure knot on a crate and tugged the next one into place.

Rino's lips twisted into a grin. "Where'd you get that sword? Looks like a familiar design."

"Belongs to the Begonian guard who gave me the scratch."

The red-haired pirate threw back his head and laughed. He punched Lock in the shoulder. "Ain't changed a bit, Lock the White."

"Neither have you."

Rino suddenly strode across the deck and grasped the arm of a lanky young crewman drinking from a wooden mug. "What the hell's that?"

"Water, Cap'n."

Reno sniffed the mug's contents. His green eyes narrowed and his teeth gleamed as he snarled, "Expensive water, boy. Stealing from the barrels below and drinking it right on deck?"

"No, Cap'n Rino. I—"

Rino dragged the boy across the deck, picked him up over his head, and flung him overboard.

Lock noticed several crew members—probably new—

staring with wide eyes at Rino. Sparrow, who had emerged from below carrying a bucket, watched with a frozen expression as the boy shrieked and splashed in the water below. She took a step toward Rino. "You can't just throw someone overboard like that! You—"

Rino laughed at her and many men joined him.

"That's what I get for letting a woman on board." Rino placed his hands on his hips. "Little beauty, that's what happens to *anyone* who doesn't follow my rules. Any Captain worth his salt keeps control of his vessel, ain't that right, Lock?"

"Sparrow, get over here," Lock called, keeping his eyes focused on the knot he was tying.

"Keep that woman in line, Lock!" Rino bellowed. "Or else *I'll* have to do it!"

"Lock, how can everybody just stand by while that man drowns?"

Lock's fierce blue eyes met hers. "Keep your mouth shut, girl. That crewman stole cargo. I'd have done the same as Rino."

Sparrow blinked. "I can't believe—"

"Think I haven't done it? Think any man in charge of a ship like this hasn't done it? This ain't a farmhouse in Begonia, Sparrow. Keep your mouth shut, do what I tell you, and we'll get to the next port safe enough."

Sparrow's chest rose and fell with agitated breathing. She hissed through clenched teeth. "I *hate* this."

"It'll be over and done before you know it."

"Your arm is bleeding. Let me check it for you."

Lock glanced at his sleeve. The arm hurt much less than his ribs.

"Hey, woman!" A short, thickly built man with balding black hair and a mangy beard shouted to Sparrow. "Got squid for you here!"

257

"Dinner," Sparrow muttered. "I'll be back to take care of your arm."

"Don't bother. I've got plenty more work to do, and it'll only tear open again. Fix it later."

"But—"

"I said fix it later!" Lock snarled.

Sparrow turned on her heel, but not before her eyes flashed rage at him.

He knew he shouldn't have been so short with her, but the idea that she'd been forced on the Lady Fire and was surrounded by scum like... *like me.*

He had to make sure she knew how important it was not to incite Rino's anger. If he was forced to defend Sparrow against the Captain, he'd have to kill him. There would be no other way. And if he took the Lady Fire—a ship as fine as his own had once been—he wasn't sure he could let it go.

* * * * *

"I can't believe this!" Sparrow muttered, slapping fat squid into an enormous pot. "Bunch of animals! Tossing people overboard! Cursing like...devils!"

For the brief moments she'd spent on deck, she'd heard more vile language than she had in her lifetime—except a few words from Lock when he was angry.

Sparrow had only been on the ship for two days, and already she hated it. She spent most of her time in the stuffy, smelly kitchen—*galley*—but at least there she could avoid the crew. Between their scuffles, bellowing, and bawdy songs, she was ready to leap overboard herself. Twice a day, she was forced to distribute the food she cooked, mostly fish and squid, but also beans, hard, flat bread, and some fruit. Though the men said little to her, she felt their eyes on her as soon as she stepped on deck. Their expressions of lust made her uncomfortable. She knew it wasn't because she was an incredibly beautiful woman, but because she was the only woman on board. Still, no one approached her, and she knew it was because they feared Lock. They feared his reputation, his size and strength. They feared the harsh expression in his pale blue eyes.

Truthfully, for the first time in months, he frightened her as well. Almost as soon as they boarded, he'd become distant, cold. Hard. She knew he had to act rough as a matter of survival—both his and hers, but she missed the Lock she'd fallen in love with. She missed the farm, Shea-Ann, and Daphne. She missed sharing her bed with Lock. Two days they'd been on the ship and he hadn't slept. He worked all day with the crew and Rino had given him a double watch at night.

She hated Rino. *Hated him*!

He was so envious of Lock his face was nearly as green as those fiendish eyes that undressed Sparrow every time she crossed his path. The other men looked at her with desire, but Rino was worse. Rino looked as if he wanted to tear her apart like a beast in heat then toss her bleeding carcass into the sea. Lock was right not to trust him, and though he'd promised to keep her safe, she wondered if he really could. Several hundred men made up Rino's crew. How could Lock defend her against so many?

She stirred the pot and began mixing ingredients to make more flatbread. Once she distributed the meal and cleaned up, she could go to sleep for the night. Hopefully Lock would join her. Rino had to let him sleep sometime. Sparrow was more concerned for his injured ribs than his lack of sleep. She'd given up worrying about his shoulder. After two attempts at stitching and bandaging it, he'd had her cauterize the gash. She'd nearly been sick when she'd burned the oozing, inflamed skin, again thinking how she'd never want to be a healer. He'd told her how to treat the wound with an herbal paste from Shea-Ann, and she prayed it would be enough to ward off infection.

"Infection, broken ribs," she muttered, using her shoulder

to brush a loose tendril of hair from her face. "I'll just be happy if he *lives* to see the next port."

He was so stubborn! The last time she'd gone on deck, she'd discreetly asked how he was feeling, and he'd snapped, "Fine! I'm busy."

She told herself he was as worried as she was and he must have been tired and sore, but still his tone had wounded her. She felt completely alone on a ship full of animals—her own lover being nearly as bad as the rest.

It was nearly dusk when she lugged food onto the deck. Men grabbed bowls and chunks of bread, nearly trampling her as they snatched, slurped, chewed, and belched. Sparrow curled her lip in disgust and approached Lock who stood by the main mast knotting a spiky length of rope.

"Here." She extended a bowl to him.

He tossed the rope aside and took the bowl. His hand brushed hers, rough and dirty, yet it made her tingle inside. The setting sun cast reddish shadows on his face. She noted his jaw and chin were stubbled from the beard growing in. Beneath his dark skin, his face looked unusually haggard. Still, his pale eyes gleamed with fury whenever Rino passed.

"I won't ask how you are." Sparrow tried to sound aloof.

Lock cupped her face in his hand, his thumb gently stroking her cheek.

"If you're gonna hump her, take her below!" Laughed a short, sturdily built man to Lock's left, exposing a missing tooth in his skinny lips.

Lock's elbow shot backwards into the man's face. The crewman dropped the bread he was eating and clutched his mouth. He leaned over the deck and spat blood. "Bastard! You knocked out my other front tooth!"

"Be glad I didn't knock off your head!"

"He'd do it, too," said a gravel-voiced, gray-haired man seated by Sparrow's feet. He chewed on a hard piece of bread. "Sailed with him on the Shana Whore once. Seen him knock off heads, chop off hands, and other things that would make you think twice 'bout crossing him. Lock the White. Never thought we'd be working the same deck."

"Just 'till the next port, he says." A third man -rather short-legged for one so tall, giving him the look of an ape— joined their group. "Ain't that right, Lock? Then Rino be rid of you."

The gray-haired man snickered. "Ain't so sure Rino wants to be rid of him. I think he likes him where he is." He glanced at Sparrow. "Heard you bought him out of slavery, girlie. That so?"

Sparrow placed a hand on her hip and lifted her chin. "I know a good hunk of manflesh when I see it."

Lock raised an eyebrow and the men laughed.

"I like you," said the ape-man. "You got spirit. You'll need it on the Lady Fire."

Sparrow glanced at Lock before she gathered the empty bowls to clean below deck. His gaze swept her once from head to foot before he turned back to his work.

Several hours later, Sparrow curled up on a blanket in the corner of the galley. Tired, she closed her eyes, though she found it difficult to relax in the midst of such a crew.

She'd begun drifting off when she felt the presence of another in the room.

"Who's there?" she demanded, reaching for the rolling pin she kept close to her blanket.

"It's all right. Just me," Lock said, groaning softly as he settled beside her.

"You must be exhausted."

"Wouldn't be so bad if my ribs weren't killing me."

"You're never going to heal like this."

"I'm fine."

"You keep saying that." Sparrow offered him part of the blanket.

He tugged her against his chest.

"I smell like fish," she said.

"Who doesn't? Kiss me."

"Won't that destroy your illusion of frigidity with your mates up on deck?"

"I said before sarcasm doesn't suit you. Just kiss me."

Sparrow slid up his body and touched her mouth to his. His lips were soft as she remembered. She kissed his upper lip then his lower before placing her mouth over his, her tongue slipping into his moist heat. He buried a hand in her hair as his tongue met hers. When the kiss broke, he lay beneath her in silence, his breathing slow and even.

Thinking he was asleep, she lit a lantern and unbuttoned his shirt to examine his ribs.

"I'll be fine," he murmured.

Her eyes shot to his. She unraveled the bandage, exposing a bruise that discolored most of his side. "That's awful. Lock, this is crazy. You can't—"

"I've had worse. Remember? Don't worry about it."

She moistened a cloth with cold seawater and placed it on his side.

"Everything's my fault anyway." His eyes slipped shut. "If I'd have asked the Empress for my freedom like you wanted me to, you wouldn't be here."

"I don't think so, Lock." She smoothed a loose white curl from his forehead. "I think once she saw you, she'd have tried to take you for herself no matter what. You wanted to avenge Thea for me. No one's ever done anything like that for me before."

"I'd do just about anything for you." He took her hand and entwined his fingers with hers as he fell asleep.

Sparrow kissed his cheek and rested her head against his shoulder. "I love you."

* * * * *

Lock awoke with Sparrow still cuddled beside him. The ship was silent, and he guessed it was several hours before dawn. His body ached and he dreaded the coming weeks. Without the possibility of resting his injuries, work would be painful – and plentiful, no doubt. He and Rino had hated each other for years, and had their positions been reversed, Lock would have treated Rino no better. His own discomfort meant little to him, however. The thought of Sparrow trapped on the Lady Fire twisted his gut. She didn't belong on a pirate ship with a bunch of stinking SothSea pigs. Sparrow was too good for that.

"Lock?" she whispered.

"Yeah?"

"I thought you'd sleep right through." Her fingers stroked the hair at his temples then moved to his chest.

"Hard to sleep when I'm spending so much time thinking. I'm sorry you ended up here."

"There's no use worrying about it. Once we dock, everything will be all right."

"You know what I'm thinking now?"

"Tell me."

"That I wish we were back on your farm in your bed." He tugged her close and whispered in her ear. "I wish my ribs were good so I could fuck you into oblivion."

"Umm. That sounds so good." She slipped down his body and tugged at his trousers.

"What the hell are you doing, girl?"

"It's the least I can do after you risked your life to kill Miska."

Lock's cock popped free and Sparrow's warm fist closed around it while her other hand grasped his balls and gently squeezed.

He drew a sharp breath, his eyes slipping shut against the pleasure of her touch. "Are you crazy? We can't do this now, Sparrow."

"Shh," she breathed against his cock head.

Lock's heart pounded when her soft, moist lips closed over the tip of his cock. Her tongue tickled the head then ran from top to base and back again. She lapped the length of him and swirled her tongue around the head. Resisting the urge to moan his pleasure, Lock's hands sifted through her hair. He tried not to squeeze her head too hard, difficult when she began sucking him so deep into her mouth he thought she might swallow his cock.

Lock's back arched and his head sank into the blankets as she lapped, sucked, and tickled his cock.

"Sparrow, you better stop," he gasped, trying to keep his voice hushed. "I can't take much more."

Ignoring him, she continued her carnal work. The sensations flooding Lock's body and concentrating around his engorged cock were enough to make his eyes cross, if they'd been open. He couldn't have forced them open if he wanted to. Trying his best to keep his panting quiet, his hands gripped her head and his hips thrust in ecstasy. He exploded, his neck throbbing and heart hammering. Somewhere in the mix of pleasure, he realized his ribs ached, but not nearly enough to keep him from enjoying one of the best orgasms of his life. Perhaps it was the danger of being discovered, or the idea that she still loved him after all, but it was a climax he'd never forget.

He lay for several moments, nearly asleep. Sparrow curled up beside him and kissed his cheek.

"I owe you, girl," he murmured.

"One day I intend to collect."

"You can wager on it."

* * * * *

Rino spat a mouthful of stew into the sea, wiped a gnarled hand across his mouth and narrowed his eyes in Sparrow's direction. "Tastes like shit."

"I can only cook with what you give me."

"Put more spice in it. Cover the taste of the eel."

Sparrow snatched the bowl from his hand. "Too much spice is not good for your stomach."

Rino grasped her upper arm and ran a tongue over his lips. "Just do what I tell you, woman."

Sparrow tugged away and walked below deck, an unsettled feeling in her breast. They'd been on the ship for almost a week, and neither Rino nor the other men had touched her. Oh, they made rude comments and the occasional bawdy gesture, but she attributed the lack of serious assault to Lock's presence. Even the Captain knew better than to push her too far. He knew Lock had little choice but to obey him, but Sparrow sensed a part of Rino didn't want to risk inciting Lock's wrath. Perhaps Rino was beginning to relax and realize she and Lock had little choice about his treatment of either of them. He kept Lock so busy that even on board the ship, she scarcely saw him. When she did, her worry only increased. Though he never complained, he didn't look well. She knew his ribs hadn't healed and had probably worsened due to heavy labor. He needed rest, but she knew he wasn't about to get it any time soon. Lock had said he wouldn't have been able to ride fast or far enough to escape the Empress's guards, but surely the work Rino forced on him was worse than riding would have been. Still, according to Lock, they were far safer at sea than on land. Sparrow wasn't so sure.

I wish I could put poison in Rino's stew, Sparrow thought as she stepped into the galley. The water was rough that morning, but the motion didn't affect her. If she hadn't been so miserable, she would have enjoyed sailing—not stuck below, but up on deck with the salty wind blowing and spray from the water cooling her face. During a few brief moments with Lock one afternoon when he'd called her to the rail and pointed to dolphins playing in the water, he'd said she was a "born sailor." She'd been a bit concerned about seasickness at first, having heard awful stories about it from Shea-Ann. Fortunately ship travel agreed with her.

"Complaining about the food," Sparrow muttered as she dumped handfuls of spice into a smaller pot of stew, just for Rino. "I'll burn his filthy tongue off. Maybe his insides will rot out. Putrid bastard."

She paused and shook her head. Her tongue was becoming as vile as the other crewmen's.

"Eh there, girlie." The ape-like man stepped into the galley. A red scarf tied at his nape half concealed his stringy black hair. His short legs were covered in cutoff pants that made them appear even shorter. He made an almost comical character, but Sparrow had to admit she rather liked him. He never spoke to her rudely and often volunteered to bring her buckets of water and fish to cook with.

"I told you my name's Sparrow." She cast him a half smile.

"You ain't never called me Ilias."

"You're right. I'm sorry, Ilias."

"No matter." He shrugged and stole a chunk of fish from the pot. His eyes teared as he spat into his hand. "Bloody hell! Too much spice, don't you think?"

"Captain's request." She touched his shoulder. "Don't worry. I made a special pot just for him."

Ilias dropped the chewed food from his hand back into the small pot and winked. "Don't tell him I done that, Sparrow, else he'll toss me over."

"I won't say a word."

* * * * *

"You know what I hate most about you, Lock?" Rino leaned against the foremast, watching Lock as he mopped the deck.

"If I don't ask, are you still going to tell me?"

"I hate how you always thought you were so much better than the rest of us. You were never just interested in spoils and cargo like normal people. You stopped at places and *talked* to *people*. Thought you were so smart cause you can read and write. You thought yourself royalty, and you're the worst of us all. No matter how many languages you speak or whether you know the history of the bloody Kennas, you're still nothing but an Archipelago whore, no better than the bitch who spat you out of her pock-ridden chute."

"The pocks she had she most likely got from you, Rino. I get a clear memory of two years ago. You standing in back of a SothSea tavern pissin' enough fire to keep a lighthouse burning for a year."

Rino laughed long and loud. "Then I been with your mama for sure. You was probably born pissin' fire. How'd you end up with that pretty little girl of yours? She's got the muscle of a farmer but the manner of a Lady. How did you convince her to buy you, or do I even want to know?"

Lock glanced at the deck, his hands tightening on the mop. Two seconds it would take him to ram the handle up the Captain's ass. Two seconds to start a brawl that would end in someone's death. Two seconds that might leave Sparrow at the mercy of Rino.

"You know what I think, Lock?" Rino grinned. "I think that little girl means more to you than a good bed-warming. I think she's got to you."

Lock glared into Rino's eyes. "I think now's a good time to stop talking about her."

Rino whistled. "I don't believe it. You're moonin' after a woman who bought you as her *slave*. You know she really can't think you're good enough for her. Women like that bed down men like us for one reason, Lock, and I thought you'd be smart enough to know it. She thinks you'll show her something wild, and I'm sure you already have. She'll get bored of you and look for someone else to fill up that innocent side of her with stone-black lust."

"Has it really been so long since you've had a woman that you spend this much time thinking about her?"

"Feeling for a woman can kill a man, Lock. Remember that."

Lock watched Rino as he sauntered away. *Feeling for her surely can kill a man, Rino, and I think that man will be you.*

* * * * *

Sparrow nearly stumbled as she hung pans on the metal hooks in the galley. The sea felt especially rough that night. Above, the crash of thunder joined the sound of waves smashing against the side of the ship. It had been hours since she'd last seen anyone, and in spite of the storm raging above, she needed to find out what was happening.

She no sooner stepped on deck when the wind struck her, strong enough to nearly push her back below. Fat drops of ice-cold rain shot from the black sky. Crewmen scattered across the deck, securing the sails and checking the ropes on cargo.

"Turn her about!" A familiar voice bellowed from the crow's nest. Sparrow glanced up at Lock who clung to the mast with one arm while the other pointed to a small island of jagged rocks in the distance. "Move! We're going to run aground!"

The ship swung fast. Sparrow grasped the rail, her heart pounding as she nearly fell overboard.

"Sparrow!" Lock shouted. "Get back below! I—"

He stopped speaking, his eyes fixed on the distance. Sparrow as well as many other crewmen glanced in the direction he was looking. A spiral of wind, even blacker than the sky, churned across the sea.

"Goddess help us," Sparrow murmured, clinging harder to the rail as an enormous wave crashed over the deck. She closed her eyes tightly as water soaked her. Her fingers slipped, but she managed to hang on.

Someone grasped her waist hauled her toward the hatch.

"Get below, Sparrow," Ilias told her, his brown eyes worried. "This is bad."

He joined the others, and Sparrow glanced up at Lock. The crow's nest swayed precariously, and she wondered how he still held his footing after the last wave.

"Get out of our way!" Rino brushed by her, almost knocking her down the hatch. The Captain paused, grasping her arm and hauling her back on deck. "Second thought, we need all the hands we can get. Check those knots."

He flung her between two crates while she plotted his death.

A bolt of lightning ripped through the sky and struck the topmast. It splintered and crashed onto the deck, pinning a crewman beneath. Sparrow gasped as the man's terrified eyes fixed on hers, blood spurting from his mouth and nose. The mast had crushed him from the middle.

The tornado whirled across the sea, rising high then dipping to touch the waves. Another wave covered the boat. Sparrow felt the water pushing her across the deck. She reached for a loose end of rope and held fast. She looked up to the crow's nest and felt her stomach drop to the bottom of the sea. Half the rails were ripped away and Lock was no longer in it.

A body suddenly covered hers. Teeth tore at her ear and a hand buried in her hair.

Rino's breath hissed close to her cheek. "Think we're rid of him, girlie, and when this storm is over, it'll be you and me." He punctuated his last words with painful thrusts of his cock against her backside.

* * * * *

Panting, Lock released the sail and dropped onto the slippery deck. Gut feeling had told him to abandon the crow's nest before the next wave hit. With the help of the knife he carried in his boot, he had managed to climb down the sail. He glanced around for Sparrow, the wind and rain rendering him almost blind. He bellowed for her before another wave crashed over the deck. Grasping the wooden rail, he managed to keep his footing as he saw several men tumble overboard into the dark, churning water.

"Sparrow!" he bellowed again. The pounding of his heart caused his ribs to ache even more. Once again, his nightmare— *his vision*—was coming true. He'd been unable to protect Sparrow from what he'd foreseen.

Suddenly, he caught sight of her lying on deck, covered by Rino's hulking form. Her fingers stretched for a slab of wood splintered from one of the fallen masts. She smashed it across the Captain's face. He fell aside. As she scrambled across the deck, he reached for her ankle and dragged her toward him.

Lock ran across the neck, but the ship tilted and he caught the mast to keep his footing. Sparrow and Rino struggled together. He saw Rino wrap her hair around his massive fist and pull. Ignoring the pain exploding across his ribs, Lock dove at Rino, his hands clutching the Captain's thick neck as he squeezed while his knee rammed into Rino's ribs.

The redhead bellowed in pain and rolled backwards, freeing Sparrow. Lock held fast as the men skidded across the deck. Another wave struck, and they slipped toward the rail. In the skirmish, they'd changed positions and faced each other, each with his hands around the other's neck. Rino's green eyes spat hatred into Lock's, but the look only flared Lock's rage. Since he'd stepped on board, he'd wanted to kill Rino but had managed to hold his temper until he'd seen the Captain on Sparrow.

Around them men shouted and thunder clapped. The wind was overpowering as the tornado neared. As Lock and Rino grappled, the ship tilted again, flinging them both overboard. Amazingly, each caught the rail, his feet dangling.

"Lock!" Sparrow shrieked and leapt toward him. His heart nearly burst through his chest in fear of her slipping, but the ape-like crewman caught her waist before another wave crashed.

"Son of a bitch!" Rino bellowed at Lock, his voice nearly lost in the wind. He kicked Lock who was grateful his broken ribs were on the other side. He doubted he could have held the rail otherwise. His leg lashed out in a kick, the ball of his foot striking Rino in the head. The Captain lost his grip and fell into the sea.

Summoning the last of his strength, Lock pulled himself on deck where he sat on his knees, panting, every breath painful. He crawled toward Sparrow and Ilias as the tornado approached, dipping its funnel into the water. Rino disappeared into the heart of the fierce, black storm. The crew clung to the ship, everyone watching in terrified silence, waiting to be blown apart by the tornado. It passed them and continued across the sea.

"Lock!" Sparrow reached for him. He pulled her close, resting his cheek against her wet blond hair.

If any gods or goddesses exist, thank you, he thought. He glanced at Ilias who sat with his back against one of the crates, looking bewildered. "Thank you," Lock said to the man.

Ilias shook his head. "Couldn't let her go over. She makes the best squid of any cook we've had...Captain."

Lock glanced around, aware that most of the men were watching him, waiting for his next action. He'd killed Rino, and by the unwritten laws of the SothSea pirates, he was now the Captain of the Lady Fire.

* * * * *

Though the tornado had passed, the sea was still fierce and Sparrow stumbled as Lock guided her below.

"Where did you put the bag from Shea-Ann?" he asked.

"In the galley." Sparrow pressed a hand to her ear, feeling warm blood against her cold fingers. She still felt the sting of Rino's teeth, and she shuddered with horror and disgust.

"Sit there." Lock, still holding her hand, brought her to a corner of the galley.

"Are you all right?" she asked. "I thought you were going to fall overboard with Rino."

"Not from the lack of his trying." Lock stooped beside her and chose a jar filled with herbal paste. He gently took her face in one hand and tilted it sideways so he could better examine her ear. She wondered how he could see in the unlit galley, since they dared not light a lantern while the storm still rocked the ship.

"How bad is it?"

He half smiled. "It won't kill you, unless you get mad dog disease from Rino."

"What?" Sparrow felt her heart drop.

"Just a bad joke, girl. You'll be all right." He cleaned the wound and applied the paste. When he'd finished, he brushed her mouth with his and stroked a tendril of sea-soaked hair from her eyes. "Stay here and rest. I'm going topside to get this ship back in order. As soon as the storm clears, we'll start repairs as well as we can."

As he stood to go, Sparrow reached for him and buried her face in his chest. Her arms tightened around him, and she felt him flinch slightly as the gesture squeezed his ribs. She loosened her grip and looked up at him. "Let me wrap those again before you go up."

He agreed, removing his wet shirt and unraveling bandage beneath. She took a dry one from the bag and bound his middle. When she'd finished, she rested her hand against his muscular chest, feeling his heartbeat against her palm.

Injured and all, his body was still a marvel of male beauty. If she hadn't been so tired, frightened, and worried, she would have wanted him then and there.

She felt her own concerns combined with attraction in the kiss he pressed to her mouth before leaving the galley.

Chapter Twenty-One

🔊

Sparrow sighed, rubbing one of her sore palms with her other aching hand. She sat on her heels and glanced around the hold at the trunks she'd just secured. Most of them had held through the storm, but Lock wanted the ropes checked again.

Lock wanted the ship repaired yesterday. If possible, he was even more diligent running the ship than he had been rebuilding the village. He was as hard on every crewman as he was on himself.

Early that morning, once the storm had passed and everyone knew Rino was dead, Sparrow had sensed tension on board. All the crewmen, first mate included, accepted Lock as the new leader—except for the second mate. At the man's first gesture of rebellion, Lock had, to Sparrow's horror, run him through with the short sword he'd taken from the Empress's guard and flung the carcass overboard. The crewmen had watched then gone about their work, attempting to turn the ship back on course and make as many repairs as they could under Lock's direction.

"You had to kill him?" Sparrow had snapped. Several of the men glanced at Lock with raised eyebrows, wondering how their new captain would react to demands from a woman.

"Get back to work, or else you'll be swimming to shore, wherever the hell it is!" Lock had growled at the men, causing backs to turn and heads to lower over busy hands. Remote blue eyes met Sparrow's. "Any act against my authority is as good as an act against my life. It's an unwritten law of the Archipelago. Every man here knows about it. We have work to do, Sparrow. I need you below."

She turned on her heel and stormed down the hatch. Halfway to the galley, Lock caught her arm and tugged her toward a hold. "In here. I'll teach you how to check these knots."

"Take your hand off me!" She'd shoved him.

"You never minded my hands before."

She'd drawn a deep breath, closed her eyes, and willed her temper under control. "That was before you started booting people overboard every half hour."

"I tossed two men: one of them threatened me, the other threatened you. Would you have rather I let Rino rip you apart?"

"I can't wait until we land somewhere and get away from this ship!"

"I would have thought you'd be in a bigger hurry to get away when Rino was Captain. Now at least you're as safe as can be. We can go anywhere we want in this ship."

"What do you mean?"

"I mean, we're no longer running, girl. We have the means to survive and survive well."

"Lock, this isn't your ship."

"Ain't it? I damn near drowned securing it, I'll say that makes it mine." He'd held her eyes, and by his expression noted the anger and disbelief she felt. "Just get to work, Sparrow. We can talk about it when she's back on course."

"Oh, we'll talk about it, Lock! You can wager on it!"

Sparrow pressed her palms to her eyes. That conversation hadn't gone well at all, and since then she hadn't spoken to Lock other than brief words regarding repairs. Part of her understood his hard manner toward the crew. They were a bunch of pirates who would as soon cut out a man's heart as look at him, but his new attitude bothered her. When they'd first met, he'd been like an animal, but after months together, he'd become human. They'd laughed and talked. They'd fallen in love. Now he'd reverted to the animal again, and if they stayed on board the Lady Fire, Sparrow was afraid she'd lose *her* Lock forever.

* * * * *

Sparrow slowly climbed onto the deck, her body aching and her ear stinging. Though she'd managed to get some rest the previous night when Lock had taken her to the galley, it had been a light, agitated sleep, and now she felt more than ready for bed. Lock hadn't slept at all, but as she stepped into the sunlight, she noticed him standing by the mast speaking to the first mate. His legs were spread in a wide stance, his feet planted firmly on the swaying deck. His arms were folded across his broad chest, the long, curved muscles visible in the mist-dampened tan vest he wore. Thick brown and white hair blew like knotted spirals around his shoulders and across his face. She knew he must have felt tired, but in spite of his injuries and lack of sleep, he looked strong enough to fight an army of Rinos.

"Come here, girl!" he called.

She resisted the urge to turn away from him and go back below. She approached, glaring at him.

He smiled and reached out to touch her face, but she stepped way. "What do you want?"

The first mate—a man of middle height and sturdy build—watched her with amused brown eyes. Lock ignored the man's expression and said to Sparrow, "Nice morning."

"For some, maybe."

The mate smiled. "I like this woman, Captain."

"So do I, if you get my meaning," Lock growled.

The man shook long, black hair over his shoulder as he walked away.

"What is wrong with you?" Sparrow demanded. "All he did was make a comment."

"Let him make it about some other woman, not about mine." Lock grasped her arms and kissed her before she had a chance to refuse. She stiffened, but as his lips gently moved against hers, his tongue tenderly tracing the shape of her mouth, she forced herself not to melt into his arms. He whispered against her ear. "You're mine, Sparrow, and I've made sure every man on this ship knows it. There won't be a repeat of what Rino did do you. Believe me."

"I'm more concerned with what Rino did to you."

"To me?"

"You're changing, Lock." She held his eyes, her fingers braced against his shoulders.

"I'm doing what I have to. Believe me about that, too." He released her, his gaze sweeping the deck. Men stood at their posts while others sat or gazed over the rails. All looked worn, and several were injured. Lock strode to the quarter deck and bellowed for attention. Sparrow stood beside Ilias as Lock spoke. "Last night's storm did damage. You all know that, but we're in decent shape. As soon as we dock and make repairs, we'll make this ship the most formidable vessel to sail out of the Archipelago. This benefits me and that means it benefits you. Some of you know me. You know I'm not easy. What I am is fair. Work with me, and you'll all go home rich men."

Sparrow noted the pirates' weary expressions turning to ones of interest. The crew shouted and cheered at Lock's words. He held up his hands for silence, and they obeyed.

"Work against me, and the bottom of the sea will be your home. Now keep this ship headed North." Lock stepped back onto the main deck and glanced at the first mate. "Mingo, you have her. I'll be in my cabin shoveling out Rino's shit." He took Sparrow's hand. "Come with me, girl."

If Lock's speech had pleased the crew, it unsettled Sparrow. What did he mean, they'd all go home rich men? Surely he didn't intend to continue pirating? What about they plans they'd made? What about marriage?

As they disappeared below, Sparrow tugged her hand from his. She was losing the man she loved. Perhaps he'd never really existed at all.

* * * * *

In the Captain's cabin—a small room, but far more comfortable than anywhere else on the ship—Lock bolted the door. He sat on the bed and tugged his shirt over his head, pausing in the middle of the motion, his ribs most likely hurting.

"We need to talk." Sparrow folded her arms across her chest and paced the cabin.

"Sparrow, I have to get some rest."

She glanced at him, noting his eyes were lined with fatigue, but he'd put on a fine show of power on deck. Besides, she was far too angry to sympathize with any discomfort he might be feeling.

"You asked me to marry you, now you want to make me some nautical whore on this floating den of wolves?"

"I don't recall saying I didn't want us to get married."

"So what do you want to do, Lock? Take wedding vows then go out pirating?"

"I'm a pirate."

"*Were.*"

"Unless you haven't noticed, I'm Captain of this vessel. What would you have me do? Sink it to suit you?"

She stared at him in open-mouthed shock. When she recovered, she unlocked the door, but he grasped her arm and slipped the bolt back into place.

"Let go of me! I can't stand to look at you right now, Lock!"

"Sparrow, I don't expect you to stay on this ship forever. I'll take you home."

"Home where? To the Archipelago?"

"I have a nice house, a secluded beach. You'd probably like it there. You'd be safe."

"Jailed by those eunuch slaves you once told me about? Maybe I can assist your mother at the brothel and help with the family profits!"

Lock's eyes flashed rage and he walked back to the bed and lay down. "Come here and get some sleep. When you've calmed down we can talk about it."

"I'm never going to calm down, Lock! You lied to me. You said you were going to try to make an honest life."

"With this ship, we can make an honest life. We can trade instead of pillage."

"Stop lying to me! This is a ship full of cutthroats, and you're the worst of them all!"

"Things look quite different when you're out of your own territory, don't they?"

"What?"

"Everything was fine for you when I was chained to the wall washing dishes. Now that I'm free again, it's harder to ignore the facts I've been telling you since the day we met."

"I never wanted you chained to my wall, Lock! It was you who drove me to it, and you're as unreasonable now as you were then! I thought you'd changed. I thought you cared about me."

"I care about you more than anything."

"Then prove it." She sat on the edge of the bed and rested her palms on his chest, staring into his pale blue eyes. "Leave this ship with me as soon as we dock. If you don't, it'll destroy us."

He tugged her onto the bed beside him and kissed her forehead. "It's not that easy. The Lady Fire is my responsibility now."

"Give it to one of the others. Ilias, maybe."

Lock laughed. "Ilias? He's a good enough crewman, but too soft. He wouldn't last a day in charge of this vessel. One thing about a pirate ship, girl, only a bastard can run it right. I fit the description in every way, if you get my meaning."

"You're a good man deep inside. I remember how you rebuilt our village, and not for any profit." She touched his face and spoke with more confidence than she felt. "I know you'll do the right thing."

She saw a flicker of emotion in his eyes — guilt, maybe?

Resting her cheek against his shoulder, she listened to the evenness of his breathing. Only when she was certain he was asleep did she turn her back to him and cry.

It seemed to take hours for Sparrow to fall asleep. Finally she succumbed to the ship's gentle rocking and the pleasant feeling of Lock's warm body so close to hers. He'd lied to her and probably to himself, but she still loved him. She had to get him away from the ship, or else the man he'd become might be lost forever. He had the potential to be good, but the temptation of the Lady Fire was like a disease to him. She'd seen some people addicted to wagering on anything from dice games to horse-races. They bore the same crazy look in their eyes as Lock when he played the part of Captain. It seemed piracy was a more terrible vice than she'd ever imagined.

When Sparrow awoke, Lock lay beside her, staring at her.

"Is it time to get up already?" she asked.

"Stay and sleep if you want. I'll be going on deck in a while."

"I'll get back to work, too."

"Wait." Lock tugged off the blanket and raised her dress.

"What are you doing?" she demanded.

"I owe you."

"Lock, we can't—"

"Why not? We're alone. No one will bother us. Besides, you once did the same to me under more dangerous circumstances."

She relaxed. He was right. The danger of Rino was past, but the newer danger frightened her even more. The danger of losing Lock to pirating forever.

"I've missed being alone with you, girl," he whispered.

He pressed soft kisses to her inner thighs while he massaged the backs of her knees with his fingertips. His tongue traced the indentation between her pelvis and thighs. Instinctively, Sparrow's hands grasped handfuls of his hair. She shivered when his tongue tickled her perineum then ran along her pussy lips. It slipped inside her, swirling and licking.

She moaned softly, hoping none of the crew could hear. Lock grasped her waist, stroking and squeezing as he continued exploring the delicate folds of moist flesh. His lips tugged gently at her clit before he sucked it.

"Oh, Lock!" Sparrow panted.

Again the tip of his tongue poked inside her. One of his hands cupped her buttocks. He pressed a finger to her anus while he lapped her clit with frustrating gentleness.

Sparrow's legs trembled and she wiggled beneath him. His strong hands held her firmly in place as he lapped her to a quaking climax. Before the last ripples of pleasure coursed through her, he slid up her body, guiding her legs to a bent-knee position and crossing them in front of his chest as his cock pushed into her liquid pussy. The strange position felt surprisingly good. It must have to him as well since, when Sparrow opened her eyes a slit to watch him, his own were closed, his expression euphoric.

"I've wanted you so much, Sparrow," he said, his voice rough with passion.

"You, too, Lock," she admitted. "I've wanted you so much it's almost painful."

"It has been painful," he sounded almost breathless as his thrusting increased.

Sparrow felt another orgasm building. She clutched the

sheet beside her, moaning and gasping as she came. He tensed, thrusting hard and fast, before stiffening and crying out his own climax.

Sparrow sighed with contentment. At least some things hadn't changed.

Chapter Twenty-Two

ഇ

The following week brought calm seas and sunny days, a welcome relief after the storm. The Lady Fire's major damages were fixed, and the crew awaited some sign of land to replenish supplies and make the last of the repairs.

The crew adjusted well to Lock's claiming of the ship. Sparrow thought many men even appeared grateful for such solid direction. Lock knew what he wanted and issued clear instructions. Sparrow knew his experience at sea kept them alive through the first days after the storm, and the men, after days of carefully watching their new Captain, accepted him completely.

Lock—to Sparrow's relief and dismay—seemed born to control a ship. At least she could walk about without fear—or at least with little fear. She remained in charge of the galley, but spent much time on deck, glad to breathe the salty sea air and enjoy the sun and wind on her skin. She and Lock didn't speak again of their plans for when the Lady Fire docked. Once the tension of restoring the ship passed, his temper improved and he often acted like the man she'd known in Begonia.

Perhaps if he treated her differently the idea of leaving him would have been easier, but he still cast her affectionate glances throughout the day. In between overseeing the running of the ship, he ducked into the galley for some brief conversation or touched her arm or hair when they passed one another on deck. She didn't doubt his love for her, but she didn't know if it could compete with his love of the sea and for the power that accompanied his position on the Lady Fire.

"Enjoying the view?"

Sparrow started at the sound of Lock's voice close to her ear. She turned from the rail where she'd been gazing into the sea and looked at him. "Trying to see more dolphins."

He smiled. "Thought you might have been searching for a merman. Legend has it, when women go to sea, mermen steal their hearts and take them below."

"My heart's already been stolen."

He bent to kiss her when Ilias bellowed from the crow's nest. "Look! Gulls!"

Both Sparrow and Lock glanced skyward. Two grayish birds dipped and soared overhead.

"Means land." Lock told her.

"Land?" Sparrow's stomach clenched. She almost dreaded the idea of docking. Now she'd know exactly how much Lock loved her.

She wanted to ask how far they were from shore, but he'd already turned and begun issuing orders. She felt the crew's excitement about docking and noticed they laughed more than usual.

By midday, a dark rise loomed in the distance. Several hours later, they docked on the shore of what appeared to be a small island.

Lock sent Ilias and several crewmen ashore in the dingy, and when they returned, informed them they'd landed on Gray Horse Isle, located between the Western continent and the Kennas.

"Not all that far from Begonia, but far enough to be out of the Empress's reach," Lock told Sparrow. "I've stopped here before. Not the wealthiest isle in the world, but self-sufficient. We can buy supplies here and make repairs."

"Can we settle here?" Sparrow asked.

He shook his head. "Wouldn't want to stay here, girl. Can cross the whole island in half a day on foot. Besides, it floods badly during storms, which come often. Water's also full of sharks—"

"All right, Lock." Sparrow raised an eyebrow. "I understand you don't want to live here."

"Now that we know where we are, plotting our course will be simple. Don't worry, girl. We'll find someplace soon."

She touched a finger to his lips. "Lately everything out of your mouth has been a lie."

"We can't stay on the ship forever. If I say we'll be docking again soon, then we will. In the meantime, let's go ashore while the weather's good. I have to barter with the sellers in the market. Won't be pretty. They know if we've stopped here to buy, we've got to be hard up."

"I want to go, too. I need some clothes."

"Ilias," Lock glanced at the man who stood a short distance away, "you'll go with Sparrow to the market. Get her whatever she wants and the two of you are in charge of buying provisions. Come with me, and I'll give you money."

"If you mean the money in the hold, it's stolen," Sparrow stated.

Lock raised an eyebrow. "And I don't know who it was stolen from, so I can't very well give it back now, can I?"

Sparrow glanced at the sea while Lock took Ilias below.

I can't live like this, she thought. *No matter how much I love him.*

* * * * *

"Can I ask you a question?" Ilias glanced at Sparrow as they walked side-by-side through the market.

When they'd arrived on the island, Lock had kissed Sparrow's cheek, taken several crewmen, and gone to barter for supplies while she and Ilias went to buy food.

"Of course." Sparrow considered the ape-like man her only friend on board the Lady Fire.

"How did you end up with Lock? I mean, I know you bought him as a slave, but how did you end up as his woman?"

Sparrow sighed. "Sometimes I wonder that myself."

"Not that he doesn't like you. No man on board would dare touch you."

"I certainly feel safe with him, if that's what you mean."

Ilias laughed. "He pays you a lot of attention, not that any man wouldn't... Sorry." Ilias shook his head. "Didn't mean no disrespect. Don't tell the Captain."

"I won't. I consider you a friend, Ilias. I—"

"No need to explain. Friendship is fine for me. Don't think I'd have the guts to fight Lock for you, anyway."

Sparrow smiled, imagining what an unfair fight that would be. "The only man I've ever wanted is Lock, but I didn't expect him to go on pirating."

"But he's a pirate." Ilias raised an eyebrow. "Most feared pirate ever to sail out of the Archipelago."

Sparrow glanced at her shoes and sighed. No matter how she tried to forget about Lock's reputation, it seemed neither of them could escape it.

"So you're saying you love him?"

"Yes, I love him."

"In a way that's good to know." Ilias offered a quirky smile. "Gives me hope that even though I'm a pirate a decent woman might want me someday, too."

"You don't have to be a pirate, Ilias. Wouldn't you like to settle somewhere and raise a family?"

"Raise a family, yes. Settle, no. It's not in my blood. I'm not from the Archipelago. I just boarded a vessel one day and that's where I ended up. My people are travelers. Gypsies, they call us."

"Really? Gypsies passed through my homeland once. They were fascinating. They provided entertainment like dancing, a magic show. They sold the most wonderful perfumed oils."

"My people have a rich culture. Many are horse tamers and musicians as well, but we rarely settle for long. It's a good life, and at times I miss it, but there's something I like about the sea."

"That's what Lock says. I know it's a part of him. That's why leaving the Lady Fire would be so difficult."

"Leave? He never said anything about leaving. Most of the crew think he'll be good for the ship—and for their pockets."

"I'm sure he will, but we'd made plans to settle."

Ilias glanced at her, his expression somber. "Begging your pardon, Sparrow, but he doesn't seem to be the settling kind."

"I know. Please don't mention what I've said to the rest of the crew."

"I'd never discuss what we talk about, Sparrow. As far as I'm concerned, none of them can be trusted."

"Thank you. Now, we'd better get this shopping done and get back to the ship."

* * * * *

That evening, almost every man on board agreed Sparrow cooked the finest meal they'd eaten in months.

"It's easy to cook with good supplies," she said to Lock as they sat side-by-side on deck eating stew and freshly baked bread.

"A bad cook can ruin good food. This is the best bread I've ever had."

"Want more?"

He shook his head. "Any more and I'll make a pig of myself."

"Since when have you worried about appearances?"

"Any more and you could roll me overboard."

"Worrying about your handsome looks. That's more like it." She stood. "I have to clean the galley. Are you standing another watch tonight?"

"No. I'll be in the cabin tonight."

She smiled coquettishly. "I'll wait for you there."

He tugged her to his chest, one hand beneath her chin as he tilted her face toward his. "I haven't seen that look in far too long."

She stood on tiptoe and kissed him before slipping from his grasp. Lock watched as she disappeared below. He wanted to bed her so badly he could just about taste it. Funny how a single look from her made his heart beat faster. Funny how a single look from her made him feel so damn guilty.

He knew he should leave the Lady Fire at the next port. He knew he should settle down and marry her, just as he'd promised. Perhaps he would. After all, what was so great about the ship? It was just another battle-tested vessel built for speed and loaded with enough cargo to make him a very rich man, not including all the treasure he had buried back on SeaSpider Island.

Sparrow seemed to be in better spirits today, after her trip to the market. Maybe she could grow accustomed to life with a pirate, after all.

No, never. She's too honest, has too much dignity. What in the hell is she doing with me to begin with?

Still, part of her must have forgiven him. She hadn't argued with him in days.

Lock had intended to retire early that night, but remained on deck until well after the moon rose. The storm had taken several crewmen, and every hand was needed for repairs. If their luck continued, they'd be leaving Gray Horse Island within the week.

When Lock opened the door of his cabin, the scent of herbal perfume oil struck him. His eyes adjusted to the dim light, and he noticed Sparrow sprawled on the bed, staring at him with lust-filled eyes, her body draped in a robe of sheer black silk. Her nipples pressed against the fabric as she crawled toward the foot of the bed like some exotic cat.

"Pretty robe." He leaned against the door, watching as she stood, the V of short, dark hair between her legs visible through the fabric. Her long, honey blond hair hung thick and glossy over her shoulders and down her back.

"Glad you like it."

He reached for her, molding her body to his while his lips explored her neck and the soft flesh behind her ear. "You smell good. Funny, but when you said you needed clothes in the market I imagined things you could wear to work in the galley."

"I got some clothes for that, too, but I thought you'd like this."

"I like it." He lifted her in his arms and carried her to the bed. While one hand pushed the robe above her knee and caressed her inner-thighs, his mouth covered one nipple, his tongue teasing it through the thin fabric until she shuddered.

"I've missed making love with you, Lock."

"So have I." He discarded the tunic along with his own clothes and covered her body with his.

He claimed her with deep kisses. He made love to her slowly, savoring each moment though his body yearned to take her in a rush, satisfying pent-up desire.

Her arms tightened around him, her legs clasping his waist as she whispered words of love in his ear. At that moment, he was ready to leave behind the Lady Fire, piracy, and anything else she might ask of him.

Later, when he pulled the blankets over their nude, sated bodies, he drifted to sleep, more torn than ever over the decisions he needed to make. He still had time. It could be weeks before they reached another port. He could make it months if he wanted to. Months of her in his cabin every night.

Months of lying to her and to himself.

You really are a pirate, Lock the White. If you were another man taking advantage of her like this, I'd have killed you long ago.

* * * * *

Nearly a week later, the Lady Fire left the dock at Gray Horse island and headed north. Sparrow stood at the rail, watching the island fade in the distance. Though she enjoyed her visit, she agreed with Lock that it wasn't the place for them to settle. It was a small, tight-knit community ruled by men. After living in Begonia, where women were looked on as equal to or better than men, Gray Horse Island was not for her. Nor was the Archipelago where she knew male dominance would be even worse.

Lock approached, his pale eyes squinting at the sunny sky. "Looks like we'll have good weather, at least for the next day or so."

"Where are we headed?"

"North."

"I can see that."

He shrugged, folding his arms across his chest and leaning his back against the rail. He gazed into her face. "Maybe Rhahas. Not the biggest settlement in the world, but they have rare spices that trade well in the east."

"Trade well?" Sparrow felt her brow furrow. "Voyages east could take months, years! What about us?"

"Sparrow, we often talked about me fishing or trading. Why has that changed? I can make us both happy."

"With a stolen pirate ship? Did you intend to trade with Rhahas for their spices, or just take what you want because they have no army to speak of?"

He lifted an eyebrow, his jaw tightening. "Depends on how welcoming they are. I—"

"Cap'n!" a gruff voice called as one of the crewmen, a

gray-haired, thickly built man dragged a skinny boy across the deck. The boy was one of the lowest workers and probably hadn't served long on any ship. He struggled against his captor who pinned his arms behind his back. "Caught this boy pickin' through the cargo. Stole a bunch of coins. Who knows what else he took before we caught him."

Lock stared hard at the boy who swallowed, his thin throat rolling, his eyes terrified. "Didn't take anything before, Captain. I swear it."

"What good is your word?"

"What should I do with him?"

Lock tapped his heel against the side of the boat.

Sparrow felt the boy's fear, and though she knew he was as much a pirate as the rest, couldn't help feeling sorry for him. Even though Lock had no more right to that cargo than anyone else on board, to him and to the crew, it was his. She also knew there had to be some punishment for anyone who stole or else he'd lose control of the ship. Most likely the poor boy would be stuck below for the rest of the journey.

"You know what the punishment for theft is," Lock said.

"Aye."

"No!" the boy shrieked and struggled so hard Sparrow thought he might break his own arms to free himself. "I don't want to die! No!"

"Die?" Sparrow stared at Lock. "You're not really going to kill him?"

"It's how we punish thieves."

"I won't go near the cargo again! I swear! Please!" The boy turned to Sparrow. "Madam—"

"What are you looking at her for?" Lock grasped the boy's jaw roughly. "You think a woman runs this ship? Is that the general idea?"

"No!"

Lock released the boy and glared at the man holding him.

"I didn't say nothing, Cap'n." The older crewman's eyes widened.

"Lock, be reasonable!" Sparrow said. "He's just a boy."

"A boy with slippery fingers."

"Didn't you ever make a mistake?"

"That was no mistake. If he'd been securing the cargo and the lid popped open and the coins jumped into his pockets, then *that* would be a mistake."

"I guess death is a fitting sentence, then." Sparrow held his eyes. "In Begonia, thieves are killed, too. On the rack. After they've nearly been whipped to death..."

Lock's teeth ground, but she knew he understood her.

"Should we ready the plank?" the gray-haired man asked.

"No."

"No, Cap'n?"

"I said no!" Lock growled. The crewman looked disappointed, and the boy relaxed visibly. Lock curled his lip. "Don't look so happy. You still have to be made an example of."

"Looks like asking Madam helped you after all," the older man snickered.

"That'll be two examples," Lock said, and the crewman looked stunned.

"What are you going to do to them?" Sparrow asked.

"None of your business. Now get below."

"But—"

"I said get below!" He grasped her arm and dragged her toward the hatch.

In the galley, Sparrow's teeth ground as she kneaded bread. "I can't stand another day of "The Cap'n!" He thinks he's the king of the ocean! I can't believe he was going to kill that boy over a few handfuls of coins!"

A shrill cry sounded from above, and Sparrow wiped her

hands on her apron as she hurried topside, muttering to herself, "Now what?"

She stepped on deck in time to see the boy on his knees, clutching a blood-soaked cloth around his left hand. The older crewman who'd brought the boy to Lock stood with his arms tied to the main mast, another man behind him, whip in hand.

Sparrow approached the boy and knelt beside him. She touched his hand. "Let me see."

He shook his head, his eyes unfocused with shock.

Ilias approached, and Sparrow asked. "What happened?"

"Lock cut off one of his fingers as punishment for theft. Could have been worse."

"Cut off his..." Sparrow glared over her shoulder at Lock who stood, his arms folded across his chest, amidst the small crowd who'd gathered to watch the whipping.

The older man's shirt was ripped, exposing his back, and at a nod from Lock, the whipping began.

Sparrow hurried to Lock, her fists clenched at her sides. "What are you doing? Have you gone mad?"

"Everyone knows what to expect when they act out of line. That's how control is kept, and I thought I told you to get below?"

Sparrow winced as leather struck flesh. "I can't believe you've ordered a whipping!"

"Just ten lashes." He shrugged. "It certainly won't kill him. As a matter of fact, Sparrow, such a light sentence is almost an insult."

Sparrow glanced at the crewman, noting five bloody cuts across his back. He winced as the sixth blow fell.

"You cut off that boy's finger!"

"It should have been his hand." Lock's pale eyes held hers with a coldness that made her shiver. "It should have been his life, but your plea saved it. It's that affection I have for you, girl."

At that moment, Sparrow would have clawed his eyes out, but she knew she couldn't best him in a physical fight and would end up humiliated.

"This is none of your business, Sparrow. Now get back below."

"Or what? You'll beat me, too? Cut off my fingers?"

Several crewmen glanced at the couple while others watched the whipping.

Lock laughed humorlessly. "Just like a woman."

She grasped his wrist, her nails biting into his flesh. She stared into his eyes, her stomach twisted with rage. "I don't know you anymore, and I *hate* you."

She turned and walked back to Ilias and the boy.

"Ilias, help him below. I'll do what I can for him." She glanced at the whipped man who was being untied from the mast. "Him, too."

Sparrow doubted she'd ever been so furious in her life. No matter where they docked next, she was going ashore and never setting foot on the Lady Fire again.

* * * * *

"Nice night." Lock approached Sparrow who stood, gazing at the sea. Moonlight shone on the water and the breeze felt cool.

"Yes."

"You look beautiful." He touched her hair, but she jerked her head away.

He let his hand drop. For over two weeks she'd given him one-word answers and hadn't allowed him to touch her, let alone kiss her.

"Ilias made up a hell of a string of limericks tonight."

"Yes."

"He had you laughing."

She started to walk away, but he grasped her hand and felt her stiffen beneath his touch. He resisted the urge to release her, feeling like an unwelcome serpent crawling up her skirt. Since that day he'd punished the men and she said she'd hated him, nothing had been the same between them. At first he thought she'd just been angry. He could understand her feelings. She wasn't accustomed to life aboard a pirate ship. He had to keep control of the men. As it was, he knew several of them thought him lenient in his punishments. They thought Sparrow had influenced him to let the boy live, and they were right to a point. Killing the boy for stealing coins seemed harsh, especially when compared to the crimes he'd committed. Still, when he'd been as young and inexperienced as the boy, he'd been careful not to steal from his captain's cargo. The boy didn't matter to him—at least not as much as Sparrow. Since that day, she'd acted like she truly hated him. She looked at him like he was a demon spat up from the smokiest hell, and he couldn't bear it.

"Sparrow, you haven't talked to me in weeks."

"Really?"

"By the twin goddesses, girl, can't you make a sentence with more than one word?"

"Perhaps."

He tugged her toward him, a hand on each shoulder. When he tried meeting her eyes, she gazed past him toward the black horizon. "Sparrow, what are you trying to do? At night you don't even let me touch you."

"I'm not your whore."

He laughed humorlessly. "There you go. Four whole words. Whoever said you're my whore?"

"You didn't have to say it. It's how you treat me. Like one of your slaves. Like one of your crewmen—except at night, that is."

"I really need a cook, but if you don't want to do it—"

"It's not the work, and you know it! It's you, Lock."

"If you're still thinking about the punishments to those crewmen, I was well within my rights."

"You've changed."

"I'm what I always said I was and you chose to ignore!"

"No. You were different. Don't you feel it?"

He wanted to deny the truth in her words, but he couldn't. He *was* different. When he'd been at the farm with her, he thought about being at sea, but the pirating part faded somewhat. He liked working on the farm, not that it was the life he'd choose for himself, but being with her was worth it. He had daydreams of marrying her and supporting them by fishing and trading on a ship he bought with honest money. It wasn't the most exciting life he imagined, but it was *good.* When he'd met the Knights in Begonia, he'd even started to have the crazy vision that he could become one of *them.* That way he could earn an honest living but not lose the excitement he craved. He could study fighting, learn more about healing—maybe even teach that old witch Shea-Ann a thing or two. But who was he kidding? He wasn't a Knight. He'd spent his entire life doing everything they abhorred. They saved lives, he took them. They gave to the poor, he stole from almost anyone. They fought for the oppressed, he fought for whatever monarch hired him as a privateer.

"Don't you feel it?" Sparrow pressed. Her palms splayed across his chest, the most intimate touch she'd awarded him in weeks.

He covered her hands with his, holding them to his heart. "This is the only life I know, Sparrow. It's what I do."

"That's an excuse, Lock. You know you can be so much more than this."

"Can I?"

"Yes. I believe you can do anything you want. Obviously you can be a pirate, but that's a waste of your true talents."

"What true talents?"

"You're intelligent, Lock. You know so much more than

these men, than men like Rino. You can learn so much more. You can be a loving man. I've seen you help Shea-Ann when she's healing. I watched you rebuild a village that was nearly destroyed. You can *create*, Lock. You don't have to kill and steal."

Lock tugged her into his arms and held her as they gazed at the sea.

When he was very young, he used to love building things out of sand. Castles. Villages. Ships. He'd pretend he was aboard his father's vessel. His father had the finest ship in the Archipelago and he taught Lock how to run it. They visited ports in exotic places he could only imagine. Of coarse it was all fantasy. He had no idea who his father was. It could have been any of the seamen his mother entertained at the brothel.

The waves always destroyed what he built. For years he tried telling his mother about the adventures he made up, but she never listened. She ignored him when he asked who his father was. One day she said his father had returned. He awaited Lock in her room at the brothel. Excited and a bit frightened, Lock made his way to the room. He found a man sure enough, but he was in no way his father. It had been the first time Lock's mother had sold him for profit.

"This isn't such a bad life, Sparrow," he said. "There's worse."

"And there's better. I can't live like this, Lock. I'm telling you I can't."

"We don't have a choice right now."

"There's always a choice." She slipped from his arms and disappeared below.

He stared at the moon, remembering that day in the brothel so long ago. "No, girl. Not always."

Chapter Twenty-Three

🔊

"Lock?"

"Thought you were asleep." Lock sat at the edge of the bed beside Sparrow, his shirt rolled up to his elbows, the front untied.

Sparrow shook her head, her eyes meeting his in the dimness.

He continued, "We'll go ashore tomorrow. No point now. It's too late."

"Good." She wondered if she sounded as strained as she felt. Ashore. This would be her last night with him. She'd been so angry at him for such a long time that she thought leaving would be simple. Now as she looked at him and knew she'd probably never see him again, she felt mostly sadness. Not average sadness, but a deep, raw ache, akin to how she'd felt when Thea died. *Lock is not dead! He's just stubborn. And stupid. And... a pirate.* He *had* told her that much from the first.

"What's wrong? I mean other than the usual you hate me and this ship." He touched her face hesitantly. She'd pushed him away so often he scarcely ever tried touching her anymore.

"I don't hate you."

"No?"

She shook her head. She didn't. She was angry with him and disappointed he refused to become the man she knew he could be. The truth was she loved him. She knew part of her would love him until the day she died.

She sat up and looped her arms around his neck. He embraced her so tightly she could scarcely breathe, but it was a wonderful feeling. She'd missed him, though they'd been living together at sea for several weeks.

"I thought you did hate me."

She shook her head. "I love you, Lock."

He looked into her eyes, the slightest smile on his lips. "That's good to hear."

"Do you still love me?"

"What kind of a question is that? Of course I do."

"Prove it," she pleaded, taking his face in her hands. "Tomorrow when we dock, leave this ship and don't look back." He didn't reply, but remained with his eyes fixed on hers with confusion, sadness, and guilt. She sighed. "You won't."

"What would we do if we left the ship? I have nothing to offer you. No home. No money. No work."

"We can build a home and find work. Damn it, Lock, I was a *princess* and was cast out of my kingdom with nothing. I survived. You survived in the Archipelago with that bitch of a mother and—"

"You deserve more than just surviving."

"I deserve to be stuck on a ship full of cutthroats waiting for you to be overthrown like you overthrew Rino? Is that what you want for me? For our children? I will *not* raise a family with a pirate! I don't care if you have nothing. You'll have dignity and honesty. Doesn't that mean anything to you?"

"Dignity?" He laughed humorlessly. "You know my life, Sparrow. You expect dignity?"

"For an intelligent man, you have no vision."

"No...What are you talking about, girl? Vision. I have more visions than I'd like."

"I'm talking about vision of the future as you make it, not something that comes to you in dreams. Stop remembering what you were and think about who you want to become."

"I can see the near future." He kissed her mouth, her neck.

Sparrow didn't argue, didn't push him away. Instead she clung to him and kissed him deeply. Her tongue slipped between his parted lips and stroked his. Lock buried his hand in her hair and wrapped his arm around her waist as he tugged her close, tilting her across his lap. Sparrow's fingers gripped the steely muscles of his shoulders and back. She wanted to memorize every inch of his magnificent body to sustain her for the rest of her life.

Lock took her upper lip gently between his, running his tongue over it before his mouth traveled across her cheek and down her neck. Lowering her to the bed, he began undressing her, licking and nipping every inch of her flesh as it was bared.

His mouth covered one nipple, his tongue teasing the stiff nub with broad strokes. At the same time, his fingertips caressed her other nipple, rolling it between his thumb and forefinger and stroking it with the pad of his thumb.

Sparrow wanted to close her eyes to better enjoy the sensations, but she couldn't keep from staring at him. She needed to see the muscles of his powerful body as he moved over her, to relish the beauty of his white and brown hair. She wanted to remember forever the expression on his handsome face as his passion built.

"I never thought I'd be so lost to one woman," he said in a husky voice as he slipped to his knees on the wooden floor, grasped her thighs, and dragged her to the edge of the bed. He lowered his face between her legs and ran the tip of his tongue down each side of her clit. Sparrow shivered with impending desire and moaned softy when his tongue rimmed her pussy lips. The bed itself was low enough to the ground that Lock could thrust into her waiting pussy from where he knelt. He straightened and slipped his thick, hard cock inside her. Sparrow's eyes closed halfway and her pulse quickened. How she would miss him!

As he thrust, one of his hands stroked her clit while his

other played with her nipples, rubbing them in tender circles and gently tugging them. The sensations on so many sensitive parts of her body were enough to fling her headlong into a fiery, moaning orgasm. He continued thrusting and stroking until she lay still beneath him.

He slipped his stiff cock from her body and tugged her fully onto the bed. Stretching out beside her, he stroked wisps of hair from her face and brushed a kiss across her lips.

Sparrow turned to him, searching his face. "What about you?"

"I can wait. Tonight is for you."

"But—"

"I want to convince you I still want your happiness, Sparrow."

"Happiness isn't just about physical love, Lock."

His gaze held hers and she thought she saw a flicker of hesitation and perhaps regret.

"It's one way I know I can please you."

"I'd rather you pleased me less in lovemaking and left the ship instead."

"Enough talk. We can have another discussion tomorrow. For tonight..." Lock's mouth devoured hers. Though she knew she should push him away, she also realized it wouldn't matter. He'd made up his mind, as she'd made up hers.

Lock rolled her onto her back and sifted his fingers through her hair. Brushing the soft mass aside, he kissed her nape then her shoulders. The tip of his tongue ran from the top of her spine to the indentation of her buttocks. One hand slipped between her legs, his fingers fluttering across her perineum then gathering moisture from her pussy. His damp fingers stroked her clit while his other arm snaked around her waist, lifting her slightly. Sparrow rose to her knees, her forearms flat against the pillow. His kisses covered her bottom.

Grasping her hips in both hands, he drew a deep breath

301

as he entered her from behind.

"Oh, Lock," she panted.

"Tell me what you want, girl."

"I want you," she said. In every way she wanted him, but as filled with pleasure as she was at the moment, it was not to last. It seemed the only way she could truly have him was in bed. Sorrow mingled with building desire in the pit of her belly. What else had she expected from a SothSea whore?

Sparrow gasped and moaned, orgasm hurling her into a quivering frenzy. His ragged breathing told her he must be close, though again he slipped, rock-hard, from her.

Rolling her onto her back, he covered her body with his, gazing deeply into her eyes. She stroked his face, trailed her fingertip over his lips and kissed him.

"Tell me what you want," he whispered. His cock pressed between them and his eyes gleamed with passion.

"I want to feel your pleasure," she said. "I want you to explode inside me. I want to hear my name on your lips when you come."

His lips curved upward in the slightest smile before he kissed her. Sparrow reached between them, curling her fist around his thick cock and guiding him to her pussy lips.

In a swift motion, he filled her and began thrusting. Ignoring her own desire to close her eyes as his slow, steady movements rekindled her passion, she watched him. His blue eyes slipped shut, his lips parted as he drew sips of air. He buried his face in her neck and kissed her, his stubbled jaw pleasantly rough against her tender flesh.

Sparrow's legs entwined with his. The bottom of her feet caressed his hair-roughened calves. Her hips lifted, meeting his thrust for thrust.

"Lock, oh, Lock!" she cried, clinging to him tightly as another marvelous orgasm built deep inside her.

The first pulses of her pussy dragged him along with her

and he called her name in a voice raw with passion. Sparrow gripped the heated muscles of his broad back as he surged inside her, his big body slamming hers into the bed.

With a groan, he rolled onto his side and held her close.

She lay in his arms, feeling the rise and fall of his chest against her back as he slept. She didn't try to sleep. She wanted to remember every moment of that night—the last she would ever spend with the pirate Lock the White.

* * * * *

"Sparrow, wait!"

Sparrow glanced over her shoulder at Ilias who jogged up the dirt road toward her.

He fell into step beside her, panting. "You walk at a good clip. Where are you going? I saw you leave the ship while I was delivering some of the Captain's supplies."

"I'm just going for a walk. I was sick of being stuck on the ship."

"Walk?" Ilias's dark eyes narrowed at the satchel and water flask Sparrow carried. "With all your belongings?"

"Ilias, just leave me alone, please. It'll be better for both of us if you go back to the ship. I don't want Lock getting any ideas."

"About what?" Ilias looked worried. "I knew it! You're running from him, aren't you? He's never mistreated you, has he? Not that there's much I could do about it, but I'd take a shot at killing him when he's asleep—"

"Ilias!" Sparrow shook his shoulder. "I don't want you trying to kill anybody, least of all Lock."

"Good, because he'd smash me into shark feed."

"He's never mistreated me—at least not physically." She closed her eyes momentarily, remembering the warmth of his body against hers the night before. If only morning had never come. "I just can't live on the Lady Fire anymore. I can't watch

303

him throw his life away and become the same monster he was when we first met. He's headed on a path of destruction, not only his own, but of anyone who gets in his way. The trouble is, even he doesn't know where his way leads."

"Well do you know anyone in these parts? Do you have any money? Anywhere to stay?"

"I'll find something. I've been in a situation like this before. I'll survive."

Ilias gently clasped her wrist and tugged her toward another pathway. "Come with me. I can help you."

"Where are we going?"

"In the market, some gypsies were selling their wares. I spoke with them. One of the women is a cousin of my mother's. They'll give you a safe place to stay. If they like you, they might even let you work with them. And they'll know how to keep you hidden when Lock comes looking for you."

Sparrow held his eyes. "So you think he'll follow me?"

"Do cows shit in the field? The man would be insane to let you go…" Ilias blushed. "Sorry, but it's the truth, Sparrow."

"I'm really going to miss you, Ilias. You've been a good friend."

"You, too. I wouldn't take anyone but a close friend to the gypsies—nor would they accept anyone but a close friend of one of their own. We're a close knit people, as you'll see."

"You know if Lock finds out what you've done he might kill you. It seems all he's capable of lately is violence."

"I think I have to risk it this time. You don't belong on the Lady Fire."

"I'll never forget this, but I think I have a plan. Once you introduce me to your friends, and if they're willing to accept me, I'll return with you to the market. You make sure you stay with Lock and I'll say I'm going back to the ship. That way he'll have no way of blaming you when I disappear."

Ilias winked. "I think you've been hanging around us

pirates too long."

Far too long for my taste, Sparrow thought as they continued over the hillside.

* * * * *

"Ilias," Lock called across the deck.

The crewman approached. "Captain?"

"Sparrow's not below. Have you seen her? She should have been back by now."

"Haven't seen her since she left us in the market this afternoon."

Lock glanced skyward, concerned. It would be dark soon. Sparrow should have been on board. "Find ten men and come ashore with me. We have to find her before nightfall."

Ilias nodded and shouted for the nearest crewmen. Lock's eyes swept the dock, hoping for some sign of her. She'd told him hours ago, she was returning to the ship. What if something had happened to her on the way back from the market? The market was no more than a ten minute walk to the ship, but someone could have robbed her, raped her, killed...*No!* He wouldn't think of it! Why had he let her go alone? Rhahas was one of the safest settlements he knew. There was little crime, and she said she was sick of him sending Ilias with her like a guard dog wherever she went. He wished he'd have sent the man with her today.

Lock took Sea Storm ashore again. He could cover more ground on horseback while the others searched on foot. They would meet back at the ship after dark.

Lock rode through the dock and the marketplace, watching as vendors packed away their wares. He questioned several people, and a few remembered seeing Sparrow earlier that day, but not recently.

He searched the nearby village and traveled the dirt road to the next settlement.

Glancing skyward, he felt fear crawling inside him. The moon had risen and he had to report back to the ship. Maybe Ilias or the others had found Sparrow. In spite of his hope, a feeling of dread made his stomach twist and his heart pound. If anything had happened to her—*anything*—he'd never forgive himself.

When he arrived at the dock, the men waited.

"She's nowhere, Captain."

"Disappeared."

"Get the rest of the men off that ship! Leave just enough crew to keep guard. I want the rest looking for her."

One of the men raised his eyes skyward and said, "But she's not—"

Lock pulled the dagger from the sheath about his waist and pressed it beneath the crewman's chin. "Do what I tell you or I'll slit your throat. And when she's found, not a hair on her head better be harmed."

Lock mounted Sea Storm and galloped toward the wood, hopeful and terrified of what he might find.

* * * * *

"What's wrong with you? You have to eat more than that!"

Sparrow glanced at the attractive gray-eyed woman seated beside her. Dressed in a flowing maroon dress, her dark hair braided down her back, the woman spoke to Sparrow in her deep, lightly-accented voice. When she addressed the members of the campsite, she used a language completely unfamiliar to Sparrow. It was the old gypsy language, exclusive to their people. Now that Sparrow had joined their group, she was determined to add their language to the vast collection already stored in her mind. At least she hoped studying something new would keep her from dwelling on Lock.

306

"I'm just not hungry right now."

"You have a fine figure and look like you know how to eat."

Sparrow looked stunned. "I'm fat?"

"Of course not! It's good to see a healthy looking woman! Our people find meat and muscle attractive on a girl, especially one as lovely as you, but you won't stay lovely if you *do not eat!*"

"I'll be fine. Mita, thank you again for letting me stay with you."

Mita waved her hand. "Ilias's mother and I were great friends as children. He's a nice young man, but if you ask me, he's making a foolish decision by joining up with those pirates. A nasty lot, but I don't have to tell *you* that."

Sparrow sighed and took a bite of bread, forcing herself to chew and swallow. Mita was right. Why should she starve herself, pining away over a man who'd chosen the life of a criminal over making a home with her?

"I know what's taken your appetite." Mita brushed a loose strand of wavy black hair behind her ear. "It's that man you're running from. Don't deny it. I've felt the same way myself."

"I'm just so frustrated because he can do so much better than the life he's chosen."

"That's true of many people. This pirate of yours has to decide for himself that change is best. He has to want it for himself. Only then can he give you the sort of life you deserve."

"That will never happen. Especially now. And even if he did decide to change, I'm not so sure I want him anymore." Sparrow lifted her chin, suddenly feeling less weepy as anger took hold of her. Because of Lock, she'd been forced out of a home she loved, away from Shea-Ann, the only family she had left. She'd believed Lock when he said they'd marry and make a life. He'd come so far, had changed so much, and one taste of piracy was enough to make him toss it all away. She wasn't sure she could ever forgive him for ruining their relationship.

"Really?" Mita watched Sparrow through her lashes. "So you're getting over the man already?"

"I think so. You know, Mita, this is the second time in my life a man has promised to marry me and backed away because he couldn't adjust to my manner of living." Sparrow stood, her fists clenched, and paced in front of the fire, staring into the flames. "You know what I say? To hell with men! Who needs them? They're more trouble than they're worth."

"Here, here!" Mita raised her wine mug.

"They're just overly-muscled, hairy, ignorant goats who think they should be in charge of the whole damn mountain!"

Several of the other gypsy women, interested by Sparrow's angry speech, approached the fire.

One of them said, "That sounds like my husband and my father!"

"Hey, woman!" the gypsy's husband snapped from where he sat with several of his friends, drinking wine.

"They think their word is law," Sparrow continued. "They think because they sleep with us we'll bow at their feet!"

"And most of the time they're lucky we even crawl into the hay with them!" shouted a heavyset, gray-haired woman with wrists adorned with heavy gold bracelets.

"Enough of this talk!" Mita's husband, leader of the gypsy clan approached. He glared at Sparrow, his hands on his hips. "If I knew you were a trouble maker, I never would have agreed to let you stay here."

"You keep silent!" Mita stood nose to nose with her husband. "She's a friend of my dear cousin's son and welcome here, by the law of our people!"

"You sit down, woman!"

"You go join your friends or else they'll be no more fine

meals prepared in this camp for the next week!" Mita patted her husband's slight pot belly. "See how you like that!"

"Well if you women want to talk foolishness, do it quietly! Some of us want to relax. We have to be up early for hunting in the morning."

"Which means it's up to us women to run the stalls at the market. Again. So leave us alone or maybe we won't divide the profit equally between the sexes!"

"You wouldn't dare lie about money!"

"You watch me!"

Sparrow stepped back, suddenly feeling guilty. She murmured, "I always did talk too much. Now I've started a fight between a perfectly happy couple."

"Perfectly happy?" A slender, dark-haired girl who stood beside Sparrow laughed. "If Mita and Prem don't have at least two good fights a day, we think one of them is ill."

Sparrow released a breath of relief.

"I think you'll get along well in this camp. The women already like you."

"The men probably want to cook me over a slow-burning fire."

The girl laughed. "Serves them right. What you said about them is often true."

"What's your name?"

"Opal. Please excuse me, but I'm going to practice my dancing. I entertain at the village tavern."

"You dance?" Sparrow remembered Lock's dance and her stomach tightened. He'd been so handsome, and now she'd never see him again.

"I learned from my mother and she learned from her mother. It's a family tradition, and you can earn a great deal of money at the tavern. Especially when some of the men get drunk. They just toss coins at my feet."

"Would you teach me?"

Opal smiled. "That's a wonderful idea! Come on. We can..." She stopped speaking as the entire camp focused their attention on a young man who'd just run into the village, dusty from the road.

"Rider approaching!" He panted. "I think it's the pirate Ilias warned us about. The one looking for Sparrow."

Sparrow's heart pounded. "Lock! I have to run. I have to—"

"You're not running anywhere," Mita said.

"But he'll—"

"The hairy goat will do nothing." Opal winked. "He won't even know you're here."

"So what are we going to do?"

"Hide her under the wagon," suggested a boy. "We can tie her to the bottom. He'd never know she's there."

"No, he'll find me," Sparrow said. "Lock's a pirate. If there's one thing they all know about is how to hide something."

Mita narrowed her eyes. "Obviously you know little about us. The man will not find you, Sparrow, and we're not going to hide you under a wagon. Ridiculous idea."

"Then what are we going to do?"

* * * * *

Lock slowed Sea Storm as they approached the gypsy camp. He didn't now how he could have missed them before, but they were probably still packing away their stalls in the market while he was searching the countryside.

"Hello!" he shouted as he approached. A tall, heavyset older man walked toward him, a woman with piercing gray eyes at his side. The woman stared at him hard, but Lock ignored her glare and said, "I'm looking for a woman."

"That's one thing we don't sell." The woman lifted her chin. "If you want whores, go to the pier—"

"I'm not looking for a whore. I'm looking for my betrothed." Lock ignored the woman's smirk. "She's about as tall as that old man over there. Blond hair, blue eyes, very beautiful."

The woman laughed. "She's probably a toothless, freckle-faced hag."

Lock resisted the urge to dump the woman in the nearest mud pile. Instead he glanced at the others. "Has anyone seen a woman who fits that description?"

The tall man shrugged. "There are many yellow-haired women."

"She's missing part of her left ear."

"Did you bite it off?" The annoying woman continued. "She's probably running away from you."

The woman's words struck him like a fist. Though he hadn't bitten Sparrow's ear, he felt responsible. He'd taken her from a happy life into a world of violence and greed. She's asked him to leave the Lady Fire, but he wanted the power of commanding a pirate ship. He'd wanted it more than he'd wanted her...

"Perhaps she's lost in the woods," someone suggested.

"Or maybe she took the ferry upriver."

"Or—"

"Thanks." Lock dismounted. "Mind if I have a look around?"

"Who do you think you are?" The woman placed her hands on her hips. "You get out of here!"

"Mita," the man held open his hands, "let him look. We've nothing to hide. All we need is for a rumor spread that we've had something to do with a missing woman and it will ruin our sales at the market." He glanced at Lock. "Come. I'll show you around our settlement."

Lock nodded and followed the man around the wagons and caravans. The man even allowed him to look inside. Lock was suspicious of such cooperation, but he saw no sign of Sparrow.

In spite of a camp full of raised eyebrows, he knelt down and inspected the bottom of the wagons and caravans. Several times he'd transported stolen goods over land by strapping them to the bottom of wagons. He searched several piles of hay the gypsies horses munched, but found nothing of importance.

He talked to some of the gypsies who understood the languages he spoke. While he conversed with a skinny young girl, he notice Sea Storm lope toward the old man by the fire. The man's wrinkled face was smeared with dirt, and a patch covered one of his eyes. Straggly gray hair hung across his brow, and his limbs looked too slim to support the protruding gut Sea Storm nuzzled. The man pushed the horse away.

"Stop it!" Lock snapped at the horse, tugging him from the man. "Sorry, friend. He usually doesn't take to people so easily."

The man shook his head and ambled to the fire, leaning on a walking stick for support. Lock watched him, thinking, *it's certainly no fun getting old, but the idea of growing old with a woman like Sparrow makes anything in life seem worthwhile.*

"Are you finished?" demanded the woman, Mita.

"Yes. Thank you."

"Luck to you," said the man who'd shown Lock around the camp.

Lock nodded, mounted Sea Storm, and with a heavy heart, rode back to the ship.

He reached the dock well past midnight. The crewmen had found no sign of Sparrow, and Lock knew they watched him with wary eyes. If he didn't take control of the ship and set sail again, there would undoubtedly be attempts on his life. He didn't care. Until he found Sparrow—dead or alive—he wasn't about to leave the dock.

"Where you going, Captain?" asked the first mate as Lock

took Sea Storm's reins and led the horse away from the pier. "Aren't you coming back aboard?"

"After I cool down my horse."

"The men are wondering when we're going to set sail."

Lock dropped the reins and approached the man, using his height to advantage as he glared down at him. "We'll go *when I say*. Now get back on board while you still have legs to walk there."

"Aye, Captain."

Lock walked Sea Storm to a field about half a mile from the dock. There, he turned the horse loose to graze. Lock should have been tired, but he was unable to rest. Fear was an unfamiliar emotion to him, but since he realized Sparrow was missing, terror such as he'd never known had built steadily within him.

Hearing hoof beats, he glanced over his shoulder, watching Ilias approach on horseback.

"Sparrow?" Lock asked.

Ilias held his eyes, and Lock sensed hesitation. "I've come to talk about Sparrow."

"What about her?" Lock demanded, taking a step closer. Ilias backed the horse away and reached for his sword. "Get off that horse and tell me what you know about her!"

"I came here to tell you, but I ain't getting off the horse. Call for yours and I ride out of here."

"Talk!"

"First, Sparrow is not hurt and she's not dead."

Lock felt as if a weight had been lifted from his belly. "Where is she?"

"I can't tell you that."

Lock's teeth clenched and he reached for the horse. Ilias kicked the animal away.

"Ilias—"

"I'm risking my life coming to you at all! I know you're a killer, and so does Sparrow. That's why she left!"

"What are you talking about?"

"She told me she couldn't stand living on the Lady Fire anymore. She said she couldn't stand seeing what you've become."

"She said that to *you*?" Lock wasn't sure if he was more angry at Sparrow or himself. She'd discussed him with another man. She'd confided in Ilias, but not in him.

"She told me many things, and I'm glad she did. I'm saying this because I consider Sparrow a friend and I know she's in love with you. Maybe if you know her reasons for leaving, you'll stop pirating and try to make yourself a decent man for her, if you can. Maybe you won't. I don't know. Maybe you love yourself more than you can ever love her. If that's the case, then it's better she left."

"Who the hell are you to be saying this to me?"

"I know. I'm a pirate, too, or at least I was. I'm not returning to the ship, either. I'm going back to my family. I don't want to end up like you, Lock. If I ever find a woman who loves me, I don't want to lose her because I'm a murdering pirate who only cares about stealing other people's goods. I don't want to be cutting off boys' fingers and constantly watching my back because nearly everyone I know wants to kill me. I don't want to end up on an auction block in Begonia—"

"I understand!" Lock waved his hand. "You've come this far, so at least tell me where she is so I can talk to her."

"I can't."

"If you don't, I'll cut your throat."

"You'd have to catch me first. Your horse is out there, and I'd have a head start."

"I'd catch you."

"While you're hunting me you could be finding Sparrow.

If you really want to kill me, you'll probably do it no matter what I say, but how do you think Sparrow would feel about it?"

"She need never know," Lock snarled, though he already knew he couldn't kill the ape-like pirate. Sparrow considered the man a friend, and when he found her, he couldn't keep such a secret, not without betraying her again.

"I'm going, Lock. I hope you don't follow me. I hope you say to hell with the Lady Fire and go find the real lady who loves you. If you do find her, I hope you don't hurt her again. She doesn't deserve it, and she's much too good for you." Ilias grinned. "I can say that since you're not my Captain anymore."

"Is she still on land? She didn't sail off on another ship, did she?" Lock demanded.

"I don't think she wants to set foot on another ship right now. Yes, she's still on land." Ilias kicked his horse to a gallop.

"Ilias!" Lock bellowed, but the man disappeared over the hill.

Lock whistled for Sea Storm and rode him back to the dock where he stepped on deck and called for the crew. The sleepy pirates gathered on deck.

"I'm leaving the Lady Fire," Lock told them.

"What for?" someone shouted.

"Likely to find that wench," chuckled another.

Lock went to his cabin and packed his few belongings. The first mate followed.

"Looks like this is your vessel now, if you can keep it," Lock told him.

"Oh, I plan on keeping it." The man folded his arms across his chest. "You're a fool, Lock the White. All this for a woman."

Lock slung the leather bag of healing supplies Shea-Ann had given him over his shoulder and left the ship. He didn't bother telling the first mate he was leaving as much for his own sake as for Sparrow's. It would have been a waste of time because the man would never understand. Lock was only grateful he'd learned enough from Sparrow and Shea-Ann to see the truth in Ilias's words.

He had to choose between Sparrow and piracy. There was no competition.

He enjoyed the adventure and power of commanding a ship, but it lost its luster if it meant a life without Sparrow.

On shore, he mounted Sea Storm and rode from the dock without looking back.

Chapter Twenty-Four

ᘓ

Sparrow braided Opal's hair, keeping her eyes fixed on the dark tendrils, though her thoughts wandered toward Lock again.

It had been over four months since she'd left the ship. That first night she'd come to the gypsies and Lock had searched their camp for her, she'd been torn between wishing he'd find her and terrified that he would. The gypsies had disguised her well, dressing her as an old man, padding the clothes she'd borrowed from one of their men, caking her face with clay to create wrinkled, dark skin, and hiding one of her eyes with a patch. She hadn't even recognized herself when she stared at her reflection in a looking glass. Lock hadn't know her at all. Sea Storm had nearly given her away, however, with an affectionate poke of his nose.

Watching Lock search the camp that night, she'd been unable to keep her eyes from him. He'd looked genuinely concerned and seemed desperate to find her. If she had been in his place and he'd been missing, she'd have been nearly insane with worry. She wished she could at least have eased his mind. She'd wanted to dive into his arms and never let go, but it couldn't be. If she'd revealed herself to him, he would have forced her back to the Lady Fire, and she couldn't stand another day on the ship. He was a pirate and had chosen a life on board the Lady Fire over one he'd planned with her.

"Hurry up, Sparrow," Opal said. "When you're done braiding my hair, I'll do yours then we have to get to the tavern before sundown."

"Sorry. My mind was drifting."

"Lock again?"

"I can't help it."

"He was very handsome. I remember that night he came to the camp looking for you. He had a beautiful body, so tall and strong. Was he terribly good at making love?"

Sparrow swatted the girl's shoulder. "I told you to stop asking me about that. I don't discuss such things."

"You know, it's funny how such a modest woman took to tavern dancing as well as you have. I've been doing it since I was a girl, and the men throw more money at you than they do at me."

"They do not."

"Imagine how much you'll make when you really know how to dance."

Sparrow tied off the braid and turned so Opal could fix her hair. "I'm glad you're teaching me." *If only Lock could see the farm girl now*, Sparrow thought. The dances Opal taught her were nearly as tempting as the Daggers of Desire.

The women finished dressing then shared a horse to the village. They'd made camp on the outskirts of the settlement four days ago. Sparrow and Opal made arrangements with the owner of the tavern and had been dancing there for the past two nights. The men who frequented the place were not only local villagers, but hunters and trappers who made their living in the surrounding woods. The group could get rough and rowdy at times, particularly when they had too much to drink, but the owner had a tall, young stable worker who kept order in the tavern by night. The previous evening, one of the men had tried to follow Opal and Sparrow after their performance, but the women had nearly clipped off his ears with the daggers they carried. Prem, an expert at throwing daggers, had been training Sparrow, and she liked the idea of learning to defend herself with a weapon. In the line of work she and Opal had chosen, self protection was necessary.

"I really like the new dresses we made," Opal said, smoothing the lavender fabric over her narrow hips as they dismounted and left the horse outside the stable.

"The silk is very nice," Sparrow agreed, lifting the skirt of her own sky blue dress so the mud wouldn't ruin the hemline.

They walked to the back door of the tavern that opened to the kitchen.

"Evening." Leah, the full-breasted serving woman greeted them with a smile. "Room's full tonight. Cook's in a rotten mood."

Sparrow glanced at the short, gnarled old man stirring a pot of stew over the fire.

"Good evening, Cook," Sparrow said.

The man grumbled and waved a hand without turning to her. She grinned and Opal raised her eyes to heaven.

"You're just in time. A few of the regulars have been asking about you." Leah grabbed two steaming bowls Cook ladled out for her and bustled to the next room.

Laughter and conversation drifted through the open door along with the sound of a flute and drums. The tavern owner's sons had been entertaining their father's guests for years, and their music accompanied the women when they danced. Sparrow and Opal removed their cloaks and followed Leah through the door. The tables and seats by the bar were filled. Several of the men cheered upon seeing the gypsies.

Opal and Sparrow danced together at first, the center of the floor becoming a whirlwind of lavender and blue silk. The silver and gold jewelry on the women's wrists and ankles chimed to the sound of the flute and drums as they spun and swayed their hips. For the next couple of hours, Sparrow and Opal took turns dancing and gathering the coins tossed on the floor.

Sparrow left the room for a moment to change into a costume of sheer black silk pantaloons and a beaded vest that just covered her breasts, leaving her curved arms and sleek abdomen bare. She draped a long, maroon veil over her head. The material hung to her sandal-clad feet. When she returned,

319

Opal was just finishing her dance. While her friend left to change her clothes, Sparrow stood in the center of the room, and to the sound of the flute, began a sensual dance she and Opal had been working on. She spun, the veil floating around her. She slipped it from her head, and opened her arms, parting the maroon silk and revealing the scanty costume beneath as she wiggled her hips. Men laughed and banged their mugs on the table. She jumped lightly onto one of the tables and swirled the veil over the heads of the wide-eyed patrons before she dropped it and shimmied, her arms moving like liquid. Sparrow smiled, genuinely enjoying herself, and knelt on the table. She bent backwards, her arms stretching sensually over her head. She nearly toppled over when she found herself staring into a pair of shocked, angry and terribly familiar blue eyes.

She righted herself, her heart pounding from more than just the dance. It had been months since she'd seen those soul-reading eyes, that shock of brown and white hair, that disgracefully sensual body...

"Lock!" She scrambled away, but he grasped her off the table and into his arms.

The patrons shouted. Across the tavern Leah screamed for help.

"Lock, let go of me!" Sparrow bellowed, struggling, but his arms tightened around her like warm bands of steel.

"What the hell do you think you're doing?" he snarled. "Dancing like some SothSea trollop!"

"As if you're one to talk!"

"Put her down!" Some of the men shouted. "She ain't finished yet!"

"You're all finished!" Lock growled.

"Hey! Put that girl down!" The tavern owner approached, wiping his hands on a tattered towel, the lantern lights reflecting off his balding head. "I've told you men a thousand times to keep your hands to yourselves!"

"Get away from her!" Opal leapt on Lock's shoulder, grasped a handful of his hair, and pulled hard.

"Let go, you crazy bitch!"

"Not until you put her down!"

Lock shoved Opal who fell onto a nearby chair, strands of his hair still caught in her fists.

"That's the second time I've lost part of my scalp over you, girl!" Lock's furious eyes focused on her. "And I'm not putting you down!"

"Cris!" the tavern owner hollered, and a tall, thickly-built youth charged into the tavern, bits of straw caught in his lank blond hair, manure smeared on his trousers. He flew at Lock's back, screeching a war cry. Lock kicked backwards, Sparrow still in his arms. His foot landed in Cris's mid-section and knocked the youth halfway across the room.

One of the patrons, apparently itching for trouble, ran at Lock who lifted Sparrow above his head and lashed out with his foot, kicking his attacker into a chair, splintering it.

"Lock, stop it!" Sparrow hissed. "What I do is none of your business!"

He lowered her so they were again eye to eye. "Everything about you is my business!"

"Since when? All you care about is the Lady Fire...watch that guy to your left!"

In a fluid movement, Lock shifted Sparrow over one shoulder and used the back of his fist to belt Cris, who had recovered from the first blow. Blood spurted from Cris's nose, spraying the table and floor. The youth grasped his face in his hands.

Again, Sparrow found herself in Lock's arms. She blinked. "I don't believe you! How dare you—"

"All right, put her down and get the hell out of here!" The tavern owner approached Lock again, this time with a crossbow in his hand.

"No!" Sparrow shouted to her employer. "Don't hurt him!"

"Don't hurt *him*?" Cris croaked, his eyes watering as he wiped his bloody nose on his sleeve.

The owner glared. "He's damn near destroyed my place!"

"I'm just here to get what's mine," Lock stated.

"I am not yours!"

"She wants nothing to do with you!" Opal shook her fist at Lock. "Haven't you done her enough damage!"

"Just put the wench down and get out of my tavern!"

"The wench is my fiancée!"

The owner looked startled. "Is that true?"

"No!" Sparrow snapped. "I mean, not anymore."

"I've had about enough of this nonsense." The owner lowered his weapon and pointed at Sparrow. "You don't come back here until you've settled things with that walking typhoon. Opal, you keep the customers entertained. I've hired you girls until midnight, if you remember correctly."

"Sparrow, you don't have to go with him." Opal's dark eyes stared hard at Lock.

"Opal, just go ahead and dance. I'll be fine."

Lock, Sparrow still in his arms, walked to the door.

"You can put me down," she said.

"Don't wager on it. I've been looking for you for four long months, and I'm not about to let you go."

Sparrow slipped her arms around his neck and smiled. "Don't *you* wager on it."

He walked behind the tavern to a short rock wall and sat on it. Sparrow slipped from his arms to perch beside him.

"Lock, what are you doing here?" she asked.

"I think that's more a question I should be asking you." His eyes swept her bare stomach and the exposed tops of her plump breasts. "Who do you think you are, doing half-naked shimmies? If that's what you wanted, why did you give me so much trouble about taking you back to the Archipelago?"

"Don't you dare!" She stuck her finger in his face, her blood pounding with rage. "You promised we'd get married and you'd make an honest life for us. You lied! Where's that floating snake pit you call a ship?"

"Probably back in the SothSeas by now."

Sparrow narrowed her eyes. "What do you mean?"

"The night you disappeared, I left the Lady Fire. Ilias told me why you ran away. He didn't tell me where you were, though."

"Did you hurt him? I swear, if you did anything to him, I'll never forgive you, Lock the White!"

"Why has he always meant so much to you? You'd never forgive me for hurting him, but I nearly got myself killed in the ring with Miska for your sake and you didn't give me so much as a kind word!"

"Because you asking to fight him when you could have gotten your freedom was utter stupidity!"

"Too right! That's the last time I get my hair torn out for an ungrateful little—"

Sparrow slapped him hard, months of pent-up anger and hurt exploding in a loud crack of flesh on flesh.

His eyes widened, the imprint of her hand visible on his cheek. "What the bloody hell was that for?"

"For your existence! For your stupidity and your lies! Any more questions?"

"Just one." His teeth ground.

She lifted her chin. "What?"

"How can I get you back?" He grasped her shoulders and kissed her.

Sparrow knew she should push him away, but the sensation of his lips against hers was too wonderful. When she'd left all those months ago, she thought she'd never see him again, but here he was, all passionate words, long, sinewy limbs, and raw desire. Sparrow closed her eyes and clung to him, her mouth opening beneath the soft, moist pressure of his tongue. His fingers entwined in her hair as he deepened the kiss.

When they finally drew apart, both were slightly breathless.

"So will you come back to me?" he murmured. "I swear to you, Sparrow, I'll never go back to pirating again. I've been working honest jobs while I've been searching for you. I've saved everything I've earned. I have enough to support you, and I figure in less than a year, I'll have enough to build a decent ship for fishing and trade."

Sparrow sighed and took his hand. She gazed at his long fingers and touched his callused palms. She often wondered how a man's hands could be hard and graceful at the same time. "I can't go back to you, Lock. Not now."

"When?"

"I don't know. I trusted you once, but I don't anymore. I'm only glad we never had a child."

He didn't speak for a moment, and she looked up.

"I admit, I'm not the best breeder, but you seemed to like me well enough in your bed." He stood and walked to the end of the fence.

Sparrow shook her head. "I didn't mean that how it sounded."

"So how did you mean it?"

"I just meant that it would have been bad for a child the way you were and the way I had to leave. It's not that I don't love you, Lock."

"At least you're past hating me and back to love again. Think you could make up your mind?"

"Do you think you could make up yours?" she snapped, her temper rising. "First you want to marry me, then you want to be a pirate, now you want to marry me again."

"I always wanted to marry you, but I was completely selfish. Ilias helped me see that…and no, I didn't harm a hair on his head. He left the Lady Fire, too, and went back to his family."

"Good." Sparrow smiled. "He was too nice for pirating."

"Yes, he was."

"You, on the other hand, seemed born for it."

"I was." He approached her and placed a fingertip under her chin, tilting her face to his. "But you changed me, Sparrow. One thing I learned the hard way, I can live without pirating, but I can't live without you."

"Yes you can."

"I don't want to."

"Lock." She turned away. "I can't marry you. Not now. Not until I'm sure I'm what you really want."

"How can I prove it?"

She met his eyes. "Keep living an honest life."

"You won't marry me, so what about courting?"

"Courting?"

"That's what I've heard it's called. Didn't do much of it in the Archipelago."

"You want to court me?" She looked skeptical.

"Is that a yes?"

Sparrow smiled. "How can I say no to such politeness?"

"Good." His eyes held hers. "So we're courting. Seems a little funny since we've bedded already, but—"

"Lock," she closed her eyes and pressed her hands to her temples, "just don't ruin the moment, all right? I have to get back to the tavern."

"You're still going to dance in there?" he demanded.

"Yes, unless you don't want to court a gypsy dancer?"

"You know that means I'll have to sit there every night and make sure no one touches you."

"Cris does a fine job of keeping the peace — or at least he did until tonight."

"From now on, he's got help."

"I'm not sure they'll allow you back in there. You did break a chair, not to mention Cris's nose. And you kicked a patron."

"I'll talk to the owner. See if I can pay for the chair. As for the two fools who attacked me, I acted in self-defense and they'll get no apology from me."

Sparrow shook her head and smiled. "Why am I not surprised?"

"One thing before you go back there."

"What?"

"Hug me."

"What?"

He opened his arms, and she embraced him. She closed her eyes and rested her cheek against his chest. It seemed like forever since they'd been so close.

"Harder," he said. She gripped the hard muscles of his back.

She prayed this time he'd keep his promise, because she doubted she could bear to part from him again.

* * * * *

Though it took some careful negotiating from both Sparrow and Lock, the tavern keeper finally agreed to allow him back inside as a patron.

"Now remember, no causing trouble," Sparrow warned before she resumed her performance.

"They can watch and whistle," he said.

"That's right."

326

"If one of them touches you, I'll break his arms."

Sparrow cast him a warning look as he settled onto an empty seat and ordered a meal from the serving maid. He scarcely noticed when the woman brought the food, as all his attention focused on Sparrow.

Seeing her again made his stomach too tense to eat, yet less than an hour ago he'd been starving, after having spent the day hunting and skinning. Since looking for Sparrow, he'd been unable to settle in one place long enough for a permanent job. At first, he'd hunted and fished enough to keep himself alive while searching for her. Then he realized, once he found her, he'd have even less to offer her than before. If he intended to marry her, he'd need some means to do so. He'd begun hunting, selling and trading meat and fur. With a wagon he'd bought, he was able to store the goods he traded for and often stopped in marketplaces where he made more sales. Though far from wealthy, he could easily support a wife, and as soon as he could settle in one place, a family as well.

You're getting ahead of yourself, Lock. She hasn't even said she'd marry you again.

He watched her as she danced, the motions of her supple body making him hungry for something other than food. He could scarcely believe he was with her again, that moments ago she'd been in his arms and in a few hours would be again.

How could you have been such a fool to have pushed her away? He hadn't considered her at all when he'd been on the Lady Fire. He thought he'd given her enough attention, but he finally realized attention hadn't been the problem. Looking back on the changes that overtook him on the pirate ship made him feel shame such as he'd never experienced. Before Sparrow, he hadn't known enough to feel ashamed of his actions. Piracy had been a step up from the brothel. It had been the highest achievement a person could aspire to in the Archipelago. Pirates were revered there as the Knights of the Ruby Order were respected in the rest of the world. Respect! No SothSea captain ever commanded respect, only fear and loathing. He must have been insane to want loathing over love.

When he'd walked into the tavern, the last thing he'd expected was to find Sparrow dancing half-naked on a table like a common wench. What was worse, she seemed to be *enjoying* it. But why shouldn't she? Hadn't he enjoyed dancing in the Empress's competition? He understood how infectious dance could be. Even watching her, he wished he could join her.

As she spun, catching a tambourine Opal tossed her, he glanced around the tavern at the other patrons. Every man had his lusty eyes fixed on Sparrow. The women, on the other hand, either glared at their male companions or focused their attention on their food and wine. Why should they be interested in watching a half-naked woman—no matter how beautiful—perform a seductive dance? If there was a male dancer, that might be a different story...

Lock smiled inwardly. Now *there* was an idea! He'd have to talk to the tavern keeper.

* * * * *

"Well, I'll say one thing, you're persistent," Opal glanced at Lock as the three of them walked back to the gypsy camp.

"I wasn't about to let her go." He reached for Sparrow's hand.

Sparrow smiled at him, loving the warmth of his touch and the affection in his eyes. She'd missed him more than she realized.

"He's incredibly stubborn," Sparrow told her friend. "Don't you remember how he searched the camp that first night?"

"I hate to admit it, but I find that kind of stubbornness very romantic." Opal sighed. "Imagine having a man chase you across a continent."

"Romantic, is it?" Lock's eyes glistened with humor as he

looked at Sparrow. "You think so?"

"Don't press your luck," she said, but tightened her grip on his hand.

Firelight from the camp shone ahead. The silhouettes of caravans, horses, and people shone against the backdrop of hills and forest. Rays of pale moonlight shimmered on the lake running through the field.

The three stopped walking, and Opal said, "I'll leave the two of you alone."

"I'll be right there," Sparrow told her.

The slender girl glanced over her shoulder, her white teeth flashing in the night as she smiled and walked to camp. "Don't hurry, my friend."

Sparrow and Lock turned toward the lake, the lush grass soft beneath their booted feet. She looked at him. "I really should be getting back. It's very late. You have to be up early in the morning to hunt, don't you?"

He paused and tugged her behind the trunk of an enormous old willow tree, out of sight of the camp. He bent, one hand cupping the back of her head as his mouth claimed hers. Sparrow slid her arms up his back and stood on tiptoe to better reach him.

"Lock, I have to go."

"I know." He drew her into his arms and sank onto the grass, his pale eyes fixed on hers. He loomed over her. Sparrow's heartbeat quickened as she felt the warm length of his body over hers. One of his legs slid between hers. His hard cock nudged her inner thigh. How she longed to reach into his trousers and wrap her fist around the pulsing steel wrapped in velvet skin! He kissed her. Though he supported most of his weight on his forearms, she felt the hardness of his chest press against her breasts. Her eyes slipped shut as his lips moved from her mouth to her neck.

"Lock, we have to stop," she murmured, lost in sensation. His lips and tongue traced the tops of her breasts while one hand untied the front of her vest. She whimpered with pleasure as his lips captured one of her nipples. It had been too long since they'd been together and his touch felt so, so good! His scent of clean skin and sensual musk aroused her to the breaking point. She buried her fingers in his hair, knowing she should stand her ground and go back to camp, but wanting nothing more than to surrender to him completely. If she gave in to him now, he'd think she wasn't serious about making him prove himself. She wanted him more than anything, but only if he'd truly given up pirating. His tongue trailed down her stomach while his warm, callused hands kneaded her breasts. His fingers moved lower and tugged at the waist of her pantaloons.

Weakness flooded her legs. She knew if she didn't stop him then, within seconds she would no longer possess the strength to do so.

"Lock," she pushed his shoulders, "I have to go back."

He raised his head, his pale eyes brilliant with desire. Moonlight accentuated the white streaks in his kinky hair. The warm breeze tossed the unruly curls across his face. She brushed them away. He smiled and kissed her belly.

"I mean it." She slipped from him and stood, her body tingling from his touch.

"I've missed you, Sparrow."

"I've missed you, too, but we have to take this slow."

He touched his fingertips to her chin, his thumb gently stroking her cheek. He nodded in understanding and kissed her forehead. "I'll walk you back to your camp."

"Where are you staying?"

"Just over the hill, on the edge of the forest."

"Maybe you can stay with us? I'll asked Prem."

He shook his head. "No thanks. It's better if I camp alone."

Sparrow smiled. Lock seemed to have changed in so

many ways, but in others, he was exactly as she remembered him. That's what made saying goodnight so difficult, because she knew just how it would feel to spend the night in his arms.

* * * * *

"Whoa." Lock tugged Sea Storm's reins. The horse stopped the wagon. Lock hopped off the wooden seat, patted the stallion's sleek rump, and stepped through the open door of the tanner's cottage.

The sturdy, middle-aged man glanced up from the table, a faded cloth band tied over his forehead, keeping lank gray hair off his face. He pointed at Lock with the chicken leg he was eating. "Got them hides you promised?"

"In my wagon."

The man tossed chicken bones out the small window behind him, wiped greasy hands on his trousers, and headed for the door. "Let's see 'em."

Lock walked to his wagon and pointed to the skins.

The tanner examined the goods. "Not bad. Give you a hundred."

"You said two."

"Looks like you weren't too careful when you were skinning. Have to take off for that."

Lock narrowed his eyes. "There's nothing wrong with those skins."

"I ain't paying two for the likes of those."

"Well I ain't handing them over to you for one."

The tanner folded his arms across his chest and held Lock's eyes. "One ten."

"One ninety," Lock said, and the tanner laughed. Lock tried again, "One seventy."

"One thirty."

"One sixty or I take them to the next town."

331

"Next town's a day's ride."

"I'm not pressed for time."

The man picked through the skins and rubbed his nose with the back of his hand. "One sixty, then. Half now, half at the end of the week."

Lock laughed, reached across the tanner, and covered the skins. "Do I look like the village idiot? Waste of my time..."

"All right. All right. Come in and I'll pay you," the man grumbled. Lock followed and watched him count out the coins on the table covered with old grime and flakes of stale bread.

Lock placed the money in the pouch at his waist and helped the tanner unload the skins. With the skins gone, his next stop was the market. Two villages back, he'd traded for bolts of silk and wanted to sell them. He drove the wagon to the village square and rented space for the day.

He was about to display the silks when he was distracted by the sound of shouting from the tavern across the road. Lock glanced over his shoulder and noticed a mob dragging a boy to the scaffold in the center of the marketplace.

The youth struggled, screaming, "I didn't do nothing!"

"Rotten thief!"

"Keep your hands in your own pockets!"

"He ain't gonna have to worry about that where he's going!"

Lock narrowed his eyes as a man in a green tunic, apparently the local sheriff, walked up the scaffold steps and strung a noose.

"No!" The boy squirmed, but several arms held him hard. "I don't want to die! I didn't take nothing!"

Lock's lip curled. He knew that boy! It was the same crewman who stole from his cargo on the Lady Fire! The one whose finger he'd chopped off.

"The little fool," Lock muttered. "Still stealing even after I lopped off his finger. Some people never learn."

The men dragged the boy up the scaffold. He stumbled, but the villagers made sure he stood straight as the noose dangled over his head. The boy's face drained of color, and even from such a distance, Lock saw him trembling.

Lock turned to his wagon then glanced back at the scaffold. He tossed his hands in the air and strode across the village, thinking to himself, *You're going to regret this, Lock. Maybe you are the village idiot after all.*

"Wait!" Lock bellowed at the crowd awaiting the execution. "Hold the hanging a minute!"

The men holding the boy, the sheriff, and the boy himself stared at Lock.

"What the hell do you want?" the sheriff demanded. "This thief picked the pocket of nearly every man in the tavern — all within five minutes."

"I didn't take nothing," the boy whimpered.

"So you actually saw him take the belongings?" Lock asked.

The men on the scaffold exchanged glances.

"So which of you saw him steal?"

"His pockets are full of coins! All of ours are gone! That's proof enough!" bellowed a ruddy-skinned man who held the boy's arms behind his back.

"So you're saying possession of coins makes a man a thief? In that case, most of us here should be hanged."

"Where would a boy like this get so much coin?" the sheriff snapped. "He's dressed in rags."

"I once knew a king who traveled the countryside dressed as a peasant all in the name of fun," Lock said.

"He's already been charged. The sentence for theft in this kingdom is death, unless someone wants to pay his way out. You want to give up a chunk of your money for a no-good thief?"

"How much?" Lock spoke the words before he could stop

himself.

"One fifty in silver."

"One fifty?" Lock snorted. "How much did he steal?"

"Doesn't matter. That's the price."

"All right," Lock sighed. "I'll pay the bloody one fifty."

Disappointed that their entertainment wouldn't come to pass, the crowd dispersed. The sheriff grasped the boy's arm and dragged him down the steps. He said to Lock, "Come to the prison house and I'll make a record of your payment, then you and the boy are free to go."

The boy stared at Lock, shock in his hazel eyes, as the three walked to the prison house.

Once he'd paid, he and the boy left under the wary eye of the sheriff.

"What the hell did you do that for, you bloody bastard?" the boy snarled, craning his scrawny neck to look up at Lock.

Lock raised an eyebrow. "Why did I save your life?"

"What do you want? My other fingers as payment? I can't believe you're still breathing after all the curses I heaped on you!"

"Oh, so you're a warlock now as well as a thief? You'd think after I cut your finger off you'd have learned your lesson."

"I said I didn't steal nothing, especially not compared to you! You slime sucking, snake-toothed, stinking donkey's arse! If I didn't think you'd bury me, I'd chop out your gullet!"

Lock whistled. "Nice way to talk to a man who just saved your scrawny arse. Maybe I should have let you pay for your crime."

"I said I didn't steal—"

Lock grasped the boy and dragged him behind the blacksmith's shop. Gripping him by the shoulders, he lifted him off the ground so they were eye to eye. "Just like you didn't steal the cargo from the Lady Fire? You took their money, and we both know it!"

The boy kicked Lock between the legs. Cursing, Lock dropped him hard on the dirt and leaned forward, his hands braced against his knees. "Son-of-a-bitch!"

The boy scrambled to his feet and ran, but Lock caught him by the back of the neck. "Let me go!"

"Not until you shut up and listen to me!"

"What for?"

"You took the money, didn't you? Didn't you?" Lock shook the youth hard.

"I took it! So what? How else am I supposed to eat?"

"Did you ever try honest work?"

"What a joke coming from you, the worst pirate to ever sail out of the SothSeas!"

"Not anymore. There's no future in piracy."

"What do you mean? When you had the Lady Fire, you could have anything you wanted."

"Not anything that mattered."

"You have no business telling me what to do!"

"I'm not telling you anything. I'm offering advice."

"I've been on my own since I was seven. Didn't need no advice then and I don't need it now."

"No parents?"

"Dead mother. No father. Why do you care?"

"We've got something in common. Never had a father and my mother should have been dead, but that doesn't mean I have to ruin my life because of them. Neither do you. Have you ever killed anybody?"

"No."

Lock studied the boy. For the first time, he sensed he was telling the truth. "Good. Then maybe you won't end up like me after all."

"I can be better than you! If I was a captain, I wouldn't give up my ship!"

"That wasn't *my* ship. It belonged to anyone who killed for it."

"Why should I stand here listening to you? You cut off me finger!" The boy held up his mutilated hand.

"And a lot of good it did either of us! You're still a lying, thieving brat, and if you don't do something about it, you'll be a killer on top of it all, because it always comes down to murder in the circle we travel in. I'm sure a missing finger hurt like hell, but it won't kill you. Not like that hangman's noose. Want to see what can kill you?"

Lock tugged off his shirt and displayed what was left of his back. He glanced over his shoulder at the boy who stared silently at the mass of scars and valleys cut in and healed over on the broad bones and hard muscles.

"That only happened because you got caught," the boy muttered.

"And so have you. Twice."

The boy folded his arms across his chest and planted his feet wide apart. "So why aren't you dead? That beating was meant to kill you."

"Someone took pity on me."

"That woman, Sparrow. If it hadn't been for her, I'd be dead, too, remember?"

"Looks like we have something else in common. She saved us both. I have a business proposition for you."

The boy's lip curled. "I don't want to deal with you. You cut me finger off."

Lock continued, "You work for me, and I'll give you a portion of the profits."

"I'll kill you in your sleep," the youth snarled.

"No you won't."

"Why not?"

"Because, you skinny little shit, you know I'd wake up before the blow landed and gut you like a fish." Lock bent so that he was almost nose to nose with the boy. He straightened and shrugged. "Also because you're no killer yet. Take a good look at me, boy. Look at what I was, what I did to you. I'm giving you the chance to change, or do you want me to turn you back over to the mob now that you've admitted you stole from the men in the tavern?"

The boy paled. "I'll stay with you…for a while."

"First things first. We go back to the market and sell the goods I have left. I've been hunting for the past few days and just spent nearly all my profit paying for your life."

"Don't throw that at me! I already gave you me finger."

"You hold a hell of a grudge."

The boy tossed Lock a furious look but followed him back to the market.

Sea Storm stood quietly in front of the wagon, munching from the feed bag Lock had given him. Everything seemed just as he'd left it. He thought someone would have tried to steal both the horse and the wagon. Not that Sea Storm would have gone, but he'd have put up a fight that would have caused even more trouble in the marketplace.

Lock tugged away the leather covering on the back of the wagon and clenched his teeth, smashing his fists against the wood and causing Sea Storm to snort.

"What?" the boy demanded.

Lock pointed to the empty wagon. "Someone stole everything. Goods. Food. Even my damn underpants!"

The boy clicked his tongue and laughed. "I said you should have minded your own business."

Lock cast him a quelling look. "Shut up and get in. I have to go back to my camp."

"You ain't got nothing now? No money? No food?"

"What money I have is none of your business, just as long

as you get paid for what we hunt and sell in the market. I'll be getting more money tonight. I have work for the evening."

"What kind of work?"

"Get that fire out of your eye. It's all honest work. From now on, that's all we do, you and me."

"Right." The boy hopped into the wagon.

"By the way, what's your name? Can't keep calling you boy."

"That's all me mother ever called me—but I call meself Janos."

"Janos, we've got work to do before tonight. Are you any good at drawing?"

"I guess so."

"Good."

"What kind of work are you going to do tonight, anyway?"

Chapter Twenty-Five

** හා**

Sparrow rode silently toward the tavern, Opal's hands on her waist from where she sat behind her on the horse. The gypsy girl chatted about the day's events, but Sparrow thought only of Lock. For the past several days, he'd stopped at their site and walked her and Opal to the tavern, but today he hadn't come. Perhaps he was tired of her already. The thought made Sparrow's stomach drop, but if he reverted to his old ways, it was better that she hadn't agreed to marry him right away.

"Sparrow, are you listening to me?"

"No."

"Thank you so much." Opal's voice dripped sarcasm.

"I'm sorry. I was just wondering where—"

"Lock is? For a woman who had no intention of taking him back, he's all you seem to talk about."

"I know I'm a fool, especially after what he did."

"I know what he did to you, but I like him. He's interesting, funny, handsome."

"He can also be arrogant, bull-headed, and rotten."

"Nobody's perfect."

"Opal, he's too old for you."

"I don't want him!" The girl giggled. "At least for anything like marriage. Tell you what, Sparrow. I'll *borrow* him until you're ready to settle down."

"You'll do no such thing!" Sparrow glared over her shoulder.

"It was only a joke. Besides, all he sees is you. It must be so nice to have a big, strong, handsome ex-pirate madly in love with you."

Sparrow sighed. At times Opal seemed so bright for her age, but at other times Sparrow wondered if she had a brain in her head. Not that she entirely disagreed. Lock could be very winning, and just the idea of being in his arms made her entire body weak.

"Where is he tonight?" Sparrow muttered.

"He's probably still getting back from the village. He's a busy man, from what I hear. He'll make some woman a wonderful husband."

"You haven't known him long enough to judge."

"Sparrow, why don't you just admit you want him back?"

"Of course I want him back, but I can't let him know how much. Not right now. Lock's difficult. I have to be careful how I handle this situation. I have to…What's going on in there?"

Both women dismounted, and approached the tavern. From inside came the sounds of female voices shouting and laughing. Several men, mugs of ale in their hands, stood grumbling outside. Upon noticing Sparrow and Opal, their sullen expressions faded.

"Finally," one of the men said.

"Lady dancers. Thank the goddess!" said another.

"What's wrong?" Sparrow asked. "Why are you all out here?"

"That man who's been following you around is in there," snorted a tall, skinny farmer, "you wouldn't believe what he's doing."

"And the women love it," added a pot-bellied man in a stained tunic. "Disgusting."

"What are they talking about?" Opal asked.

Sparrow heard giddy shrieks from the women inside, and she muttered, "I think know."

She stepped into the tavern, Opal close behind her.

Women and a few irritated men filled the room. In the center, surrounded by giggling ladies, Lock performed the most seductive of dances. Barefoot, dressed in a black leather vest and leather trousers that fitted to the hard length of his legs, revealing the enticing bulge of his crotch, he smiled and moved his hips and arms sensually. The open vest exposed his broad chest and muscled abdomen, thorns and branches painted across his skin, masking old scars.

Coins littered the floor at Lock's feet, and every now and then a skinny boy scurried to the center of the room and gathered the money into a cloth pouch.

I know that boy. Sparrow suddenly saw the missing pinky finger. *The boy from the Lady Fire! What's he doing here?*

Opal laughed, clapped her hands, and went to join the women closest to Lock. Sparrow grasped her arm. "We have to get ready for our own performance, if we still work here, that is."

"He's very good, Sparrow!"

"Come on!" Sparrow took Opal's wrist and dragged her to the tavern owner who grinned as he sold mugs of ale to several women.

"Sparrow! Opal! Business is better than ever!"

"You never told us you hired another dancer," Sparrow said.

"Don't worry, you're certainly not replaced. He's going to dance an hour or so in the early evening then you girls have the rest of the night. I didn't think it was a good idea at first, but he said I didn't have to pay him for the first two weeks. He'd just take whatever he earned from the patrons. I never realized how much women would like to watch a man dance. Crazy, isn't it?"

"No crazier than the men who ogle us," Opal said.

"The men don't seem to like it much," Sparrow noted, smiling inwardly. Though she didn't like the idea of women lusting after Lock, she had to admit she found some justice in his performance. Why shouldn't the village women enjoy the same entertainment as the men?

"They'll get over it." The tavern owner waved his hand. "It's only one short hour a few nights a week."

Sparrow's eyes fixed on Lock as he moved. His gaze suddenly met hers and he winked. Sparrow tried to repress her smile, but only partially succeeded. There was no man like Lock. Anywhere.

The boy stepped out of the way as Lock spun, and Sparrow called to him. "Janos! What are you doing here with Lock?"

The boy smiled. "Sparrow! Good to see you."

"What's going on?"

"Work. The pirate and me is business partners."

Sparrow resisted the urge to laugh since the boy looked so serious. "Business partners? I'm glad to see you're off the ship, at least."

"Things ain't much better on dry land, I tell you. Was nearly hanged this mornin'."

Sparrow looked horrified. "Why?"

"Some men said I stole from them. Same old story."

She sighed and folded her arms across her chest. "Was it true?"

"I don't want to spread no rumors."

"Janos, what are we going to do with you?" Sparrow ruffled his curly red hair. "How did you and Lock end up together? How's your finger?"

"Don't hurt at all no more. The son-of-a-bitch—I mean Lock—got me out of the hangin'. Can't figure out why, but I won't complain about it."

Sparrow glanced at Lock and half smiled. *So he got Janos out of the hanging. Maybe he really has changed this time.*

She hoped so because she knew she couldn't give him up

again, no matter what.

* * * * *

Lock shoved damp hair from his eyes as he stepped into the kitchen where Sparrow waited for her turn to dance. Opal had claimed the tavern floor as soon as Lock finished, but not before tossing him a saucy wink.

"We made a killin'!" Janos grinned as he hurried to keep up with Lock's long strides. He peered into a sack full of coins.

"We?" Lock raised an eyebrow.

"Never thought women would throw money at a man just for screwin' air."

"Screwing air?"

"Sure. The way you dance, that's what it looks like. Speakin' of screwin', imagine how much you could make if you bedded them down…"

Lock shot the boy a look that said exactly what he thought of the idea. Janos gazed back at the money pouch. "Just a thought."

"So how much did you make?" Sparrow cast him a haughty look as she approached, a sheer veil draped over her body, scarcely concealing her pantaloons and beaded vest beneath.

He took the pouch from Janos then held out his hand.

"What?" The boy looked innocent.

"Empty your pockets."

"But I didn't take nothin'."

"I think I might tattoo that phrase across your face," Lock muttered. "Empty them. I didn't dance my ass off so you could keep half the profits."

"I didn't take nearly half," Janos muttered, fishing in his pockets and tossing into the pouch the coins he'd taken. "And you said you'd pay me for working for you. I been crawling on my hands and knees for the past hour picking up coins."

Sparrow peered in the pouch and Lock pulled the strings tightly, nearly catching her nose. She glared at him. "That's not right. You make more than I do and you've only been here a night."

"I can't help it if the men are stingier than the women. Besides, you get a fee from the owner, too."

"Are you going to pay me or what?" Janos demanded. "At least let me get something to eat. I'm starved."

Lock glanced at the skinny boy and divided the money between them. "You look like you could use it. Out of what I gave you, I want you to go to the market tomorrow and get some supplies for our camp."

"Why should it come out of my share?"

"Don't you ever shut up? You're worse than a woman."

"I resent that!" Sparrow lifted her chin.

"Sparrow, you know I didn't mean you."

"I'm sure he meant it. He's obnoxious, ain't he?" Janos grinned at Sparrow before he stepped back into the main room to order food.

"He can be." Sparrow folded her arms beneath her breasts. Except for the cook who stood grumbling over his stew pot, they were alone in the kitchen. She placed a hand on Lock's bare chest. "Janos told me what you did today. You saved him from being hanged."

Lock shook his head. "Good for him, but I get the feeling it's going to be bad for me. He'll probably try to kill me in my sleep."

"You did cut off his finger."

"Yes, and I just saved his neck. That boy attracts trouble — and it's going to be like chewing rocks to get him to keep his hands off other people's belongings. Speaking of belongings, everything in my wagon got stolen this afternoon, so it's a good thing I got the extra work here."

"All your things are gone?"

"Even my underpants."

Sparrow laughed, and Lock felt a smile playing around his own lips. "Think that's funny, do you, girl?"

"I'm sorry." Sparrow swiped the tears streaming from her eyes as she leaned against the wall, dissolved in laughter. "Who would want your underpants?"

"They were good wool ones for the winter."

Sparrow collapsed on the floor, unable to control her mirth.

"Took my frying pan, my razor—"

"What do you need a razor for?" She pointed to his white streaked beard.

"To shave my privates before I wear the wool underwear." He tossed her a sarcastic look and folded his arms across his chest. "Will you get up from there. It's not all that funny. Good thing I didn't keep the money I've earned in the wagon or else four months of work would have been gone to the wind."

"Where are your earnings, then?"

"Buried over half this continent. I couldn't very well take it with me in the wagon while I was trailing you all over creation."

"Buried?" Her laughter resumed. "You're not even a pirate anymore, but you're still burying your money!"

"Glad to see how much I'm amusing you tonight."

She stood and slid her arms around his waist. "I'm sorry. I've almost forgotten why I fell in love with you. You make me laugh and you make me crazy."

He cupped her cheek and kissed her, his eyes slipping shut, enjoying the sensation of her lips and her firm curves pressed close to his body.

"Sparrow, get out there!" Opal said as she stepped into the kitchen.

Sparrow tugged away from Lock, blew him a kiss over her shoulder, and hurried to the floor.

"That was quite a performance you gave," Opal said to Lock. "Sparrow told me you could dance, but I wasn't sure."

"Have you been teaching her?"

"Yes. She does well. The men love her."

"Do they?" Lock wondered if his irritation was apparent.

"She has a beautiful body."

"Yes, she does." Lock walked out to the table where Janos was shoving in a variety of foods.

"Slow down before you kill yourself." Lock snatched a slice of bread from Janos's plate.

"So? You never know when it's going to be your last meal." The boy's words were garbled as he spoke with a full mouth.

Lock's gaze fixed on Sparrow as she danced. Most of the women had dispersed, and the room was now filled with men, drinking, eating, and ogling Sparrow and Opal.

Someone nudged Lock in the shoulder, and he glanced at a plump, dark-haired woman. She offered him a lusty smile. "That was a fine performance."

"Thank you."

"Last time I saw such a stud, my husband borrowed his brother's breeding bull."

Lock resisted the urge to raise his eyes.

The woman's hand slid up his arm. "Looking for some company later on tonight?"

Lock smiled at her. "Lovely as you are, I'm already spoken for."

The woman sighed. "Oh well. Who's the lucky woman?"

Lock pointed at Sparrow.

The woman curled her lip as she watched Sparrow tug the veil from her fit, rounded body. "I should have guessed.

Will you be here again tomorrow?"

"Yes, I will."

"See you then." The woman removed her hand from Lock's arm and left.

"You're a bloody fool," Janos said, a piece of apple sticking out of the corner of his mouth. "You could be making money bedding these wenches."

"Don't you know what self-respect is?" Lock took a chunk of meat from his plate, and Janos nearly stabbed him with his knife.

"Get your own. I'm hungry," Janos ordered.

"For a skinny little thing you eat like a half-starved pig."

Janos cast Lock a sidelong look. "Better than having a face like one."

Lock cursed under his breath and waved for Leah to take his order. He was beginning to understand why the sheriff wanted to hang the boy.

* * * * *

Lock and Sparrow walked together to the gypsy camp, Opal and Janos ahead of them, the horses plodding alongside each of the youths.

"They seem to get along well," Sparrow nodded toward the boy and girl. "Janos is actually being polite."

"Probably just wants to get close enough to her to steal her purse."

Sparrow laughed. "Opal would cut off the rest of his fingers, believe me."

"Did I tell you how beautiful you look tonight?"

"Yes," she gazed at him through her lashes, "but you can tell me again."

He kissed her hair. "You're beautiful."

"Eh, Lock!" Janos called over his shoulder. "It's a sailor's sky tonight, ain't it?"

The group looked at the stars and moon gleaming brightly in the clear sky.

"I'd say so." Lock took Sparrow's hand as they walked.

"What do you mean, a sailor's sky?" Opal asked.

"No storm in sight. Perfect for navigatin'," Janos explained.

Lock smiled slightly. "Imagine being at sea right now. Cool, salty breeze. The ship rocking like a cradle. What a night to stare at the waves."

Sparrow felt a twinge of apprehension. "You miss the sea."

"I miss the sea, but it's not forever. I'll have enough for a ship soon, and—"

"A ship!" Janos eyes widened. "You're going back to pirating? And you had me buying all that rubbish about honest livin'. I knew you didn't really turn in to a woman, Lock the White!"

Lock gently smacked the back of Janos's head. "What do you mean a woman? I'm not going back to pirating, and neither are you. It's going to be a ship for fishing and trade."

"Ah shit," Janos muttered. "At least it'll be a ship. And if it ain't a pirate ship, I guess you won't be cuttin' off any more of me fingers." Janos turned his big, green eyes to Opal. "He cut off me pinky finger, you know."

"So I heard."

"Ain't that brutal?"

"Yes, it is." Opal shot Lock a disgusted look then turned the same face to Janos. "But don't expect too much sympathy. He could have killed you for stealing, and you still haven't learned your lesson, even after losing a finger."

Janos whistled and turned to Lock and Sparrow. "She's a rough woman, ain't she?"

"I think you should stay at our camp tonight," Opal

suggested to Lock, "especially since all your belongings have been stolen. You can have a good meal, share our fire. The others would like to meet you."

"We've met, remember?"

"Yes, but that wasn't a social visit. You practically tore apart our camp looking for Sparrow."

"I hardly call that tearing apart a camp," Lock said. "I just looked around a little."

"You looked under the beds in our caravans."

He shrugged. "She could have been there. Who knew you'd have her dressed like a fat, wrinkled old man?"

"Sea Storm knew me." Sparrow patted the stallion's flank.

"I should have paid more attention to him." Lock tickled her, and she playfully slapped his hands away. "Thanks for the offer, but Janos and I will be fine at our own camp."

"Speak for yourself," the boy snorted. "If I can get a good meal and better company than you, I'm takin' it."

"Meal? You haven't stopped eating since we got to the tavern."

"I wish you'd stay." Sparrow looked up at Lock.

"You do?"

She nodded and slipped her hand into his.

"If you want to be a stubborn fool, go ahead," Janos stated. "I'm spendin' the night with them."

"Then I guess I'll have to stay to keep you out of trouble."

"Me? Trouble?"

At the top of the next hill, the gypsy camp was visible below. The caravans and wagons stood in a semi-circle. Several fires burned, a few people seated by the flames.

"Almost everyone is in bed," Sparrow said.

"Sounds good to me." Opal yawned. "After a snack."

"I'm for that," Janos said.

"That's a surprise," Opal glanced at the boy. "Come on. I'll see what's left over from supper."

"Opal, would you take the horse with you? I want to show Lock the river."

Janos winked at Lock. "I'll take Sea Storm, so all you'll have to worry about is looking at the river."

"That boy is almost more trouble than he's worth," Lock muttered, watching Opal, Janos, and the horses hurry toward the camp.

"You like him very much, don't you?" Sparrow tugged him toward the next hill.

"He has potential but hasn't had much of a chance."

"I think you're feeling guilty about cutting off his finger."

"I am not. If Rino had been Captain, the boy would have been shark food."

"So you did him a favor by maiming him?"

"Can't you let anything go, girl?"

"Then why did you help him, if not out of guilt?"

Lock shrugged. The truth was, Janos reminded him a little of himself as a boy. No guidance, no one who gave a damn about him. Maybe if someone had showed him a different way of life, he wouldn't have grown into the sort of man who thought it was acceptable to lop off people's appendages.

"So what did you want to show me at the river?"

"Just follow me."

The field was well lit until they reached the woods. Moonlight even shone through the trees, allowing them to pick their way down a path. As they walked, Lock enjoyed the sensation of Sparrow's small hand in his, the sound of her voice when she spoke, and the simple feeling that they were truly together again. Since he'd found her, she hadn't once looked at him with the hatred he'd seen on the ship, and for that he was grateful to whatever power ruled the universe.

Ahead Lock saw a clearing in the moss-covered trees. A

cascade emptied into a basin that ran into a small brook.

"Isn't it pretty?" She slipped off her cloak, sandals, and vest. Her arms covering her bare breasts, she cast him a coquettish look over her shoulder before stepping beneath the cascade.

Lock watched her for a moment. Her eyes closed, her face upturned to the dark water pouring from the overhanging rocks, she reminded him of a water sprite spoken of in eastern legends.

Sparrow had changed since they'd parted. She seemed more free somehow, as if a part of her had bloomed and he was lucky enough to experience the full beauty of the flower. Still, he knew part of her didn't trust him, and she *had* trusted him once. She wasn't as innocent as when they'd first met, and he knew he was responsible.

"Are you coming in?" she called. Her long, fawn-colored hair hung in wet tendrils over her shoulders and down her back, pieces clinging to her firm, full breasts.

Lock removed his clothes and stepped into the water. It felt cool but refreshing against his skin. Though it wasn't the ocean, even such a small cascade filled him with excitement. The only thing he loved more than the water was Sparrow.

He tugged her close and kissed her, water gushing over their heads. Her arms slid around him; her soft breasts pressed against his chest.

"The gypsies will be moving on sometime next week," Sparrow said.

"Are you going with them?"

"Yes."

"Then it looks like I'll be going with you."

"You still plan on following me?" She opened her eyes, blinking through the pouring water.

"I'm going to follow you until you either tell me to go or consent to marry me."

351

"I know you want to go back to sea."

˙ "I want you." He took her face in his hands and kissed her again. "I'd rather spend the rest of my life in a desert as long as you're beside me than spend another moment at sea without you."

"I want to believe you, Lock." She rested her cheek against his chest. Her palms splayed against his back, her fingers gripping muscle.

"I know I lied to you. I know I hurt you and I wish I could take back what I did. I wish I could change so many parts of my life, but I can't. All I have is the present and the future. I want to share them with you."

"I just need some time, Lock."

"You'll be well worth the wait."

When they finished swimming, they walked back to camp. Almost everyone was asleep. Sparrow took two blankets from the caravan she shared with Opal while Lock rekindled one of the fires outside. They lay on the blankets, Sparrow snug in his arms.

"This is almost too much to ask of me, you know," he murmured in her ear before kissing the hollow between her shoulder and neck.

Sparrow shivered with desire and sighed. "It's not easy for me either, Lock. Especially when you...do...that..."

Her voice drifted off as his hand slipped beneath her vest and fondled her breast. His thumb rolled one of her nipples. He smiled when he felt her pulse quicken.

"We can't Lock," she whispered, turning to him. Her beautiful eyes held his, wide with passion that seemed as difficult for her to restrain as it was for him. She tried moving away, but he held her fast. "If you don't stop, I won't be able to resist you, so I have to go back in the caravan."

Disappointment washed over him. His cock ached with desire and his lips longed to taste every inch of her, but if she wasn't ready, he wouldn't force her and risk losing her again.

The idea of life without Sparrow was too painful.

Brushing a kiss across her brow, he held her to his chest and closed his eyes. "I'll stop, so don't leave."

Sparrow snuggled close to him, one of her arms wrapping around his waist. Her breath fanned his chest, her eyelashes tickling one of his nipples. His erection pressed against her hip, arousing him more than he wanted to admit. Sighing, he prepared himself for a sleepless night of magnificent torment, holding the woman he most desired yet unable to claim her as his own.

Chapter Twenty-Six

ഇ

Over the following month, the gypsies traveled through two more towns, finally stopping at the seaside village of Rose Cove on the southern most tip of the continent. Though small, Rose Cove possessed an active marketplace, being located near several major kingdoms as well as within fairly close sailing distance of the Isles of Kenna.

The gypsies decided to stay for a while, considering how well their goods sold in the marketplace. Lock and Janos set up their camp nearby. The boy had a talent for woodcarving, in particular creating lovely wind chimes that sold so well in the village he was offered a permanent job working with one of the local craftsmen.

"You should take it," Lock told the boy one evening when they sat around a fire in the gypsy camp, sharing a meal with Opal and Sparrow.

The boy shrugged. "Don't know if I'm one for settlin' down."

"Maybe it's about time," Lock said. "You haven't stolen anything in months, and you're making a good living selling those chimes."

"I guess. It's nice knowing the money in me pocket is really mine." The boy stared hard at Lock. "And what about you? This seems like the kind of place you've been talking about movin' to, the kind of place you wanted to build your ship. I know you got enough money to do it."

Lock glanced at Sparrow. "Not sure I'm ready yet."

"Maybe you should," Sparrow said quietly. "It's what you said you want."

"It's one of the things I said I want, not the most important."

She held his eyes, a slight smile tugging the corners of her fine lips.

"It would be profitable," Janos said. "When you go off tradin', you can take some of my chimes, then we could both make more money."

"This would be a nice place to settle," Lock admitted. "Eventually. What do you say, Sparrow?"

"It's very nice."

He glanced at the fire and leaned back on his elbows. He rather hoped she'd sound more enthusiastic. Perhaps she'd changed her mind about him completely and he'd been making an ass of himself following her all over the continent. *Well, it wouldn't be the first time you've been an ass, Lock the White. And she's well worth the risk.*

"I'm takin' the job!" Janos slapped his fist into his palm. "Why the hell not?"

"Good for you!" Opal lifted her mug of tea to him, and the others joined her.

"You know, I hate to admit it, but I'm gonna miss travelin' with you," Janos told Lock. "You ain't so bad."

"Neither are you." He took a swallow of ale. "By the way, sorry about your finger."

"You should be." Janos reached for a chicken wing, and nothing more was said on the matter as the group discussed possibilities for the future.

When the others had retired for the night, Lock and Sparrow sat close to the fire, his arm around her. She leaned her head against his shoulder and entangled her fingers with his.

"Prem said the gypsies will be moving again soon," she said.

"Where to this time?"

"Not sure yet."

"Are you going with them?" He asked that question each time the gypsies left a village or town, and the answer was always the same. He didn't know why he even bothered asking. His hair would probably go completely white by the time she decided to marry him, if ever.

Sparrow looked at him, her eyes glistening in the firelight. She shook her head. "Not this time."

His stomach fluttered and he wasn't certain if his disbelief was visible in his eyes. She smiled and looped her arms around his neck as he kissed her.

* * * * *

The following afternoon, Sparrow and Lock married in the temple on the outskirts of the village. Janos, Opal, Prem, and Mita witnessed the joining, and afterward the gypsies provided a fine celebration.

Lock had intended to travel alone to retrieve the money he'd buried while following Sparrow, but she insisted on accompanying him. He was glad. Another separation from her was the last thing he wanted.

Once they'd gathered the money, they'd return to Rose Cove, build a house, and then he'd find a crew of men interested in trade and begin building his ship.

Later, they set up their camp away from the others. A breeze kept the warm night comfortable. Lock turned Sea Storm out to pasture, then he and Sparrow went for a midnight swim in a nearby brook. Wrapped in soft plaid robes they'd bought each other as wedding gifts in the market that morning, they walked back to the fire.

"Are you happy?" he asked.

"Very happy." She rubbed her cheek, cool from the brook's water, against his. "Are you?"

"I've never been so happy." He kissed the top of her head

and stood, walking to the wagon. She added another log to the fire then sat, giddy with joy. Since she'd met Lock, she wanted him. He'd been such a rogue back then, but somehow she'd sensed they were meant to be together.

She felt his hands brush the hair from her back and drape it over her shoulder. Warm lips touched her bare nape before he slipped a slender rope of braided brown leather around her neck and fastened it loosely. A delicate gold bird hung from the leather, and she touched it with her fingertips. "What's this?"

"Another wedding present. I bought it months ago and was waiting for the right time to give it to you."

She smiled. "It's a sparrow. Thank you, Lock. I love it."

"What about me?"

She laughed and hugged him. "I love you more than anything."

They slipped off their robes and climbed beneath the blankets by the fire, Sparrow curled against his chest. He stroked tangled hair from her forehead and kissed her.

"So this is our wedding night." She smiled, running a fingertip down his nose.

His lips turned up in a wolfish grin as he slid his hands down her back and cupped her naked buttocks. "Good thing I don't have to waste time being gentle."

"Gentle!" She gripped a handful of his kinky hair. "Since when have you ever been gentle?"

"You always said you like it rough, Princess." He rolled her onto her back and covered her body with his, running his tongue down her neck while one hand caressed her breasts. "And I always aim to please."

"In what little time you work with."

His startled gaze flew to her face, and she laughed. "I was only teasing."

"Were you, girl?" He slid down her body, raining kisses

over her breasts, belly, and hips. "We'll see if you're in the mood for humor in about an hour or two."

"What lofty goals you set." She tried to sound mocking which was difficult to do when his lips tugged at her clit and his tongue thrust into her pussy, swirling and tasting. She clutched handfuls of his two-toned hair and closed her eyes, her body aflame. The marvelous, relentless lapping of his warm, wet tongue over her clit flung her into orgasm. She convulsed, moaning and panting. "Goddess help me. Lock!"

She heard the laughter in his voice. "What's wrong, girl? Tired already."

"You must be joking." She gasped as he resumed the fantastic torture. "You still have a lot to teach me."

"You're a luscious student."

"I love you, Lock." Her eyes opened halfway, and she gazed at him.

He stared at her, all humor gone from his handsome face. He reached for her hands and entwined his fingers with hers. "I love you too, Sparrow."

"Say it again."

"I love you."

Sparrow knew she'd never heard words so beautiful.

Bending his head, he returned to her aching clit and ran the tip of his tongue along the ultra-sensitive sides of it. She quivered, her legs clamping his shoulders while his hands kneaded her buttocks and clutched her hips. This time when she came, the sensations were almost too powerful. She lay in blackness, aware only of the waves of pleasure breaking over her convulsing body.

"I need you, Sparrow," he said in a husky voice. "I need you so badly."

Sparrow reached for him, pulling him close. He slid into her, groaning with desire. Her legs wrapped around his, her feet pressing him closer, deeper, while her fingertips stroked his back and ribs. She felt his heart pounding, though his thrusts were long and slow. Soft lips covered hers in a tender kiss. His tongue rimmed her mouth then thrust inside, meeting hers. He kissed her so deeply she thought he might draw her very soul out of her body and into his. She would welcome such a joining, for she felt they already shared two parts of one soul.

Another orgasm built deep inside her. The exquisite pressure was almost unbearable. He must have felt the same, for she felt his heart racing, keeping time with hers as his thrusts increased. Suddenly Sparrow exploded, her cry of pure passion absorbed by his kiss. As she clung to him with all her strength, riding out her pleasure, she felt him stiffen and surge into her with several fast, hard thrusts. Tearing his mouth from hers, he gasped out his orgasm. He collapsed, his big, hard body pinning hers to the mattress. She felt his every harsh breath mingling with hers as she languidly stroked his curly hair.

"I love you, Lock," she whispered.

"I love you, too."

She smiled as he rolled onto his side, holding her close.

* * * * *

Two weeks later, the gypsies broke camp.

Though Sparrow found saying goodbye to Opal and her friends difficult, her new life with Lock thrilled her. Her only concern was that he wouldn't be happy settling down. She didn't doubt his love for her, but she knew he needed passion beyond the bedroom. Perhaps when his ship was built and he returned to sea, his adventurous spirit would be satisfied.

"Where are you going next?" Sparrow asked Prem and Mita as the two stood beside their wagon, ready to leave Rose Cove.

"Begonia," Mita replied. "It's been quite a while since we've been there."

Sparrow nodded, smiling gratefully. She knew the gypsies had avoided Begonia while she traveled with them.

"Would you take a message to my friend Shea-Ann?" Sparrow asked.

"Of course."

Sparrow embraced the couple. "I'll miss you. You're always welcome in our home."

"And you're always welcome in our camp." Mita glanced at Lock. "You, too, as long as you're with her."

"Thanks." Lock grinned. "I think."

Sparrow and Lock watched as the caravans and wagons disappeared over the hill.

"Tomorrow we'll leave," Lock told her. "Sure you want to go digging up money for the next month or so?"

"I'm *not* letting you out of my sight again." She grasped his wrist as they returned to their camp.

"I might not let you out of my arms again." He picked her up, kissing her neck, his beard tickling her skin.

She clung to him, giggling. "I think I can live with that."

* * * * *

By the end of the summer, Sparrow and Lock had collected the money he'd hidden and built a house on the outskirts of Rose Cove. Sparrow cleared space for gardening and once the house was finished, Lock, along with a hired crew, began building his new ship. Shea-Ann sent a message that she and Daphne were doing well in Begonia, but they missed Sparrow and would visit as soon as she could get away. Sparrow looked forward to seeing her old nanny again, and even Lock seemed happy about Shea-Ann's visit.

"I can't wait to see her again," Sparrow told Lock as they sat down to dinner the day she received Shea-Ann's letter.

"I'm almost looking forward to seeing the witch, myself."

"When she visits, do you think you two could try to get along?" Sparrow scolded.

"If I tried to get along with her, I think she'd be terribly disappointed."

"You're incorrigible."

"Maybe once, girl, but I'm quite tame now."

"Not from what I remember about last night."

He grinned and kissed her. "I'm going to get some exercise then I'll be back and really give you something to remember."

"Modest as always."

He winked and stepped outside.

Sparrow cleared the table then followed him. She sat on the fence behind their house, watching Lock practice his martial arts forms in the field where Sea Storm grazed. She thought how utterly content she was in her marriage. Though Lock spent his days farming and working on the ship, nights were devoted to her. They talked and danced together, swam in the ocean just outside their door, and made love on the beach. Lock was an attentive and satisfying husband, and she knew he genuinely enjoyed their life together. Still, she sometimes wondered if part of him was bored.

Her gaze followed his every movement, loving the play of his muscles as he blocked and kicked. Every chiseled inch of his tall form seemed to lure her. Simply watching his long, rock-hard thighs and calves as he shifted stances was enough to make her wet.

When he finished practicing, he peeled off his sweaty vest and approached her. Rather than appearing tired by his practice, his expression was as lusty as she felt.

"I need a swim," he said, wiping his broad chest with the rolled up vest.

"No you don't." She tossed him a coquettish look and beckoned to him with one finger. He reached for her, and she ran toward the house. He chased her, catching her with a few long strides and lifting her in his arms.

"Lock!" She giggled as his beard tickled her neck. She clung to him as he kicked open the door and closed it, placing her on a stool by the wall so she was a bit closer to his height.

His mouth covered hers, and she ran her hands over his sweat-slicked back and shoulders, feeling him slide off his trousers and kick them aside. She closed her eyes as his cock, hot and steely like the rest of his body, slid into her pussy.

She fastened her legs around his waist and he growled, walked two steps to the bed, and flung them both on it.

Sparrow clutched his back, her body straining to keep time with thrusts so hard and fast she thought she might die of pleasure. Lock's warm, panting breath fanned her neck. His hands squeezed her buttocks and caressed her ribs.

"Oh, Lock, don't stop!" she gasped, threading her fingers through the damp hair at his temples.

His mouth covered hers as he thrust harder, faster, while she wrapped her legs around him and lost herself in the ride. She cried out, desire stabbing her. Her entire body pulsed, her pussy clenching his cock, her fingers gripping his hard, wet back. Tearing his mouth from hers, he growled his desire as he climaxed.

"Sparrow, I love you so much!" he gasped, his body crushing hers, but she didn't care. It was the most marvelous feeling in the world, being pinned beneath him.

After a moment, he moved slightly aside, tugging her to his chest, before they both fell into a deep, satisfied sleep.

* * * * *

Lightning ripped a jagged streak through the sky, disappearing into the tossing black ocean. Thunder was disguised only by the crash of waves as they washed over the deck of the sinking ship.

Waves swept men overboard while others clung to the mast or fought their way through the deadly black sea to a lifeboat scarcely

362

safer than the vessel.

The scanty crew battled for life against the indomitable tide.

* * * * *

Lock leapt awake to a clap of thunder that shook the house. He threw off the sheets and reached for his trousers. Though drenched in sweat, he trembled like he hadn't since he'd been tortured in Begonia.

He knew from experience his dream hadn't been ordinary. It was real. It was clear, just as when he'd dreamed his own whipping so many years ago and the vision of Sparrow and the storm at sea, except this dream wasn't of something to come. It was happening *now*. He knew it, and this time, he could stop it.

Sparrow woke just as he was heading for the door.

"Lock, what's wrong?"

He heard her voice in the distance, but his mind still spun with the nightmare. He raced to the barn and guided Sea-Storm into the blinding rain, not bothering with saddle or bridle.

Sparrow, barefoot, wearing only her cloak, grasped his arm hard. "Lock, what are you doing?"

"Ship's sinking off the west beach. Go to the village and get help. Have them wait on shore."

"How do you know there's a ship sinking?" she demanded.

"I saw it in a dream."

"Just because you had a few dreams that came true—"

"Means I know the difference between one that's foolishness and one that's a vision."

"What are you going to do?"

"Take the ship out." He mounted Sea-Storm and using hands and knees, nudged the animal down the path toward the beach.

"Lock! You can't take the ship out in this storm! It's not completely finished and you don't have a crew! You'll be killed!"

"Maybe, but if I don't go, they won't make it. Do as I tell you, Sparrow!"

He kicked the white stallion to a gallop and didn't stop until he reached his ship tossing in the dock amidst the raging storm.

Squinting against the rain and wind, he turned the ship out to sea.

Waves crashed over the ship. Several times he thought he'd capsize and wondered if Sparrow was right. She'd looked at him as if he was mad. Perhaps he was, for there was no ship in…There! Just ahead the vessel was halfway down. Several men leapt from the rails and joined the others who struggled to keep their heads above the waves. The lifeboat had already sunk.

One of the men noticed Lock and swam for his ship. He threw the swimmer a line and hauled him on deck. Two other men followed. Lock saw that there were two swimming with the burden of a companion in distress.

Kicking off his boots, shirt, and trousers, he asked one of the men nearest him, "Can you control this vessel?"

The man nodded, and Lock jumped into the freezing water. Having spent most of his life in the ocean, Lock was an excellent swimmer and had on more than one occasion plucked companions from the sea during wrecks. He swam toward the two men aiding their injured companion and took the wounded one to the ship before dragging three more men aboard and climbing on deck himself where he sat on his knees, gasping, tendrils of wet hair streaming in his face.

"How many of you were lost?" Lock panted.

"We're it," said a tall, slender man with a dark, wiry beard. "We're all here."

"All?" Lock narrowed his eyes at his passengers. Though the ship was far too full for a craft of its size, there were no more than twelve on board and two large, tawny dogs— scarcely any for the size of the ship, which had almost disappeared beneath the water.

"Because of the battles with Zaltana, there were few to send on this mission," the bearded man continued as he stooped by one of his wounded comrades and did his best to stop the bleeding from a gash on his arm. Lock noticed both the men wore a black uniform with a circle of red thorns embroidered around a ruby over their hearts. The man who'd been talking wore a green sash about his narrow waist. He suddenly realized they were all Knights of the Ruby Order.

Lock took control of his vessel, knowing they had to get away from the sinking ship quickly lest they be dragged down with it.

A tall, slim redhead with an even redder beard and eyes almost as pale as Lock's approached him. This man also wore a green sash over his wet black tunic. He touched Lock's arm. "You listened when the Spirits spoke. Thank you."

"Eh?" Lock demanded as he fought the storm for control of the ship.

"Your vision," the redhead told him.

"How did you know about that?"

Though he didn't reply, a streak of lightning revealed the redhead's smile.

Lock sighed with relief when he saw the shoreline. Sparrow and several villagers ran toward them as they docked.

"Goddess!" Sparrow murmured, staring at the men on board. "You were right, Lock!"

"I told you," he said. "Some of these men are wounded, and they'll need places to stay for the night."

"Knights of the Ruby Order?" a villager said. "All of you?"

"We are," said the one with the dark beard.

Several villagers volunteered their homes and took the wounded as Lock and the healthy passengers carried them off the ship.

"Can we put up a few, girl?" Lock glanced at Sparrow.

"Of course," she said. "We have plenty of room."

Lock and Sparrow's home was closest to the beach, so they helped the two bearded Knights with green sashes and another lanky comrade with short, black hair haul three of the wounded to the house. The two dogs followed.

Inside, Sparrow lit lanterns and fetched a bucket of water.

The Knights settled the wounded. While the redhead worked on their injuries, the one with the dark beard said, "I'm going to the village to help the others."

"I'll go with you." The black-haired knight stood. Both paused as they reached the door and thanked Lock for his assistance.

"Most of us wouldn't have survived without your help." The black-haired one extended his hand to Lock.

"Was nothing. No bother."

"My name is Torn. This is Crag." He pointed to his companion with the dark, wiry beard.

"We're in your debt," Crag said.

"Not at all."

As the two Knights left the house, Lock kindled the fire.

"Mate of the Key, help me," the redhead stated. Lock glanced over his shoulder, and the Knight smiled. "Yes. Help me bind this leg. Good practice for you."

Lock approached and applied pressure to the cut on the man's thigh. This Knight had dark hair and deep blue eyes. Both dogs hovered around him like drooling gargoyles. He patted them weakly and gasped as Lock began cleaning the wound according to the redhead's instructions. Lock didn't take his eyes from his task and marveled that the redhead could so easily instruct and work at the same time.

Lock's charge cursed under his breath as the former pirate applied more pressure. "Don't know your own strength, man!"

"What do you call these beasts?" Lock motioned with his head towards the dogs in an attempt to keep the man's mind off his injury.

"That's Roland. And the pretty one's Melinda."

Lock chuckled, stealing a quick glance at the dog's snubbed and wrinkled black face. "She's a beauty all right."

"I'm Rain. What's your name?"

"Mate of the Key," the redhead muttered.

"Mate of the Key!" Rain snapped. "What the hell is that supposed to mean, Blaze?"

"My name's Lock."

The redhead cast Rain a knowing look. "As I said, Mate of the Key."

"You'll get used to Blaze," Rain told Lock. Again, he glanced at his redheaded companion who was murmuring to himself as he stitched a gash in the head of an unconscious Knight. Rain added, "No. I lied. Most of us never get used to Blaze, but he has a good heart and is the best healer in our Order. Lock's your name? Why does that sound so familiar?"

"Erik's acquaintance," Blaze supplied.

"Sir Erik?" Lock asked. "I met him and another Knight, Warrant, in Begonia."

"Oh, right." Rain nodded. "He told us about your skill in the ring and how you killed Miska."

To Lock, it seemed so long ago that he and Sparrow had lived in Begonia. It had been the best and worst time of his life. He thought it was strange how he and the Knights of the Ruby Order had crossed paths twice.

Sparrow stepped inside carrying two buckets of water. She glanced at Lock with curiosity as he helped Blaze set

Rain's broken leg.

"Good," Blaze said. "You'll be a fine addition."

"To what?"

"Pay him no mind." Rain waved his hand in Blaze's direction.

"Ignore what you don't understand and you'll understand it no better next year," Blaze told him.

"I've known you over fifteen years, Blaze, and I still don't understand!"

Sparrow filled a bowl with water and brought it to Blaze so he could clean blood from his charge's face. The redheaded Knight smiled at her. "Thank you, Little Bird."

She giggled. "How did you know my name?"

"Thought your name was Sparrow," Lock muttered.

Blaze shrugged. "Sparrow. Little Bird."

"I like that," Sparrow said. "What can I do to help?"

For the next several hours, they cared for the injured. Afterward, Sparrow prepared a quick meal of bread and fruit. Just as they were about to eat, Torn and Crag returned.

"That was an admirable display of courage," Torn said to Lock. "But I wonder what you were doing out in the middle of a storm?"

Blaze glanced at Lock. "Guided by the Spirits."

"In a way I guess I was. I dreamed your ship was sinking. I've had dreams before that came true, and I knew this one was the same."

"You risked your life to help us," Crag said. "And simply for a dream. Few people would have done that."

"Lock's a rare man." Sparrow rested a hand on her husband's arm.

"Not really. I understand the sea, that's all. I've been in enough storms and wrecks to know what to expect."

"In a half built fishing ship?" Rain looked skeptical.

"No." Blaze stared at Lock. "The blood on his hands is not from fish alone."

"I've never heard it put quite that way." Lock raised an eyebrow. "I've sailed all over the world and seen my share of battles. I'm not proud to say I caused most of them. I was a SothSea pirate."

"I see. " Torn's eyes swept Lock. "How did you end up here?"

"Striving for redemption." Lock winked at Sparrow, a gesture of affection without humor.

"Well, you've made a hell of a good start," Rain said, tearing a chunk of bread with his teeth. "You're—"

"Lock the White," Crag said. "I've heard of you."

"Lock the White?" Torn narrowed his eyes. "I thought you were dead. Apparently Erik must have thought so, too. He spoke of a man called Lock whom he wanted to recruit, but evidently didn't realize you were the pirate."

Sparrow said, "Lock the White *is* dead. My Lock is alive."

"I can't erase what I've done, Sparrow."

"None of us can," Crag told him. "But just because we can't change what we've done doesn't mean we can't improve what we do. You're lucky to have realized that."

"I had some help." Lock slid his arm around Sparrow and drew her to his side. "From my…little bird."

Sparrow smiled at him.

"Why were there so few on board?" Lock asked. "That was a good sized vessel."

"We went to lend aid to a small southern island Zaltana was invading." Torn shook his head. "They never give up."

Crag took a swallow of tea and said, "They never will. Trust me."

"What about you?" Rain nodded in Lock's direction. "How did a SothSea pirate end up in the ring at Begonia and on a fishing ship out here?"

369

"It's a long story."

"We have time." Blaze's blue eyes were wide with interest. In spite of the man's strange ways, Lock liked him.

He sighed and began, "My ship went down off the coast of Lower Kenna. The crew died at sea, but the last thing I remember is swimming..."

* * * * *

The Knights exchanged glances when Lock finished his story.

"You've had a harsh guide on the path to redemption," Blaze said. "But perhaps not unjustified."

Lock raised his mug to the redhead. "That's right enough."

"Still, many men would have taken the first ship back to the Archipelago," Rain reflected. "And the Lock the White we heard of never would have risked his life to rescue a bunch of drowning men he didn't know."

Lock gave a wry chuckle. "Or who he did know."

"We've lost many this year because of Zaltana," Torn said. "And we have few ships and fewer able sailors. We could use a man with your skill."

"Have you thought any more about joining the Knighthood?" Rain asked. "I think Erik might have been right about you."

Lock shook his head. "How can I be a Knight?"

"Why not?" Sparrow asked quietly. "You're a great sailor, a master of hand-to-hand combat. Your skills are wasted here, Lock. I've always known that."

"Erik raved about your prowess in the ring," Blaze said.

"He knows a fighting form similar to yours," Sparrow explained. "I once saw Knights give a demonstration at a palace in the North."

Blaze smiled. "Yes. I remember now. I...Fourth daughter. Princess."

"Not anymore," Sparrow said.

"The spirits spoke. I would offer condolences for your family's fall, but you're content without the royal robes."

"Yes, I am."

"They say you speak in many ways."

"Speak in many...Yes." Sparrow understood. "I'm fluent in ten languages—actually eleven, since I spent time living with the gypsies."

Rain whistled. "You'd be a help when we travel. Too bad you're not a man. Ever think of becoming a Dame in the Opal Order?"

"No. That's not for me. I want to be a wife and mother, though the traveling part sounds interesting. Could you Knights use a female ambassador?"

Torn looked thoughtful. "I'll discuss it with Mahir. If you're interested, Lock, I can arrange for a meeting with our leader and an evaluation."

"Wait a moment." Lock stood and paced the room. "I can't be a Knight. You know what I've done in the past! You stand for righteousness, goodness. You stand for those I crushed. I can't join you."

"Do you think we're all pure?" Crag curled his lip. "Far from it, I assure you."

"Even the purest among us have regrets," Blaze stated.

"Lock," Crag stood and faced the pirate, "before I joined the Order, I was a Captain in the Zaltanian army. I know about slaughter. I was part of it."

"Now he stands among the madmen of our Order." Blaze nodded toward Crag's green sash and touched his own.

"What does that mean?" Lock asked.

"The green sash faction goes into battle without weapons." Rain shook his head. "They don't kill and are the best healers in the Knighthood. Blaze leads them. He's third in command of the entire Order. There are only about ten of them who wear that sash, and if you ask me, they are madmen."

"I wouldn't go *that* far," Lock said. "Nor would I ever join that faction. When I'm fighting, give me a good blade."

"Here, here!" Rain punched Lock amiably in the leg.

"Training for the Order is rigorous," Blaze said. "But I sense you're accustomed to hardship."

"Work doesn't bother me, and learning keeps you young."

"You will be separated from your wife for a time while you train," Torn said.

Lock glanced at Sparrow, and she told him, "I understand. To see you using your talents will be worth it. No matter how happy we are here, Lock, part of you needs adventure. And I'll always be there when you come back."

Torn nodded, his expression solemn. "You both should travel to the Order with us."

"You'll be given a quick evaluation," Blaze said. "Torn is second in command."

Lock and Sparrow exchanged looks then glanced at the dark-haired Knight's smooth, attractive face and slightly protruding front teeth.

"I'm sorry, but you look so young," Sparrow said.

"Torn was raised in the Order. Mahir, our leader, is his foster father," Rain said. "He didn't get any special privileges, though. Torn's one of the toughest men you'll ever meet, in the Order or anywhere. There are stories of his deeds—"

"That can be saved for later." Torn shook his head. "One thing about most of these Knights. They talk too much."

"To keep us busy when you station us in the field for weeks on end."

"Better to be a madman than a crone," Blaze murmured.

Rain growled, "If my leg wasn't bad, Blaze—"

"He'd kick your tail like he did last week," Torn said. "Enough of this. It's late and we're keeping our hostess up. We can all use some sleep."

Lock and Sparrow retired to their bed. She lay in his arms and whispered, "Do you think you'll be happy as a Knight?"

"If I have what it takes to become one."

"I don't have a single doubt."

Chapter Twenty-Seven

 හ

When Lock, Sparrow, and the Knights finally reached the Ruby Order's fortress in their kingdom of Rubyshire, the families of several of the Knights awaited them in the courtyard.

Sparrow looked around the Knights' home. A massive stone wall surrounded the inner palace. The courtyard was vast and filled with trees and flowers. Windows of many chambers shone in the high walls. Outside in the fields, Knights had been training with weapons and on horseback while others farmed with their families. The Order was completely self-sufficient, a small world of its own.

"Crag!" A small, blond-haired woman shouted, hurrying toward the tall, slender Knight with the wiry brown beard. She held an infant in her arms, and two young children followed at her heels.

"Lily!" The Knight beamed.

"Pa!" the children chimed, clinging to the Knight, one tugging on his green sash.

Sparrow smiled as the Knight grasped the woman and kissed her soundly on the mouth then embraced the children before turning to the infant. As Sparrow watched Crag with his family, she could scarcely believe he'd once been a Captain in the Zaltanian army.

"Another baby?" Rain, using a walking stick to support his healing leg, approached Crag and his wife. His dogs licked the children who began playing with the tawny beasts. "Congratulations. Looks like a beauty."

"Nice going, Crag!" another Knight called.

Crag's wife said, "He had a little help, you know!"

"That may be us someday," Lock whispered close to Sparrow's ear.

She smiled up at him. "I can scarcely wait."

"Follow me," Blaze said to the couple. "I'll find you a room."

They followed the redhead into the great hall. Though large, it was simply decorated with rows of long, oak tables and chairs. Several people sat eating at the tables or socializing. She saw Torn standing by the fireplace kissing a tall, dark-haired woman.

"Torn's mate," Blaze explained. "Charming."

"Are you married, Blaze?" Sparrow asked.

The Knight laughed. "In a dream, perhaps."

They stopped in an upstairs hall, and Blaze opened the door to a small guest chamber. Inside was a bed, trunk, and table with a pitcher of water. In spite of the palace's lavish size, the Knights lived simply within it.

"Rest. Torn will call for you when it's time to meet the Leader of Swords and Sewing Needles," Blaze said, leaving the two alone.

"I think he meant the leader, Sir Mahir," Lock explained. "Blaze isn't easy to follow, but if you listen hard enough, you can understand."

"He's tried to help you understand your dreams, hasn't he?"

"He says my dreams are a privilege. I can't control them, but I can learn to guide them."

"Perhaps he's right."

"Are you sure you'll want to live like this, Sparrow? I might be sent away for months. During training, I'll have scarcely any time for us."

"I know." Sparrow touched his cheek. "Do you want this, Lock?"

"Yes." His pale eyes held hers. "The only thing I've ever wanted more than this is you."

"Then this is how I want to live."

"I love you, Sparrow."

"I love you , too, Lock."

* * * * *

Sparrow sat in the great hall in the fortress of the Knights of the Ruby Order talking with Torn's wife, Honey Wine, ruler of the Sophianna. They awaited their husbands who were speaking privately with Mahir.

Sparrow noted that Honey Wine was a tall, strong woman with a beautiful face and eyes that spoke of the deepest pain and joy. Though Honey Wine was now a leader, Knights of the Ruby Order: Lockd Mistress in her land, she had once been a member of the royal guard. When she'd spoken against a brutal fighting ring, she'd been stripped of her rank and forced to work as a healer in the dungeon. There she met Torn who had been captured while on a secret mission for the Order.

Torn had been tortured while imprisoned, and Honey Wine forced to watch.

"I understand what you must have felt when you saw Lock beaten in the village," Honey Wine said.

"I didn't even know him then, but I couldn't stand seeing him like that, even though he probably deserved it. I'm glad I took him. No matter what he's done in the past, he's a good man."

"If you hadn't saved him, Torn and the others would most likely have died at sea. I'm forever grateful to you both."

"I'm just happy none of them drowned. It was miraculous they all survived."

"Danger is all too common in the life they've chosen."

"What's it like being married to a Knight?" Sparrow asked. "Are you afraid when he's called away on missions?"

"Always," Honey Wine said, "but it's Torn's life. The Knighthood is inside him, and not just because he was raised here. If it's meant for Lock, you'll understand what I mean."

It was several hours before Lock returned with Torn, Blaze, and Mahir. They joined the women and other Knights at the table for the evening meal, and Lock told Sparrow he'd been accepted to train for the Order.

Sparrow embraced him tightly and smiled. She was genuinely happy for him, but part of her already missed him.

* * * * *

Lock and Sparrow sold their home in Rose Cove and gave their ship to Janos who wished Lock luck in his endeavor to become a Knight. Training began immediately, and from then on, he wore the gray tunic of a trainee and spent from early morning until late at night sharpening his fighting skills on the field and learning the healing arts. For one year, he was to learn the basic skills of Knighthood, then for two years work in his area of expertise. With a lack of good seamen, Mahir wanted Lock to captain a ship after his training.

The Knights spent many long hours working. Lock and Sparrow scarcely saw one another, difficult considering they'd only just married. Though she missed him, Sparrow tried not to complain too much about their lack of time together — at least to him. When she, Lily, and Honey Wine got together, they openly aired their grievances, though the other wives offered her assurance as well.

"It's not usually bad for me and Crag," Lily explained one evening when she, Sparrow, and Honey Wine shared a meal in the courtyard. "Unless he's drafted for a special mission, I travel with him. I'm a midwife, and his specialty is healing, so we work together — similar to the way you and Lock will once he's Knighted and given his own ship."

"It's wonderful that Mahir is preparing you to act as an ambassador for the Order," Honey Wine said. "That way you and Lock will work together, and since he's going to be a ship's captain, you'll get to travel to so many exotic places. It's difficult for me and Torn. I have to run affairs of state, so we hardly ever travel together."

"But I'm sure you make it worth your while when you are together." Lily smiled at her friend. "The morning after he gets back from a mission, you have a glow about you. Wonder what that could be from?"

Sparrow glanced at the jug of wine she shared with her companions. Lock's training had affected their love life as well. Often times when he returned from the field and assignments, he was too tired to do anything but sleep, particularly since he'd been having difficulty conforming to the Order's strict lifestyle. Due to insubordination and several scuffles that his superiors deemed avoidable, he was often given extra duties.

"Don't worry, Sparrow." Honey Wine patted her shoulder. "Lock won't be a trainee forever."

"I just want him to be happy, but I'm concerned with the trouble he has—or should I say the trouble he causes."

Lily grinned. "I remember when Crag was a trainee. He had a few reprimands himself. Your Lock is a good man, and he'll do much better when he's in charge of his own ship. Sir Erik's been keeping a careful eye on him."

And I'll bet he cringes every time Lock opens his big mouth or finishes a tavern fight, Sparrow thought to herself. Why had she ever thought joining the Order would curb his wild nature? Still, she knew once he made it to the dubbing, his courage and strength would be an asset the Ruby Order. Evidently they thought so, too.

After the women finished their meal and said good night, Sparrow walked to the room she shared with Lock. It was large enough for them to live comfortably, and contained a bed, trunk, table, and bookshelf. Sparrow undressed and slipped into her nightshirt. She chose a book and sat at the table with a mug of tea. Lock had been away for nearly three days—one day longer than expected. The moon was high in the sky outside their window when he stepped into the room, looking tired.

Sparrow stood and embraced him. His arms slid around her and he held her tightly.

"I thought you'd be back earlier."

"Got stuck with extra guard duty." He shrugged his shoulders. "My back is killing me."

"Extra guard duty?" Sparrow took the tunic he pulled off and set it aside for washing. She noted it was filthy with dirt and blood, but didn't bother asking where the blood had come from. She knew he'd been sent to assist the healers who were lending aid to a mining colony that had a cave-in four days ago.

"Told Sir Warrant he was wrong about the way he divided the men for rebuilding. Should have kept my big mouth shut, but he was willing to let it pass when he realized I was right. Then, just hours before I'm ready to come back home, some big miner starts giving me trouble, so I gave him some trouble. Got me a shift on guard duty on the Fortress wall on what should have been my time off."

"So you've been home since this morning and I didn't even know?"

"I was on duty, girl. Came home as soon as I could. I have to meet Blaze in the morning to help him make medicines in his herbarium." Lock sat on the edge of the bed and rubbed his bloodshot eyes. He took Sparrow's hand and tugged her beside him. "I'm sorry. I wanted to see you, too."

"Honestly, Lock, can't you behave?" Sparrow felt torn between irritation and sympathy. She climbed behind him on the bed and brushed aside hair as unruly as he was. Her fingers massaged the taut muscles of his shoulders and back. He released a guttural moan of satisfaction. "It's bad enough how much time you spend working without acting up and having more shifts added on. Don't you ever want to see me?"

"I always say I'm going to keep my mouth shut, but it just

doesn't work, girl. Rub a little to the left…"

Sparrow moved her hands, finding a particularly knotted muscle just below his nape. "Well don't get yourself thrown out before you get dubbed, or all this work will be for nothing."

Lock stretched out on the bed and tugged her to his chest.

"Other than you, this is the only thing worthwhile I've ever had in my life," he said. "I have to become a Knight, Sparrow. There was a time when I thought it was impossible for me, but it's not."

"I know it's not." She squeezed him. From the moment she'd seen him, something inside her knew he was a man of courage and quality. He might not be the most polished of men, but he was what Knights were made of. She kissed his chest. "You'll be a Knight, Lock. I know you will."

She wasn't sure if he heard her, since he was fast asleep.

* * * * *

Somehow, Lock and his temper made it through the first crucial year of training. After that, he was often sent away for months at a time as a crew member on different ships of the Order. If Sparrow had missed him before, it was nothing compared to those lonely months while he was away. Though she didn't always see him at home, he was stationed nearby. At least none of the assignments lasted longer than two months. However his final mission before dubbing was to the far east, a journey that could take up to two years.

The day he left, Sparrow stood at the dock and clung to him tightly before he boarded the ship. "I love you so much. I'll miss you."

"I'll miss you, too, girl." He kissed her deeply, his eyes reflecting her sadness. "Just think. When this is over, I'll be a ship's captain again. Now that Mahir has officially made you an ambassador for the Order, you'll be able to travel with me."

"I can scarcely wait."

"Lock!" One of the Knights waved to him from the deck. "Get up here!"

He brushed a final kiss across Sparrow's mouth and boarded.

She watched as the ship vanished on the horizon. Sparrow hugged her waist and sighed. She knew this separation was to be the longest, but when he returned, Lock would be dubbed a Knight of the Ruby Order. She wanted to tell him a secret she'd been keeping for the past several days, but he had enough to worry about without knowing he was leaving her with a child. Once it was born, she'd send him a message and hope it would reach him.

"Sparrow." Honey Wine approached and placed a hand on her shoulder. "How are you feeling?"

"I miss him."

"I know." The Mistress placed an arm around her. "This time will pass more quickly than you realize. Torn has often told me Lock is a fine addition to the Order. They need men with his skills."

"He's had so many reprimands because of his temper."

Honey Wine shook her head. "He's not the only Knight to engage in brawls while traveling, even though the others say he attracts trouble like flies to a pig's rear end, but I think he's mellowed."

"Not where it counts." Sparrow touched a hand to her stomach. One thing about their small separations while he was at sea, they invigorated their love life. Just last night, he'd made love to her for so long she'd nearly fallen asleep before he'd finished. He'd said he didn't want her to forget him while he was away, as if such a thing could ever happen.

Honey Wine laughed. "So do you have any names picked out?"

* * * * *

381

Though Sparrow wished Lock wasn't away, preparing for her baby kept her occupied. Her pregnancy was pleasant, and most of the wives, particularly Honey Wine and Lily, were helpful to her, though Honey Wine was only around as often as her duties to her kingdom would allow.

One evening, Sparrow sat with her two friends by the river outside the Knights' fortress. They watched Lily's children and Honey Wine's daughter splashing in the water, and talked about the approaching winter.

A teenage boy wearing the gray robe of a trainee approached with a message for Sparrow.

She unwrapped the parchment with excited fingers and grinned as she told her friends, "It's from Lock."

"How is he?" Honey Wine asked.

Sparrow's eyes scanned the parchment, and she touched the bold black lettering, thinking that Lock's hands had also touched the letter. She smiled at some of his promises of how they were going to celebrate when he returned, but kept those parts of the message to herself. She told her companions, "He said they'll be leaving for home in three weeks. They've stopped in Upper Kenna. He said they sometimes work for days at a time with little rest or food. There have been a lot of skirmishes with Zaltana, even so far east. He said he's tired, but a good tired."

"He's a Knight, that's for sure," Honey Wine said.

"Have you told him about the baby?" Lily asked.

"No. As soon as it's born, I'll send a message."

"You better sharpen your quill," Lily told her. "You're due any day now."

"I'm just glad you're here to deliver it."

Chapter Twenty-Eight

ℬ

"I can't believe we're on our way home." Sir Erik said as he and Lock sat on deck of a ship called the Ocean Star, oldest of the Ruby Order's small fleet, but one of the finest. It had carried the group of Knights to and from the far east, through two storms and several battles with stray Zaltanian troops. Now they were so close to home they could almost smell the wild flowers that littered the hillside behind the Order's fortress.

Lock thought of Sparrow so often during their separation. Each night, she was his last thought before falling asleep. In the midst of battle and disease-ridden towns where the Knights stopped to lend aid, the thought of returning to her often kept him from giving in to utter despair. He'd spent his life fighting, but becoming a Knight meant more than soldiering. He'd finally become a healer, and with that came greater responsibility than he'd ever imagined. At times the Order perplexed him. They fought and healed. One moment his sword sliced a man's gut, the next he stitched someone's war wound.

"You finally made it," Erik continued. "When we get home, you'll be dubbed."

"I've learned not to count on my wager until the horse crosses the finish." Lock took a long drink from a wine flask and passed it to Erik.

The Knight swallowed a mouthful. "I'm glad you decided to join us. I had a feeling about you all those years ago when I saw you fight Miska."

"The hardest part for me has been walking in line."

Erik grinned. "You've been doing well. Haven't had a

fight in three weeks."

"We haven't docked in three weeks."

"I only hope you remember what it's been like for you once you've got your own ship. You'll have young trainees on your crew, and they'll be looking to you as an example."

"That's a haunting thought," Lock muttered. "All jokes aside, I hope I can help them learn from my mistakes. I...What's going on over there?"

The men stood, glancing off the port side where a small ship approached.

Sir Rain and the ship's Captain, Sir Otto, approached the rail and exchanged words with the two men sailing the ship. Moments later, the filthy men in bloodstained, tattered clothes were brought on board. One nearly collapsed on deck, but Blaze, caught him and began administering to their injuries while Rain and Otto talked with them.

The other Knights, at the Captain's command, kept their distance and continued with their work.

"I wonder who they are?" Lock and Erik returned to their place on deck to continue their time off duty.

"I'd say we're about to get into another battle. Any insight on the matter?"

The Knights were by now familiar with Lock's visions. Though they still came at random, with Blaze's help, he was able to better understand the messages they brought. It had been months since he'd had such a dream, however, so he could offer Erik no reply.

"Then I guess we'll have to wait." Erik glanced across the deck to where Blaze, Rain, and Otto spoke quietly to the newcomers.

Within the hour, the entire crew gathered on deck for Otto's announcement.

"By now I'm sure you all know two men were brought on board. They're from an island called Black Haven just east of here. Sonian Slavers have invaded their island and shipped off many of their people. The ones who remain behind have been trying to hold their own in the only village left that hasn't been destroyed. Many are wounded and dying. We're heading for Black Haven now. Sonian Slavers don't travel in large groups, but their warriors are well trained. Prepare yourselves for battle and heavy casualties."

Otto dismissed the men, and everyone set to work readying weapons and healing supplies.

Lock was assisting Blaze with herbal remedies when Rain approached, his tawny, bull-faced dogs at his side.

"Lock, I know you've been assigned as a healer for this journey, but we're going to need our strongest fighters in the front lines." Rain glanced at Blaze. "Sorry to take him from you."

"No need for apology," Blaze replied.

"Truth is, we could use you up there as well," Rain said to Blaze, and Lock understood why. Sir Blaze, though he wore the green sash which signified his vow that he'd never touch a weapon, was the most skilled of any Knight in hand-to-hand combat. Lock had trained with him often, and always ended up with the bruises to prove it. At times the power in Blaze's tall, slender body amazed him. Though Lock was physically stronger, Blaze was like liquid steel: bendable, yet unyielding.

"I would go willingly," Blaze said. "However, experienced healers are few here."

"I know," Rain said. "We're going to have our work cut out for us."

The dark-haired Knight left the hold, his dogs behind him.

Lock followed, glancing over his shoulder at Blaze. "Good luck."

"And to you."

"Lock," Rain said before the reached the deck, "I want to tell you something before we go out there."

"What?"

"Are you familiar with Sonian Slavers?"

Lock shook his head. He'd seen and learned much in his years at sea, but these particular slavers were unknown to him.

"Few people do. They're from far north and are a small but fierce tribe. They like to take prisoners in battle and have a reputation for whipping them to death. I thought you might want to know."

Lock's stomach twisted and he felt a momentary rush of panic that subsided so quickly it might never have been. "It doesn't matter to me. I'm part of the Order, and we're in this together."

"I thought you'd feel that way."

"Thanks for the warning."

Rain nodded. "Let's go. We have work to do."

* * * * *

"Another attack coming!" Erik bellowed through the broken door of the long house, the only building left standing on the entire island of Black Haven.

Lock heard him, the information registering in the back of his mind, as more urgent matters held his attention. One of the islanders had been injured fighting the slavers that morning, and his leg required immediate amputation just below the knee. While Blaze performed the surgery, Lock held the patient immobile, not a simple task, as the process was excruciating and islander large and strong.

"Almost finished," Blaze said.

The man shrieked and cursed but Lock kept him from moving.

All around, islanders and Knights scurried to protect the house and the wounded. Tables were overturned and placed in front of the windows. Two men hurried to repair the door that had been knocked off its hinges during an earlier attack.

An arrow flew through the door, just missing Lock's head.

"Bloody hell." He glanced at the arrow embedded in the wall beside him. "Blaze, hurry up!"

"Patience."

"Go to hell!" the islander screamed.

"We're already there," Lock muttered.

Another trainee, little more than a boy, approached Lock, his eyes frantic. "Sir Rain wants you outside."

Blaze was bandaging the stump, so the trainee took Lock's place in assisting him.

Lock grabbed his sword and headed for the door, almost grateful to join the battle. At times he preferred fighting to healing. There were less complications on the field.

Outside, the crew of Knights fought with a group of Sonian Slavers dressed in thick plates of armor. The Sonians carried double swords and wielded them with amazing skill. Before he had a chance to think, Lock found himself fighting two slavers. He killed both, but others appeared. As Rain had said, they were fierce fighters. Lock's blood seeped from shallow wounds that might have been fatal, if not for his skill.

Finally, the Knights began driving the slavers back, but the Sonians refused to give up easily. If they couldn't take their prisoners, they would destroy their enemies.

Flaming arrows soared through the air and set fire to the long house.

As he spun to block a blow from behind, Lock noticed Blaze and several trainees attempting to evacuate the house. Lock glanced at what was left of the village. Rain and the others had control of the foot soldiers, most of whom had already retreated. Several Knights headed for the forest from which the Sonian archers fired their arrows.

Lock sheathed his sword and ran toward the longhouse, joining the others in clearing out the wounded before the building burned to ashes.

The house was thick with smoke, and flames ate through the ceiling.

"Almost everyone is out!" Blaze called. "Just a few more at the back."

Lock, Blaze, and two trainees forced their way to the back of the house. Lock's eyes stung and he and the others coughed as they breathed the thickening smoke. He squinted, noticing several people, groping their way along the floor amidst flames. He heard a creak from overhead and glanced up, his heart pounding.

"The roof's falling in!" Lock bellowed. "Hurry!"

Blaze grabbed two children. Lock slung an unconscious man over his shoulder and took the wrist of a woman who was nearly blind from the smoke. The Knights guided the four to safety, but they'd seen at least three others left behind.

Together, Lock and Blaze headed back inside. A particularly loud creak caused Lock to look up again. A beam cracked and nearly fell. Lock caught it and held it up. "Get them, Blaze!"

The Knight's pale eyes widened slightly as he stared at the size of the beam Lock held. "But—"

"Go!" Lock hissed, unsure of how long he could support the weight of the beam. Already his arms and shoulders felt ready to break.

Blaze disappeared into the smoke. To Lock it seemed like forever before the Knight reappeared, a woman in his arms, a boy and girl clinging to his robe. He rushed them to the door.

Lock grunted and heaved the beam upward before he leapt for the door just as the roof collapsed. No sooner had he jumped clear of the building when an arrow struck him in the leg. Lock fell forward. When he looked up, he found himself surrounded by Sonian Slavers, several sword tips poking his flesh.

"Hell!" Lock muttered, his heart pounding. He was going

to die without ever seeing Sparrow again.

Suddenly two of the slavers dropped to the dirt. The remaining three glanced at their companions, turning their swords from Lock, but not in time.

Blaze's foot struck one between the legs and another in the face before the men realized they were being attacked. The last slaver twirled his swords, slashing and stabbing at the auburn-haired Knight who dodged every blow. Weaponless, the Knight used a piece of wood as a shield. He blocked two sword swipes, kicked one of the blades from the slaver's hand, and dropped to the ground, one long leg lashing out in a sweep that knocked his opponent to the dirt. Another quick kick in the head rendered him unconscious.

Lock glanced around and saw Knights and islanders driving off the few remaining slavers, then focused his full attention on his leg. Blaze had already knelt beside him, examining the wound.

"Thank you," Lock told his friend, gritting his teeth as the arrow was removed. "You saved my life."

"Thank *you*," Blaze said. "Your strength is as admirable as your courage."

"Anybody would have done the same."

"Not anybody." Blaze bound the wound. "We'll care for this on the ship."

Rain and his dogs, all three covered in dirt and blood, approached. "The island is secure. Some of the Knights are staying behind to help rebuild. As soon as we reach home, we'll send a fresh crew." He glanced at Lock's leg. "You'll need to rest that for a while. Looks like you're on light duty for the remainder of the journey. Good work, men. This was no easy test for any of us."

* * * * *

Several hours later, Lock lay in one of the holds, his bandaged leg propped on a sack of supplies. Blaze had cleaned the wound and said Lock should heal well, though it would take time.

Lock folded his arms behind his head. "At least I'm off duty for a few days." The injury was uncomfortable, but he'd had far worse. When he'd found himself surrounded by slavers, he had anticipated another whipping. He'd take the leg wound over that any day.

He closed his eyes, hoping he could fall asleep and dream about Sparrow, but footsteps drew his attention to the hatch. Blaze, followed by a young island boy with a black and white bird perched on his shoulder, approached.

"You gifted him with life, he gifts you with a soaring companion," Blaze said.

"Huh?" Lock asked, grateful for all Blaze's help, but a bit too tired to figure out his riddles.

"If it hadn't been for you, me, my mother, and my sister would have died in the fire," the boy said. He raised his arm and the bird hopped on his wrist, its curved, yellow beak reminding Lock of a colorful anchor. "We haven't much left after these battles, but we'd like you to have one of our birds."

"That's not necessary," Lock said. The last thing he needed when he came home to Sparrow was a bird on his shoulder. She'd think he was more daft than ever.

"Please." The boy extended his wrist. The bird settled onto Lock's broad shoulder.

"Hello," the bird croaked, and Lock felt his eyes widen in surprise.

"Our family has bred and trained these birds for years," the boy explained. "Unfortunately, most of them were lost when the island was seized, but we've recovered a few."

"Hello," the bird said again.

"How are you?" Lock said, then raised his eyes to the ceiling. He'd just spoken to a bird!

"He learns quickly," the boy said. "We've taught him

several words, but with patience, you can teach him more."

"You don't have to give him to me. It was no trouble."

"You were wounded because of us."

"No. I attract trouble. Ask anyone on board. Blaze?" He looked to the auburn-haired Knight for help, but only received an amused smile.

"We insist," the boy said. He climbed up the hatch, Blaze behind him.

"Hey!" Lock shouted. "I don't need a bird! I don't — "

"How about an ale?" The bird fixed its glossy black eyes on Lock.

"I think I need a barrel of it," he muttered, then sat up straighter, an idea forming in his mind. "Can you say Sparrow?"

"How about an ale?"

Lock sighed. It was going to be an interesting trip home.

* * * * *

Lock stood on deck of the Ocean Star as it docked in the waters in a coastal village two days from home. He watched several Knights board, men as eager as Lock and the crew to return home after long assignments.

Home. Lock sighed, squinting against the sunlight. *Sparrow.* And the dubbing. For the first time in his life, a year and eight months at sea had challenged him. He'd been separated from Sparrow and knew this assignment would decide whether or not he was of the right quality to enter the Ruby Order. There had been plenty of hard work, fighting, sleepless nights, and rough weather, but for the first time in his life, he felt proud of his actions. The Knights had given aid wherever it was required and had even picked up several new recruits after the battle at Black Haven. These men all wore gray tunics similar to Lock's. He glanced down at his own. It was tattered from use, but it fit more comfortably. *Much like myself,* he thought.

"Bloody hell," a voice croaked close to Lock's ear.

He glanced at the black and white bird and snapped, "I told you not to say that."

"How about an ale?"

"That's not what I've been teaching you." Lock shrugged his shoulder and the bird stretched its wings.

"Comfort approaches." Blaze joined Lock at the rail, squinting at the glare of sunlight on water.

"We're almost home. I know."

"Your leg?"

"Feels much better." Lock raised the stick he'd been using for support and walked several steps. "Be rid of this thing soon. I can't wait to kick again."

"And dance." Blaze grinned.

"I only showed you because you asked. They'd probably never dub me if they saw me dance."

"Not as long as you keep clothed." Blaze extended his arm, and the bird hopped from Lock's shoulder to the Knight's wrist. "Like a breathing flower, this creature."

"Bloody hell," snapped the bird.

Blaze shook his head, raising his eyes to heaven. "Mate of the Key, you're a bad influence on an innocent."

"So my wife has told me."

One of the Knights who'd just boarded approached Lock and offered him a slip of parchment. "This message arrived for you with one of our troops headed south."

Several other Knights and trainees crowded around the newcomers to retrieve messages from home.

Lock broke the seal and read Sparrow's words, unable to control his smile. He turned to Blaze and the Knights also reading their letters and said, "I have a daughter!"

His companions congratulated him.

"Didn't know Sparrow was expecting," one of the Knights remarked.

"Neither did I," Lock said, flooded with elation. The events of the past year and eight months slipped from his mind, and all he could think about was seeing his family.

"A dubbing and a daughter. Not bad at all, Lock. Not bad at all," said another Knight.

Two days from home, Lock thought. *Now it's going to seem like forever. A daughter. I wonder what she looks like?*

* * * * *

Sparrow stood at the dock as Lock's ship approached. She glanced at the chubby baby girl tucked against her shoulder and smiled, her heart pounding with anticipation. She could scarcely wait to see Lock and show him his daughter.

As the ship neared, she noticed him immediately. He stood on deck, taller than every other Knight on board, his kinky, waist-length hair now more white than brown, his beard gleaming silvery in the sunlight. A black and white bird clung to his shoulder. Sparrow laughed. Obviously he had as much to tell her as she had to tell him. He waved, and she waved back.

As he stepped on shore, she noticed he carried a walking stick and his gait was a bit awkward as he hurried to her. He placed a steely arm around her waist and kissed her, his tongue tracing the shape of her mouth, exploring every moist corner and crevice that he hadn't felt in too long. Then he stared at his daughter.

"She's beautiful, Sparrow," he said. "She looks just like you."

"You're hurt." Sparrow glanced at his leg.

"It's nothing." He kissed her hair. "In another few days, I'll be rid of this bloody stick."

"Hello," the bird said.

Sparrow stared at it. "Should that thing be near the baby?"

"He's harmless."

"That beak looks like it could snap a finger off. Where in the world did you get it?"

"Long story."

The bird's tiny black eyes fixed on Sparrow. "Bloody hell."

Sparrow's eyes widened. "Lock! Did you teach it to curse like that?"

"Not intentionally."

"A fine example you're going to be for your daughter," she teased.

"I'm going to try," he spoke seriously.

Sparrow stood on tiptoe and kissed him. "You're going to be a wonderful father. What better example than a Knight? I love you, Lock. I've missed you so much. I have so much to tell you."

"I have so much to tell *you*." He accepted the baby and held the small body close to his broad chest. "What did you call her?"

"Shea-Ann."

Lock laughed and slapped a hand to his forehead. "Say it isn't so, girl!"

"Sorry." Sparrow grinned. "She's like a mother to me. By the way, she's here at the fortress visiting. She came to see the baby and your dubbing. She said she'll believe it when she sees it."

"I made it, girl, so she'll sure as hell be seeing it."

"Blaze said the ceremony is set for the end of this week. There are twenty of you being Knighted."

"Torn boarded the Ocean Star a day ago. He said after the dubbing, I'm to oversee the building of a new ship. Afterward,

I'll be the Captain. He said it's completely mine, so long as I do well by the Order. I'll even get to name her."

Sparrow gazed at the man who'd once been a feared and treacherous pirate. He'd come such a long way and taken her with him. "Lock, I'm so proud of you."

His smile faded to a look of pure love. "I'm grateful to you. You saved my life in every way, Sparrow."

"Because I knew it was a life worth saving."

The bird whistled and said, "I love Sparrow."

She smiled.

"I *did* teach him that." Lock grinned.

That night, Sparrow and Lock spent quietly in their room with their daughter.

"Once I'm Knighted, we can think about moving out of the fortress and maybe building a house of our own on the coast of Rubyshire," Lock said, once Shea-Ann was tucked into her cradle and he and Sparrow lay in bed, cuddled naked in each other's arms.

"That would be wonderful." She kissed his chest. "Especially if we have more children."

Lock tilted her chin upward and brushed her lips with a kiss. "We can start trying for another whenever you feel you're ready."

"I think I'd like to wait a few months before starting on another baby, but we can certainly go through the motions." She straddled him, gazing coquettishly into his eyes. She leaned forward, kissing him, then drew back, her expression concerned. "Unless you're not up to it because of the injury—"

"I'm feeling fine, girl," he grasped her hips then cupped her face in his hands. "Ever since I've been away, I've been dreaming of lying with you like this."

She smiled tenderly. "You have?"

"Sparrow, through some of the roughest times - and believe me, it did get rough - I thought of you and all we've gone through together. I knew I could make it through just about anything. You're like some magical anchor in a stormy sea, saving me from hitting the rocks."

"That's beautiful." She caressed the base of his throat, leaned forward, and kissed him. "All I thought of was you, too, Lock."

Sparrow slipped down his body, pushing his thighs apart and kneeling between them. Clasping the base of his erection, she gazed at him and said, "I want to give you a welcome home present."

His pale eyes narrowed and his lips parted as his breathing quickened with anticipation. "I'd be a fool to argue with that."

Grinning, Sparrow lowered her head, her hair caressing his abdomen as she ran her tongue up and down his shaft. She lapped his cock head, feeling his body tense as pleasure grew along with his thick, steely rod.

How many nights had Sparrow closed her eyes and imagined his taste and scent? She'd longed to feel his body and hear his voice. Now it was real, and she wanted to devour every inch of him. Her tongue ran along the underside of his erection before she took the head between her lips and sucked in a quick, steady rhythm that soon had him panting. By the subtle jerking of his hips, she knew he was trying to restrain himself from thrusting hard.

"Oh, Sparrow," he murmured in a strained voice, trying to keep quiet to avoid waking the baby. "You'd better stop, girl. After so long away from you, I haven't got much control left."

Sparrow released his cock and gazed at him. She squeezed his hard, hair-roughened thighs and whispered, "It's all right, Lock. Give in. I want to feel you come."

He groaned when she lowered her head again and took as much of his balls as she could fit into her mouth. Her tongue tickled and teased the sac before running up the length of his cock. Again she took the head between her lips and sucked. One hand kneaded his balls while the other held his shaft, squeezing and stroking.

The barrage of feelings were too much. Lock had dreamed of this moment for so long and now that it was here, with more raw sensation that he could have imagined. He broke. Gasping, his hands clutching the sheets, he surged into her warm, wet mouth. Sparrow closed her eyes, accepting the brunt of his passion. Her pussy was drenched from arousing him, her clit throbbing. Just feeling him come pushed her over the edge as well and she climaxed simply from the emotional stimulation of exciting him.

He relaxed onto the mattress and Sparrow sprawled between his parted thighs, one hand still curved around his softening cock. They lay, unmoving, as their breath and heartbeat returned to normal.

Finally Lock chuckled and said, "Damn, it's good to be home."

Sparrow lifted her head to meet his gaze and grinned. "Well, damn, it's good to have you back."

Chapter Twenty-Nine

🔊

The Sparrow Song docked in the harbor of Lock's old house on the Archipelago. He stood on the deck of the ship entrusted to him by the Order, a ship he'd designed, helped build, and named after the love of his life. Lock stared at the familiar beach, feeling strangely detached. He suddenly realized that even though he'd lived on SeaSpider Island almost all his life, he'd never felt like it was home. He wanted nothing more than to sail from the Archipelago and never set eyes on it again, but there was something he had to do first.

"So this is where you used to live." Sparrow approached, leaning on the rail. The wind tossed her long hair and spray from the sea dappled her face. It had been a year since he'd been dubbed, five years since they'd met. In spite of pain so terrible he still shuddered at the memory, he was glad for the day he'd been tortured. It had killed Lock the White, but had birthed Sir Lock, Captain of the Sparrow Song and husband to the most beautiful woman he'd ever known. Sparrow continued, "It's lovely."

"No, it just appears that way." He turned toward his crew. "Ready?"

Carrying shovels, the men followed Lock and Sparrow to shore where they began digging the forest and beach, taking back the gold, silver, and jewels he'd pirated for so many years.

Though he couldn't return the goods to their rightful owners, he intended to give it to people in need. It belonged to them more than it ever had to him. He'd been glad when Mahir and Torn had approved his plan to return to the Archipelago. For the first time, he felt like a true Knight. As

Sparrow had once told him, he couldn't erase his past, but he could improve his future.

"I can hardly wait to get back to Shea-Ann," Sparrow said as she and Lock dug beneath the shade of a tree just outside his house.

The building was empty, all the contents taken or ruined. Storms had battered the walls and destroyed the roof. Obviously the servants had abandoned it years ago, or were taken by other masters. Lock didn't care. If he could have knocked the entire place completely to the sand, he would have done so.

"Which one?" He winked.

"Both of them. Our daughter and her temporary nanny."

"There was no way I was taking her with us on this mission," Lock said. "I didn't even want you to come."

Sparrow paused in her digging, her eyes on his. "There was no way I was letting you come back here alone."

"Alone? I've a ship full of Knights and trainees."

"Somehow I doubt they'd give you a hug when you need one."

Lock smiled and touched a hand to her cheek. "When I'm away at battle, I miss those hugs."

"So do I." She leaned forward as he bent to kiss her.

"So it's true," came a husky voice from behind them.

Lock's stomach tightened with disgust. He and Sparrow turned to his mother who stood, her arms folded beneath full breasts exposed in a sheer red dress. Her hair was piled on her head, a red flower the same color as her painted lips adorning the thick brown and gray mass. Lock noted she'd aged well and was still attractive, but her blue eyes were as cold as ever. She continued, "Someone said you'd returned and were wearing the tunic of the Ruby Order. I said that was a crazy story."

"Who is this?" Sparrow demanded.

"No, who is *this*?" Shanna's gaze fixed on Sparrow.

Sparrow stepped in front of Lock, staring at the madam. "I'm his wife."

Shanna's eyes widened a bit, then she broke into uncontrollable laugher. "His *wife*? You're *married*?"

"Sparrow, this is my mother." Lock's voice dripped contempt.

He saw the look of fury cross Sparrow's gentle face.

"This is unbelievable." Shanna circled the couple, completely ignoring Sparrow, her eyes only for Lock and the black uniform he wore. "How can you possibly be a Knight? I've heard only honorable men are Knights."

"He is honorable!" Sparrow snapped.

"How did you manage to fool this little girl, Lock? Did you tell her what you *are*?"

"Sparrow knows everything."

Shanna raised an eyebrow. "After marrying you, I'm sure she does. You were the best whore I ever had—and the most profitable pirate to trade with."

"You repulsive bitch!" Sparrow dove at Shanna, but Lock caught her arms and tugged her against his chest.

He kissed her hair and said, "Ignore her. She's not worthy of your attention."

"Oh, how chivalrous!" Shanna batted her lashes and pressed a hand to her heart before she clenched her fists and scowled, "I thought you were dead. You'd have been better off. It seems the Ruby Order isn't as selective as everyone thinks, if they took you."

"I can't believe how jealous you are of your own son!" Sparrow said.

"He was much more than a son, little girl." Shanna took a step closer to Lock.

Sparrow struggled against his hold and kicked at the madam.

Shanna shook her head and walked away. "What a terrible waste of man flesh and thievery."

Lock held Sparrow until Shanna disappeared. When he released her, she shoved him.

"Don't ever do that again, Lock! If I want to punch somebody in the nose, it's my business!"

"Sparrow, you don't have a nasty bone in your body. She's not worth your effort."

"After what she did to you, she belongs dead!"

"To us she is dead. Are you going to help me dig up this trunk, or what?"

"Since when is your temper so soft?" Sparrow still fumed as she continued digging. "Crag told me how he had to bail you out of prison for a tavern fight during that trip to Tanek last month."

"What would you have had me do, girl? The man was looking for trouble. He came at me with two swords."

"Crag said you knocked six men unconscious."

"He had friends?" Lock offered her a helpless look. Sparrow smiled, and Lock knew her anger was slipping. "How about tonight I knock you unconscious with something other than my fist?"

Sparrow giggled. "Want another daughter, do you?"

"Daughter. Son. Either is fine with me."

"I'll see what I can do."

The Knights dug until dusk before returning to their ship. They could have dug for days, but the Sparrow Song was gaining the interest of pirate ships. They didn't want to cause trouble in the Archipelago if they could help it. Still, they had trunks full of goods worth enough to make a commoner a king.

Lock watched the last of the Knights loading trunks into a dingy. He asked the nearest trainee, "Have you seen my wife?"

"Said she had some business in the village, Sir," the boy replied.

Lock clenched this teeth. He should have guessed Sparrow wouldn't leave the Archipelago without letting Shanna know just what she thought of her.

"Tell them we'll be back within the hour," Lock said to the boy before running down the path to the village.

* * * * *

Sparrow knew the bordello from Lock's descriptions. The sight of the two-floor building with men and women half-dressed and summoning guests outside it, made her sick to her stomach. She thought of how empty their lives were, how empty Lock's had been. He'd dragged himself out of the Archipelago, and his mother had condemned him for it. Being a mother herself, she couldn't imagine any woman treating a child as Shanna had treated Lock. He was right of course. She should mean nothing to them, but Sparrow couldn't release the anger she felt towards the madam.

Several bare-breasted women glanced curiously at Sparrow as she stepped into the bordello.

Inside, prostitutes entertained pirates on couches and rugs. The air was thick with pipe smoke, old sweat, and perfume. Lock had told her of the smell, but it was the first time she'd ever experienced it, and she understood his loathing.

Shanna sat on a bamboo chair drinking from a silver goblet. She placed the drink aside and stood up on seeing Sparrow.

"My little daughter-in-law." The madam smirked. "Come about a job, or are you looking for Lock? He'd probably like a romp before he goes. And if you think he's going to stay with you forever, you're wrong. His heart is here, and he has no soul."

"You have no soul!" Sparrow snapped.

"What good is a soul, dear? You can't make a profit with it."

Sparrow drew a deep breath, her rage fading to disgust. "Lock was right. You're not worth our time."

Sparrow walked to the door, and Shanna said, "That's because he's had most everyone here enough times. Want some advice on how to keep him awake at night, little girl?"

Sparrow spun and struck Shanna so hard in the face that the Madam landed on her backside on a sheepskin rug.

"Well, maybe you're more like him than I thought," Shanna muttered, wiping a trickle of blood from her split lip.

"Sparrow."

Sparrow turned to the doorway where Lock stood. He extended his hand to her, and she took it.

Together they walked to the shore and boarded the Sparrow Song.

As they drifted from the harbor, they stood on deck, gazing at the sky. Lock slid his arm around her, and she rested her cheek against his chest. His bird hopped from his shoulder to Sparrow's and said, "I love Sparrow."

"He took the words right out of my mouth," Lock murmured against her hair. He gazed skyward. "It's a new moon."

"Yes." Sparrow smiled, pressing her body closer to his. "How very apt."

Epilogue
Six Months Later
Somewhere in the Chaston Ocean

ဆ

Blood splattered Sir Blaze's face as he fought, empty handed, amidst a mass of shrieking, sword-wielding men. Blaze's foster daughter, Dame Sun, half dragged by a tall, black-haired, ebony-skinned man, turned, raising her arm in time to stop the deadly blow aimed at her head as Blaze raced towards the couple.

Stone buzzards circled in the sky as battle raged amidst the bloodied sands of Upper Kenna.

* * * * *

Lock leapt out of his cot, gasping, his heart pounding. He stared, wide-eyed around the chamber, taking a moment to rejoin the solid world.

"What is it, love?" Sparrow, sat up, running a hand through her long, fawn-colored hair and blinking sleep from her eyes. She stood, touching a hand to the Knight's perspiring face. "Another dream?"

"Vision."

"Vision. I'm sorry." Sparrow slipped her small hand into his.

"I have to go to the Kennas." Lock dragged on trousers and his black tunic. He jerked his mass of kinky brown and white hair into a tail at his nape, his gaze fixed on Sparrow. "There's some kind of battle going on. Blaze and Sun are in the thick of it. And there was a dark man I didn't recognize."

"Enemy?"

"I don't know. I'll drop you at the nearest port."

Sparrow shook her head. "I'm going with you."

"No. I won't argue about it, girl."

"Good to know that." She also dressed. "It would be a waste of valuable time."

"I mean it. Don't push me on this, Sparrow!" Lock growled.

"Be reasonable. If there's trouble going on, I'll be invaluable to you. I speak all the dialects of the Kennas. By the Spirit, Lock, that's why I'm on board the damn ship with you in the first place! I'm an ambassador for the Ruby Order!"

"Ambassador, not a warrior."

"While you're fighting with me, you could be turning this ship around. You know I'm right."

The anger in Lock's voice was a contrast to the tender kiss he pressed to her forehead. "Doesn't mean I have to like it."

He strode out of the cabin, and Sparrow hurried to keep up with him. He told his first mate to assemble the crew.

Within moments, the ship turned, its sails billowing and its sharp nose cutting the water as it sped toward the Kennas, to Blaze, his foster daughter, and the mysterious dark-skinned man.

The End

Also by Kate Hill

ɞ

eBooks:

Alien Affairs 1: Doing Thyme

Alien Affairs 2: Moonlight on Water

Alien Affairs 3: Menage a Tasia

Alien Affairs 4: Pandora's Box

Ancient Blood: Cryptic Trysts

Ancient Blood: Darkness Therein

Ancient Blood: Deep Red

Ancient Blood: God of the Grim

Ancient Blood: Handsome Bastard

Ancient Blood: Immaculate

Ancient Blood: In Black

Ancient Blood: Infernal

Ancient Blood: Much More Than Blood

Ancient Blood: Revenge of the Court Jester

Ancient Blood: The Blood Doctor

Ancient Blood: The Holiday Stalking

Back To Haunt You

By Honor Bound: His Sister's Kiss

Ellora's Cavemen: Jewels of the Nile I *(anthology)*

Horsemen 1: Dream Stallion

Horsemen 2: Captive Stallion

Horsemen 3: Highland Stallion

Horsemen 4: Winter Stallion

Horsemen 5: Victory Stallion

Knights of the Ruby Order 1: Torn

Knights of the Ruby Order 2: Crag

Knights of the Ruby Order 3: Lock

Knights of the Ruby Order 4: Mica

Knights of the Ruby Order 5: Blaze

Licking Fire

Marriage in Moonlust

Moonlust Privateer

Naked Souls

Northman's Passion

Raptvyn's Rogue

Rediscovering Thor

Silver Cuffs

Windswept

Print Books:

Ancient Blood: Unquenchable

By Honor Bound *(anthology)*

Dusky Kisses

Ellora's Cavemen: Jewels of the Nile I *(anthology)*

Forever Midnight *(anthology)*

Horsemen 1: Dream Stallion

Horsemen 2: Captive Stallion

Horsemen 3: Highland Stallion

Knights of the Ruby Order 1 & 2: Torn and Crag

About the Author

෨

A lifelong fan of action and romance, Kate Hill likes heroes with a touch of something wicked and wild. Her short fiction and poetry have appeared in publications both on and off the Internet. When she's not working on her books, Kate enjoys dancing, martial arts, and researching vampires and Viking history.

෨

The author welcomes comments from readers. You can find her website and email address on her author bio page at www.ellorascave.com.

Tell Us What You Think

We appreciate hearing reader opinions about our books. You can email us at Comments@EllorasCave.com.

Why an electronic book?

We live in the Information Age—an exciting time in the history of human civilization, in which technology rules supreme and continues to progress in leaps and bounds every minute of every day. For a multitude of reasons, more and more avid literary fans are opting to purchase e-books instead of paper books. The question from those not yet initiated into the world of electronic reading is simply: *Why?*

1. *Price.* An electronic title at Ellora's Cave Publishing and Cerridwen Press runs anywhere from 40% to 75% less than the cover price of the exact same title in paperback format. Why? Basic mathematics and cost. It is less expensive to publish an e-book (no paper and printing, no warehousing and shipping) than it is to publish a paperback, so the savings are passed along to the consumer.

2. *Space.* Running out of room in your house for your books? That is one worry you will never have with electronic books. For a low one-time cost, you can purchase a handheld device specifically designed for e-reading. Many e-readers have large, convenient screens for viewing. Better yet, hundreds of titles can be stored within your new library—on a single microchip. There are a variety of e-readers from different manufacturers. You can also read e-books on your PC or laptop computer. (Please note that Ellora's Cave does not endorse any specific brands.

You can check our websites at www.ellorascave.com or www.cerridwenpress.com for information we make available to new consumers.)

3. *Mobility.* Because your new e-library consists of only a microchip within a small, easily transportable e-reader, your entire cache of books can be taken with you wherever you go.

4. *Personal Viewing Preferences.* Are the words you are currently reading too small? Too large? Too... ANNOYING? Paperback books cannot be modified according to personal preferences, but e-books can.

5. *Instant Gratification.* Is it the middle of the night and all the bookstores near you are closed? Are you tired of waiting days, sometimes weeks, for bookstores to ship the novels you bought? Ellora's Cave Publishing sells instantaneous downloads twenty-four hours a day, seven days a week, every day of the year. Our webstore is never closed. Our e-book delivery system is 100% automated, meaning your order is filled as soon as you pay for it.

Those are a few of the top reasons why electronic books are replacing paperbacks for many avid readers.

As always, Ellora's Cave and Cerridwen Press welcome your questions and comments. We invite you to email us at Comments@ellorascave.com or write to us directly at Ellora's Cave Publishing Inc., 1056 Home Avenue, Akron, OH 44310-3502.

MAKE EACH DAY MORE *EXCITING* WITH OUR

ELLORA'S CAVEMEN CALENDAR

WWW.ELLORASCAVE.COM

ELLORA'S CAVE
Romanticon

Annual convention
for women who
refuse to behave

ELLORA'S CAVE

ROMANTICA PUBLISHING

Discover for yourself why readers can't get enough of the multiple award-winning publisher

Ellora's Cave.

Whether you prefer e-books or paperbacks,

be sure to visit EC on the web at
www.ellorascave.com

for an erotic reading experience that will leave you breathless.

CPSIA information can be obtained at www.ICGtesting.com
Printed in the USA
LVOW05s0951250813

349523LV00001B/118/P

9 781419 964329